Milo stuffed the handkerchief back in the pocket of his tan pants. "The deceased wasn't a local," he said in his laconic voice. "According to Marlow Whipp, he came into the grocery store just before closing, about five to seven. He tried to say something, and then collapsed." Never a fast talker, Milo slowed to a snail's pace. The little cluster of neighbors drew closer. "His name is Kelvin Greene, from Seattle. He was twenty-seven years old and lived somewhere out in the Rainier Valley area. It looks as if he'd been shot in the head." Milo's long face wore a disgusted look. "Marlow called us. Marlow swears he didn't shoot him, though he keeps a gun under the counter. Kelvin died before the ambulance could get here. He was black. Any more questions, or can I get the hell out of here and do my job?"

Also by Mary Daheim
Published by Ballantine Books:

THE ALPINE ADVOCATE
THE ALPINE BETRAYAL
THE ALPINE CHRISTMAS

THE ALPINE
DECOY

Mary Daheim

BALLANTINE BOOKS • NEW YORK

Copyright © 1994 by Mary Daheim

All rights reserved under International and Pan-American Copyright Conventions. Published in the United States of America by Ballantine Books, a division of Random House, Inc., New York, and simultaneously in Canada by Random House of Canada Limited, Toronto.

Library of Congress Catalog Card Number: 94-94193

ISBN 0-345-38841-0

Manufactured in the United States of America

First Edition: September 1994

10 9 8 7 6 5 4 3

Chapter One

THERE'S NO FOOL like an old fool, unless it's a middle-aged fool. Like me.

The letter from the Washington Newspaper Publishers Association was very businesslike; the invitation to the seminar on advertising revenue was suitably formal. So why was my heart racing like an out-of-control dishwasher?

The answer was simple, and so was I. According to the program schedule, the panelists included Tom Cavanaugh of San Francisco, former reporter and editor, currently owner of seventeen weeklies and four small dailies throughout the western United States and Canada. According to my pudding-like head, Tom Cavanaugh was my former lover and permanent father of my only son, Adam. I hadn't seen Tom in almost two years. The prospect both thrilled and terrified me.

"Your sleeve's on fire," said Vida Runkel, my House & Home editor. "Be careful, you're going to burn your arm."

I jumped, slapping at my beige linen jacket. Sure enough, I'd scorched the fabric on the coffeemaker in *The Alpine Advocate*'s editorial office.

"Damn!" I exclaimed, wincing at the heat that seared my fingers. "I don't exactly have a lavish spring wardrobe."

Vida was sitting at her desk, peering at me over the rims of her tortoiseshell glasses. "Trim the sleeves, then roll them back. That look came in a few years ago and it's still around. I ought to know—I get all the fashion handouts." She returned to her typing, a wonder of two-fingered wizardry on a machine almost as old as she was.

Removing my singed jacket and pouring a cup of coffee, I studied the WNPA letter more closely. "I should send Ed

1

Bronsky to this. They're holding the summer meeting at Lake Chelan."

"You should hold Ed under water at Lake Chelan. I don't know why you put up with him. He's the worst ad manager I've ever met." Vida didn't pause in her typing.

It wasn't the first time that Vida and I had argued over Ed Bronsky's ineptitude. Indeed, Ed wasn't inept so much as he was negative. In a town like Alpine, Washington, with four thousand souls held hostage by semi-isolation on Stevens Pass, Ed couldn't see any reason why local retailers needed to advertise in the first place. There was one furniture emporium, one pharmacy, one sporting goods store, one bakery—and, until the past year, one source of food. A few months back Safeway had opened to give the Grocery Basket a run for everybody's money.

"Maybe the seminar would motivate Ed," I said, but sounded dubious to my own ears.

"Dynamite wouldn't motivate Ed," Vida replied, and this time she did stop typing, not to concentrate on our conversation or her latest story, but because she was finished. She whipped the paper out of the ancient upright and gave me her gimlet eye. "Why don't you go, Emma? Chelan is a short drive from here. Why, you wouldn't even have to spend the night if you didn't want to."

Her innocent look didn't fool me, and though I hate to admit it, I blushed. The mail had just arrived. Vida couldn't possibly have seen the WNPA invitation. It was addressed to me: Emma Lord, Editor and Publisher. I had opened it a mere five minutes ago with my own two hands. But somehow Vida knew. She always knew. It was her way.

"I shouldn't take the time," I mumbled. "It's in mid-June, and I was away for almost a week at Easter. That was just a month ago."

"So? It's another month until mid-June." Vida shook her broad shoulders, making her lime, magenta, and white striped blouse ripple in various directions across her impressive bosom. "You know it's worthless to send Ed. He'll pooh-pooh any innovations. But if you go, you can collect all sorts of new ideas and insist that he knuckle down. Really, Emma, it gets my goat how you turn a blind eye to his laziness and indifference. Just because your predecessor hired Ed, doesn't mean you have to keep him."

My predecessor, Marius Vandeventer, had founded *The Alpine Advocate* back in the Thirties and sold it to me at the start of the Nineties. I'd inherited Vida and Ed from Marius, but had hired my sole reporter, Carla Steinmetz, and our office manager, Ginny Burmeister, on my own. Carla was eager, but dizzy; Ginny was methodical, but diligent. I felt I was batting about five hundred, which wasn't bad. The thought put me on the defensive.

"Ed has a wife and children," I said, resorting to my usual weary defense. "With the logging business gone to hell, there are enough people out of work in Alpine without adding Ed to the list. Besides, he's improved. Really, he has."

With a toss of her unruly gray curls, Vida snorted. "That's only because you watch him like a hawk and Ginny helps so much."

Even though Vida was right, I would have argued further if Carla Steinmetz hadn't burst into the office, carrying a white paper sack from the Upper Crust Bakery.

"Sorry I'm late," she said, waving the sack at Vida and me. "Here, it's glazed twisters. You'd better eat them before Ed gets back from the Rotary Club breakfast meeting."

I glanced at my watch. It was almost ten. Ed should have returned by now. And Carla was definitely tardy.

"Where were you?" I asked, hoping against hope she'd been out getting a hot story.

Carla passed the bakery bag first to Vida, then to me. "At the doctor's. You know I've had an earache for three days. Libby, my new roommate, said I couldn't go on like this."

In all probability, neither could Libby. Carla had hardly talked of anything else since coming in Monday morning, holding her head. I could imagine how she'd complained at home. Libby—Liberty, actually—Boyd was a brash young woman who drove a Ford pickup truck, lifted weights, and had recently been posted to the ranger station at Icicle Creek. She and Carla had moved in together May first. I wondered how long the wholesome, athletic, down-to-earth Libby would survive in the company of my flighty, ebullient, comfort-loving reporter. I'd met Libby only once. She struck me as long on valor, but short on patience.

Carla had swept her long black hair back and leaned forward just enough to show off the wad of cotton stuffed in her left ear. "See? Dr. Flake put drops in it. I think they've helped already."

"Good," I said, not without sympathy. "Earaches can be nasty."

Carla and I munched on our twisters. Vida, however, let hers sit on the desk, untouched. It wasn't like her. She was gazing at Carla, expectancy written all over her majestic figure.

"Well?"

Carla was getting herself a mug of coffee. "Well, what?"

Vida made a face. "Well, what about the new nurse?"

With another flip of her long locks, Carla hopped into the chair behind her desk. "The new nurse?" Her black eyes were very round. "Why, Vida, you must know all about her. Your niece is the receptionist, after all."

Vida's nieces, nephews, and other relations, by family and by marriage, were everywhere. The tribal network of Runkels on her late husband's side and Blatts by blood formed the basis of her limitless knowledge of Alpine. She narrowed her eyes at Carla.

"Marje has been on vacation for two weeks, and you know it. She went to Mexico to get sick."

At first Carla looked surprised, then she turned smug. "That's right, I didn't see her this morning. Doc Dewey's wife was working the desk." Carla took a big bite of her twister. "What do you want to know, Vida?"

Vida's right hand closed over the twister that lay on her desk in a gesture that suggested it might have legs and try to escape. Or, perhaps, that she would like to do the same to Carla's neck. "I'm curious, of course," she replied with dignity. "Marilynn Lewis is the first black person we've ever had living in Alpine. I think she's either very brave or very foolish."

Carla was still looking smug, even superior. "You're supposed to say African-American," she declared. "I think Dr. Dewey and Dr. Flake were very brave to hire her. I gather it was Dr. Flake's idea, since he's more progressive than Doc Dewey."

There was almost twenty years' age difference between Alpine's two physicians, but the town's perception was based on more than the generation gap. Peyton Flake was a recent arrival and new to private practice. Gerald Dewey was a local, the son of Alpine's late and much-beloved Cecil Dewey, who had attended three generations of Skykomish County residents. During the years that the father and son had practiced together, they were known as Young Doc and Old Doc. Gerald Dewey was still called Young Doc by most Alpiners, and it appeared that for good or for ill, his indigenous roots were perceived as making him far more hidebound—and thus more reliable—than the upstart newcomer. But the senior Dewey hadn't felt a need to build his practice; his son relied on the clinic's virtual monopoly. Peyton Flake was much more aggressive: He foresaw potential patients defecting along the Stevens Pass corridor, driving to doctors in Sultan, Monroe, Snohomish, and even as far away as Everett. Flake worked actively to keep current patients and recruit new ones. Consequently, the active chart file was growing, and with it, the need for a new nurse.

"I just happened to see Marilynn Lewis leaving work the other night," Vida remarked. "The clinic is right on my way home." The explanation may or may not have been an excuse for satisfying Vida's rampant curiosity.

Having devoured her twister, Carla settled down to deliver serious information. "She's young, maybe my age or a little older, pretty, seems sharp, and very nice. I heard she's rooming with the Campbells, at least until she finds a place of her own."

Swiftly, Vida digested Carla's account. "Yes, Jean and Lloyd Campbell have taken her in." She made it sound as if they'd acquired a stray cat, but I knew better. While Alpine abounded in prejudiced people, Vida wasn't one of them. "I'm not sure how they're all managing, with Cyndi living at home and Shane back from Seattle."

I racked my brain as I often did when Vida started rattling off families and their histories. One of the hazards of moving to a small town is learning who's who. It's bad enough for the average newcomer, but for somebody like me with a job where names are not only news, but the primary source of income, it's overwhelming. After three years in Alpine, Vida and the other natives can still stump me. Small-town dwellers throw out unfamiliar names like a challenge. Recent arrivals drown in a sea of first, last, maiden, and married names. As well as nicknames. Meanwhile, the true-born smirk, reminding the newcomers of their outsider status.

At least I'd been around long enough to know that Lloyd Campbell owned Alpine Appliance and was close to sixty. His wife, Jean, worked part-time at the Presbyterian church, which numbered Vida among its members. Cyndi was their daughter, also around Carla's age, and the receptionist at the Public Utilities District office. Shane, I assumed, was their son, but I knew nothing about him.

Vida guessed as much. "Shane is the middle Campbell child," she informed me, licking twister glaze off her fingers. "He's been living and working in Seattle for the past two or three years. I think he was with Fred Meyer. I heard he moved back here because the chain planned to open a store at the Alpine Mall."

"They keep putting it off," I noted. "I had Ed call their Oregon headquarters just last week." As a former Portland resident and employee of *The Oregonian*, I was well acquainted with the Fred Meyer stores; they featured everything from apparel to groceries to electronics to jewelry. While I would welcome their convenience as well as their advertising, I realized that they might be hesitant about a new venture in a town as economically depressed as Alpine. I also realized that our local merchants would be upset. The small specialty stores featuring books, CDs, china, jewelry, stereos, and shoes wouldn't welcome the competition.

Carla was going through her in-basket. She stopped and called to me just as I was heading back into my small, cluttered office. "Emma—should we do a story on Marilynn Lewis? I mean, it *is* news that she's here—and that she's African-American."

I considered the idea. "No, not yet. She's been here—what? A couple of weeks? Let's give her a chance to get settled in. I don't want to draw attention to her and make her a target of any bigots. Let's face it, the news isn't that she's here; it's that she's African-American. I'm not sure Marilynn would regard that as a positive story angle. If you want to do a newcomer feature, interview Libby Boyd. Isn't she the first female forest ranger to be posted up here?"

Vida confirmed that she was. Carla, however, gave an indifferent shrug. "Women doing what used to be men's work isn't news anymore. Besides, she hasn't been in the job long enough to know how it feels. She had an office assignment in Seattle."

Carla, however, didn't press the Marilynn Lewis story, and Vida didn't comment. I took the scorched jacket into my office along with my coffee and went back to work. Briefly, I thought about Marilynn Lewis. She *was* very brave, perhaps a trifle foolish. I wondered why she'd exchanged the relative anonymity of the Big City for the scrutiny of a small town. But I didn't think about it too long. I had problems of my own, and at the moment, they were all named Tom Cavanaugh.

"Those Anasazi Indians have got ruins older than you are, Mom," said my son over the phone. "Uncle Ben thinks he can get me on a dig. Aren't you hyped?"

"Sure, I think it's great." I reached for my take-out burger. I gathered that Ben thought it was great, too. My brother had seemed enthused that his nephew was going to join him for the summer in Tuba City, Arizona. Naturally, I would have preferred that Adam spend at least some of his time helping Ben out at the mission church on the Navajo reservation, but it seemed that my only child's interests were centered on the artifacts in the ancient tribal villages. At least, I chided myself, he *had* an interest. There were times when I felt Adam was drifting, from one university to another, from one girlfriend to the next, from one professed major to the latest career of the week. . . .

But Adam had maintained his enthusiasm for Native-American culture ever since Ben's visit to Alpine in December. My son had been determined to join my brother in Tuba City, and would fly from the University of Alaska at Fairbanks directly into Phoenix in June. He would then take a bus to Flagstaff where Ben would meet him. Adam would come to Alpine at the beginning of August, about the same time the temperature hit a hundred and twenty in northern Arizona. With any luck, Ben might get away for a week or so then, too. But as the only Catholic priest in the vicinity, it was possible that he'd be stuck until his regular vacation came due at the end of the year.

While Adam waxed on about digging in the digs, I contemplated telling him about his father's scheduled appearance at the WNPA conference. But Adam had seen Tom since I had. After twenty years of estrangement, they had finally met in San Francisco last November. The meeting had gone well. If Adam had resented his father's absence from the scene, it hadn't showed. Maybe my son—our son—understood that Tom's defection hadn't been voluntary. Twenty-two years ago, when I discovered I was pregnant by a married man, I'd told Tom to get lost. Reluctantly, he'd complied. After all, he had a family of his own. It wasn't his fault that his wife was crazier than a loon. At the time, I wasn't feeling entirely stable myself.

But Tom had stayed married. His wife, Sandra, had stayed crazy. And Adam and I had created our own little world. It was only by coincidence that Tom had showed up in Alpine a year ago last autumn. At least it *seemed* a coincidence at the time. He had given me invaluable advice about running a weekly newspaper, and I had given him my pardon for a crime he never committed. But I still wasn't willing to give him Adam. That had only happened after much soul-searching and many letters from Tom, asking to see his illegitimate son.

"You know," said Adam, as if reading my mind, "I've got enough money to fly into Seattle and come up to Alpine before I go to Arizona."

The money had come from Tom, providing airfare for Adam to visit me and Ben and the pope, if he wanted to. Tom had been very generous, trying to make up in one year for two decades of paternal absenteeism.

"Well," I hedged, "that's up to you. I'd love to have you come, of course. But if you're returning to Fairbanks next year, you'll need to save up."

"I don't know about that," Adam replied. "I'm thinking

about transferring to Cal-Berkeley. They don't have an archaeology major up here. Or is it anthropology?" As ever, Adam sounded vague on the subject of his future.

"What's wrong with the UDUB?" I demanded, referring to the University of Washington in Seattle which had been good enough for me.

"There's WAZZU, too," Adam remarked. The nickname stood for Washington State University, some three hundred miles away in Pullman. "But I like the Bay Area. San Fran is cool."

San Fran was indeed cool. It was also home base for Adam's father. I had mixed feelings about that. "Talk to Ben. He gives good advice."

To my mild surprise, Adam agreed. We talked some more, about his classes, which bored him, about his latest girlfriend, who thrilled him, about his part-time job with the state highway department, which fatigued him. He was still trying to convince me it would be terrific for him to stop off in Seattle and Alpine en route to Tuba City. I didn't argue further; I'd be too glad to have my only son with me to squelch the idea.

I had just hung up when Milo Dodge loped into my office. Since it was Thursday, the day after our weekly publication, I wasn't as frantically engaged as usual. So far there had been only a dozen irate phone calls from readers. This week they pounced on two issues. One was Vida's account of the perennially controversial Junior Miss Alpine competition. The other was my recent editorial devoted to resurfacing the county road that led out of town to the ranger station. It was pretty tame stuff, but some of our subscribers felt that any public work demanded new taxes. They weren't entirely wrong.

Milo is the sheriff of Skykomish County, and just because we are both single and share the same decade of birth, people often think we should be madly in love. We are not. Milo is involved with a potteress from Startup named Honoria Whitman who gets around in a wheelchair, courtesy of her late husband who once threw her down a flight of stairs. I am involved with my newspaper. Or so I like to tell myself.

"People sure are dumb," Milo declared as he settled his

shambling body into one of the two chairs positioned on the opposite side of my desk. "Are you eating that salad?"

"I sure am," I retorted, stabbing at the lettuce with a plastic fork. "If you were so hungry, why didn't you call? We could have gone out to lunch."

Milo scratched at something on his neck. "I thought about it, but we got a call from that new nurse at Dr. Flake's. Some jerk is writing her threatening letters."

I swallowed quickly. "Marilynn Lewis? We were just talking about her this morning."

Milo's long face grew longer. "She's gotten three of them. Two are obviously from the same nutcase, but the third may be from somebody else."

"Antiblack?" I asked, polishing off the burger dip.

Milo nodded. He is a few years older than I am, in his midforties, with graying sandy hair, hazel eyes, and a laconic manner that fools a lot of people. I am not one of them. "It's to be expected. There haven't been any minorities around Alpine since the Orientals worked the mines back before World War I. Oh, we get tourists who aren't lily-white, but they don't stick around, so the locals tolerate them. But this Lewis woman seems inclined to stay. Some of the reactionaries resent that."

"You're right: they're dumb." I pushed the plastic container of salad at Milo. "Here, have some. I'm getting full." It wasn't exactly true, but bigotry has a way of taking the edge off my appetite. "Do you know who sent them?"

Milo shook his head. "It could be anybody. Ms. Lewis isn't all that upset, but after the third one, she felt she ought to notify us. I'm afraid we can't do much about it."

I sat back and watched Milo finish my salad. Absently, he drank my Coke. Unconsciously, he gobbled up the last four milk chocolate Easter eggs I'd been saving for a month. I sighed.

"It's not a story," Milo asserted, mistaking my reaction.

"You mean 'Sheriff Charged With Piggery'? Damn it, Milo, I've been keeping those chocolate eggs in the refrigerator since Easter."

"Oh." Milo had the grace to look sheepish. "Sorry. I wasn't thinking. You didn't figure I came here to see about running something on those letters, did you?"

I shook my head. "I assumed you came her to steal my lunch. It's too bad, because I was thinking about asking you and Honoria to dinner tonight."

"Honoria's in Seattle until Sunday," Milo replied. "There's some kind of ceramic and pottery show at the Center. I could come, though."

Not having been serious about the dinner invitation, I found myself hoisted with my own petard. I surrendered with good grace. "You're right," I agreed as Milo eased himself onto his feet. "It's not a story."

Milo nodded. "The letters'll go away. People'll get used to having a black person around. I guess she's a pretty good nurse."

"She'll offer Alpine a positive image of African-Americans," I said, wondering if Carla had any twisters left over. It was unlikely, since Ed had returned from breakfast and stuffed himself at Carla's expense. "I'm glad she's here. With so many commuters from Everett and even Seattle, it's about time we got some racial mix."

Milo inclined his head. Somehow, I wished he'd given me a vigorous nod instead.

Ed Bronsky was trying to explain why we didn't need to publish a special section on the new bowling alley. I saw the event as an occasion for various Alpine merchants and organizations to take out ads congratulating the Erdahl family on opening Alpine's Fast Lanes; Ed saw it as a nuisance.

"Do you know how long it takes me to lay out a four-page insert?" Ed looked as if he was first oarsman on a Roman slave galley.

"Actually, Ed," I persisted, "Ginny gives you all kinds of help. If we get enough ads, we could actually turn a profit for the first week of June."

Ed's heavy face fell at the sound of an obscenity like *profit*. He was about my age, not quite medium height, wide of shoulder, and broad of beam. The only person I knew who had a worse shape than Ed was his wife, Shirley.

As if on cue, Ginny Burmeister entered the news office. She expressed mild enthusiasm over the proposed insert, which was about as excited as Ginny ever gets. Ed didn't take kindly to her positive stance.

"You're still young, Ginny," he said in his lugubrious voice. "You can stand hard work and long hours. You don't have to go out and beat your feet on the sidewalks, hustling every day."

"Like who?" Vida looked up from proofing the obituary of ninety-three-year-old Axel Swensen, who had worked the big cut-off saw in the original Alpine mill. "Ed, the last time you hustled was when Carla cut Ginny's birthday cake. You slipped in a puddle of punch and landed right in the frosting. Carla took a picture to prove it, but as usual, she forgot to load her camera."

It was going on five. I didn't feel like listening to my staff wrangle anymore for the day. "We're going to do the insert, and that's that," I declared firmly. "You know, Ed, maybe it's time you rethought your career. I sometimes get the impression you don't really like advertising."

Even as the words tumbled out of my mouth, I regretted them. I rarely took a staff member to task, and when I did, it was always in private. I was dismayed as I watched Ed redden and seem to creep inside the collar of his rumpled raincoat.

"I *love* advertising," he protested. "My father was a salesman for John Deere. It's in my blood. Free enterprise, the American way, the whole idea of *commerce*—why, I wouldn't know how to do anything else!"

I didn't doubt that for a minute. But I refrained from saying so. "Then try changing your attitude," I said, making my voice sound less harsh. "You give the wrong impression. It's very frustrating for me sometimes." I smiled, if a bit feebly.

Seemingly placated, Ed rummaged around his desk, made incoherent noises about pursuing the insert idea, and then left. Twenty minutes early. Ginny returned to the front office to finish her daily chores, and Vida announced she was heading home, too. In her case, I didn't mind. I knew she had to cover a party up at the ski lodge that night. One of the county commissioners was retiring due to ill health or perennial intoxication, or both.

Just as Vida left, Carla returned, holding her head. "My

ear is hurting again. I went over to the high school to inter-view the music teacher about the Methodist Church's ban on rap recordings, and I got the most awful stabbing pains. Do you think I should see Dr. Flake before he leaves for the day?"

I advised her to go. "Are you sure the music teacher didn't make you listen to some of those recordings?" I asked dryly.

Carla didn't find my remark amusing. "Are you kidding? The Methodists—and some of the other churches, too—are making sure Platters on the Sky won't carry any of the re-cordings with those stupid explicit-lyrics stickers on them. Whatever happened to free speech and all those amend-ments? Ouch!" Carla grabbed her ear.

Back in my office, I made a note to write an editorial on censorship. I also made a quick grocery list. Milo was strictly a meat-and-potatoes man so I jotted down rib steak, which I knew was on special at the Grocery Basket, the fix-ings for a Caesar salad, and a bottle of red wine. I'd make my own french fries and pick up dessert at the Upper Crust.

The phone rang just as I was debating whether or not I should wear my damaged linen jacket. Milo Dodge's la-conic voice was on the other end of the line.

"I may be late," he said. "Closer to eight than seven."

"That's fine," I assured him. "I have to shop and cook first." I could have been ready for Milo by seven o'clock, but if he came later I wouldn't have to rush. I might even have time to check the mail and phone messages at home.

Milo, however, didn't hear my reply. He was off the line, speaking to one of his deputies. I thought I recognized the usually chipper voice of Jack Mullins. Except Jack didn't sound so chipper.

"What's that, Emma?" Milo said into the phone. "Sorry, I got interrupted."

"What's going on?" I asked, exchanging my role as host-ess for that of journalist.

Milo let out a groan. "More dumb stunts. It's just as well I don't say anything. You might be tempted to run it in the paper."

The sheriff of Skykomish County knows better than to pull that line on me. All I had to do was walk down the street to his office and check over the daily log. "Okay, Milo," I sighed, "what happened?"

He hesitated, then gave in. "It's our new nurse. She got a little surprise in the mail today." Again, he paused, and I could picture his long face grimacing. "Somebody sent her a black crow. Dead. Now that's pretty ugly, Emma."

It sure was. But could it be news? I was afraid so. Nevertheless, I made a judgment. "I'm not running that," I said, on a note of outrage.

"Good," Milo said. "But it could get worse."

I sighed again. Milo was right. It could, and it did.

Chapter Two

HALFWAY DOWN AISLE 2-A at the Grocery Basket, I realized that Carla might be about to make one of her classic journalism mistakes. Having gone to see Peyton Flake, she would probably hear the story of Marilynn Lewis and the dead crow. It was likely that my eager young reporter would grill the new nurse about her experience. While I could easily veto the article before it got into print, I felt it was equally important to spare Marilynn the embarrassment of Carla's questions.

Tossing salad oil and anchovies into the cart with the rest of my groceries, I raced to the checkout stand. I cut short the usual pleasantries with fellow shoppers, the checker, and the courtesy clerk. Five minutes later, I was at the clinic where Nancy Dewey was closing the office for the day.

Young Doc Dewey's wife was closer to fifty than forty, but well preserved, mainly due to good bones and fine gray eyes that retained a youthful sparkle. She had helped put Gerald Dewey through medical school by working at the University Book Store in Seattle. Now that her two children were raised and married, Nancy Dewey filled her leisure hours by alternating as a backup at her husband's clinic and as a salesperson at her father's stereo store at the Alpine Mall.

"You looking for Carla?" she asked, with a smile that was a trifle pinched.

I said I was. Carla, however, was in the back, being examined by Peyton Flake. She wouldn't be long, Nancy assured me.

I leaned on the counter that separated the receptionist's station from the waiting room. "Is Marilynn Lewis still here? I haven't officially met her." I tried to keep my expression bland.

Nancy Dewey gave me a sharp look. My attempts at subterfuge almost always fail. "She went home about an hour ago." Nancy paused, apparently waiting for me to blurt out the real reason for my visit.

I capitulated. "Was she upset?"

"Wouldn't you be?" Nancy gave the day calendar an angry flip to the next page. "Imagine, the gall of some people! Oh, I know we've got plenty of rednecks and bigots in this town. But to go out of your way to make somebody miserable—that takes a real mean streak. We had four patients waiting when Marilynn opened that blasted box."

As usual, I mentally calculated how long it would take the four onlookers to pass the news around Alpine. Whatever the time frame, the gossip mill would work faster—and more efficiently—than we could at *The Advocate*. Maybe my concern about sparing Marilynn embarrassment was in vain.

"What did she do with it? The box, I mean. And the crow," I added, as an afterthought.

Nancy switched the phone to the answering service before she replied. "I made her give box and bird to the sheriff. No return address, of course, and the handwriting was crude. A local postmark, but sufficient stamps so that it wouldn't have to go across the post office counter. Cowardly, as you might expect." Her fine eyes snapped with anger.

Sadly, I shook my head. I didn't know what to say. It was doubtful that Marilynn Lewis had ever experienced such an insult in Seattle. Not that there weren't bigots in the Big City, but Marilynn wouldn't be singled out. In Alpine, it was different. She was, in effect, a pioneer. She must have realized that when she moved to town. I said as much to Nancy Dewey.

Nancy shrugged. "I suppose she was prepared for the worst, but she probably expected better. You know how most people are: eternal optimists." It was clear from Nancy's tone that life had taught her otherwise. She leaned across the counter, lowering her voice as if the waiting room were filled with eager listeners. "Gerry wasn't crazy about the hiring. In fact, Flake didn't tell him Marilynn was black. He interviewed her in Seattle, so my husband never saw her until she showed up for work."

I hated to ask the question, but I couldn't avoid it. "And Gerry was upset?"

"Oh, no!" Nancy shook her head with vigor. "Not for himself, that is. Heck, Gerry had a black roommate in college. It was the Sixties, for heavens' sake! But that's the point, Emma—people like Gerry, who've lived away from Alpine, usually aren't prejudiced. Unfortunately, most of the locals have spent ninety-nine percent of their lives in Skykomish County. Then there are the newcomers who moved up here to get away from urban problems. That combination makes up our practice. I can't blame Gerry for worrying about local reactions."

"He should only worry about Marilynn's qualifications as a nurse," I noted in my primmest voice.

Nancy nodded. "Which are excellent. Though," she added, "it's mostly hospital experience. Orthopedics and emergency room. But if you can handle the E.R., you can do anything."

Carla came out from the examining room area with Peyton Flake at her heels. My staff reporter is barely five feet tall; Flake is six-four. They made an odd pair. Carla's long black hair fell over her shoulders, while Flake's wavy brown locks were held back in a ponytail. As ever, his professional attire was more than casual. It was almost disreputable. His blue jeans were ragged at the cuffs, his flannel shirt was rumpled, and the white coat he wore in deference to Gerald Dewey needed both cleaning and pressing.

"Bastards," said Flake, yanking the stethoscope from around his neck. "If I find out who did that to Marilynn, I'll kill the sons-of-bitches." He wheeled on Nancy who was coming out of the receptionist's area. "I've already told your husband that if this crap keeps up, I'm quitting. I won't live in a lame-assed town where people aren't treated like people."

Nancy Dewey didn't even blink. I gathered she was accustomed to Peyton Flake's outbursts. "You've got surgery at eight tomorrow," she said calmly. "Mrs. Whipp, knee replacement."

Flake's face fell. "I've never done a knee. Oh, well." He shrugged and went out the door.

Carla was staring at me. "What are you doing here? I've got to go to the pharmacy and get some antibiotics."

I asked her if she'd seen Marilynn, but the nurse had left before Carla arrived. Relieved, I bade Nancy Dewey good night and accompanied Carla outside. As it turned out, Carla didn't know anything about the dead crow. No surprise there—my reporter is often the last to know anything. She expressed dismay, but in a detached sort of way. It was obvious that Carla's priority was her aching ear. I watched her hurry across Pine Street and head for Parker's Pharmacy two blocks away, between Third and Fourth on Front.

Coincidences in Alpine often aren't very remarkable. With only four thousand people, it isn't unusual to run into somebody you've just been talking about. Or at least to meet up with one of their cousins. In this case, it was an Alpine Appliance van parked across the street at the community hospital. A young man with straw-colored hair was coming out of the emergency entrance as I unlocked the door to my green Jaguar. I wondered if he might be Shane Campbell, whose parents were providing board and room for Marilynn Lewis.

I used my guise as journalist to find out. "Equipment problems?" I shouted.

Startled, the young man stopped in the act of locking the rear doors of the van. He said nothing, but gazed at me while two cars and a pickup truck passed between us on Third Street.

I crossed to meet him and identified myself. "I thought there might be a crisis at the hospital," I explained. "You know—electricity, heat, water. That's news in a small town."

"It is?" The young man obviously didn't think so. "No, nothing like that. Mrs. Whipp just checked in and insisted on renting a VCR. I dropped it off on my way home." He gave me a halfhearted smile and headed for the driver's side of the van.

"Are you Shane?" I called after him.

Turning to look over his shoulder, he nodded. "Right. Do

you need something? We've got a sale on gas barbecues this week."

I gaped. "You do? How come your dad didn't take out an ad?"

Shane lifted his broad shoulders, which were covered by a brown jacket with ALPINE APPLIANCE emblazoned in crimson letters. "I thought he did. Come to think of it, I didn't see it in the paper yesterday."

I hadn't seen it, either. Inwardly, I cursed Ed Bronsky. Had he forgotten to run the ad? Had he discouraged Lloyd Campbell from placing it in the first place? Had Ed made it so small that he could have mounted it on the head of a pin? I vowed to call Ed as soon as I got home.

My original intentions had been sabotaged by my ad manager's apparent dereliction of duty. Whatever tactful approach I had devised flew right out of my head. I considered offering my sympathy to the Campbell family's boarder, but held back. If Shane had been out delivering appliances all afternoon, he might not have heard about Marilynn Lewis and the dead crow. My feigned innocence hadn't fooled Nancy Dewey, so I tried acting dumb with Shane Campbell. Having had more practice at the latter than the former over the years, I was sure of success.

"How's Marilynn Lewis doing? I still haven't met her. Is she settling in okay?"

My queries seemed innocuous, but Shane Campbell's fair skin flushed. "She's doing all right," he mumbled, suddenly absorbed in the clipboard he was carrying. "She's anxious to get her own place. That's not easy in a little town like Alpine."

It wasn't. Carla had roomed in two different private homes before finally getting an apartment in a new, but pricey complex. Ginny Burmeister had given up trying to find affordable housing, but as a native, she had the option of living at home with her parents. I was aware that it might be more difficult for Marilynn Lewis to find a permanent niche. While it would be illegal for anyone in Alpine to discriminate, it wouldn't be impossible. It never was.

"You must be kind of crowded," I remarked, edging

away from the curb and closer to Shane. "Your sister still lives with your folks, doesn't she?"

The flush faded. Shane apparently felt he was on safer ground discussing his sister. "Cyndi? Yeah, she's the only one of us who's never left the nest. Our older sister, Wendy, got married five or six years ago. She teaches at the high school."

Quickly, I made the connection. Wendy Campbell must be Wendy Wilson: English, lit, speech, and debate. Her husband, Todd, was the local Public Utilities District manager. Cyndi obviously worked for her brother-in-law as the PUD receptionist. I'd met Wendy at several high school functions and talked to Todd on many occasions. I had also seen Cyndi at the PUD office. The Campbell family portrait was coming into focus.

It was apparent that Shane was anxious to shove off. It was also evident that he wasn't entirely comfortable discussing his family's boarder. I felt sad about that. Stupid me, I keep hoping that each upcoming generation will be more tolerant. If the sixtyish senior Campbells were broadminded enough to invite an African-American woman to share their roof, I would have thought their son would be even more progressive. But children often take the opposite course, if only to be perverse.

Shane Campbell drove off, and so did I. The afternoon sun was low over the evergreens that surround my cozy log house high on the hill above Alpine. I found no surprises in either my mail or on my answering machine. Ed Bronsky, however, sounded flabbergasted when I called to ask him about the ad for Alpine Appliance.

"Now that's the darnedest thing, Emma," he said, in an uneasy voice. "I had that dummy all laid out and looking spiffy. But there was this typo—well, not a typo, really, a mistake—something about the price. I put it down as $29.99, but it was $299.99. When Lloyd Campbell told me to fix it, I said, 'Gee, Lloyd, what kind of a sale is *that*? Three hundred bucks to cook something you could do on your stove? What happens if it rains? Which it will, because it always does.' Then he got mad and said to forget it. So I did."

I groaned. Ed was impossible. I would have to call Lloyd

Campbell first thing in the morning and try to talk him into running another ad, probably at a drastic discount, just to keep him happy. Better yet, I'd go over to Alpine Appliance in person.

"The next time that happens, tell me right away," I snarled into the phone. "I mean it, Ed. We can't afford to upset our advertisers. If you keep this up, I can't afford *you*." I slammed down the phone and fumed for almost two minutes.

I was trying to settle my nerves with a stiff bourbon and my recipe for Caesar salad when Ed's wife, Shirley, called.

"Ed's in tears," she announced in her squeaky voice, which always reminded me of one of the Three Little Pigs. In fact, Ed and Shirley looked like two of the pigs; their children looked like five more. "I hate to interfere, Emma, but you've been coming down awfully hard on him lately."

Shirley was right—it was only in recent weeks that Ed had begun to wear away my patience. But she was wrong if she thought I was going to relent. Ed had a responsibility not just to me, but to the rest of the staff—and to the community. If *The Advocate* didn't carry the message from local retailers, there was a very real danger that a weekly shopper could move into the area. Shoppers, with their glossy ads and neglect of news, were the journalist's nightmare. I had seen them in my dreams, resting on front porches, stuffed in mail boxes, lying on sidewalks, covering the earth like a toxic blanket.

But there was no arguing with Shirley, who always met reason with a whine. "Look," I said, keeping control of my temper, "Ed and I will sort this out at work. Go dry his tears, and while you're at it, put some starch in his backbone. I've got to get dinner."

"So do I," Shirley replied, the whine now in place. "Seven mouths to feed. Do you know how it feels to get *threats*?"

I sure did. As an editor and publisher, they were part of the job description. But for once, I didn't dwell on myself. Rather, I thought of Marilynn Lewis and the ugly letters and the dead crow. There was real menace in those kinds of threats.

I, however, was a paper tiger, and Shirley Bronsky knew it.

Milo Dodge ate everything but the plates. While his lanky frame didn't look it, he could have given the porcine Bronskys a run for their money when it came to forking up food. Still, I wasn't displeased. Sometimes I get bored cooking for only myself.

It was over coffee that I finally broached the subject of Marilynn Lewis. I would have done it sooner, but Milo had undergone a more recent crisis, caused by our local loony, Crazy Eights Neffel, who had poured kerosene all over the statue of town founder Carl Clemans and attempted to ignite it with an empty cigarette lighter. The lighter wasn't the only thing that didn't work; Crazy Eights's brain had been haywire for years. At seventysomething he refused to retire from mischief-making. Some said he was simpleminded; others, that he was a genius gone awry. Vida would say no more than that he was a nut, but always added in a protective tone that he was "*Alpine*'s nut." She had taken a picture, passing by on her way to the ski lodge. Milo had taken Crazy Eights to jail and locked him up for the night.

"Nancy Dewey's right," Milo said as we sat in the living room, with the front door open to allow the mild spring breeze inside the house. "No return address, mailed through a corner box, postmarked yesterday."

"Did the handwriting match any of the letters Marilynn received earlier?"

"Hard to tell. We'd have to get a handwriting expert to figure that out." Milo sipped his coffee.

"Will you?" I had a feeling Milo might be inclined to let the entire episode off the hook.

The sheriff considered, his long legs propped up on my coffee table. "That depends. On Marilynn, mainly."

I was quiet for a moment, wondering if Milo were wishing Marilynn and her dead crow and her threatening letters out of his life. Crazy Eights Neffel might be mad as a hatter, but Milo was used to him. And Crazy Eights was white.

"What's the connection?" I finally asked. Seeing Milo's

justifiably baffled look, I elucidated: "Between Marilynn and the Campbells. Their appliance store does fine, so they don't need the money. They aren't in the rooming house business. In fact, they must be all jammed up with Shane back home."

Milo rubbed the back of his neck. "Not really. I suppose Marilynn has Wendy's old room. The Campbell house is pretty big. You know the place? It's in that block with the cemetery on one side and the high school on the other."

I recognized the street, which featured a half-dozen large frame homes, at least two stories tall, with spacious yards. The bank president lived there, as did the owner of Barton's Bootery and the local optometrist.

"Still," I argued, "why the Campbells? They've never taken in boarders before."

Judging from the blank look on Milo's face, the thought had never occurred to him. "Maybe Dr. Flake asked them. The woman has to live somewhere." He continued to look blank, so I dropped the subject. It was apparent that Milo wasn't overly concerned with Marilynn Lewis's place of residence.

The sheriff and I had our usual evening, which, as usual, did not include a sexual orgy. He talked of steelheading, which was—as usual—poor. I regaled him with my tales of Ed Bronsky's ineptitude. He countered with a sloughing off on the part of his deputies. I pointed out that Carla wasn't improving as fast as I wished. We agreed that people in general don't take pride in their work. Then Milo went home.

Keeping true to my own work ethic, the next morning I went straight to Alpine Appliance. Although the store doesn't open until ten o'clock, Lloyd Campbell shows up at eight. When I arrived, he was in his small office drinking coffee and leafing through a television manufacturer's manual.

"Emma," he said, getting up and offering his hand. "I haven't seen you since the high school band concert last month at Old Mill Park. How's it going?"

Fine, I told him, sitting down and accepting his offer of coffee. Lloyd's hair had faded to silver, but may have once been the same straw color as his son's. His blue eyes crin-

kled at the corners, and his stocky figure showed only the
slightest signs of flab. He was a genial man, as befitted a
salesman who had gotten his start selling Fuller Brush
products door-to-door in neighboring Snohomish County.
We exchanged general pleasantries before we got down to
the specifics of Ed Bronsky. Lloyd accepted my apologies,
but refused to deal further with Ed.

"The sale ends Tuesday," Lloyd pointed out. "I couldn't
change the date—the manufacturer helped pay for the ad. It
was a co-op deal, part of a national campaign. I shouldn't
have let Ed get me so riled up—I guess I shot myself in the
foot, but he can be pretty aggravating."

Unfortunately, I understood. Ed certainly could aggravate
a body. I coaxed, I soothed, I sucked up. Lloyd listened
patiently, occasionally making a pertinent comment or com-
plaining about the local economy.

"People aren't buying unless it's something they absolutely have to have," he informed me. "A stove, a water
heater, a washer. In all these years, I've stayed open from
ten until five-thirty, five days a week. You know the motto
around here: if you can't make it in five, you won't make
it in six. But so many wives are working, even in Alpine.
I'm thinking about opening up on Saturdays, at least until
one o'clock."

Lloyd Campbell's philosophy about the workweek wasn't
new to me. I'd heard it from most of the local merchants.
Indeed, before I'd arrived in Alpine, there had been a ti-
tanic battle over whether the Alpine Mall would be open on
Sundays. It wasn't for the first six months, and the radical
change occurred only after the Christmas season when the
store owners discovered that they could actually sell merchandise to paying customers on the Sabbath.

After ten minutes, Lloyd and I had hammered out an advertising compromise, which involved a free quarter page
in the bowling alley special and putting Ginny Burmeister
on the Alpine Appliance account. Ginny should be pleased,
and Ed would be relieved. I supposed I was getting off
cheap.

"Now when Marius Vandeventer owned the paper . . ."
Lloyd had leaned back in his chair and was gazing up at
the tube lighting in the ceiling.

I've lost count of the times I've heard that phrase. Since Marius Vandeventer sold *The Alpine Advocate* to me three years ago and retired to Santa Fe, he's achieved sainthood. It was not always so. In his early years, Marius's left-wing leanings were despised by people of a more conservative nature; as a senior citizen, his rampant Republicanism had choked most of Alpine's more liberal thinkers. And throughout his reign over *The Advocate*, it was said that an editorial endorsement of any local candidate, regardless of party affiliation, was tantamount to the kiss of death.

But now that Marius was gone, local attitudes had changed. I might not be able to fill his shoes, but I was wearing them. It wasn't much consolation to know that when I retired or left town or died, I, too, would become sanctified.

So I let Lloyd Campbell ramble on, my mind wandering to other ideas for the bowling alley special, to the School's Out edition, even to the Fourth of July promotions. I came up short when I heard Lloyd mention Marilynn Lewis's name.

". . . wouldn't have put up with treating Marilynn like that for a minute." Lloyd smacked his fist on the desk for emphasis. "What do you think, Emma?"

I could hardly tell Lloyd what I was thinking. What I surmised was that he had been talking about Marius Vandeventer's policy on prejudice. To cover my lapse of attention, I hedged:

"I think these things have to be weighed carefully. I'd have to speak with Marilynn first. I haven't met her yet, you know." I sat back in the captain's chair and tried to look pensive.

Lloyd squinted at the calendar on the near wall. It showed a picture of Mount Baldy, covered with snow. The calendar was sponsored by Alpine Appliance. "What's today? Friday? How about coming over for dinner? You can meet Marilynn. Let me call Jean and see if she can rustle up something edible."

I started to protest, but Lloyd was already punching in his home phone number. Or so I assumed. As it turned out, he had called the Presbyterian church. Jean Campbell didn't answer, but whoever did managed to put her on the line almost at once.

Lloyd's conversation was brief and to the point. Replacing the receiver, he beamed at me. "There. You're on for seven o'clock. Don't worry, I didn't have to twist Jean's arm. I forgot, Wendy and Todd are coming over tonight. Jean says it's no trouble to toss another spud in the pot."

I started to convey my appreciation when the phone rang under Lloyd's hand. Never taking his eyes off me, he listened, smiled, and nodded. "Good idea," he said. Then he hung up.

"That was Jean. She wants to know if you'll invite Vida, too. Jean and Vida are quite the chums at church," he explained.

While I knew that my House & Home editor was a staunch Presbyterian, I wasn't aware that she and Jean Campbell were particularly close friends. But that was typical of Vida—she knew everyone, people told her everything, she went everywhere. Yet she was basically a very private person. Those closest to her were virtually all family members. Given the vast number of Runkel-Blatt kinfolk, there was hardly room for outsiders in Vida's crowded world.

Vida, however, was perfectly willing to join the Campbells for dinner. "Jean got new Oriental rugs after Christmas," she said, circling photos on a sheet of contact prints. "I haven't seen them yet. Grace Grundle said the Campbells paid more for the rugs than they did for their house when they bought it in 'fifty-nine. Of course, we were in a recession that year." She licked at the end of her grease pencil.

"You'll also get to see Marilynn Lewis up close," I pointed out.

Vida looked at me over the rims of her glasses. Her face was impassive. "So will you."

I spent the next half hour with Ed and Ginny. Ed professed to be still upset, but judging from the number of jelly doughnuts he devoured, I doubted it. Ginny was mildly pleased by being assigned to the Alpine Appliance account. I wondered if she realized she was building quite a little empire in addition to her front office duties. I also wondered when she'd get around to asking for a raise.

I was halfway through my public swimming pool editorial for next week when Carla sauntered into my office and announced that she was feeling much better.

"I even went jogging this morning," she said, draping herself over the back of one of my visitors' chairs. "Libby tells me that I'm not in good shape. Guess what I saw."

"Milo let Crazy Eights Neffel out of jail?"

After almost three years in Alpine, Crazy Eights was old news to Carla. "He's always in jail or some place like that," she sniffed. "What's so funny about an old man wearing his underwear outside of his clothes? Or walking around with a live duck on his head? I don't think he should be allowed to ride a tricycle down the middle of Front Street. It isn't safe."

"It sure isn't," I agreed, "especially with drivers like Durwood Parker driving everywhere but in the legal lane." In his own way, Durwood was as great a menace as Crazy Eights. But Durwood wasn't crazy; he was merely the worst driver I'd ever had the misfortune to run into—or *almost*, having made a quick left turn to avoid him in the Alpine Mall parking lot.

Our digression had steered me away from Carla's morning run. But since the topic was herself, Carla picked up where we'd left off. "So there I was, going around the track up at the high school field, and he came out from behind the scoreboard. He saw me and hurried away. Weird, huh?"

I blinked. "Weird? Why? Who was it?"

Carla shrugged, allowing her long black hair to tumble over the front of her sleeveless chambray shirt. "That's just it—I didn't recognize him. Would you expect me to?"

Yes. No. Maybe. I was all at sea. Was my mind going? I'd already managed to lose track of Lloyd Campbell's conversation; now I was foundering with Carla. But reason—and experience—told me that this time it wasn't my fault.

"Wait a minute, Carla—you've left something out. We got distracted," I added, lest she think me too critical. "If you don't know who this guy is, why are you telling me about him?"

Slowly, Carla stood up straight. She looked puzzled, then

put her hands to her head. "Oh! I get it! I forgot!" She gave me her big, infectious smile. "I didn't describe him! He wasn't that close, but I've been practicing my powers of observation. You know, what you keep telling me about paying attention with the journalist's eye?" She spoke very fast and I nodded. "He was fairly young, twenties, I'd guess, five-ten, maybe six-foot, average build, really short hair—a fade, I think you call it—Stussy shirt, baggy khaki pants, probably tennis shoes, but I couldn't be sure." Carla looked very proud of herself, then her face fell. "Oh! I almost forgot!" She gave me an apologetic smile. "He was black. That's the part I left out."

Chapter Three

MY FIRST REACTION—other than an urge to kick Carla—was that the stranger had come to Alpine High School to recruit for a college sports team. Or that he was a tourist, out to join Carla for a morning jog on the track. Perhaps he was a teacher, interviewing for a job in the upcoming school year. He might be a forest ranger, newly posted to the area, or sent from one of the state agencies on a fact-finding mission. He could even be a nature lover, making sure that nobody was taking potshots at the spotted owl. I couldn't think of a more endangered species in Alpine than an African-American environmentalist.

But on second thought, I feared that he was probably none of the above. Never mind that my initial responses made perfect sense. My gut reaction told me that the black man at the high school field wasn't in town on official business. I hoped I was wrong.

"So he hurried away?" I asked, remembering to transfer and save my swimming pool editorial before we had one of our frequent power failures.

Carla nodded. "Yeah, you know, sort of furtive. As if he didn't expect anyone to be there except him. I knew Coach Ridley had scheduled track-and-field practice for this afternoon because I interviewed him about the big meet coming up in Seattle. Of course, it *was* early—just after seven o'clock. I wouldn't dream of being late two days in a row." Carla had assumed an air of virtue.

I let Carla's assertion pass. Seven A.M. wasn't all that early for activity at the high school field. Practice for various sports often took place before classes started. But this particular Friday in May wasn't one of those days. I confessed that I was at a loss for an explanation.

After Carla drifted away, I resumed regaling my reader-
ship with the need for a bond issue to build a public pool.
The site was ready and waiting, right on Alpine Way, where
the original bowling alley had stood, and a series of enter-
prises, including a pool hall, a swap shop, and a buffet-style
restaurant, had tried and failed to make a go of it.

I was attempting to dispel the myth that swimming in the
river was good enough for Alpine's founders, even in January at fifteen below, when I heard Vida arguing heatedly
over the phone. By the time I entered the news office, she'd
banged down the receiver.

"Edina Puckett! Honestly!" Vida raised her arms and
flexed her muscles like a weight lifter. I suspected she
wanted to put a hammerlock on Edina. "Why can't people
use *sense*? This Junior Miss controversy has all these parents
at each other's throats!"

I knew the story behind the story of the previous weekend's local Junior Miss pageant. As usual, Vida had covered it and taken some rather fuzzy photos. Also as usual,
Vida had discreetly chosen to report only the bare bones of
what had actually happened. According to her, the annual
competition brought out the worst in Alpine's mothers, fathers, and children, too. Hair pulling, name-calling, and
hysterics could set the stage for family feuds that lasted a
lifetime.

This year the talent segment had featured everything
from whisking eggs to hand puppets made out of milk cartons. The most serious incident had been caused by fifteen-
year-old Kerri Rhodes, daughter of the Venison Inn's
bartender, Oren, and his wife, Sunny, the resident Avon
Lady. Kerri's talent was tap-dancing with a pig named
Kash. Wearing matching yellow tutus, Kash and Kerri had
hoofed their way through "Old MacDonald Had a Farm."
On the last "E-I-E-I-O," Kash had become overly excited
and wet the boards. No one seemed to notice, thus setting
the stage—literally—for Trisha Puckett and her unicycle.
Trisha, sixteen, skidded four feet before crashing in full
view of the audience. Only her dignity had been seriously
hurt, but her parents, Edina and Clayton Puckett, were
threatening to sue Oren and Sunny Rhodes. Naturally, *The*

Advocate would say nothing until formal charges had been filed.

The disaster would never have occurred, argued Pageant Chairman Stilts Cederberg, if the contestants had stuck to the rules that banned the use of wheels.

"Wheels?" I asked, somewhat dazed.

"Wheels," Vida responded firmly. "The rule was originally made for musical instruments. In the old days, some of the contestants played tunes on mill machinery. You know, band saws, donkey engines, re-covered oil drums. Back in 'forty-five, Veda Kay MacAvoy won for her rendition of 'The White Cliffs of Dover' on the original mill whistle."

"On wheels?" I asked, trying to keep a straight face.

"No, of course not. Why would you put the mill whistle on wheels? It was the handcar that was a problem that year. The Gustavson twins stole it from the railroad tracks, and it flew off the stage and landed in the audience while they were singing 'Tea for Two.' Millard O'Toole suffered three fractured ribs, and Mrs. Pidduck's glasses got broken." Looking severe, Vida returned to her typewriter.

The rest of the day was uneventful. Over the phone, I interviewed a state official in Olympia about the latest plan for selective logging, talked to Mayor Fuzzy Baugh concerning his new antilitter program, and spent almost half an hour listening to a highway department engineer drone on about the problems involved in resurfacing the road to the Icicle Creek campground. Shortly before five, I found myself staring at the WNPA invitation. The deadline for registration was May 21, a week away. I had seven days to jitter and dither.

Putting the information aside, I grimaced. My brother, Ben, had problems making decisions. His indecisiveness irked me. But I was no better. Indeed, I often excused my own waffling on the grounds that journalists aren't supposed to take sides, except on the editorial page. I grimaced some more. This wasn't politics or a social issue or a matter of morality—this was my life. I was Emma Lord: forty-two years old, five-foot-four, brown haired, brown eyed, passably good-looking, reasonably intelligent, a mother, a journalist, a homeowner, a university graduate, a Roman

Catholic, a Democrat, a voting resident of Alpine, Washington, Skykomish County. And I couldn't make up my mind about going to Lake Chelan. I turned off my word processor and decided to go home.

Vida was standing by her desk, adjusting her gold straw hat with its matching gold piping on the brim. It was new, and looked ridiculous, though no more so than most of Vida's headgear. She was gazing into a small mirror affixed to the door of her filing cabinet.

"I got this through a catalogue," she said. "Isn't it smart?" I was chasing an answer when she went on talking. "Tommy called. You were on the phone, so I took it."

I gaped at Vida. She was the only person I knew who dared to call Tom Cavanaugh "Tommy." "Tom called? Today?"

Satisfied with the set of her straw hat, Vida gave me a nonchalant look. "You were on the phone with that long-winded engineer. Tommy just bought a newspaper in the San Fernando Valley. His daughter auditioned this week for a part in a play. His son wants to join a soccer team in Europe. Sandra robbed a bank." Vida reached for her worn alligator handbag and a copy of *The Seattle Times*. "Are you going to pick me up or shall I walk? The Campbells live only three blocks from my house."

"Vida!" I was leaning on Ed's desk, gritting my teeth. "I haven't talked to Tom since February! Why didn't you tell me he called?"

Digging into her purse, Vida pulled out her car keys. "You were busy," she answered reasonably. "Besides, he had to go someplace. The Pacific Union Club? Something like that. And visit Sandra. She's been institutionalized again. The robbery, you know."

I didn't know who to feel sorry for: Tom, Sandra—or me. While Tom's wife had been involved in a number of shoplifting incidents, bank robbery was new. I could hardly believe it. In fact, I didn't.

"Vida—are you talking armed and dangerous? When did this happen? Where? What did Tom say?"

Vida had started for the door. Over her shoulder, she threw me a faintly exasperated look. "I didn't ask for details, Emma. You know I don't like to pry. Besides, Ginny was signaling that Ellie Pierce from the Burl Creek Thimble Club was on line three. They had their annual election last night."

I let Vida go. But before she pulled her big Buick away from the curb, I ran after her, shouting that I'd pick her up at five to seven. She gave a toot of her horn in acknowledgment and headed up Fourth Street toward her home on Cascade.

In the sanctuary of my log house, I considered calling Tom. But Vida had said he was going out. I'd wait until morning. The rates would still be down, and it sounded as if he were alone in his handsome brick mansion high above the bay. Or so I imagined it, never having seen the place.

But I had seen the Campbell house, many times. I hadn't, however, assigned an owner to the big, three-story white home on the corner of Seventh and Tyee. A white picket fence, a wraparound porch, and a widow's walk lent a gracious New England air. The garden was abloom with azaleas, rhododendrons, mountain laurel, wallflowers, Dutch iris, and tulips.

Jean Campbell greeted us warmly. She was a big woman, as tall as Vida, but heavier without being fat. Her graying brown hair was swept back into a french roll with little wispy curls dancing at her high forehead and smooth temples. In her sensible two-inch heels, she was almost a head taller than her husband.

"We're having London broil," she announced. "Safeway had a special on flank steak. I saw it in *The Advocate*." She gave me a big smile, showing off the slight gap between her front teeth. "Come, sit, we'll have a drink while we wait for the poor working stiffs. Shane had a late delivery of the Tolbergs' new gas range, and Todd got tied up at the PUD."

Jean Campbell's idea of a drink was sparkling cider, which was fine with me and appropriate to the family's standing as staunch Presbyterians. I had considered having a bourbon and water when I got home, but didn't want to show up at the Campbells' reeking of alcohol and thus perpetuating the myth that all Catholics are die-hard drunks.

If many Alpiners are prejudiced against people of color, they also have some pretty strange notions about other re-

ligions. While the Scandinavian Lutherans dominate the local population, I'm aware that Baptists don't trust Methodists, Congregationalists look askance at the Pentecostals,
and everybody thinks the Episcopalians are almost as
strange as the Catholics. I keep waiting for somebody to
figure out that Carla is a Jew.

Cyndi Campbell was the first of the younger set to appear. She greeted Vida and me with subdued enthusiasm. A
pretty young woman with her father's fair coloring and naturally pink cheeks, Cyndi wore a tan tunic top over a
matching crocheted skirt. To my surprise, she smoked like
a chimney. I envied her, having quit shortly before buying
The Alpine Advocate. I was sure I'd made the right decision
about the newspaper; I wasn't sure I should have given up
the cigarettes.

"How long have you been at the PUD?" I asked, in an
effort to make conversation and to avoid snatching the pack
out of her small, graceful hands.

"Three years," Cyndi replied, crossing her legs under the
short skirt and exhaling deeply. "I went to Shoreline Community College in north Seattle for a couple of years and
got my associate of arts degree. I tried the UDUB for two
quarters, but it didn't feel right. Too big." She exhaled
some more.

I gave Cyndi a sympathetic smile. "It can seem that way,
if you're not used to crowds. You like living in Alpine, I
take it?"

Cyndi's green eyes darted from father to mother. "I
guess. Seattle's too big. I visited on weekends while Shane
was living there. I thought I might like it better when I
wasn't going to school, but I didn't. Still, I wouldn't mind
living in a bigger town than Alpine—like Bellingham or
Everett." Her attitude suggested she was throwing out a
challenge to her parents.

Jean Campbell's response was to head for the kitchen.
"The flank steak ought to be marinated by now," she said,
over her shoulder. "Fifteen minutes until dinner." I gathered
she had paused in the hallway, perhaps to call upstairs.
"Shane! Are you up there? Come down, have some cider!
Marilynn?"

But no one appeared. The aroma of garlic wafted into the

comfortable living room with its pink flowered drapes and matching sofa. Vida was ogling the Oriental rugs. Her expression was a mixture of admiration and envy. Lloyd Campbell tossed a travel brochure at her.

"Spain," he said. "We're thinking of going there this fall."

"Spain," Vida repeated, tearing her eyes off the carpeting. "My daughters insisted I go. It's very hot. Sort of like an old Montana in the summer."

Lloyd didn't seem discouraged. "Scads of history, though. Art, too. And I hear the beaches are terrific. We went to England and France six years ago."

Scanning the brochure, Vida nodded. "I know. I did the story after you got back. The English were stuffy and the French were rude. But you liked Oxford and the Loire Valley." She tossed the brochure back to Lloyd. "Who doesn't? It's criminal to hate either of them. Why don't you go to Italy instead of Spain? Rome is fascinating and Florence has all sorts of art treasures."

But Lloyd shook his head. "Too many Catholics. You know, the Vatican, and all those priests." He glanced at me and flushed. "Sorry, Emma, but I hear those people over there aren't like Americans. It's different."

"That's probably because it's Europe." My tone was dry.

We were saved from further embarrassment by the arrival of Wendy and Todd Wilson. Wendy was taller than her sister, not quite as pretty, but more outgoing. Her dark blonde hair hung in a carelessly combed pageboy; the hem of her blue wrap skirt was uneven; her navy jacket was draped at an odd angle. Her clothes looked expensive, yet everything about Wendy Campbell Wilson seemed off balance. She almost tripped over the magazine rack that stood next to the flowered sofa.

"Well!" Wendy lunged first at Vida, then at me. "Surprise! Mom said we were having unexpected company. Vida, do you remember the wedding story you wrote about us? You said I wore a borrowed blue *farter*." Wendy threw back her head and laughed in a gusty manner.

Vida drew back, her eyes narrowed. "I got my bifocals that week. I couldn't read proof properly." She shifted her gaze in my direction, as if daring me to make an untoward comment.

Todd Wilson had slumped into a rose-colored armchair. "God, Wendy," he said, in a tired voice, "you women remember the damnedest things! That was seven years ago."

His wife gave him a sharp glance. "Eight, come June. I'll bet you don't even remember which day."

Todd didn't contradict Wendy. "I don't remember yesterday. Life at the PUD wipes out my memory. It wipes me out, too. That wind last weekend knocked down a bunch of branches on the line to the fish hatchery. I spent all afternoon sawing down trees and trying not to deck that mouthy guy from the State Fisheries Department." Todd's close-set brown eyes traveled across the room to his sister-in-law. "Was today a bitch or was it not, Cyndi?"

Cyndi let her head loll back on the sofa. "It always is. The middle of the month, all those cutoff dates for the deadbeats. I get tired of answering the phone and listening to their excuses. They won't wait until I can connect them to Danielle in credit."

"Not them." Todd waved a freckled hand in dismissal. He was a pleasant-looking fellow in his midthirties, with wavy brown hair highlighted by hints of red. His forehead, however, was prematurely creased. "I mean the complaints about the water-shortage surcharge. We either got water or we don't. This year's not as bad as last, but you'd think we were personally responsible for the lack of rain. Hell, this last February was the driest on record for—"

Todd's complaint was cut short by the appearance of Shane Campbell, now wearing blue jeans and a pale blue shirt. He greeted us all with a diffident wave, then went directly to the kitchen. I saw Wendy's gaze follow her brother out of the room. She didn't look pleased.

"Shane should go back to Seattle," she declared. "He's the perfect example of the you-can't-go-home-again syndrome."

"Shut up," snapped Cyndi. "Shane's doing fine. He's waiting for Fred Meyer."

Wendy leaned forward in the white leather club chair, all traces of her earlier good humor gone. "You shut up, Cyndi. Why do you and Shane always take sides against me? I'm only thinking about what's best for him. You haven't thought about anybody but yourself since the day you were born."

In his recliner next to the fireplace, Lloyd Campbell chuckled. "Come on, kids, knock it off. We've got company." He turned his genial face to Vida and me. "Siblings. They never get over squabbling. What about your three girls, Vida?"

Vida considered. "They debate. They also live in different towns. That helps."

Lloyd inclined his head, conceding the point. Before he could ask for my opinion, Jean returned from the kitchen. "We're almost ready," she said, a bit breathlessly. "Shane is watching the meat. Would anyone care for more sparkling cider?"

"More?" Todd made a face. "Wendy and I haven't had *any*. You got a beer? I've had a hell of a day."

Jean frowned at her son-in-law, but Lloyd got up from his recliner. "Believe it or not, Todd, I have a six-pack stashed away in the woodshed. I was saving it for a fishing trip."

Moments later, Todd Wilson was caressing his can of beer as if it were a family pet. His wife ignored him. His sister-in-law looked envious. Lloyd Campbell made another trip into the kitchen and disappeared. I wondered if he'd liberated a second beer for himself and was drinking it in the backyard.

Our hostess could be seen through the French doors that separated the living room from the dining room. Jean had brought out two serving bowls; she returned with a bread basket; on the third trip, she carried a large platter.

"Dinner," she called, then went back into the kitchen.

Wendy led us into the dining room with its solid oak table and chairs, a big breakfront jammed with china, and a buffet decorated with a pair of brass candlesticks and a bouquet of tulips.

Swiftly, I counted the place settings. There were nine. Eight of us had already shown up. Marilynn Lewis was missing. Shane carried in a big bowl of salad; Jean brought a ladle for the gravy. We were still in the act of sitting down when we heard the sirens.

Vida craned her neck in the direction of the double window that looked out onto Seventh Street. It was still broad daylight. "That's the sheriff," she said.

Lloyd eased himself into his chair at the head of the table. "Probably a wreck out there at the four-way stop. Damned fools come tearing down First Hill Road and don't bother to see if anybody's coming off Highway 187. Kids, I'll bet." He passed the potatoes to Wendy on his left.

Wendy pursed her lips. "We need a real traffic light there. We've had two assemblies on traffic safety already this year at the high school, but nobody listens. Drivers' ed, yes—that works pretty well. But not everybody takes it . . ."

Her voice trailed off as another siren sounded nearby. "Ambulance," said Vida, taking the meat platter from Shane. Her eyes flickered around the table, lighting on the vacant chair between Cyndi and Todd. "Where's Marilynn?"

The question had been on my mind ever since we arrived half an hour earlier. Glances seemed to fly around the table: Lloyd at Jean, Jean at Shane, Shane at Cyndi, Cyndi at both Wendy and Todd.

It was Shane who finally spoke. "She was going to be late. She said not to wait for her."

Wendy gave a little snort. "Well, we didn't." She spooned green beans onto her plate.

The awkward lull that ensued was broken by Jean Campbell, who urged us not to skimp on the meat. "It isn't often that flank steak's on special, so I always get plenty of it. And I hate having leftovers. Lloyd won't eat them." She gave her husband a benevolent smile.

The mood seemed to relax, though I noticed that Vida was leaning back in her chair, as if listening for further action from outside.

Apparently, Lloyd also noticed her attitude. "You should have brought your camera, Vida. Front-page car crashes always get readers' attention, I'll bet."

But Vida shook her head. "Those sirens didn't go all the way to the intersection. In fact, they didn't even go past your house. It sounded to me as if they stopped a couple of blocks up Spruce."

Spruce was the next east-west artery, between Tyee and my own street, Fir. It went past the high school field before petering out at Highway 187 and First Hill Road. I felt a wave of uneasiness creep over me. I didn't know why.

No one argued with Vida's pronouncement about the sirens. Instead, Wendy began to talk about the essays her American lit students had handed in that day. Her parents wore interested expressions; her siblings looked bored; her husband left the dining room, possibly searching for his father-in-law's stash of beer.

"They can't get it through their heads that science fiction isn't literature. Neither are romances or spy stories or those thrillers that make your hair stand on end." Wendy was pontificating, using her fork for emphasis. "I'm not asking them to read Hawthorne or Henry James—I'd settle for Hemingway, even J. D. Salinger. I had one kid who turned in a paper on a comic book version of *Call of the Wild*!"

Jean Campbell wore a look of concern. "Salinger? I remember when you and Shane and Cyndi read his book. It was awfully frank. I don't think Hemingway is suitable, either. What's wrong with Sir Walter Scott and Louisa May Alcott?"

"The smokers' grocery." It was Vida who spoke, tapping her fingers on the linen tablecloth.

Everyone, including Todd, who had returned from the kitchen beerless, stared at Vida.

"The what?" asked Jean, diverted from her diatribe against immoral literature.

"That little store across from the high school," Vida explained. "You know, where the students go to smoke. And do heaven knows what else these days." Her face puckered in disapproval.

Wendy buttered a chunk of sourdough bread. "They don't go there anymore except to buy candy and pop. After old Mr. Whipp retired, his son cleaned the place up. That's probably why he's going broke."

Shane was looking out the window, though there was nothing to see except the backyard and a large blue house across the alley. Dark clouds were moving in over the mountains. Our fine spring weather seemed about to break.

"Do you suppose the store got robbed?" Shane asked in an apprehensive voice.

Lloyd Campbell chuckled. "You've spent too much time in Seattle, son. We haven't had a real robbery in Alpine since the 7-Eleven got held up three years ago. Even then, the robbers were from Everett."

"A robber wouldn't get much from Marlow Whipp," Wendy asserted with authority. "I go in there once in a while to buy gum or a can of diet pop, and there's never anybody around. I'd guess he loses as much to the kids who shoplift as he makes off the ones who pay."

Jean Campbell was pressing more food on all of us. Her forehead creased as she offered Vida a second chance at the potatoes. "I hope Marlow hasn't had a heart attack. He's not a kid anymore. We went to school together. He was always nice, rather quiet, and not much of a scholar. He couldn't spell, and he was even worse at math. I wonder how he manages to keep his accounts straight."

"Math!" Vida sniffed. "As I recall, Marlow flunked shop twice. No mechanical aptitude. Still, he may be dumb as a bag of sawdust, but he comes from sturdy stock. His parents are still alive and kicking. Reva Whipp got a new knee this morning, and she's well over eighty."

"Vida and I were in school together," said Lloyd Campbell, giving me a wink. "Of course she was a couple of years ahead of me."

"Light-years," snapped Vida, "in more ways than one."

Everyone laughed, though not without a trace of awkwardness. The Campbell family wasn't as accustomed as I was to Vida's tart tongue.

We all grew silent as the front door opened. My eyes watched the doorway into the long hall that led from the living room, past the dining room, and on into the kitchen. A moment later, a dream came walking out of Africa. Shane Campbell looked as if he were awed by the sight, and I couldn't blame him. Marilynn Lewis wasn't merely young, slim, and pretty, as Carla had mentioned. She was dazzling, with classic high cheekbones, wide-set limpid brown eyes, and sculpted features that might have adorned royalty from Ethiopia. I thought of the Queen of Sheba, of Aïda, of all the goddesses I'd seen portrayed in African art exhibits over

the years. She moved with grace; she dominated the room.
Yet it struck me that she was scared to death.

"I'm so sorry," she apologized breathlessly, pushing her
heavy dark hair away from her face. "I had to look at an
apartment in that building across from the clinic." She sat
down between Cyndi and Todd.

Lloyd introduced Vida and me to Marilynn Lewis. Her
smile was charming, if tremulous. Jean urged her to eat,
then asked if she liked the apartment.

Marilynn frowned as she speared a slice of London broil.
"It's an old building, you know, but it's certainly convenient since I don't have a car. I told the manager I'd consider it." She kept her brown eyes on her plate.

Vida finally leaned forward in her chair. "The manager?
Isn't that Dolph Terrill? He's a nincompoop, Marilynn.
Don't agree to his first offer. He won't remember what he
said, and it will be too expensive anyway. Dolph doesn't do
a thing to keep that place up. He's lazy and drinks too
much."

Over the bowl of green beans, Marilynn gave Vida a shy,
nervous look. "Mr. Terrill drinks? Maybe that's why he
seemed . . . odd."

"Odd!" Vida tossed her head, almost losing her straw hat
in the process. "Pay no attention to anything he says. There
aren't that many apartments available in Alpine, so you
have to take what you can get, but you don't have to take
it at Dolph Terrill's first price. Do you want me to talk
sense into him?"

Marilynn's face relaxed a bit. It was clear that she was
surprised by Vida's offer. "That's awfully nice of you,
Mrs. . . . Runkel, is it? You know Mr. Terrill well?"

"Certainly," Vida replied. "I used to baby-sit him. He
was a horror even then. You wouldn't believe what I caught
him doing to the family collie. Her name was Venus. Do I
need to say more?" Vida's gray-eyed gaze ran darkly
around the table. Everyone but Todd looked away.

"Say, Marilynn," Lloyd put in to mercifully change the
subject, "you didn't happen to walk home on Spruce Street,
did you?"

Marilynn frowned some more. "No, I came up Tyee.

Spruce is the next block over, isn't it? That would have been out of my way."

"Of course it would," Lloyd replied in his genial voice. "I just wondered. We think there's been some kind of ruckus over on Spruce. Sirens and such. You hear them?"

Marilynn considered. "Maybe. I heard the train whistling. I don't remember. I was thinking about the apartment."

Vida got to her feet, straightening her straw hat in the process. "Excuse me. I can't stand it another minute. I'm going over to Spruce and see what's going on." She glared at me in reproach. "Newspaper people have to keep abreast of current events. They owe it to their readers. Are you coming, Emma?"

Not for the first time did I feel as if our roles were reversed. I might be the editor and publisher, but Vida was the heart and soul of *The Alpine Advocate*. Her nose for news was as great as her natural curiosity. Indeed, they walked arm-in-arm through the streets of Alpine. Feeling rebuked, I also got to my feet.

"Vida's right," I said in an apologetic voice. "We ought to at least check out what's happening. We'll be right back."

Jean Campbell's voice floated behind us: "I'll hold off on dessert. It's cherry cheesecake."

Going down the front walk, Vida announced that it would be faster to go on foot than to take my car. The threat of rain didn't deter her in the least. "Unless I'm crazy, those sirens stopped less than two blocks away." She marched ahead of me in her splayfooted manner. "They haven't left yet. If they had, we'd have heard the sirens again."

As usual, Vida was right. The city's only ambulance, along with one of the four county sheriff's cars, was parked in front of the Spruce Street Grocery. I also recognized Milo Dodge's Cherokee Chief. Whatever had happened was important enough to take the sheriff away from his official off-duty hours.

Marlow Whipp was out on the sidewalk, talking earnestly with Milo and Deputy Bill Blatt, Vida's nephew. Several neighbors were also there, exchanging apprehensive remarks. At least a dozen perspiring teenagers carrying track shoes were craning for a better look. Vida was heading straight for Bill Blatt when the ambulance attendants and another deputy, Dwight Gould, emerged from the little grocery story with a stretcher. It was covered with black canvas. I suppressed a small groan.

Milo saw us, but kept talking to Bill Blatt and Marlow Whipp. Vida, however, was undaunted.

"Well?" she demanded, seizing her nephew by the collar of his regulation jacket. "What happened? Who's that?" She gestured at the covered stretcher, which was now being wheeled past us to the ambulance.

It was Marlow who answered, his Adam's apple bobbing up and down. "I never saw him before. I swear it." Marlow Whipp was a small man, in his midfifties, with faded brown hair and protuberant blue eyes, which now appeared dazed. "He came into the store, tried to say something, and collapsed. Honest to God!"

Milo Dodge put a hand on Marlow's shoulder. "It's okay, relax. Go inside and sit down. But don't touch anything." Realizing the ambiguity of his words, Milo grabbed Marlow more firmly. "On second thought, Dwight'll drive you down to the office. We'll get a statement and make you some coffee."

The ambulance doors were closed; Marlow Whipp was led away by Dwight Gould. With an apologetic look for his aunt, Bill Blatt followed his fellow deputy to the squad car. Milo Dodge pulled out a red bandanna handkerchief and blew his nose.

"Damned allergies," he muttered, as the first drops of rain began to fall. "Doc Dewey says it's the cottonwoods. I never used to have any problems."

"Your system changes every seven years," Vida responded, somewhat crossly. "Now what on earth's going on, Milo? Was that person dead?"

The ambulance pulled away from the curb, but at legal speed. The siren didn't go on; the lights didn't flash. Vida's question was answered. Several of the onlookers shook their heads. Most of the high school athletes began to drift away.

Milo stuffed the handkerchief back in the pocket of his

tan pants. "The deceased wasn't a local," he said in his laconic voice. "According to Marlow Whipp, he came into
the grocery store just before closing, about five to seven.
He tried to say something, and then collapsed." Never a fast
talker, Milo slowed to a snail's pace. The little cluster of
neighbors drew closer. "His name is Kelvin Greene, from
Seattle. He was twenty-seven years old and lived somewhere out in the Rainier Valley area. It looks as if he was
shot in the head." Milo's long face wore a disgusted look.
"Marlow called us. Marlow swears he didn't shoot him,
though he keeps a gun under the counter. Kelvin died before the ambulance could get here. He was black. Any
more questions, or can I get the hell out of here and do my
job?"

Chapter Four

VIDA AND I were torn. We both felt the professional urge to follow Milo to his office, but we had to consider our social obligations, too. We reasoned that since the paper wasn't due out again until Wednesday and the sheriff would prefer that we make ourselves scarce until he had control of this latest tragedy, we might as well go back to the Campbells' and eat dessert.

"When in doubt, eat cheesecake," Vida asserted as we briskly walked away from Marlow Whipp's little store. Though her words were flippant, her face was grim.

The rain was coming down quite hard by the time we reached our destination. Jean Campbell, looking worried, met us at the door. "What's happening?" she asked as we shook off raindrops and stamped our feet on the welcome mat.

"There's been a shooting," Vida replied, heading for the dining room. She paused at the foot of the table by Jean's vacant chair. Her gray eyes skimmed the other diners. Perhaps I imagined that her glance lingered just a trifle overlong on Marilynn Lewis. "It's no one we know. We might as well enjoy that delicious cheesecake."

We did, though naturally the others pressed us for details. As ever, Vida was regarded as the source of all knowledge. Only Marilynn, another outsider, fixed her curious gaze on me.

"I thought small towns were supposed to be quiet," she murmured at me behind Cyndi's back. "Does this kind of violence happen very often?"

Vida had honed her hearing on whispered comments during roll call at social clubs, on discreet remarks four rows away at high school band concerts, on breathless seduction attempts at cocktail parties. Even across the table, her keen ears caught Marilynn's words. Vida shot me a warning glance.

"Well," I mumbled, "Alpine has its share of . . . problems. People are people, after all. Sometimes they go haywire."

Marilynn's beautiful face remained troubled. "But who was killed? I mean, if it's no one we know, it's still *somebody*."

Vida turned away from her tête-à-tête with Shane. "The sheriff will release the name of the victim in due course. Right now, he doesn't know any details. That's why Emma and I came back here." She shrugged her wide shoulders. "There's no real news yet."

At the other end of the table, Lloyd Campbell was passing sugar and cream for coffee. "That's the trouble—we push for growth to pump up the economy, but when newcomers move in, there's often trouble. It seems to me we don't know what we're asking for."

"Lloyd!" Jean's voice was low and sharp. Her eyes darted in Marilynn's direction.

Lloyd blanched. "Oh, good Godfrey, Jean, you know I don't mean Marilynn here. Or Emma," he added, smiling sheepishly at both of us. My inclusion, I felt, was a nice touch. Consciously or otherwise, it was as if Lloyd were making the point that strangers come in all hues. "I mean all the riffraff that drifts in and out of a town like Alpine. It always has. Look how the hoboes used to ride the rails through here in the Twenties and Thirties."

"Goodness," Jean laughed, her manner a bit stilted, "that was before *my* time! Speak for yourself, Lloyd."

"I remember," Vida declared. "I was a small child during the Depression, but I certainly recall how my father and some of the other men kept an eye out for any vacant buildings where the hoboes might move in and start a fire. We were always so afraid of fire—especially in the forest. There just wasn't the means to fight a blaze in those days."

The conversation eased forward along the lines of danger, progress, and rumors of a new bond issue to increase the size of Skykomish County's emergency facilities. By the time we had finished dessert and moved back into the living room, we were once again on safe ground. Wendy had resumed airing her complaints about teenage illiteracy; Lloyd expounded on the wonders of high-definition TV, which he insisted was just around the corner; Cyndi critiqued the romantic comedy playing at the Whistling Marmot Movie Theatre; Todd asked Shane if he'd like to go fly-fishing on Sunday up at Surprise Lake; Jean and Vida discussed Pastor Purebeck's stance on marital infidelity that, happily, did not include any hanky-panky on their minister's part, but did display a surprisingly broad-minded attitude. At least for a Presbyterian. Or so it seemed to me. But then I had my own set of prejudices.

"I'm a Methodist," Marilynn Lewis confided. "I haven't been to church since I got here, but I understand the local minister is very respected. I've heard that from some of Dr. Flake and Dr. Dewey's patients."

I'd met the Reverend Minton Phelps on several occasions, and he seemed both respected and respectable. At least he hadn't dropped his pants in public, which was more than could be said for the previous Pentecostal minister—who had done just that shortly before I arrived in Alpine. My perverse, puckish sense of humor dictated that I relate the incident to Marilynn, who laughed merrily at the anecdote, some of which I made up since I hadn't been an eyewitness.

"Really, Ms. Lord," she said, still giggling, "I think I'm going to like it here in Alpine. I've met several awfully nice people." Abruptly, she sobered and lowered her dark eyes. "Of course, there are some jerks, too. But that's true everywhere, isn't it?"

"I'm afraid so." I, too, had turned serious. "You mustn't mind them. In some ways, this town is kind of backward. Isolated. Ingrown. Some of the locals need educating. And call me Emma."

Marilynn's smile resurfaced, though it was a little lopsided. "You aren't from here, either, I guess."

"No." Briefly, I recounted my history. Born and raised in Seattle, three years at the University of Washington, an internship at *The Times*, a journalism degree from the University of Oregon, eighteen years in Portland on *The Oregonian*. Parents killed in an auto accident, brother a priest in Arizona, son a student in Alaska. I omitted the part about my married lover and my unmarried pregnancy.

Marilynn reciprocated. She had been born in Oakland, but her family had moved to Seattle just before she entered high school. Her father was dead; her mother had remarried and moved back to California. After graduating from the UDUB's School of Nursing, she had gone to work at Virginia Mason Hospital. Four years later, she had decided she needed a change, both personally and professionally. I had the feeling she had omitted something, too.

"It's an adjustment," I said, referring to small-town life. "I still miss the city in many ways."

Marilynn nodded. "I do, too. I think." Her gaze traveled around the living room, taking in the Campbell family and Vida, who was regaling Wendy and Jean with an account of last year's Memorial Day ceremonies wherein Crazy Eights Neffel had decorated the town's World War I monument with balloon animals. Shane was at the window, peering into the rain. He struck me as edgy, especially when a solicitous Cyndi approached him from behind, and made him jump. "The first few weeks are the hardest, I suppose," Marilynn remarked, her forehead creasing.

I waited for her to go on, but she didn't. "People in Alpine have to adjust, too," I said, hoping my voice was compassionate. "They're not used to minorities living here."

Marilynn's eyes narrowed for just an instant. "No. But they don't have to be so mean. You heard about the crow? And the letters?"

Relieved that she had finally broached the subject, I nodded. "I get to hear just about everything in my line of work. Naturally, I'm appalled. But I can't say I'm surprised. You have no idea who sent them?"

"No." She stared down at the glass-topped coffee table. "I've met quite a few people already. You do, in a doctor's office. But they seemed . . . okay. Oh, some of them looked shocked when they walked in and saw me the first couple of days." Suddenly, she laughed. "I felt like wearing a sign that read, 'Yes, I'm a person of color. No, you're not.' It's kind of weird, being an object of curiosity. And fear."

"Fear," I echoed. "Yes, you're right. It *is* fear. Irrational, but it's there."

Marilynn's laughter faded. "It's ridiculous," she declared, sounding quite severe. "What on earth is there to be afraid of?"

"Nothing," I replied. Naturally, I meant it. And, of course, I was wrong.

Vida and I left the Campbell house just before nine. As I expected, she insisted that we drive down to the sheriff's office. Vida couldn't contain her curiosity another minute. Neither could I.

The rain had stopped. It was dark now, with a scattering of stars above the mountain ridges that ringed the town. Milo Dodge, Bill Blatt, and Dwight Gould were on the job as expected. Doc Dewey had joined them, in his capacity as the Skykomish County coroner. The body, I assumed, had been taken to the morgue, which was located in the basement of Alpine Community Hospital.

". . . Fio Rito, down in Kittitas County, outside of Ellensburg," Doc Dewey was saying as he poured his apparently cold coffee onto an artificial fern. "I took my brother-in-law from Seattle there for opening day, and we did all right."

Dwight Gould was shaking his head. "You got to go farther than that for any real fishing. I'm heading up north to British Columbia in August. We'll camp out, and you'd better believe I'll come back with so many trout you guys'll . . ." Dwight stopped, his square face looking vaguely embarrassed. "Hi, Mrs. Runkel, Mrs. Lord. We're just winding down."

"Well, wind up," Vida demanded. "What's going on? Have you got any information about the victim, or are you four fools just trading fish stories?"

Milo, who had his feet up on his metal desk, reached for a computer printout. "Simmer down, Vida. We're doing our job. This Kelvin guy was a doper, at least he'd been picked up for dealing. I figure he came here to corrupt the locals. Seattle's getting too crowded."

Vida made an impatient gesture with her hand. "The locals are already corrupt enough without having outsiders help them along. As long as you've got an Elks Club, you're going to have corruption. Now tell us the real reason he came to Alpine."

Milo—and his deputies—looked blank. "Hell, Vida," Milo replied, passing a weary hand over his high forehead, "how do we know? Maybe he was just passing through. We haven't started our investigation. Doc here has to do an autopsy."

Vida turned to Gerald Dewey, whose round face evinced ignorance—or was it innocence? I had the feeling that our law enforcement and medical officials weren't exactly falling all over themselves to figure out who had killed Kelvin Greene. The assumption was disturbing.

"Well?" Vida had her fists on her hips. "What are you waiting for, Gerry? Did you freeze-dry the corpse so you could natter away with Milo and his merry band of lamebrained men?" She whirled around to fix her nephew with a withering stare. "This man was shot. What kind of bullet? What sort of gun? When? Where? Who? The press—and the public—needs to know."

"Shit." Milo removed his feet from the desk. He looked at Doc Dewey. "Do your stuff, Doc. Lois Lane here is about to make us crazy."

Vida snorted. Doc Dewey headed for the exit. "Your father wouldn't have been so negligent," she called after him. "Doc Dewey Senior was an admirable man."

Milo was now standing up. "It's after nine," he announced. "I'll start my questioning in the morning." With his jaw set, he gazed first at me, then at Vida. "Given the ethnic roots of the victim, we'll begin with Marilynn Lewis."

I had a sudden urge to pour cold coffee over Milo.

It's rare that I have a weekend all to myself. News is made seven days a week. If Vida and Carla can't cover events on Saturdays or Sundays, I take over. On this third weekend of May, the Lutheran church was holding its annual Spring Food and Fun Festival, which required Vida's attendance. She was also going to Axel Swensen's funeral in the morning. Carla was scheduled to take pictures of the high school baseball game between Alpine and Sultan. I assigned myself the task of keeping tabs on Milo Dodge and the murder investigation.

Figuring that it would take Milo until midmorning to come up with anything substantial, I used the time to clean house. I was vacuuming the living room when I thought I heard the phone ring. I picked up the receiver just before the call was switched over to my answering machine.

My voice was breathless when I said hello; it didn't get any better when I heard who was at the other end.

"Well, hello there, Emma," said Tom Cavanaugh in his usual mellow tones. "I thought you might be outside working in your yard."

"I should be," I replied, sitting down with a plop on the chair next to my desk. "I'm housecleaning." I giggled. I could have strangled myself.

"Adam called this morning," Tom said. "He may be flying down to the Bay Area for a few days after school gets out."

I stopped giggling. I felt my face take on a stern expression. I still wasn't used to sharing Adam. "That's up to him. He likes San Francisco." I knew my voice had turned stiff.

"Most people do," Tom said, sounding not quite as casual as usual. "I'll be able to take some time off to show him around. He'd probably like to stay down at Fisherman's Wharf again."

I bit back the urge to ask why Tom didn't invite him to bed down in one of what I assumed to be a plethora of spare rooms at the Cavanaugh mansion. Adam had not yet met his half siblings. I figured Tom hadn't broken the news to them that he had another child.

"Adam finishes up just before the Memorial Day weekend," I noted, trying to relax. "I expect you'll have plenty of leeway before you head up here for the conference at Lake Chelan."

"Definitely," Tom assured me. "I don't plan on coming until the day before it starts. Are you attending?"

Hearing the new formal note in his voice, I bristled. "I doubt it. It's a busy time. Maybe I'll send Ed Bronsky."

The slight pause at the other end evoked a mental picture of Tom on the verge of delivering a flippant barb, but thinking better of it. "Ed could use some helpful hints. Maybe he and I could have a drink together."

"How thoughtful." Now I'd sunk to sarcasm. I literally kicked myself. "I mean, it probably won't do any good. Ed's a mess."

"Then why are you sending him?" Tom sounded reasonable, but I knew better.

"It'd make more sense to send Ginny Burmeister," I replied, and realized that was true.

"The conference isn't aimed at underlings, Emma." Tom also could be stern.

"Well . . . I've got almost a week to think about it." I shrugged, obviously for my own sake rather than Tom's. It was time to move away from the hostile topic of the WNPA. "How's everything going down there?"

"Terrific," Tom answered. "The kids are fine, Sandra's great, business is booming. How about Alpine?"

"Wonderful," I replied. "I get to like this town more every day. The people are so warm and friendly, and after a rocky first quarter, the economy is really roaring now that spring is here." I, too, could lie through my teeth.

"It sounds like you've found a real niche for yourself." Tom's voice held no expression. "I'll have Adam call you when he gets here. *If* he gets here."

"Thanks." Wildly, I cast around for a way to keep Tom on the line while still saving face. "Are you flying up?" The question was idiotic. How else would a wealthy newspaper magnate cover the seven-hundred-plus miles between San Francisco and Alpine? "I mean, into Sea-Tac—or . . . ?" Where? I didn't have the foggiest idea if there was an airport at Lake Chelan. A real airport, as opposed to a landing field. . . . My brain was disintegrating before its time.

"I'm driving," Tom replied, and I thought I caught the hint of amusement in his words. "I own a couple of weeklies in northern California and one in central Oregon. I haven't called on any of them in almost a year. It should be a nice trip. I can do it in three days if my local folks don't present me with any big problems."

I thought of Tom, driving alone through the rolling farmland north of the Bay Area, on to the Siskiyou Mountains, and across the high desert country of central Oregon. He was right—it would be a wonderful trip. It would be even better if I were with him. . . .

"I miss Oregon," I said. "It was home for almost twenty years."

"Take a vacation down there," Tom suggested, his voice again casual before it dropped an octave: "Give yourself a break, Emma. Life's too short."

"I know." I sounded wispy.

"I've got to go. I'll see you, kid."

"Right. Bye."

He'd see me. Did Tom mean that literally? I hoped so. I thought not. I kicked myself again.

"She's lying," Milo Dodge stated flatly. "I'd bet my badge that Marilynn Lewis knew Kelvin Greene."

I grimaced at Milo over my schooner of beer. The sheriff was officially off duty, and therefore entitled to drink himself stupid, if he wanted to. Fortunately, Milo doesn't do that very often. "You're jumping to conclusions," I said in a peevish voice. "Good grief, Milo, there are thousands of African-Americans in Seattle. They don't all know each other. Why *should* Marilynn know this Kelvin Greene?"

Milo stifled a sneeze, then waved in a vague manner at a couple of workmen in overalls who had just entered Mugs Ahoy. "Why should Kelvin Greene come to Alpine? Face it, Emma, when was the last time a black guy came here without a backpack or a wife and kiddies? We get tourists, campers, hikers, skiers—maybe somebody on business from the state. But casual visitors who are black? I don't recall a one."

I wasn't convinced. But neither would I argue further with Milo. My eyes scanned the gloomy interior of Mugs Ahoy, where a dozen customers sat at tired tables drinking domestic beer and watching an NBA play-off game. An early Saturday afternoon doesn't bring out the best of the tavern's atmosphere. The truth is, there isn't any. But Milo had been thirsty. Autopsies, he said, had that effect on him.

"Tell me about the bullet," I said. Seeing Milo give me a quizzical look, I elaborated. "You know what I mean— the ballistics stuff. Where was he shot? With what? Where and when?"

Milo ran a big hand through his graying sandy hair. "Hell, Emma, this isn't television. We don't have any lab reports yet. Monday, I expect." He signaled to the owner, Abe Loomis, to bring another round.

Milo's beeper went off before Abe could draw our new schooners. "Damn," the sheriff muttered, waving at Abe to desist. As Milo headed for the wooden phone booth next to the rest rooms, I contemplated the decor. A generous soul might have called it minimalist; I opted for cheap. Most of the art was neon beer signs, touting local brands, including a couple of microbreweries. Two fading photographs of Alpine's early logging days hung on each side of the mirror behind the bar. A rack of elk antlers dipped crookedly over the entryway to the telephone and rest rooms. The most unusual item was on the far wall by the booths: a crosscut saw had been painted in oils, showing a tranquil mountain valley, complete with sparkling stream, cozy cabin, and a prancing pony. If such a place existed around Alpine, I'd never seen it. But the thought was nice—for a saw painting.

Milo returned at a faster gait than his usual lope. He was wiping his nose and didn't look pleased. "Your ace reporter has a hot tip. Do you want to tag along?"

"Carla? About what?" I grabbed my handbag as Milo tossed a five-dollar bill onto the grooved table.

"Not Carla. Vida." Milo gave Abe Loomis a semisalute.

"Vida's my House & Home editor," I asserted, racing to keep up with the sheriff's long strides. "Really, Milo, you ought to know the difference by . . ."

But Milo wasn't listening. His Cherokee Chief was parked outside in the loading zone. The afternoon was sunny and warm, with only a faint breeze stirring the curtains in the open windows of the apartment house across the street. It was, I knew, the building Marilynn Lewis had visited the previous evening. Filling the block, the Alpine Arms was four stories of sturdy, if unimaginative, brick. I guessed it was probably put up shortly after World War II.

"Where *is* Vida?" I demanded after we were heading east on Pine Street, past the Baptist and Methodist churches, past John Engstrom Memorial Park, and past the golden arches of McDonald's. Above the town, Baldy was still covered with snow, as if to remind us that here among the mountains, we were never far from winter.

"Vida called from the funeral reception at the Lutheran church, but she said to meet her at the cemetery." Milo braked for the arterial at Pine and Highway 187. "She'd better not be having one of her harebrained ideas."

"Vida's ideas are never harebrained," I countered. "She merely thinks beyond the ordinary."

Milo didn't reply. Two minutes later, we were winding up the cemetery road. Alpine's dead are buried as they lived, on a hillside. The older section, with its elaborate granite tombstones and marble monuments, is located next to the laurel hedge that separates the graveyard from the highway. Here lie the miners, the millworkers, the movers and shakers who founded the town. Farther up are their children, with more modest markers, and a few American flags to commemorate the veterans from two World Wars, Korea, and Vietnam. High on the hill are the new burial sites for those who came to Alpine in the Age of Aquarius, and found not Paradise, but a long commute to Everett. To my surprise, it was here that Axel Swensen had been laid to rest.

Attired in a black nylon swing coat and a wide-brimmed black straw hat, Vida stood under a green canopy next to the freshly turned mound of earth. Sprays of flowers covered the ground. Vida was reading the enclosure cards.

"The Gustavsons," she murmured. "That would be Harold and Tessa. Duane and Evelyn Gustavson didn't know Axel that well." The Gustavsons, as I was aware, were somehow related to Vida. "Erdahls—lovely glads. The Petersens sent a wreath." Briskly, she straightened up. "Delphine Corson did very well off of old Axel," Vida noted, referring to the local florist and owner of Posies Unlimited. She saw my curious gaze and, as often is the case with Vida, read my mind. "Axel outlived everybody in his family. They ran out of room in the original plot. That's why he's up here."

"Right, right," Milo said, with a trace of impatience. "Now what's your big news, Vida? Emma and I left a couple of tall cold ones to haul our butts over here."

Vida pursed her lips. "Really, Milo, sometimes you're

very crude. I happen to know that Emma isn't all that fond of beer."

It was true. I would have preferred a large turkey sand-wich with a side of potato salad. But sometimes I have to make great sacrifices for my career in journalism. Trying not to smile, I watched Vida give Milo one last glare, then stalk over to the canopy's edge and stand by a stone marker with raised brass letters.

"Art Fremstad," Vida said, now gazing somberly at Milo. "Your late deputy."

Milo reached for his hat, realized he wasn't wearing one, and took off his sunglasses instead. "Poor Art." He stared down at the grave. Deputy Fremstad had met a violent end six years ago. He had not yet turned thirty.

Standing next to Vida, I said a silent prayer. And waited for Milo to speak. Or for Vida to make her point. The spring breeze caused Vida's lightweight coat to flutter around her thighs. She held onto her hat with one hand, then pointed at the marker with the other.

"Well? Don't you see it?"

Milo did. He bent down, peering at the headstone. I took a couple of steps to look over his shoulder. "What is it?" I asked, afraid that I could guess. "Blood?"

Vida jerked her head in assent. "I should think so. You'll need a scraping, Milo."

The sheriff bolted upright, his rear end banging into my hip in the process. "Of course I will! Damn it, Vida, you act as if I don't know my own business! Sorry, Emma." He gave me an apologetic look.

But I had turned to Vida. "Hold it—are you saying you think Kelvin Greene was shot here at the cemetery? Why?"

Vida shrugged. "I'm guessing, naturally. But the man must have been shot somewhere in the vicinity. He couldn't run very far with a bullet in his head. Where else?" Vida swept a hand at our surroundings: All I could see was the cemetery, but beyond the far reaches of the laurel hedge on the south was the high school, the football field, the track, and the handsome older homes that included the Campbell residence. To the east, the Icicle Creek development lay on the other side of Highway 187. North, across Cedar Street, was a neighborhood of more modest houses. The cemetery was a good guess, but it wasn't the only possibility. I said as much.

"The track and the football field are right across the street from Marlow Whipp's store. The shooting might have taken place there."

Vida shook her head. "No, no. Coach Ridley had his track team practicing until early evening, remember? I heard Carla mention it." She turned to Milo. "I assume you've spoken to Coach. Did he or any of the athletes see anything unusual?"

Milo didn't meet Vida's unblinking gaze. "They were just leaving when I got there. Bill and Dwight had shooed most of them away." His voice was a bit of a mumble.

"You really ought to ask Coach," Vida declared, giving Milo another disapproving look. "Honestly, I feel you're dragging your feet on this, Milo. If the rest of us can work on a weekend, why not you?"

Vida's reproach clearly stung. "Hell, I've worked more weekends than anybody else in Skykomish County! I can't make miracles. We need the lab work before we can start coming to any conclusions. It isn't as if this is Mayor Baugh or one of the county commissioners. The dead guy's a stranger, maybe a drifter, certainly a small-time perp. Do you see anybody marching on my office to demand that we make an immediate arrest?"

Vida's expression turned very bland. "No." Under her straw hat and behind her glasses, she looked faintly owlish. "That's precisely what I'm saying. Nobody cares about Kelvin Greene. Including you." With a swish of her coat, Vida stalked off from under the shade of the canopy and headed for her car.

Chapter Five

An hour later, I caught up with Vida by accident. I was heading for Dutch Bamberg's video store while she was coming out of the children's shop across the street. Still attired in her funeral wear, Vida was now lugging a large bag emblazoned with crimson letters that read KIDS' KORNER. It had taken two and a half years of living in Alpine before I realized that the capital letters weren't just a random attempt at cuteness, but actually spelled out the first name of the proprietor, Ione Erdahl.

"Roger's birthday is week after next," Vida announced, tapping the shopping bag. "I bought him clothes. He wants a chemistry set, but he's still too young."

And dangerous, I reflected, as visions of Vida's terrifying grandson exploded in my mind's eye. At almost ten, Roger's potential for mischief rivaled that of several Middle East dictators. I was still reeling from his St. Valentine's Day escapade when he'd played Cupid and shot an arrow into Darla Puckett's backside. Unfortunately, Mrs. Puckett was bending over my desk at the time, choosing a photograph of her late husband. Darla landed in my lap, Roger fled into Front Street, and traffic came to a screeching halt. A Blue Sky Dairy truck rear-ended Averill Fairbanks's Chevy Caprice, and Durwood Parker drove onto the sidewalk, demolishing a city planter, a lamp standard, and the Venison Inn's lunch-special sign. Vida blamed Darla for offering Roger such a tempting target.

I preferred to keep Roger not only out of sight, but completely out of mind. "I was going to rent a movie for tonight," I said, having no pride when it came to admitting to Vida that my Saturday evenings were dull indeed. "How about going out for dinner? Café de Flore, maybe?"

Vida wrinkled her nose. French cuisine wasn't her favorite. "Well ... I suppose I could get something sensible," she allowed, proving that as usual, she was a good sport.

"My treat," I said impulsively, and was immediately sorry. A full-course dinner for two at the French restaurant a few miles west of Alpine on Highway 2 could cost a bundle.

"Nonsense," Vida replied, rescuing me from my own generosity. "We'll go dutch. Sevenish?"

I nodded. "My car, if not my treat?"

Vida agreed, then headed for her Buick, the shopping bag swinging at her side. I watched her pull out from the curb. With a sense of alarm, I noted that she was heading not for home, but toward the mall. The toy store was located there. It carried chemistry sets. With a shudder, I hurried to the sanctuary of my green Jag.

I didn't get far. Carla and Ginny were coming down Pine Street, apparently headed for Videos-to-Go. Despite the asset of youth, their Saturday nights weren't much more exciting than my own. I sympathized. There was definitely a dearth of eligible men in Alpine.

But when I started to commiserate, my two nubile, young employees proved me wrong.

"We went out last night to the Icicle Creek Tavern," Carla said, flipping her long black hair over one shoulder. She glanced at Ginny. "It was kind of fun, huh?"

Ginny's serious face turned even more thoughtful than usual. "I guess. *You* had fun, anyway. I told you, you should have had Libby go instead of me. Your new roommate could put up with anybody."

Carla giggled, always a jarring sound. I suppressed a smile, thinking that Ginny was right—Libby Boyd was putting up with Carla, after all. "Libby has a boyfriend," Carla countered. "So what if Rick Erlandson's hair *is* weird? I mean, bright orange isn't his color. But he works at the bank, Ginny. He can't be a complete dweeb."

"Maybe not." Ginny gave me a persecuted look. "Carla always gets the real guys. I get what's left."

Curious, I turned to Carla. "Who was it? Crazy Eights Neffel?"

Carla giggled again, and I was sorry I'd asked. "No, no, *no!*" More giggles. I didn't know if I could stand it. "Peyton Flake. He's really pretty cool. For a doctor."

I all but reeled. Somehow, Peyton Flake's eligibility had eluded me. Yes, I knew he was single. Yes, I realized he was in his early thirties. Certainly I was aware that he was well educated and that his potential for income was excellent. But I had seen him strictly in his professional capacity, as a physician. As for Carla . . . I was dumbfounded. She was pretty, more than pretty, really, and while I considered her dizzy, she was basically intelligent. At least she was a university graduate. Her social skills were adequate, and her interests were reasonably wide. But I had viewed her, too, as a vocation, not as a person. She was a journalist, and didn't always live up to expectations. At least to *mine.* Now I was the one to giggle.

"Well, for heaven's sake! I had no idea I was watching romance blossom under my very nose!"

Ginny sneered; Carla scoffed. "Not really," Carla replied. "Not yet," she added, a bit smugly. "But we did have fun."

Ginny didn't seem so sure. "It was interesting. Especially the part about Cyndi Campbell." She darted a sidelong look at Carla.

"Oh!" Carla bounced on the sidewalk, drawing the attention of a couple of passersby. "That's right! Guess what, Emma? Cyndi had been in the Icicle Creek Tavern that afternoon with a black dude. Everybody was talking about it. What do you want to bet it was the guy who got shot last night?"

My happy face turned down. "Kelvin Greene? Wait— who told you this?"

Carla started to answer, then turned again to Ginny. "Who was it? That Rafferty guy who tends bar? Or our waitress, Denise Petersen?"

"Denise," Ginny answered after careful consideration. "She was kind of thrilled about it. But she waited until Peyts went to the men's room to mention it. You know, because he has a black nurse for him. I guess she didn't want to embarrass Peyts."

I wasn't sure if I was more stunned by the news of Cyndi Campbell drinking beer with an African-American or by my staff's nickname for Dr. Peyton Flake. Shock was coming upon shock. I felt like clinging to the nearby lamp-post.

"Now hold on here," I admonished, sounding more like the boss than just another female engaging in girl talk. "When was Cyndi at the tavern with this person who may or may not have been Kelvin Greene?"

"Kelvin Greene?" Carla gave me her most wide-eyed stare. "Is that his name? Gee—I don't know. It was in the afternoon. Isn't that what Denise said?"

Ginny nodded. "They just talked. I mean, it wasn't like a *date*." My office manager seemed aghast at the mere thought, then tried to explain herself: "I mean there's nothing wrong with Cyndi dating a black man. Lots of celebrities do it. I see them in *People* magazine all the time. They even intermarry." Ginny's fair skin was flushed.

But romantic implications weren't my primary concern. Milo seemed convinced that Kelvin Greene had come to Alpine because he knew Marilynn Lewis. But what if he had been acquainted with Cyndi Campbell instead? I had to admit it was a strange coincidence that both young women lived under the same roof.

My staffers started off down the street, but Carla stopped before they reached the corner. "I got the baseball pictures," she called over her shoulder. "We won, eight to five, but the Buckers' mascot got stolen."

I visualized the high school mascot, a large, lumpy stuffed dummy named Swede in a plaid shirt and brown pants. Except for appearances at games and pep rallies, the ersatz sawmill bucker resided in the trophy case at the high school.

"Sultan poor sports?" I inquired.

"Probably," Carla replied. "They must have taken it during the night because Coach Ridley said it was gone when they went to get it this morning."

"Great." I could foresee a series of incidents between the two student bodies, with mascots, trophies, uniforms, and possibly even innocent freshmen being hauled up and down Highway 2 between Alpine and Sultan. The school year was ending, and with it, a certain madness always set in. I would have to run a small story, though I hated to encourage further mayhem. With any luck, Swede would be returned by deadline.

I called Milo as soon as I got home, but he was out. I left a message on his machine, then spent the rest of the afternoon weeding my garden. Out with the dandelions, the thistles, the clover, the buttercups, the bindweed, the nightshade, even the common vetch, which blooms prettily enough in late May, but chokes everything else. By five-thirty, I had filled a huge plastic garbage bag and was feeling exceedingly virtuous. I even had the wounds to show for my efforts. Several scratches marred my arms, and I'd gashed a finger with a rose thorn. It was still bleeding, but I felt impervious to pain. I stood back to admire the fruit of my labor. The rhododendrons were at their peak, the azaleas were brilliant, the iris and poppies looked lush. Like most Pacific Northwest gardens, mine reveled in the spring. Summer would be more sparse, with sporadic bursts of roses, two weeks' worth of gladioli, and, if I got lucky, enough dahlias to make a small splash.

I was envisioning the months to come when a horn honked in my ear. I turned to see an official Forest Service pickup parked by my mailbox. The back was jammed with tools and brush. I wondered if there was room for my trash bag. The city charged extra for yard collection.

Libby Boyd leaned out of the cab. "Hey—Ms. Lord! Are you ready to run an engagement story yet?"

Brushing dirt off my hands, I approached the truck. Libby's olive skin glowed with good health. Her strawberry blonde hair was cropped close to her head, with what I assumed to be natural curls dancing around her heart-shaped face. She had a sunny smile and sparkling blue eyes, the aura of a charming cherub. Libby's radiant vitality made me feel like a slob. A *dirty* slob, given my grubby clothes and earth-ladened flesh.

"Are you talking about Dr. Flake and Carla?" I asked, somewhat flabbergasted.

Libby laughed, an infectious sound. "Aren't they a pair? I'm kidding, of course. At least, I think I am. Hey, you're bleeding! What happened?" She sobered, her white, even teeth coming down on her lower lip.

I dismissed my injury, which I'd already forgotten. But Libby was insistent, rummaging in the glove compartment. "You could get an infection. I've got a first-aid kit in here. At least, I thought I did. That's odd—it's gone."

Libby's concern touched me. I had visions of her trailing Carla around their apartment, making sure my dizzy reporter had brushed her teeth, turned off the stove, and wouldn't leave without her keys. Carla needed someone like that in her life.

My impression was bolstered by Libby's next words: "You know, I worry about Carla. She's man-starved. I'm afraid she'll fall head over heels for the first guy who pays her any attention around here."

I, too, turned serious. Carla's emotional state hadn't troubled me in the least. I gave Libby Boyd a hard stare. "Peyton Flake's a decent man," I asserted, hoping to ease my conscience.

"Oh, sure, he's cool," Libby replied, turning away to search for something on the passenger seat. "I don't know Carla as well as you do, so I ought to keep my mouth shut. But she seems sort of vulnerable to me." Libby reached out through the window to hand me a sheet of paper. An inch of pale skin around her left wrist indicated that she'd already acquired an early tan. Maybe she cheated, and it was induced by the electric beach. But that didn't seem to fit Libby's healthy image. "Here, this is the summer fact sheet for the campgrounds," she explained. "I should have given it to Carla, but I forgot last night. You might as well have it because she'll probably lose it if I give it to her over the weekend."

I glanced at the official U.S. Forest Service heading. "Thanks, Libby. And thanks for being concerned about Carla."

Libby lifted her shoulders, which were covered in the tan uniform of a park ranger. Obviously, she had drawn Saturday duty. "Carla's okay. I'm not knocking Peyts. He's probably good for her. Every couple needs balance. One partner is always stronger than the other. That's what makes it work. Stability is the key to life." She gave me a worldly smile.

The pickup roared off down Fir Street, where it made a

deft turn onto Third. I was moved by Libby Boyd's com-
passion. If Peyton Flake was good for Carla, so was Libby.
I wondered if Carla realized that she had been lucky in her
choice of a roommate. I hoped she'd be as lucky in love.

Milo had called while I was outside. After hauling the
trash bag to the garbage can next to the carport, I applied
a Band-Aid to my finger and opened a can of Pepsi. Then
I phoned Milo back, telling him about Cyndi Campbell and
her rendezvous with an African-American male at the Icicle
Creek Tavern. The sheriff asked if I'd gotten a description.

"I heard this secondhand," I retorted in a vexed voice.
"Go ask Denise Petersen. Better yet, talk to Cyndi
Campbell."

Milo said he would, come Monday. It was his poker
night. They were playing their monthly game in the back
room at Harvey's Hardware and Sporting Goods. Huffy and
not sorry for it, I hung up.

Vida and I drove down Stevens Pass among tall corridors
of evergreens, bathed in the late day's golden sunlight. Traffic was fairly heavy both ways, with weekend travelers going between the western and eastern halves of the state.

The Café de Flore was also busy, and I was glad that I'd
thought to call in a seven-fifteen reservation. We sat next to
a window that overlooked Anthracite Creek. A Downy
woodpecker hammered at the trunk of a tall cedar. Out by
what I guessed was a storehouse, a gray squirrel rooted in
the ground by a clump of blue speedwell. I ordered a vodka
gimlet and tried to put aside all thoughts of murder and
mayhem.

Of course, with Vida as my companion, that was impossible. On the short drive to the restaurant, I'd told her about
the sighting of Cyndi Campbell at the Icicle Creek Tavern.
Vida's interest far exceeded that of Milo. Now, stirring her
Tom Collins with a swizzle stick, she made a face. "Honestly, Emma, Milo is being unusually impossible, even for
a man." Before I could respond, she swiveled in her chair,
taking in the rest of the dining room. "I thought so," she
murmured. "At the long table, against the far wall—Wendy
and Todd Wilson, with some of the high school faculty."

Vida was right. The Wilsons had been joined by Coach

Rip Ridley and his wife, Dixie; the principal, Karl Freeman, whose spouse, an elementary teacher, was named
Molly; and Steve and Donna Wickstrom. Steve taught science and math; Donna's first husband had been Art
Fremstad, on whose headstone Vida thought she'd spotted
blood. The four couples seemed to be relishing at least two
different types of wine and a large tray of hors d'oeuvres.

Vida, however, was ready to cut to the chase. "If I remember my French, I recognize roast chicken and potatoes.
That sounds safe." She put the menu aside and tried again
to turn discreetly in her chair. "More wine for the high
school faculty," she said in an undertone, though there was
no possibility of being overheard from across the room in
the busy restaurant. "The waiter is positively *fawning*. My,
my!"

"That's the owner," I said. "He's French. His wife is
from California."

If I thought I possessed a fragment of information that
Vida didn't know, I was wrong. "So it is," she agreed, removing her glasses to stare. "Jean-Nicol Saint-Something-
or-Other. His wife is Becky. She's four months pregnant."

I sighed. "Marje Blatt?"

Vida nodded. "Of course. My niece knows how I like to
hear about new babies. The Saint-Whoevers live between
Index and Gold Bar, but Becky finds it easier to see Dr.
Flake than someone farther down the highway because she
can come in on her way to the restaurant."

Vida declined a second drink. So did I, though I couldn't
resist ordering a slice of the liver pâté. Vida sneered. "It
does taste like paste, you must admit. Now what awful
thing are you ordering for dinner?"

I'd decided on the oysters in cider. Vida professed indifference. "Panfried or raw—I wouldn't eat oysters any other
way. Really, Emma, you're like so many Americans—if the
French baked a gopher and stuck sprigs of parsley in its
ears, you'd think it was delicious."

"It might be," I allowed. "The gang from the high school
is certainly enjoying their meal. They just brought the fish
course."

Vida swiveled again. "Honestly, I should have sat where

you're sitting. This is so awkward! Why don't they have a mirror on that wall behind you?"

"Why don't you go over and say hello?" I was serious. "You know all of them. Maybe they're celebrating something. It could be a news item."

"I already thought of that." Vida gave me a reproachful look. "I'll wait until they're having dessert. They'll be full and sleepy then. Their guard will be down."

I felt my eyes open wide. "You're not going to ask Wendy what her sister was doing at the Icicle Creek Tavern with a man who is probably dead, are you?"

Vida looked affronted. "Certainly not! That's hardly the sort of thing to mention in the middle of a social gathering. I'll drop by tomorrow and offer her some hyacinth bulbs. I dug a few up by mistake last week. Extra bulbs always come in handy. So do tubers."

Somehow, Vida and I managed to avoid analyzing the recent murder during the rest of our dinner. The meal was excellent, and even she had to admit that the roast chicken was properly cooked. Despite her carping over French food, Vida's performance in the kitchen is, at best, uneven. She gardens much better than she cooks.

We were finishing our demitasses when Vida announced she was going to drop by the Wilson table. "I'll commiserate about the kidnapped mascot. On my way to the rest room," she added, as if needing to excuse herself to me as well as to Wendy and the other diners. I sat back and watched as Vida worked the room. The high school faculty weren't the only people she knew. Though I recognized only one other couple who happened to be my fellow parishioners at St. Mildred's, Vida made four interim stops: two older women, who laughed uproariously at her greeting; a family of five, with mother, father, and three adult children exchanging what I presumed to be birthday presents; a handsome older couple whose sophistication seemed out of place for Skykomish County; and three men of Vida's own age, one of whom either turned his hearing aid up or off when she approached.

Vida hit the Wilson gathering on her return from the rest room. Molly Freeman kissed her on the cheek. Karl Freeman hugged her warmly. Coach Ridley vigorously shook

BRETAGNE

her hand. Dixie Ridley gave a languid wave. I couldn't see
the Wickstroms, who were temporarily hidden by the arrival of Jean-Nicol and a silver wine bucket at the next table. Wendy and Todd Wilson seemed polite, if not effusive,
in their greeting. Vida chatted for a full five minutes, leaving only after the waitress had presented the bill.

"Well!" she gasped, sitting back down and polishing off
her demitasse in a gulp. "Five hundred and eighty-four dollars and twelve cents! It's not even a special occasion, just
a chummy night out! And Todd Wilson insisted it was his
treat! Why, with a generous tip, that's almost seven hundred
dollars!"

I, too, was stunned. "What does it mean? Job security for
Wendy at the high school? That must be close to two
weeks' take-home for a teacher. What do you think Todd
earns at the PUD?"

Vida turned thoughtful. "We ran those salaries awhile
back. I think his would be around forty thousand by now.
That's certainly not the kind of salary to splurge on seven-
hundred-dollar dinners. The Wilsons live high on the hog in
general, when you think about it. Wendy has lovely clothes,
though she doesn't wear them well, and they both drive
nice cars. In fact, they have three."

"No kids," I pointed out.

"True." Vida chewed on her lower lip. "Still, their home
in the Icicle Creek development is one of the more expensive houses."

Across the room, I saw the Wilson party laughing over
their after-dinner drinks. I wondered what the more
straightlaced parents would think about the principal and
three of his teachers tossing off goblets of French wine and
stuffing themselves with Bretagne delicacies. If someone
raised the issue at the next PTA meeting, it wouldn't be the
first time. Only last January, there had been a protest about
several faculty members drinking champagne, dancing with
other people's spouses, and wearing silly hats on New
Year's Eve.

"Maybe," I ventured, after we had paid our own compar-
atively modest bill of sixty-five dollars plus tip, "Lloyd has
been generous with his earnings from Alpine Appliance. He
seems to have done quite well over the years."

Vida was grappling with her cotton jacket. "Don't even think about it. Lloyd is a Scot, and you know how tight-fisted they are. Oh, they travel now and then, they spend money on their house, but they're careful. Bargains, cut-rate, wholesale. To give an example, consider the flank steak."

I was scarcely qualified to argue with Vida. We made our exit just ahead of the Wilsons and their guests. I was relieved, preferring to be ahead of them on the highway. After only one drink and a dozen oysters, I could lay a solid claim to sobriety.

Nor was I sorry. Vida and I had enjoyed a delicious meal, and as she would have put it, "a nice visit." We were home before ten o'clock. If my Saturday night hadn't been fraught with excitement, it had been replete with friendship. I could ask for nothing more.

After changing into my bathrobe, I took the WNPA registration form out of my briefcase and filled it in. I would mail it on the way to Mass in the morning. Somewhere between the Café de Flore and the bridge over the Skykomish River, I had made up my mind to go to Lake Chelan.

Chapter Six

THE VISITING PRIEST from Monroe made short work of Sunday Mass. Not only did he keep his homily to under ten minutes, but he was seen pulling out from behind the rectory while the rest of us were still chatting in the vestibule.

"I miss Father Fitz," Francine Wells lamented, referring to our former pastor who had suffered a series of strokes the previous December and was now in a nursing home for priests.

"I hear we're getting someone new when the Chancery makes the assignments in June," Roseanna Bayard confided. "I'm glad. It's one thing to run a parish as a mission church, but it's another matter when there's a school."

I had to agree with both Francine and Roseanna. We had seen at least a half-dozen different priests on the altar of St. Mildred's since New Year's. I was about to say as much when Francine jabbed me in the arm and lowered her voice:

"Say, Emma—what's this about that black man who was shot at Marlow Whipp's store the other night? Was he really robbing the place? I wouldn't figure Marlow to have more than small change in the register."

Roseanna nodded vigorously. "I guess it was just awful. The robber was armed, and Marlow wrestled him to the ground to get the gun. Then he shot the guy as he was running out of the store. Gee!"

As expected, the gossip mill had been busy. And wrong. Both Roseanna and Francine were intelligent women. In addition to helping her husband, Buddy, run Bayard's Picture-Perfect Photography Studio, Roseanna tutored children with reading problems. Francine owned her own business, an upscale women's apparel store that did remarkably well in a beer-and-bowling town such as Alpine. Yet my fellow parishioners were quite willing to accept hearsay as gospel truth.

I attempted to clarify the matter, choosing my words with a journalist's care. "It wasn't an attempted robbery. The victim came into Marlow's store and collapsed. Apparently, he'd already been shot somewhere else. He died inside the store. Marlow insists he'd never seen the man before in his life."

Francine bent her carefully coiffed head closer; Roseanna leaned in my direction, her blonde pageboy swinging at her wide shoulders. Buddy Bayard had also joined our little group, along with a half-dozen other parishioners.

"Somewhere else?" Roseanna breathed. "You mean . . . he was murdered?"

I fell back on Milo's lame excuses. "The sheriff doesn't know the details yet. He's waiting for the lab report."

Roseanna and Francine exchanged quick glances. "He was a black man, right?" Roseanna saw my faint nod. "Edna Mae Dalrymple said she saw him hanging around Old Mill Park Friday morning on her way to work at the library. Now where on earth did he come from—unless he was a friend of that new nurse's?"

"A boyfriend, I'll bet," Francine said, straightening up and smoothing the lapels of her Anne Klein jacket. "He's probably from one of those gangs in Seattle. I lived there for almost fifteen years before I divorced Warren. I never went near the Central District." She gave a little shudder.

The Central District is Seattle's version of a ghetto, and while it has its share of inner-city crime, it is considered an up-and-coming neighborhood in many ways. Most Seattle-ites have no qualms about going there, and often do, if only to get their teeth into Fran's chocolates and Ezell's chicken.

Roseanna was nodding. "The last time I was in downtown Seattle, three black kids followed me down Fourth Avenue after I left The Bon Marché. I just knew they were going to grab my purse. I all but ran around the corner and went back in the Pine Street entrance. I waited until they were gone."

I tried to refrain from rolling my eyes. I'd heard the Big City horror stories before, always capped with the great sigh of relief uttered when the out-of-towners finally reached the safety of Highway 2. Indeed, their paranoia was contagious. On a trip to Seattle the previous February, I had stopped at a cash machine before heading home. The bank was closed, the parking lot was deserted, and it was almost dark. An African-American man in his early thirties was lingering near the cash machine, ostensibly reading something from a small notebook. I became so nervous that I botched my PIN number twice. While the automatic teller finally spewed out my forty bucks, the man went up to a pay phone a few feet away and made a call. He turned out to be a real estate agent, scheduling an appointment to show a two-hundred-thousand-dollar condo on Queen Anne Hill. I felt so silly that I departed as furtively as if I'd been passing counterfeit money at the bank.

It was pointless to argue with Roseanna, Francine, or any other Alpiners who regarded Seattle as a den of iniquity. The city's evil justifies their very existence as small-towners. So there they stay in their splendid rural isolation, absolved of guilt for the wider world's social ills.

But I stay there, too, so I kept my mouth shut. When I speak out, it's usually through the editorial page. I state my opinions professionally, not personally. I have to get along; I have to make a living. And I don't want to get run out of town.

Extricating myself from the little group, I headed for the Jag and home. With no pressing plans for the day, I thought about calling Marilynn Lewis. Perhaps she'd like to have lunch or go for a short hike. After finishing the Sunday paper, I phoned the Campbell house. Jean answered on the fourth ring. I thanked her again for a lovely dinner, then asked for Marilynn.

"She went to church—the Methodist church," Jean answered in a voice that suddenly had grown stilted. "We just got back. The phone was ringing when we came in the house. I imagine she'll be along shortly. She walked."

Marilynn returned my call about fifteen minutes later. She expressed surprise at my invitation. "I'd like to see Deception Falls," she said, sounding rather shy. "It's not far, is it?"

It wasn't, being only a couple of miles up the pass. Nor

would we have to hike, which was fine with me. I told her
I'd pack a lunch. There were picnic tables at the falls, and
we could eat there. Marilynn sounded very pleased.

An hour later, I was in front of the Campbell house,
waiting for Marilynn. Cyndi was out in the yard, cleaning
off the lawn furniture. She came over to the Jag and said
hello.

"What's new on that guy who got killed Friday night?"
she asked, leaning against the door of my car.

The question seemed natural; her body language did not.
Cyndi appeared to be bracing herself on the Jaguar. "Not
much," I replied, wondering how to tactfully broach the
subject of her rendezvous at the Icicle Creek Tavern. Vida,
of course, would use blunderbuss tactics. Encouraged by
her example, I threw caution to the winds. "Did you know
him?"

Cyndi's green eyes widened and she backed away a couple of steps. "Heavens, no! How could I?" She stared at
me, and I could almost see the wheels spinning in her head.
Cyndi knew as well as I did that if she'd been spotted with
Kelvin Greene at the tavern, most of Alpine had heard the
story by now. She uttered a nervous laugh. "Oddly enough,
I ran into a black man that afternoon. I had to deliver something for Todd to the Icicle Creek Tavern, and there was
this guy who wanted to know how to get to the ski lodge.
I gave him directions." Her gaze had shifted to the hood of
my car.

I had two choices: to believe or not to believe. I didn't
know which to take. "I wonder if he ever got there," I remarked, trying to leave my options open.

Visibly relaxing, Cyndi shrugged. "I don't know. That
was about three o'clock, maybe even four. It took forever
to make him understand. I guess he wasn't too bright."

"Do you think he was the one who got shot?" Out of the
corner of my eye, I saw Marilynn Lewis walking down the
garden path.

My query seemed to surprise Cyndi. "Well . . . yes, I
suppose. There couldn't have been two of them, could
there?"

Somehow, her reply made me want to smile. But I
didn't. And while two African-American males descending

upon Alpine was clearly beyond Cyndi's comprehension, it certainly wasn't a laughing matter.

But Marilynn's arrival cut our conversation short. Cyndi wished us a good time, and we drove off down Tyee Street to Alpine Way. For starters, I kept to neutral topics, such as Marilynn's search for housing. She was undecided about Dolph Terrill's apartments, since the unit she'd looked at was in need of repair. On the other hand, there weren't many rentals for single people in Alpine.

"The Campbells are very kind about letting me stay on as long as I want," Marilynn said as we crossed the bridge over the Skykomish River. "But I don't like to impose."

I told her I'd have Ginny check out this week's classifieds before we went to press. If there was a new listing, Marilynn would get first dibs.

"That's awfully nice of you, Ms. . . . Emma." She gave me a soft smile.

"It's not easy to find a place," I replied. "Carla, my reporter, has moved three times in three years. She's still not terribly happy where she is now." It was true, since Carla's ideal apartment didn't exist in Alpine. The unit she shared with Libby Boyd was in the town's newest complex, across Alpine Way from The Pines—or Stump Hill, as the development was known before three dozen handsome houses were built among the trees. Indeed, Carla could not have afforded the monthly rent for The Pines Village if she hadn't found a roommate. "I could ask Carla if there are any vacancies coming up," I said. "I think they have some one-bedroom units."

Marilynn seemed pleased by that offer, too. Indeed, Marilynn seemed pleased with any small act of kindness. I wondered if she'd spent her entire life being ignored or rebuffed. It didn't seem likely, not in the city. But perhaps Alpine had dealt her a quick lesson in rejection.

The six picnic tables at Deception Falls were filled. Most of the visitors were families, some with teenagers, others with babies in backpacks, and the rest with children in between, clustered around the picnic tables and the stationary grills. The mountain air was tinged with wood smoke and barbecue aromas.

Other visitors studied the historical display that described

James B. Hill's determination to complete the railroad link
between the Twin Cities and Puget Sound. At the trail head,
groups milled about with cameras, video recorders, and eager
children. The license plates in the parking lot covered the
map: Washington, Oregon, Idaho, California, British Columbia, Alberta, North Dakota, Pennsylvania, Illinois, and Ver-
mont. We decided to visit the falls first.

Marilynn reveled in the tall evergreens, the lingering
patches of snow caught among the cliffs, the birds that
hopped over the ground in search of a handout. She particularly liked the falls, with the tumbling white water dashing
over the rocks and cascading down the mountainside. At
the upper falls, which roared under the highway itself, the
spray dashed against our faces. We saw a pair of water ou-
zels, dipping their trim gray bodies atop a boulder as round
as a basketball. We noted the recent blowdown, which
struck me as excessive. But there had been some severe
windstorms in the past few months. It was no wonder that
so many trees had been toppled.

Along the path to the lower falls, we paused to read the
informational panels. No trees in this forest were older than
two hundred and eighty years. Somewhere around the beginning of the eighteenth century, a great fire had wiped out
everything, including the giants that were said to be over
six hundred years old. I gazed upward, awed by the western
red cedar, the Douglas and Pacific silver firs, and the western hemlock. These were mighty trees, venerable trees,
wearing soft emerald moss and gray-green lichen.

Back at the picnic area, a camper from Burnaby, British
Columbia, was being loaded. With friendly smiles,
Marilynn and I snagged the Canadians' table as soon as
they removed their plastic cloth. I had selected a modest
menu of chicken sandwiches, macaroni salad, potato chips,
and lemonade. Marilynn, however, seem delighted.

"I haven't been on a picnic since I was a Girl Scout,"
she exclaimed as we unpacked the hamper. The view was
of the highway, not the falls, but we couldn't complain.
"When I lived in Seattle, I hardly ever got outside the city,"
she mused, gazing at our fellow nature lovers. "I'll bet a lot
of people in town never come to places like this."

It was certainly possible. Growing up in the city, I'd

been lucky. My family had enjoyed regular outings in the country. By chance, my parents, my brother, and I had picnicked several times at Deception Falls. My happy memories may have played a part in my decision to buy *The Advocate*. The stopoff hadn't been so busy in those days. Now, it bustled with car and foot traffic. In vain, I scanned the other tables for an African-American. The only ethnic group represented was a Japanese family, who, judging from their boisterous behavior, probably were three generations removed from the Orient. Two leggy teenaged daughters were hassling their somewhat younger, whining brother; Mom and Dad were arguing over whether the hamburgers were cooked through. It seemed to me that East had met West, and West had won. It also seemed that I was making some ethnic judgments of my own.

We were finishing our lunch when Marilynn broached the subject of the harassment. "I thought I might hear from the sheriff about the letters and that awful crow, but I haven't so far. I suppose none of it can be traced."

"It's the weekend," I pointed out. "Nothing else has happened, I hope?" I couldn't help but wonder if the death of a black man might trigger new forms of harassment against Marilynn.

But she shook her head, the big gold hoop earrings swinging. "Nothing in the mail yesterday. Today's Sunday, though. I suppose some show of racism is inevitable."

Unfortunately, it was. "Does it bother you?" I asked bluntly.

Marilynn considered, her dark eyes staring at the ground. "Not too much. It was the whispering that bothered me. I know some of those people were trying to connect me with the man who was shot."

"But there's no connection?" To my dismay, I couldn't keep the question out of my voice.

"No." Marilynn got up from the bench, wandering over to the dormant grill. A sudden silence fell between us. I shifted uneasily on my side of the bench. I'd berated Milo for trying to tie Marilynn Lewis to Kelvin Greene. Yet I realized I was equally guilty. Surely the arrival of a black woman in town and the appearance of a black man was a coincidence. Watching Marilynn's tall, slim, graceful form,

I couldn't imagine her involvement in anything sordid. But, of course, I'd felt that way about other people—and been quite wrong. Vida wouldn't be so naive.

"I'll have to try hiking," Marilynn announced, facing me again and looking serene. "Skiing, too, next winter. Do you ski?"

"I used to, but I sort of quit." I gave Marilynn a lame smile. "I wasn't very good at it. My coordination stinks."

"I like to swim," Marilynn said, watching a nutcracker swoop down to forage for picnic leftovers. My father had always called the handsome, noisy birds Camp Robbers. The nutcracker found his snack and flew off into a huge hemlock. "There's no public pool here, is there?" Marilynn asked, shielding her eyes as she followed the bird's flight.

"No, there isn't." I explained my campaign to build a pool on the former bowling alley site. "Carla's apartment has a small pool," I added.

"Carla seems nice," Marilynn commented, sitting back down at the picnic table. "Is it true she's dating Dr. Flake?"

Marilynn already seemed tuned into the rumor mill. "They've gone out," I hedged. "I'm not sure it's a romance. Yet."

"He's a wonderful man," Marilynn said, watching a chipmunk scurry past. "In some ways, I think he's more upset about the hate mail than I am."

I didn't doubt it. Peyton Flake struck me as the type who would take such intimidation personally. In Flake's case, it was ego as much as righteousness. He had hired Marilynn Lewis; he would be outraged if anyone questioned his judgment.

Our talk turned to more mundane matters, including a comparison between working in hospitals and private practice. Marilynn commented on the differences in treating big-city versus small-town patients. The most unusual case she'd had so far was Ellsworth Overholt who had brought in his guernsey cow to be examined by Doc Dewey. Doc had urged him to see the vet. Ellsworth refused, saying that he and Dr. Medved hadn't spoken in fifteen years after a dispute at a Grange Hall potluck and dance. The cow was driven off to a less controversial vet in Monroe.

We were loading the picnic hamper into the Jag when

Libby Boyd approached us. She was wearing her ranger's uniform, and I realized that I'd never seen her in the classic wide-brimmed hat. Maybe Vida had stolen it.

"Have you met Marilynn Lewis, Dr. Flake's nurse?" I inquired, taking Marilynn by the arm.

Libby's blue eyes shrewdly assessed the other woman. "No. In fact, I've only met Dr. Flake a couple of times, when he came to pick up Carla. Hi, you're working for a fine doctor, I hear. Are you still living with the Campbells?"

A bit stiffly, Marilynn allowed that she was. Libby's calculating manner retreated. Marilynn's tension remained. To cover what I sensed as awkwardness, I asked Libby if she had to work through the weekend.

"I sure do, six days in a row," Libby replied. "I'm the new kid on the block, so I get the last choice on the schedule. Ten hours a day, too, from eight until six. And I'm lucky if I get home before seven. There's always some little kid who falls in the creek or a tourist who's lost a camera. But it's fun, much better than being cooped up in an office." She gave us a humorous look.

Marilynn, however, wasn't smiling. "I like being in an office," she declared, sounding a bit defensive. "It's a definite improvement over hospital work."

"Oh?" Libby was cool, yet pleasant. "I suppose it would be. I've never been in a hospital in my life."

"Except when you were born," I threw out, hoping to lighten the mood.

But Libby turned absolutely frigid. "No. I was born in a converted bus, somewhere between Santa Fe and the Sangre de Cristo Mountains. My parents were hippies. They didn't believe in hospitals—or money—or having a home. The wind blew them all over North America. It finally blew them both away, from me and from each other. Luckily, I landed on my feet in Seattle. This is as far as I care to wander. I'm putting down roots in Alpine." She gave both Marilynn and me a defiant look, as if we might be about to hustle her onto a passing Greyhound bus.

The moment was saved by a towheaded twelve year old who wanted to know if he could take home a garter snake he'd captured. The snake was trying to crawl out of his shirt pocket. We bade farewell to Libby, the boy, and the snake.

On the way home, I refrained from mentioning the meeting with Libby Boyd. It had not been a comfortable interlude, though I wasn't sure why. Instead, I told Marilynn she would get used to small-town eccentricities. The bizarre quickly becomes the ordinary. Irrational behavior often goes unquestioned, even by a journalist like me. Marilynn allowed that was probably so, but that she wasn't quite used to it yet.

"There are similarities, too," she said as we stopped in front of the Campbell house. "I think people in Alpine can be just as wicked as people in the city."

I didn't argue. But I wondered exactly what she meant.

Vida had delivered her hyacinth bulbs to Wendy Wilson about the same time that I was unpacking the picnic hamper at Deception Falls. Wendy had been very vague about her sister's encounter with a black stranger at the Icicle Creek Tavern. At first, she had feigned downright ignorance, Vida revealed, then she had admitted—lamely—that Cyndi "ran into some guy" and gave him directions to the ranger station.

"It was the ski lodge in Cyndi's version to me," I noted.

Vida harrumphed. "Cyndi—and Wendy—ought to get their stories straight. It was neither, of course. What do you suppose it was?"

"We don't know it was the same man," I pointed out as we waited for the coffee to finish brewing.

But Vida gave me her gimlet eye. "Who else? Come, come, Emma, it's not likely there would be two of them." Her comment echoed Cyndi Campbell's. Somehow Vida's remark didn't strike me as funny.

Ginny brought the mail around just after ten. She looked worried, and I wondered if she was still stewing over her pairing with Rick Erlandson. I suspected that the double date had probably been Carla's idea.

But Ginny had reevaluated the evening. "Rick's really very nice. He's just sort of quiet." I kept my face expressionless. Ginny wasn't exactly a firecracker. "I think that orange hair is his big protest against the world. He won't speak out, so he dyes his hair a funny color. He'll grow out of it."

So, I thought, would his hair.

Ginny, who was usually not loquacious, kept talking. "It's these letters," she continued, placing three single sheets of paper in front of me. "They're all from people who want you to write more about the logging issue. You know, like the editorial you did in December. But I think they're wrong." She took a deep breath and stared at me with a very somber expression. "I think you were wrong. I mean, in theory, it's wonderful to support the timber industry. But it's not very realistic, is it?"

Ever since the president's timber summit in Portland the previous winter, I had suffered qualms about my unabashed endorsement of Washington State's loggers. While I hadn't leapt on a soap box to demand the resumption of clear-cutting, I had certainly cast my lot with the forest products people. It was, I felt, my duty as a resident of Alpine. Certainly my big-city background had groomed me as a spiritual environmentalist. I'd been converted to a pro-logging stance by living in a small town where so many faces had grown bleak and so many lives had lost hope. People came first. The loggers were proud, so were their families. They were steeped in the tradition of the forest, a vocation handed down from generation to generation. It seemed impossible that they could retrain, regroup, and recant.

But the winds of change were sweeping down the mountainsides. I could see it in Ginny's level gray-eyed gaze. I could read it in news stories about other logging communities. I could hear it on the evening news, out of Washington, D.C., Seattle, and the state capitol in Olympia.

"I've always hoped for a compromise," I told Ginny, who was looking at me as if I might actually have some real answers. "I prefer biding my time to see what's going to happen at the federal level."

Ginny inclined her head, then brushed at a stray strand of auburn hair. "I guess. But what do men like my Uncle Cord do in the meantime? Darrington is going to sponsor a wild-flower festival this summer. Why can't we do something here that will provide jobs and help the economy?"

Darrington was yet another logging town, some seventy

miles north on the Mountain Loop Highway. I had heard rumors of their civic project in the past few weeks. "We've got Loggerama," I pointed out, and immediately realized that our annual celebration could be considered passé, a mere reminder of what had been, rather than what could be.

"We could put on a Scandinavian festival," Ginny said. "That's Alpine's heritage, too. Like for Midsummer Eve, to celebrate the solstice."

I stared at Ginny, then broke into a smile. I never thought of my office manager as having the slightest amount of imagination. Obviously, I had misjudged her. "That's not a bad idea," I said. "I could talk about it at the next Chamber of Commerce meeting. You could come along."

Ginny looked pleased. Indeed, the hint of a blush touched her fair skin. Shyly, she brought forth yet another letter, which she had been concealing behind her back. "This one isn't about logging, but you're not going to like it."

The single page of typing had the usual share of misspellings, though I had the feeling they might have been intentional. The letter was short and to the point:

"Dear Publicher—It looks to me like we got trubble here in Alpine. You let those city dudes get a foot in the door and the next thing you know, they ruin the whole place. They get innocent people hooked while they make lots of money off suckers, all of which is tipikel of those ignerent crazed savages. I say we pass a law to keep them out of town. Yours truely, A Loyal Reader."

I pride myself on running every letter sent to *The Advocate*—as long as it's signed. I was grateful that this particular imbecile had chosen to remain anonymous. Instead of tossing the missive into the wastebasket, as I usually did with crank mail, I saved it so that Milo could compare it to the letters Marilynn Lewis had received.

Milo had the lab report shortly after eleven that morning. Kelvin Greene had been shot in the head at a distance of no more than four feet, no less than three. The .22-caliber full-metal-jacket slug had been found lodged about an inch from his left ear. It was possible that he could have lived for hours with the bullet in his head. It was also unlikely.

"If you're thinking Kelvin sat around drinking beer at the

Icicle Creek Tavern after he got plugged, forget it," Milo said in his laconic voice. "Realistically, he was probably shot five to ten minutes before he died in Marlow Whipp's store."

"What kind of a gun?" I asked, making notes.

"Probably a handgun," Milo replied. He paused to blow his nose, not a pleasing sound. "Let's face it, the killer would have been noticed carrying a rifle around town this time of year. It's not hunting season."

"What about the blood up at the cemetery?" I glanced out through my open door at Vida. She was immersed in typing a story, her bowler hat askew.

"It's a match," Milo admitted grudgingly. "If that canopy hadn't been up for Axel Swensen's funeral, the rain would probably have washed it away."

"Footprints?" I inquired without much hope.

Milo chuckled. "After a funeral? Sure, about forty sets. The only thing we can pinpoint there is that the Peabody brothers—the grave diggers—finished around five on Friday. The cemetery officially closes at sundown, which means about eight this time of year. But I don't suppose the killer or the victim came by car. It's easy enough to crawl through that laurel hedge."

I had one more question. "Was Kelvin Greene armed?"

Milo was blowing his nose again. I wished the hay fever season would pass. "There was no gun on him. But it's possible that the killer used it. That would indicate a struggle, though, and there's no sign of that with Kelvin."

In the news office, Vida's instincts were at work. She was coming toward me, the bowler hat now riding on the rims of her glasses. "Say, Milo," I added as an afterthought, "did you check with the Icicle Creek Tavern to see if the stranger who was drinking beer with Cyndi Campbell matched Kelvin Greene's description?"

Milo made a disparaging noise, which was an improvement over his sneezing. "Yeah, Dwight Gould talked to Denise and that Rafferty kid with the beard who tends bar during the day shift. They couldn't be sure. All blacks guys look alike to them."

I tried not to gnash my teeth. "Do they look alike to Cyndi Campbell?"

Milo sounded impatient. "Do you want me to ask Cyndi to come down and ID the corpse? Come on, Emma, isn't that kind of a cruel thing to do to a nice girl like her? From what I hear, all she did was give him directions to Alpine Falls."

My anger boiled up, but I squashed it and settled for sarcasm. "Very good, Milo. You've just won *The Advocate*'s coveted award for Mutt of the Month. See you in the funny papers." I hung up, gently.

"We don't carry the funny papers," Vida noted tartly. "What did Milo do now?"

I explained. Vida made a face and tipped her hat back on her head. She agreed with me that Milo was "being difficult." She also agreed that we should go to lunch.

As usual, the Venison Inn was filled with people Vida knew. As time went on, I recognized more and more of the locals, but it was always Vida who was the focus of attention. A salutation for Regis Bartleby, Episcopal rector. A nod to Harvey Adcock, hardware-store owner. A smile for Jeannie Clay, the dental hygienist. A wave to Chaz Phipps, who worked at the ski lodge. We made our way like a royal progress, acknowledging, greeting, smiling en route to the last empty booth at the rear of the restaurant.

"My new diet's a washout," Vida announced. "All these fads are worthless. This one calls for nothing solid after four o'clock, just water. Now what do you suppose I do all night?" She nodded before I could hazard a guess. "That's right: up and down, down and up to the bathroom. Maybe it's the exercise that takes off the weight. But I need my sleep." She turned to our waitress and ordered a pastrami melt on rye with a side of fries and potato salad. "Oh—and a strawberry malted milk. No coffee for me after noon." She gave me a virtuous look.

Across the aisle and down one booth, Jeannie Clay was being joined by Marje Blatt. Marje spotted her aunt and flew over to our table.

"Guess what!" she breathed, her small bosom rising under her crisp white uniform. "The sheriff just came to the clinic to talk to Marilynn Lewis about that murder Friday night! Is it true you found the body, Aunt Vida?"

"Certainly not," sniffed Vida. "Emma and I covered the story, of course. That's our job."

Marje is in her midtwenties and possesses a wholesome prettiness. Spiritually, she is a petite version of her aunt. Marje is brisk, efficient, and seemingly without guile. She is also curious by nature.

"I wanted to stay to find out what was happening, but Dr. Flake thought we should leave for lunch." She motioned at Jeannie, who was practically falling out of the booth in an attempt to overhear. "I don't think Dr. Flake was very happy to see Milo Dodge come to the office while we still had patients."

"Milo has to do his job, too," Vida replied primly. "Maybe you can ask Dr. Flake—or Marilynn—what Milo wanted to know." Her smile was benign; her eyes were like stilettos.

Marje started to turn away. "I'll call you tonight. I have to tell you about my trip to Cabo San Lucas."

"Yes, you do. I'll wait to hear from you." Vida gave a jerky nod of dismissal. I half-expected Marje to salute.

I, however, did not intend to wait for secondhand news. Feeling somewhat deceitful, I told Vida I had to go to Parker's Pharmacy after lunch to get some Excedrin. And I did, but instead of returning to *The Advocate*, I continued along Front Street to the sheriff's office. Milo was in, eating a double cheeseburger and wiping his nose.

"So," I said, sitting down in his visitor's chair and assuming my most knowing air, "what did Marilynn have to say?"

Milo curled his lip over his cheeseburger. "Damn. I'm glad I'm a law enforcement officer. If I were a crook, I wouldn't stand a chance of getting away with anything in this town."

"Oh?" I gave him an arch little smile. "Does that mean you've caught your killer?"

Milo's glare would have daunted someone who hadn't raised a son on her own. I may not understand men, but I know their limits. Under that indolent exterior, Milo Dodge has a temper. It's not difficult to rouse, but easily extinguished.

"Stick your sarcasm in your ear, Emma," Milo snapped.

"If you're so fired up for me to make an arrest, I could haul that nurse in right now. Who else in this town is likely to have plugged that guy? She doesn't have an alibi, either."

Inside, I froze. But I kept calm, seemingly casual. "Does Marilynn admit she knew Kelvin Greene?"

"Hell, no." Milo took a swig of coffee from a heavy white mug. "But she's lying. I'd bet on it."

There was no point in arguing. Not just now. "She does have an alibi. She was apartment-hunting after work Friday."

Milo made a gesture of dismissal with his free hand. "Dolph Terrill is her alibi. First of all, the old rummy says she came by on Thursday. Then he says it was Friday after lunch. Finally, maybe before dinner. He can't remember his own name. In fact, when Dwight Gould questioned him, Dolph fell off the front porch."

"Great." I sighed. "What do you do next?"

Swallowing a pill, which I presumed was for his allergies, Milo flinched slightly. "Check with our liaison in Seattle. Get more information on Kelvin Greene. Find out why he came to Alpine." His face relaxed a bit. "Say, Emma—did you hear a shot Friday night? You and Vida were at the Campbells', right?"

I nodded. "Yes—and no," I replied slowly, working my way through the memory of our arrival at the Campbell house. "We got there right around seven. I don't remember hearing any shots. If there were, they could have come from the practice field. Coach Ridley had his kids going through their paces for the track meet that's coming up. Starter guns." I gave Milo a curious look. "Weird timing, huh?"

"Lucky timing, for the killer." Milo's expression was wry. "And yes, I did talk to Rip Ridley. He didn't see anything or anybody unusual by the high school. Neither did his athletes. They're worked up anyway, since Swede got snatched. There's no sign that anybody broke into the high school, though. Damned odd." Obviously baffled, Milo shook his head.

It seemed to me that the sheriff was showing more concern over Bucker Swede's disappearance than Kelvin

Greene's murder. "But a black male was hanging out by the high school field that morning." Trying to get Milo back on track, I told him about Carla's report. "It was so early that it might mean Kelvin got to town the previous night. Have you found a car?"

Milo became smug. "Sam Heppner found it yesterday. A 'ninety-one Trans AM, parked up in the cul-de-sac at the end of Fifth Street by the Tolberg farm."

I raised my eyebrows. My log house was located on Fir, between Fourth and Fifth. The forest began where my backyard ended. The cul-de-sac was a mere hundred yards from my home. It was also an equal distance to the high school track.

"That's not a cheap car, right?" The only thing I knew about automobiles was that I'd always coveted a Jaguar. I'd bought mine used, four years ago. I intended to drive it until the wheels fell off.

"They don't give them away," Milo replied. "Greene's the registered owner, so he didn't steal it." The sheriff looked disappointed.

"Has Marlow recovered from having a dying man drop in?" In my mean-minded way, I figured that most of Whipp's customers were already dead.

Milo's hazel eyes flickered over me and came to rest on his nasal spray. "So it seems. Though . . ." He shrugged, leaving the little word hanging.

I pounced. "Though what? Come on, Dodge, air your doubts."

But Milo put his feet on his desk and his arms behind his head. "I don't know, Emma. I don't think he'd ever seen this character before in his life. Still, Marlow is acting strange. I suppose it's the shock."

"Maybe." But I was certain Milo did indeed have doubts. If the sheriff did, so did I. It was Milo's certainties that worried me. Especially when it came to Marilynn Lewis.

Chapter Seven

ED BRONSKY SEEMED to be trying. Usually, he was only trying my patience, but in this third week of May, my ad manager was actually putting forth some effort. In a fit of remorse after work on Friday, he had tried to apologize to Lloyd Campbell. Gunning the Bronsky family station wagon up First Hill Road in hot pursuit of Lloyd's Alpine Appliance van, Ed hadn't quite succeeded. The old station wagon stalled twice, and Lloyd was gone by the time Ed reached the van. But Ed had further proved his newfound diligence by talking Dutch Bamberg into four inches instead of his usual two, along with a discount coupon for midweek video rentals. He also came up with an original layout for Alpine Fine Fabrics, rather than relying on his tired clip-art file. And wonder of wonders, he found a new display advertiser, Skykomish Credit Counselors, which had previously been buried in the classified section.

I praised Ed to the skies. Diffidently, he brushed off my fulsome words. "I guess it was time I tried some new tricks. It took some doing with Dutch Bamberg—he's stubborn as a mule. They don't call him Dutch for nothing. But we can't wait forever for Fred Meyer and Starbuck's to get here and zap things up. Shirley and I had a real heart-to-heart talk over the weekend. She sort of stoked my engine." Ed chuckled and leered, not a pretty combination, but given the circumstances, I kept smiling.

By late Monday, we seemed to have the paper under control. Still, I held off writing the homicide story in case there were any late-breaking developments. I checked in with Milo just before heading home, but he'd already left work. Deputy Sam Heppner informed me that Honoria Whitman was back from Seattle. The sheriff had gone a-wooing. And, I realized, I'd forgotten to show Milo the letter I'd received from the bigot. If I had time on Tuesday, I'd do it then. But the day before we go to press gets pretty hectic. The bigot could keep. Unfortunately, they always do.

I stopped at the library to return a couple of overdue books and to find something new to read. The Alpine Library shares space with senior services, which, in turn, adjoins the civic center. All are housed in the old high school, a two-story red brick building that dates from the 1920s. The county library system's budget has been cut, so recent releases are hard to come by. I put in three reserves and checked out a couple of older espionage novels I'd missed along the line.

Edna Mae Dalrymple was on duty. A nervous, efficient sprite of a woman, Edna Mae is the head librarian and one of my fellow bridge players. "Guess who came in to get a library card," she whispered. Edna Mae always whispers, except at the card table where she is inclined to shriek and squeal as well as fidget and twitch. She also likes to answer her own questions. "The new nurse, that's who. I'm so thrilled that she's a reader."

"Well, why not?" I asked boldly.

Edna Mae's overbite gripped her lower lip as she frowned and gestured at the nonfiction stacks. I turned, seeing Jean Campbell absorbed in the house and garden section.

"Ms. Lewis has a tremendous responsibility on her shoulders," Edna Mae confided. "Imagine, coming here on her own and bearing the brunt of an unintegrated town like Alpine! It's very important for her to step right in, doing all the things Alpiners do. Church works, service clubs, library books, bridge—if she plays. I'd like to recruit her for our 'Speak Up, Speak Out' series. Last month we had Coach Ridley."

The library speaker series had also had me, in my first six months as editor and publisher of *The Advocate*. Four people showed up, two of whom had been deaf as posts. A third, Toots Bergstrom, had eaten her lunch. Noisily. I couldn't recommend Marilynn's participation, but I was loath to say so to Edna Mae.

"Well . . . certainly," I temporized. Maybe Marilynn could speak on geriatrics nursing.

I was about to leave when I saw Jean Campbell approach the desk with two large gardening books. She smiled a bit tensely when she saw me. I waited while Edna Mae checked out Jean's selections.

"I'm trying some new perennials," Jean said, as we walked together through the glass double doors. She displayed the books she'd chosen, both of which were devoted to Pacific Northwest gardens. "I'm tired of annuals. They're just too much trouble. I had some lovely peonies about to bloom, but they got trampled. I suppose it was a dog. People should keep their pets tied up."

Not owning any animals, I readily agreed. "By the way," I went on before Jean could head for her Chevy, which was parked three spaces away from my Jag, "tell Marilynn there weren't any new apartment ads in this week's classifieds. And Carla doesn't know of anybody who's moving out of The Pines Village."

"Oh." Jean stared at her shoes, then gave me another tense smile. "Well. I'm sure Marilynn will find something soon. I told her she should strike a bargain with Dolph Terrill and offer to do some of the repairs if he'd lower the rent."

"And?" My own smile was full of encouragement.

Jean's forced cheer fled. "Marilynn said it was more work than she could handle. Cracks in the walls, plaster peeling, balky plumbing. Maybe Shane could help. She really should have a place of her own."

"I suppose it is kind of crowded," I allowed.

"Well . . . it's not that so much as . . . I think she'd be happier on her own. She's used to it. Though I believe she had a roommate in Seattle." Jean moved about a bit awkwardly on the pavement. "And then there've been so many phone calls last night and today. We should have thought about giving her a separate line, but that's such a bother if she's not going to stay with us."

"Phone calls?" I strove to look innocent. It's not an easy guise for a prying journalist.

Jean's mouth tightened. "I don't know what it's all about. I took half-a-dozen calls for her today—and, of course, she was at work. They were friends, I suppose." Again, she seemed absorbed in her shoes.

"Not local calls?" In the distance, the courthouse clock chimed the half hour. Traffic on First Street was moving at a brisk pace—at least by Alpine standards.

Jean shook her head. "No. Marilynn hasn't made many friends yet. She hasn't had time, really." Glancing at her watch, she flashed another unconvincing smile. "I've got to dash. I'm picking Marilynn up at the clinic."

All the way home, I wondered about those phone calls. I hadn't watched the news over the weekend. As a print journalist, I disdain TV newscasts except during the week when I figure I might pick up an item with a local tie-in. Maybe the Seattle stations had carried a story about Kelvin Greene's murder. Perhaps it had appeared in the Monday morning edition of the *Seattle Post-Intelligencer*. If so, had Marilynn's rash of calls been triggered by Kelvin's death? I hoped not.

My curiosity had to be put on hold. There was nothing about the murder on the early editions of the three Seattle newscasts. Nor was there anything in the Northwest section of the evening *Times*. I immersed myself in one of my espionage thrillers and tried to forget about Kelvin Greene and Marilynn Lewis.

Yet even in my own mind, their names were linked. That bothered me. What if Milo was right? Shortly before ten, I called Vida.

"Stupid bridal shower," Vida fulminated. "I just got home. Darla Puckett's granddaughter, all of seventeen, marrying a high school dropout from Gold Bar. The theme was a zip code. Now how am I going to write about *that*?"

I gaped at the receiver. "A zip code?"

"They served tapioca. With maraschino cherries, pronounced by the bride-to-be as *marsh-o-lino*. Where do these nincompoops come from?" Vida was, as she herself would put it, fit to be tied.

"A zip code?" I repeated.

"Yes, yes, and not even from around here. Nine-oh-two-something-or-other. Maybe that's where they're going to live. Wherever it is, it'll be a hovel. They don't have siccum."

Enlightenment was dawning. "I think it's a TV show," I offered. "It's called *90210*. Very popular with teenagers."

"So is unwanted pregnancy," Vida snapped. "Why can't they have a *real* theme, with a pansy arch, or play Reach for the Ring? Honestly!"

I waited for Vida's pique to pass. Then I asked if she'd found out anything from Marje Blatt. For once, she didn't know any more than I did about Milo's call on Marilynn Lewis. Marje, however, had reported that Chaz Phipps from the ski lodge had seen an African American in the parking lot around four-thirty. Chaz had thought he was a guest checking in, but he never registered.

"Maybe," I suggested, "Kelvin really did want directions from Cyndi to the lodge."

Vida was still prickly. "For what? To pass time?" She was more interested in her nephew's report. After concluding her conversation with Marje and before going to the bridal shower, Vida had talked to Bill Blatt.

"The information is sketchy," Vida said, now simmered down. "Kelvin Greene was a small-time crook: three arrests, no convictions, all drug related. We knew that. He's been living with a woman named Winola Prince, out in Rainier Valley. She moved in with him about a month ago. It appears she's a decent woman, and is quite upset over Kelvin's demise. Winola's a licensed practical nurse. She works at Virginia Mason Hospital, which is where Marilynn Lewis worked before she came to Alpine." Vida paused, and I could almost see her smirk. "Doesn't that beat all?"

Milo Dodge's visit to the Alpine Medical Clinic had not gone unnoticed. By midmorning on Tuesday, I had heard from Mayor Fuzzy Baugh, Henry Bardeen at the ski lodge, Francine Wells of Francine's Fine Apparel, and Averill Fairbanks of UFO fame. Averill said he thought that black people had been brought to earth by space aliens about the same time that Mount Mazama blew up in Oregon to create Crater Lake. I told Averill he ought to check his theory out with NASA or the NAACP, whichever group's phone number he could find first through Directory Assistance.

Everyone seemed agog at the possibility that a black man had been shot by a black woman, right here in Alpine. And just about everyone did think it was possible, even likely. More sightings of Kelvin Greene had been reported, including at the mall, the courthouse, the Icicle Creek campground, and riding one of the Dithers Sisters' Appaloosas down First Hill Road. Maybe, I'd suggested to the last caller, they'd also seen Zorro. I felt like tearing my hair. I actually gave it a yank when I got the second letter in the morning mail.

"Dear Publicher," it read, "Rumors are flying. Where will they go? The mall? Downtown? Out into the naiberhoods? Once they get started, there's no stopping them. They will take us all over, and make us there slaves. Yours truely, A Loyal Reader."

I snatched up both letters and marched the two blocks to Milo's office. He expressed mild interest.

"They're not the same as the ones Marilynn Lewis got," he said, without a second glance. "It looks like we're dealing with yet another goofball." He yawned, sneezed, and sat back in his faux-leather chair.

I should have inquired after Honoria Whitman, but in my perverse way, I refused to ask. Besides, I was angry, not only at the malicious letter writer, but at Milo.

"What's going on with this Winola Prince?" I demanded. "Does she actually know Marilynn Lewis, or did they merely happen to work in the same hospital?"

Milo blinked at me, his face otherwise impassive. "Gosh, Emma, when are you going to stop treating me as if I were head of the gestapo? Don't you have a newspaper to put out today?"

"I can't put it out until I have all the facts in this Kelvin Greene story," I answered in a waspish voice. "Now give, Dodge. You're right, I'm up against a deadline. Have you talked to Marilynn about Winola?"

Milo made a fist, crooked his arm, and held out his wrist to display his Timex watch. "See this? It's eight minutes to eleven. I've had a busy morning. I'll get around to Nurse Lewis after lunch."

"And scare Doc Dewey and Peyton Flake's patients to death in the process? Give them a break at the clinic, Dodge. Take Marilynn out for coffee."

The suggestion obviously startled Milo. My first reaction

was that he felt I was violating law enforcement ethics. Then it dawned on me that maybe he was alarmed at the thought of being seen in public with a black woman. I asked him outright.

"Hell, no!" Milo glowered at me. "It's just that . . . How often do I take a suspect out . . . Shit, it'd look like a date!"

"Are you through spluttering?" I couldn't keep the amusement off my face.

Milo was actually blushing. I forced myself not to laugh. We were silent for a few moments, and I could tell that he was thinking, hard. "Marilynn Lewis is a damned attractive young woman," he finally said. "It wouldn't look right—under the circumstances—for me, as a single man, to take her out for coffee. Be reasonable, Emma. What would people in this town say if I were seen going around with *any* single, good-looking woman?"

That did it. Milo and I have been everywhere together in the past three years, except to bed. I jumped out of my chair, stalked to the door, and slammed it behind me. Yes, it was true that I didn't understand men. When it comes to interpersonal relationships, the density of their brains absolutely amazes me. They are a race apart, or, as Vida is wont to say: *Men aren't like other people.* I simply can't fathom the male mind.

Marching back up Front Street, I knew that Milo was thinking the same thing about women. The difference was that he wasn't thinking about what I was thinking at all.

The front-page story about Kelvin Greene's murder was relatively brief. For all of Milo's bravado about suspecting Marilynn Lewis, I didn't see that he had a shred of evidence. To protect him, as well as Marilynn, I merely stated that the sheriff was conducting an investigation. Except for mentioning that the victim was a Seattle resident, I couldn't say much about his background for fear of legal repercussions. I had no list of survivors, other than the grieving Winola Prince. Good taste dictated that I leave out her name.

Vida and I have argued over some of the newer wrinkles in obituaries, where live-in lovers, including homosexuals, are listed as a matter of course. Vida has been opposed on the grounds that only lawful relatives should be included. I gained an edge over her last summer when I pointed out that Cass Pidduck's obit listed survivors as his sons, Darrell and Conrad; their wives, Mary Jo and Jessica; five grandchildren; six great-grandchildren; numerous nieces and nephews; and his beloved dog, Flyswatter.

Nor could I publicly speculate when and where the shooting had taken place. "Greene apparently died from a head wound shortly after entering the grocery store," I wrote, having properly kept Marlow Whipp's role to that of accidental observer. The story took up four inches, and was the second lead, after the planning commission's latest bungling effort to make Front and Pine streets one-way thoroughfares. I boxed the Bucker Swede item, but buried it on page eight.

By two o'clock, we had the paper well in hand. Ed was bustling around the office, showing more signs of life than I'd seen in him since Roger put a whoopee cushion on his chair the previous April Fool's Day. Carla was finishing a major feature on the upcoming high school production of *Our Town*. The story wasn't any great shakes, but she had taken some fine pictures. Vida was struggling to get in all the weddings, showers, and end-of-school-year celebrations that fill the calendar in May and continue through June.

I had just rapped out a last-minute item about the need for strawberry pickers when inspiration hit. Dialing Seattle Directory Assistance, I asked for Winola Prince's number. There was no listing. I tried for Kelvin Greene and hit pay dirt.

But no one answered. Winola was either at work or helping make arrangements for Kelvin's funeral. I understood that the body would be released that afternoon. Perhaps Winola might come to Alpine. I called the morgue over at the hospital, but was told that the remains had been shipped to Driggers Funeral Home. The owner, Al Driggers, sounded as appropriately lifeless as ever.

"We've been asked to send the body to Seattle," he said. "Mrs. Greene—the mother—made the request."

So Kelvin Greene had a mother. I sighed as I hung up the phone. It's always easier to deal with disembodied bodies. But corpses who leave mothers, fathers, wives, and children are far more disturbing. It's okay for me not to care about dead people I never knew. It's not okay—it's not possible—for me not to care about the people they leave behind.

I called Al back. I should include Mrs. Greene's name in the story. "It's Alva," he said, all emotion carefully drained from his voice.

"A father?" I asked, pen poised.

"Not mentioned. There's a child, though. Mrs. Greene said something about finding a neighbor to watch her grandson." Al's words took on a shade of warmth.

"A name?" I inquired.

But Al didn't know. "She called him her grandbaby. But she definitely referred to him as Kelvin's boy."

I decided to omit the reference to a child. This wasn't an official obituary, but a news story. I'd try to reach Winola Prince later. When I told Vida what I'd learned, she grew thoughtful.

"You could call Marilynn, I suppose."

"I don't want to. Not yet."

Vida nodded. "I know. It's difficult. I'd so hoped there was no connection between this Kelvin and poor Marilynn. That's why I didn't say anything when we got back to the Campbells' house from Marlow Whipp's store. I didn't want the rest of them to jump to conclusions. Or for Marilynn to think we were making any assumptions."

"I thought as much," I said, recalling Vida's uncustomary reticence. Rarely have I felt as fond of Vida as I did at that moment. Rarely have I felt as fond of any woman except my own mother.

With the usual sense of Tuesday relief, I left a note for Kip MacDuff and signed the press order so that the paper could be driven to the printer in Monroe early Wednesday morning. Arriving home, I felt restless. After changing clothes, I went out into the yard. Despite my weekend efforts, there was still plenty of work to be done. Shrubs needed pruning, the grass could use a mowing, and more weeds seemed to have sprung up overnight. I concentrated on the front flower bed, which grows almost to the street. There are no sidewalks where I live. The planning commission keeps promising to put a Local Improvement District bond issue on an upcoming ballot, but in over three years it hasn't happened yet. Maybe it was time to write another L.I.D. editorial.

The pansies I'd set out two weeks earlier were blooming nicely, though threatening to get leggy. My iris were on the wane, but the trio of columbine looked lovely. As ever, my peonies were a disappointment. There were only two buds showing on the pink clump, and the deep red variety hadn't come up at all.

On my knees, pulling up clover, I recalled Jean Campbell's complaint about her peonies. She thought a dog had trampled them. But the Campbell house was protected by a white picket fence. It was only about waist high, so perhaps a dog had jumped it. Still, I wondered. Dogs don't trample, they dig. The cemetery was four doors away. If someone had gone through the Campbells' yard, the flowers might have been crushed by the trespasser. . . .

Inside the house, my phone rang. It was Milo, sounding abject. "Emma, are you still mad?" he asked.

Of course I wasn't, not really. Men aren't responsible for being insensitive boobs. I put down my weeder and sat in the chair by my desk. "Forget it, Milo. It was deadline day. You know I'm always touchy on Tuesdays."

His sigh of relief was audible. "I went to see Marilynn after she finished work," he said, obviously glad to change the subject. "She admitted she knew Kelvin Greene."

If Milo had blown a trumpet in my ear, he couldn't have sounded more self-righteous. "So you're vindicated, huh? When do you cuff her?"

He uttered a small chuckle. "You know it's not that easy. Kelvin was seeing her roommate. Winola Prince. Marilynn insists she didn't know him very well. The funny thing is," he went on in a musing voice, "I believe her."

"Well, hooray!" It was my turn to feel a sense of relief. But it didn't last long. Reality set in like a load of lead, weighing me down, telling me that if Marilynn Lewis was innocent, who on earth in Alpine would have had any reason to shoot Kelvin Greene? "Did Marilynn know why Kelvin came to town?"

Milo admitted that Marilynn had no idea. I asked if he'd

contacted Winola Prince. He hadn't been able to reach her, either. He had, however, spoken with Alva Greene.

"The woman's a clam," he declared. "I got the impression she's had a few brushes with the law, probably because of her kids. Kelvin had a couple of brothers and some sisters. I figure they've had problems."

Stretching the long phone cord, I was able to reach my liquor cabinet. It was after six-thirty, and I was entitled to a bit of bourbon. "So what happens next?" I asked.

Milo chuckled again, this time more heartily. "You think we're sitting on our dead butts? We've made inquiries. Kelvin arrived early Friday morning or got here Thursday night and slept in his car. He didn't check into either of the motels, the hotel, or the ski lodge. He wasn't seen anywhere along the Stevens Pass corridor. But several people saw him Friday in Alpine. The mall, the ski lodge, the tavern, the campground. He got fish and chips to go at the Burger Barn somewhere around noon. It looks like he was killing time, probably until he could meet his killer. The waitress and the bartender at the Icicle Creek Tavern thought he showed up there about three-thirty. Yes, he had a beer with Cyndi Campbell who, according to Denise Petersen, was flirting with him. Denise insists that Cyndi and Kelvin came to the tavern together. But Denise is off her rocker. She and Cyndi went to high school together, and Cyndi beat her out for Timber Queen the year they were seniors."

"Well, certainly, that makes Denise a famous liar," I remarked, with an irony that would be lost on Milo. However, it was probably an accurate assessment. Old grudges die hard in Alpine. "I take it you think Cyndi was doing more than giving directions to at least three different destinations?"

Milo seemed puzzled by the question, but had an answer anyway. "I admit that most people don't sit down and drink beer with strangers while they tell them how to get someplace. But Bill Blatt says Cyndi is sticking to her story. She'd never seen Kelvin Greene before in her life."

"So," I noted, hauling out a fifth of bourbon that was almost empty, "Cyndi says it was Kelvin Greene at the Icicle Creek Tavern? How does she know?"

"She described him, including his clothes. He had a

small scar on his upper lip. She remembered that. Cyndi might seem like an airhead, but she's observant." Milo's voice conveyed approval.

The phone cord didn't quite reach the ice compartment of my refrigerator. But my mind had made a leap of its own—to tomorrow. I complimented Milo on his diligence, then hung up and poured my drink. Before taking my chicken pot pie out of the oven, I called Vida, relaying Milo's information. She wasn't as generous with our sheriff.

"If Cyndi knew Kelvin Greene," she said in a crisp voice, "I'd bet some of the other Campbells knew him, too. Cyndi hasn't spent a lot of time in Seattle, but Shane has. There's got to be more of a connection up at the house on Tyee Street than Marilynn. Or Cyndi."

I agreed. "Can you hold down the fort tomorrow?" I asked slyly. "It's Wednesday, and things should be slow."

Vida's manner grew suspicious. "Why? Where are you going?"

I told her about my decision to attend the conference at Lake Chelan. She approved. Then I added that my wardrobe needed refurbishing. "Francine's summer clothes aren't my style this year," I fibbed. "I want to do some shopping in Seattle."

"Shopping?" Vida demanded sharply. "Or probing?"

"Both," I answered candidly.

"Good," Vida replied. "I'll go with you. Carla and Ed can hold down the fort. As long as Ginny's there to watch them." She hung up before I could argue.

Chapter Eight

I'D ALMOST CALLED Vida back and asked her to stay in Alpine. She was right about my intentions—I hoped to track down Winola Prince and maybe Alva Greene, too. But I was equally sincere in my desire to get some new, fiendishly smart clothes. With Vida along, I'd be lucky to make a quick stop at the Northgate Mall. She hated to shop—except for Roger.

"According to the *P-I*, Kelvin's funeral is Friday," Vida said, patting the morning edition in the well between the Jaguar's bucket seats. "That should mean that Winola is at work. Assuming, of course, she's on a day shift."

As usual, Vida's mind was running on the same track as mine. We had left Alpine at eight-thirty, after a brief check at the office where all seemed well, probably because Ed and Carla hadn't yet arrived. It was just after ten when I pulled off the freeway to head for Virginia Mason Hospital on Seattle's First Hill, or as it's more commonly known, Pill Hill. Located above the downtown area, the neighborhood is crammed with hospitals, clinics, pharmacies, and medical specialists. It's also jammed with cars. I left Vida in a loading zone and ran two blocks to the main entrance. After a five-minute wait, I learned that Winola Prince was working the orthopedic floor. She would be on her lunch break at eleven.

We parked in the hospital garage, which had surprisingly reasonable fees for the Big City. About the only charge for parking in Alpine is if a car is left in Milo Dodge's slot outside the sheriff's office. There are some definite benefits to small-town living.

"You let me handle this," Vida urged, as we made our way through the hospital's maze of halls and elevators.

"You find the cafeteria, and I'll bring Winola along. Order me some pie, if they have it. Anything but blueberry or rhubarb."

They had apple, blackberry, and custard. The apple looked safest. I got coffee. For fifteen minutes, I watched the parade of doctors, nurses, medical technicians, and visitors that marched past my corner table. People who work in hospitals always strike me as guarded. They evince neither hope nor despair. On rubber-soled shoes, they move softly, as if afraid to upset the balance of the odds that determine life and death. Maybe they're just afraid of slipping on the frequently scrubbed floors. But I sense detachment, perhaps a wish that their hearts were as protected as their feet. It's tough enough being a journalist; writing about illness and accidents can cause depression or callousness, or both. Facing death on a daily basis must require a different dimension of the human soul.

I wondered what Vida would use for an excuse to drag Winola Prince to an interview. In this case, she couldn't claim to be a relative of Marilynn's. She wouldn't impersonate an officer of the law. She wouldn't dare assume Jean Campbell's identity.

To my amazement, Vida told Winola the truth. "Here, Emma, meet Winola Prince," she said, a hand at the young nurse's elbow. "She's going to help us with our story about poor Kelvin."

Winola Prince looked as if she hadn't slept for a long time. She was slender by nature, and her face had a gaunt look that made her dark eyes enormous. She wore no makeup, and her light blue blouse and slacks hung limply, as if they, along with their wearer, had lost their starch. Winola sat down with a weary, grateful air. Vida bustled off to get her some food.

I was clearing my throat and trying to come up with a tactful remark when Winola asked a question of her own: "What kind of people you got in Alpine that'd kill my Kelvin? That Mrs. Runkel says your sheriff don't know nothin'."

"He doesn't, yet," I replied, feeling a need to defend Milo. "The investigation has just started. That's one reason we're here. We want to find out if you—or anybody who knew Kelvin—might know what led to his death."

Winola's hand strayed to the cornrows of hair that were held in place with turquoise beads. Her name tag—w. PRINCE, LPN—was crooked. "I don't know nothin' 'bout him goin' to Alpine. Kelvin didn't always tell me everything." She not only looked sad, but sulky, as past wrongs festered in her present pain.

I had opened a notebook and was pretending to scan scribblings that actually made up my grocery list. "You and Marilynn Lewis were roommates for how long?"

Winola screwed up one eye, concentrating. "Two years? Not that long—from a year ago last summer."

"Were she and Kelvin friends?" I hoped I'd phrased the question innocuously.

"Friends?" Winola stared at me, then at her hands with their long, curved fingernails. "No. Marilynn never liked Kelvin much. She can be high and mighty sometimes. Don't ask why. She got herself all messed up with that Jerome, didn't she? What was so fine 'bout him? I told her, 'Girl, you one dumb bitch. Jerome ain't no smoother than my man. You *wrong*.' " Winola's dark eyes glittered briefly, showing a fire I thought had been doused by grief. "What difference it make—now?" The fire went out.

Vida arrived with a tray containing creamed chicken, rice pilaf, broccoli, a roll, applesauce, fruit salad, and a bowl of vegetable soup. "You're too thin, Winola. You can't be eating properly. Here, start with the soup." Brusquely, Vida pulled a packet of soda crackers from her pocket.

Winola's plucked eyebrows arched. Astonishment and resentment crossed her gaunt face. Tensing, I expected her to rail at Vida. But she didn't. Her narrow shoulders slumped as she picked up a spoon. Vida could cross racial barriers, conquer strangers, and comfort the bereaved with soda crackers.

I waited for Winola to taste her soup. "I'm sorry, I'm not sure what you're talking about," I said, as much for Vida's benefit as my own. "Who's Jerome?"

Tearing the cellophane off the crackers, Winola eyed me with suspicion. "I thought you knew Marilynn. How come you askin' 'bout Jerome?"

Vida gave a sad shake of her head, making the perky magenta beret slip a notch. "Marilynn won't talk about Jerome," she said. "Too tragic, it seems."

Winola tried the chicken. It looked lethal in its sea of jaundiced yellow sauce, but she ate without comment. When she finally spoke again, her voice was listless. "Jerome was a musician. He did coke. Marilynn hated that, but she loved Jerome more than was good for her. They'd fight. Oh, Lordy, how they'd fight!" Winola rolled her eyes and shook her head. "He wanted to move in, but Marilynn, she finally say no. Then he beat her up some more. I come home once and found her passed out. She wouldn't go to the hospital—she said it would embarrass her! Shit, she be half dead!" Winola shuddered in revulsion at the memory.

I shuddered, too. Vida, eating her pie, frowned. "Really, Winola, we had no idea what a terrible ordeal Marilynn went through with Jerome. I can certainly understand why she moved to Alpine. Let's hope he doesn't find out where she is and come looking for her."

With her fork in the broccoli, Winola turned a puzzled face on Vida. "What you talkin' 'bout? You believe in ghosts?"

Vida's knowing guise cracked a jot. "Ghosts? Why, yes," she answered, recovering quickly. "I do indeed. My Uncle Osbert is a ghost. He haunts the holding pond across from the golf course."

Averting my eyes lest Winola see the rampant disbelief that shone there, I coughed. "Excuse me, I've never glimpsed Uncle Osbert."

Winola, however, wasn't as credulous as Vida had hoped. She put down her fork and her mouth set in a stern line. "Mrs. Runkel, I do think you must be a fraud. Why you comin' around here, snoopin' and sniffin'? Marilynn's got troubles enough without people like you pryin' into her life. Leave her be, she wants to start over. It's a damned shame Kelvin went to Alpine!" Angrily, Winola stood up, almost knocking her chair over. Tears had filled her eyes and her thin body was trembling. "I don't want your lunch and I don't want your lies! Go back where you come from! I got to be buryin' my man!" On rubber-soled shoes, Winola fled the cafeteria. Several of the staff members watched curiously; a few of them put their heads together. Their manner was sympathetic. The hospital grapevine seemed to flourish as vigorously as Alpine's.

Vida ate the last bite of pie, then sat with her chin on her hand. "My. We didn't acquit ourselves very well, did we?"

I didn't know what to say. "Jerome is dead," I commented at last. "Where do we find out how he got that way?"

Vida reached over to scoop up some of Winola's untouched fruit salad. "Milo can do that," she replied absently. "It would help to have a last name for this Jerome." She buttered Winola's roll. "Poor Marilynn. I hope she's not the sort of woman who has a weakness for bad apples."

"It sounds as if they both did," I remarked, watching two earnest young men, who appeared to be interns, sit down at the table next to us.

"Both?" Vida looked up from Winola's applesauce. "You mean Marilynn and Winola?"

I nodded. "Kelvin Greene may not have beaten Winola, but he sounds like a loser."

"Yes, he does," Vida agreed. "He lost his life. So, I gather, did Jerome." She tried the rice pilaf. "I wonder what those two women had in common besides dead beaux?"

Puzzled, I frowned at Vida. "They're both nurses. They worked here together. They're about the same age." I didn't add that they were also both black.

Vida, however, was shaking her head. "No, no. Oh, certainly they have superficial things in common. But they couldn't be more unalike. Winola—let's face facts—is somewhat coarse. It has nothing to do with race, you understand. I could name twenty equally coarse white women in Alpine, but I'd rather not, because it's sufficient to have to talk to them on the phone every so often. You know who I mean. They're common, and their ethnic roots are all over the globe." She gave me a hard stare. Names whirled around in my head. I could only come up with a dozen, offhand. "Marilynn is cultured, charming, self-possessed, if self-effacing," Vida continued, no doubt with a parade of Alpine vulgarians marching through her head. "Really, so much of racial prejudice is based on how people speak. It may not be fair, but think how we react to all sorts of accents—the Deep South, Texas, Brooklyn, and, of course, foreigners. George Bernard Shaw was an old fool about some things, but he was right about that. Look at Eliza Doolittle. Marilynn sounds like a lady. Why would she choose someone like Winola as a roommate?"

"Why would Carla choose Libby?" I countered. "They're opposites, too, in many ways."

Finishing off the soda crackers, Vida considered. "True, but only up to a point. Oh, well—I'm sure I don't know." Brushing off her pleated skirt, Vida got to her feet. "Now I suppose you'll want to go shopping?"

I grimaced a bit. "Actually, I thought we'd have lunch."

Adjusting her beret, Vida began to stride from the cafeteria. "Goodness, not yet! I couldn't eat a thing! That pie was awfully filling." In passing, she nodded absently at various bewildered staff members as if she'd known them all her life.

Maybe she had. Nothing about Vida would surprise me.

Twenty-two years had passed since my internship at *The Seattle Times*. I still recognized the bylines of a few old-timers, but I had no real contacts there. Vida, however, insisted I exert what little influence I might possess.

"I thought you said we'd leave this part to Milo," I argued, as we drove away from Pill Hill and headed for Fairview Avenue where the *Times'* editorial and advertising offices are located.

"I thought it over," she replied, sunk down in the bucket seat next to me. "Milo will scoff at us. We're right here, practically on top of *The Times*. We shouldn't pass up the opportunity."

I hadn't been inside the building since I left in 1971 to go to Mississippi and have my baby. I'd walked out on the job, my senior year at the University of Washington, my tiny apartment in the U District—and Tom. Not a word, not a look, not a tear. Ben, in his first year on the Mississippi Delta, had greeted me in a daze. As a priest, he knew he had to take me in and give me comfort. As a big brother, I knew he wanted to kick me in the butt and send me back to Tom.

Vida and I got as far as the security guard, a cheerful

man in his fifties. We explained our place in the journalistic fraternity while he scanned names on a lengthy list.

"I don't think any of our crime reporters are in," he said, with polite regret. "Would you settle for somebody on the city desk?"

Vida wouldn't. "What about your morgue?" she asked.

But the guard shook his head. "It's not open to the public anymore. Too many requests. You have to go through channels."

"Channels!" Vida was exasperated. "See here, young man, we've come all the way from Alpine on this murder-investigation story. We started out with one body—now we have two. Would you like to try for three?" She leaned on the desk, the beret slanting down over one eye.

The guard, who looked more amused than intimidated, picked up his phone. "Let me see what I can do."

Ten minutes later, we were immersed in microfiche. "We could have done this at the public library," I muttered. "Why are we starting with August?"

"*You're* starting with August," Vida snapped. "I have September. That's because I'm assuming Jerome hasn't been dead for more than nine or ten months. Think about it, Emma. Marilynn came to Alpine less than a month ago. If this beau of hers was killed, it could have happened as recently as April. But if his killer was caught, then there would have been a trial. That wouldn't have taken place right away, not in King County. Let's say it was early in the spring. So that would put the actual murder back in the late summer or early fall." Vida lifted her chin and peered at the microfiche through her tortoiseshell-rimmed glasses.

At a nearby machine, a balding man with a thin mustache gave us a dirty look. I assumed he was a staffer, and not pleased with strangers using the newspaper's facilities. A few moments later, I heard him mutter something about "stats lie" and "scumbag Seahawks." He left. I moved on to October.

"It might be a small story," I cautioned Vida, who seemed to be taking forever to get through September. I had the feeling she was catching up on items she'd missed along the way.

"Yes, yes," she replied testily. "I know how to read a met daily."

I didn't doubt it. Still, I'd finished August and October by the time she started on November. The room was stuffy, without adequate ventilation. My stomach was growling. It was almost one o'clock, and breakfast had been meager. A chic young woman with an expensive haircut glided over to the files. I wondered how much they paid reporters these days at *The Times*. I had a feeling they made more than I did as an editor-publisher. I thought of Carla, eking out her four hundred a week, and I felt guilty. No wonder she couldn't afford a six-hundred-dollar apartment on her own. Maybe I should give her a raise. Ed, too, if he continued to perform. And Ginny, who certainly deserved an increase in salary.

"Bingo!" Vida exclaimed, startling the sleek-looking young woman in her three-hundred-dollar summer suit. Leaning over, Vida beamed at me. "Jerome Cole, twenty-nine, was shot and killed the day after Thanksgiving in an apartment on Capitol Hill. Here, Emma, read this. It's short, but let's hope there's a follow-up."

There was. The following day, a neighbor, Wesley Charles, had been arrested for the murder of Jerome Cole. Again, the story was brief, and confined to the local section of the paper.

I burrowed through December; Vida took January. On December tenth, Wesley Charles was arraigned for murder. He entered a plea of not guilty.

We didn't find another reference until early March. The trial was set; the jurors were being chosen. On March eleventh, a verdict was handed down after two hours of deliberation: Wesley Charles was found guilty of second-degree homicide. A week later, he was sentenced to twenty years in prison. He still claimed to be not guilty. His attorney vowed to appeal.

Marilynn Lewis's name was mentioned only once, in connection with the murder site. According to the testimony of a mutual friend, Kelvin Greene, Wesley Charles had bragged that he was "going to do Jerome Cole." Charles, said Greene, had a romantic interest in the woman who lived in the apartment where Cole was shot. Her name was Marilynn Lewis. Winola Prince wasn't mentioned.

I had finally managed to steer Vida to a restaurant on Lake Union. It was almost two, and I was afraid we'd miss the lunch setting. The hostess at Chandler's Crabhouse assured us we weren't too late. Vida insisted she couldn't eat more than a small salad, then ordered a ten-dollar crab Louie and ate most of the bread that arrived before the entrée. I chose the Copper River salmon special.

"Now what do you think?" Vida demanded after our drink orders had gone to the bar. "This poor Wesley fellow was defending Marilynn from another savage beating?"

I shrugged. "That didn't come through in the trial. Wesley kept insisting he was innocent."

"His attorney was an idiot," Vida declared, as the waitress brought her white wine and my screwdriver. "He tried to prove that someone else had killed Jerome Cole. He failed miserably, with some hogwash about a stranger in a leather jacket. The interesting part is Kelvin Greene. At least as far as we're concerned. Now why did he come to Alpine?"

A terrible thought flew through my mind. Judging from the look on Vida's face, it had struck her, too. "Oh, no!" I breathed. "Not Marilynn!"

"What do you mean?" Vida uttered the question through lips that scarcely moved.

I took a quick sip of my screwdriver. "What if Marilynn was somehow implicated in Jerome Cole's murder? What if Kelvin Greene was blackmailing her?"

Vida remained expressionless. "*Implicated?* Is that what you really mean?"

It wasn't exactly, but I refused to play out the shocking scenario that had leapt into my brain. Would a smitten Wesley Charles take the rap for Marilynn Lewis? But he hadn't—not really. He had claimed to be innocent. "It's fair to say that Kelvin Greene came to Alpine to see Marilynn Lewis," I said slowly. "His visit probably had something to do with Jerome Cole's murder. Maybe he had additional information. Maybe Marilynn wasn't even there when it happened. Maybe Kelvin was bringing a love letter from

Wesley or a last-gasp message from Jerome or . . ." My voice trailed off.

Vida sniffed. "You make it sound so civilized. Whatever the reason, the result is that Kelvin got killed, too. I wonder where Wesley Charles is incarcerated." Without another word, Vida got up and marched toward the front of the restaurant. The waitress arrived with our entrées before Vida returned. Not wanting my salmon to get cold, I began eating. When Vida finally resumed her seat, she was looking vexed.

"I called the state Department of Corrections," she said, spearing a crab leg out of her salad, "and got put on hold. I heard half of Simon and Garfunkel's entire repertoire while I waited. I'd hoped that Wesley Charles had been sent to the reformatory at Monroe, but he's still down at Shelton, waiting to be processed. He probably won't be sent to Monroe until June. We're going to have to leave this part to Milo after all."

"Oh." I, too, was disappointed. We could have stopped at the reformatory on our way back to Alpine. Shelton, located on a southwest arm of lower Puget Sound, was a two-hour drive from Seattle. "We're going to have to badger Milo."

Vida gave a single sharp nod. "Of course we are. And we may not like the results."

I knew that. The more we learned about Marilynn Lewis's background, the less I liked it. But I still liked Marilynn Lewis. I couldn't believe she'd killed Kelvin Greene or anyone else, no matter what the provocation.

I also knew I could be wrong.

Chapter Nine

IT'S A WONDER I didn't end up buying a chenille bathrobe and fuzzy slippers with glass eyes and whiskers. Vida spun me around Nordstrom's like a top, chased me up Fifth Avenue as if I'd stolen her purse, and absolutely refused to stop at more than one boutique in the Westlake Center. Nothing, she insisted, was worth trying on, and the prices were outrageous.

"Ivory—too hard to keep clean," she remarked, stomping past a table full of cotton and rayon sweaters. "Pants with a pleat! *Eeeek!*" "Silk dupioni? It sounds like an Italian dessert." "Oh, good heavens! Platform shoes! I thought they went out with FDR!"

But I persevered. A long striped skirt with a side slit, a short-sleeved taupe sweater, a gauzy wrap-around white blouse, black leggings, a caramel trench dress in viscose rayon, and—yes—platform brown mock-crocodile sandals.

Vida was still exclaiming over my extravagance when we reached the turnoff for Stevens Pass. "Honestly! Not one item on sale! Emma, do you realize you spent almost a thousand dollars?"

I didn't, of course. On the rare occasions that I splurge, I don't keep track of what I spend. That takes all the fun out of it. And since I refurbish my wardrobe only about every two years, I try not to feel guilty. Still, I couldn't help but gulp.

"A thousand dollars? Really?" I not only felt guilty, I felt sunk. In my head, I began to tot up the articles I'd purchased. Vida was right. I drove slowly through Monroe, noting the rooftops of the reformatory, and wondering how soon I'd join Wesley Charles there—as a bankrupt. Then I remembered that women aren't sent to Monroe; they're put away at Purdy, on the Kitsap Peninsula. Growing more gloomy, I tried to calculate how close I'd come to maxing out my bank cards.

"Do you see this skirt?" Vida inquired, pointing to her pleats. "It's twenty years old, Penney's. It cost fifteen dollars." She thrust out her floral-clad bust from under the boxy gray jacket. "The blouse was nine ninety-nine at the Everett Mall. The jacket came from my sister-in-law, Geraldine. It didn't look right on her, and she was too lazy to return it to Sears."

We were going through Sultan, past the sporting goods store, the Hoot Owl Mini Mart, the Sportsman Inn, and the Dutch Cup Motel and Restaurant. "Besides," Vida went on, "he won't even notice."

I took my eyes off the road just long enough to give Vida an exasperated glare. There was no point in feigning innocence with Vida. "That's not true. Tom notices things. He always liked me to look ... nice." I felt a faint flush come over my cheeks as I gunned the Jag past Startup.

"Perhaps." Vida was looking very prim, her eyes directed at the jagged peaks that rose above the highway. "Women are very silly, you know. They spend oodles of money on clothes and cosmetics to make themselves attractive for a man. But if the man truly loves a woman, he doesn't care if she's wearing a grocery bag. It's only appropriate to get all gussied up and act foolish in the very beginning, to be noticed. After that, you might as well save your money and wear housecoats."

"But it makes me feel better about myself to know I look good," I argued. "It gives me confidence."

"Oh, pooh, it gives you piles of bills! Really, Emma," Vida went on, very serious, "at your age, you should have plenty of confidence. Now if it were Carla, chasing after Dr. Flake, that'd be different. She's only twenty-four."

We were beginning to climb up into the mountains. Crossing the South Fork of the Skykomish River, we approached the entrance to the Snoqualmie National Forest. The river would weave back and forth across the highway almost as far as Alpine.

I reflected on Carla and Dr. Flake; I thought about Tom and me. Peyton Flake was single; Tom wasn't. If Carla wanted to chase Peyts from Mount Baldy to Beckler Peak, no one should criticize her for it. But I had just spent a grand on seducing a married man. I was profligate in more ways than one.

I was also lonely. At the two-thousand-foot level, the river narrowed, tumbling among huge boulders. I had a vision of myself in the gauzy white wrap-around blouse with the deep neckline and the clinging black leggings and my hair cut in a new gamine style and my makeup applied just right. And Tom, standing in the middle of a hotel lobby I could only imagine, cocking his head to one side and giving me his big grin.

"So I won't take a trip this year," I said in a defiant voice. "I didn't want to go anywhere anyway."

Vida turned to gaze at me. She chuckled very softly. "Except to Chelan."

We drove through stands of western hemlock, cottonwoods, and cedar. Tall foxgloves waved in the wind and glossy-leafed salal grew in big green clumps. There were ferns everywhere, and cattails, slim and straight.

I didn't reply to Vida. I didn't have to.

It was almost six-thirty when I dropped Vida off at her house. On a whim, I turned left instead of right on Spruce Street. Marlow Whipp's small store was still open, as I had hoped.

Marlow, however, gave a start when I entered. He peered at me as if I were a stranger, and in a sense, I was. I had never been in the store until now, and though I might have seen Marlow around town, my first real look at him had come on the night of Kelvin Greene's murder.

"How can I help you?" Marlow asked, moving a bit uneasily behind the counter.

The store was very small, with a minimal stock of just about everything. He had cans of soup, toothpaste, butter, ice cream, toilet paper, macaroni, pet food, pantyhose, eggs, beer, tuna, candy, gum, and cigarettes. He even had three small tins of pâté, though I guessed they had been on the shelf since the Reagan era. The only concession to modern marketing was a gleaming brass espresso machine that I guessed was newly installed. I hadn't noticed a sign advertising Marlow's innovation, though I assumed it could improve business. I made a mental note to mention it to Ed Bronsky.

I introduced myself, reminding him that we had encountered, if not met, the previous Friday. Marlow put a hand to his faded brown hair.

"Oh! That was terrible! Can you imagine? A guy like *that* comes in here and dies?"

I put on my most innocent air. "A guy like . . . what?"

Marlow swallowed hard, his Adam's apple bobbing up and down above the undershirt that showed beneath his plaid flannel. "Well . . . a black guy, a stranger, a person who wouldn't normally come here." He waved his hands in a helpless gesture.

"Did you think he was going to rob you?" I heard the wry note in my voice, but Marlow didn't seem to notice.

"I didn't know what to think." Marlow shook his head. "I didn't have much time to think at all. He walked in and sort of staggered." Marlow pointed to an old-fashioned barrel near the door where he kept his hard candy. "He fell against that, and then came forward. He tried to say something, but he never got it out. Then *kerplunk*—he landed facedown right where you're standing!"

I glanced at the worn floorboards. If Milo had made an outline of the body, it was now gone. "Why do you think he came here?" I inquired.

Marlow looked genuinely mystified by the question. "Why? Well, why not? I mean, where else would he go that time of night?"

"A house?" I suggested. "There's a house next door, there are houses all over the place, at least on this side of Spruce. And wasn't there activity at the high school field across the street? If the man wanted help, why not go there?"

It appeared that the thought had never occurred to Marlow Whipp. But instead of considering it, he leaned one elbow on the counter and his blue eyes grew wary. "So what are you trying to say, Mrs. Lord?"

I wasn't sure. I suppose I'd been trying to flesh out the scenario. It appeared that Kelvin Greene had been shot at the cemetery, right by Axel Swensen's newly dug grave. If that was true, then Kelvin might have stumbled from the cemetery, up the service road to Spruce, crossed Seventh Street, and seen the sign for the grocery store. Would a dying black man be sufficiently rational to realize that he might not receive help from a private residence in a small town like Alpine? Was that why Kelvin Greene had sought sanctuary in a more public place? Maybe he had merely wanted to be sure that someone was on hand to give him aid. I tried to summarize my thoughts for Marlow Whipp.

Marlow, however, wasn't in a speculative mood. "Who said he got shot at the cemetery? It didn't say so in your newspaper. I figure somebody plugged him up in the woods. Hell, it could have been an accident. You know how it is with some of those guys and their guns. They'll shoot at anything that moves. A black guy like that probably looked like a bear."

I didn't bother to keep from rolling my eyes. Marlow slapped his hand on a post that was decorated with cans of chewing tobacco. "Hell, Mrs. Lord, what are you getting at? The only thing I know for sure is that I didn't shoot the son of a bitch, and I never saw him before in my life. I told Dodge that, and he believes me. Now why don't you all go away and leave me alone?" Marlow's voice was somewhere between a rasp and a whine.

Giving Marlow a flinty smile, I nodded at the espresso machine. "I wouldn't mind taking a cup home with me. Can you do a mocha?"

Marlow stared at the big brass vat as if he'd never seen it before. "A mocha? I don't know. . . . I'm just learning how to run that rig. The principal at the high school talked me into it. He swears the teachers—and some of the kids— will go nuts for it."

"They will," I assured him. "It should perk up your business. So to speak." I kept a straight face, certain Marlow would miss the unintended pun.

He did. "Yeah, maybe. I do all right. You'd be surprised how much candy and gum those kids buy."

"And beer and cigarettes?" I added, now giving him a conspiratorial smile.

Marlow ducked his head. "Well . . . cigarettes, maybe. Some of them *are* eighteen. I don't encourage them and I don't smoke myself. Never did. But I can't turn them away if they're of age."

I let the lie pass. I also passed on waiting for Marlow to figure out how to make a mocha. But I did buy some gum and a pound of butter. The butter cost almost half again as much as I would have paid at the Grocery Basket or Safeway.

Still, I wondered how Marlow Whipp stayed in business. I also wondered if Milo Dodge wondered. And then I wondered why it mattered. I drove home, still wondering.

Vida was giving a dinner party. "Just us girls," she announced Thursday morning while Ginny and Carla fussed with the coffeemaker. "We four, plus Libby Boyd, Marilynn Lewis, and Cyndi Campbell. Friday, seven-thirty."

I had misgivings about Libby and Marilynn at the same dinner table, but I couldn't say why. So I kept my mouth shut. Carla, however, did not.

"I may be going in to Seattle Friday night," she said, flipping her long black hair over her shoulders. "Peyts wants to have dinner at that new restaurant on the water. Palisades or something?"

Vida shrugged. "In that case, I won't invite Libby. I was only doing that so she wouldn't feel excluded. Did you say she had a beau? Where is he—Seattle?"

Carla was fiddling with a fingernail. "What? She doesn't talk about him much. Libby's private. She had a rough youth. I think she obsesses about being respectable. Don't get her started on her parents, though. She says they were total potheads, always protesting something and being thrown in jail." Getting an emery board out of her desk, she began filing away. "Of course, I don't see her that much. She works weird hours."

"Good," Vida declared. "Then you won't get sick of each other. It's important for roommates to be independent."

Ed arrived late, but filled with good intentions. "I got four inches instead of two out of the pet store this week. They're introducing a new line of dog and cat food. Henry Bardeen up at the ski lodge has a summer promotion, including a special for the restaurant. There's a rumor Payless may be coming in. Shall I check it out?"

Overcome by Ed's burst of energy, I practically reeled around the news office. "Gosh, Ed, why not? We should probably start in on the Fourth of July insert, too."

"Right-o," Ed agreed, wedging himself into his chair. He started humming. Dazed, I headed for my office, but was stopped by the sound of Todd Wilson's voice. He had arrived in the company of Francine Wells, who had come to see Ed about yet another ad. Todd, however, was calling on Carla. The PUD was doing maintenance work the last week of May, and there would be some limited power outages. Todd wanted to make sure that their customers were forewarned.

I listened to hear if my address was included. It wasn't, but Vida's home was among those that would be without electricity for almost three hours on May twenty-eighth. Luckily, it was during the day when she'd be at work.

"I better not lose anything in my freezer," she warned Todd.

"You shouldn't," Todd assured her, "except maybe ice cream. That's why we warn people." He gave her a big smile.

"Ice cream!" Vida exclaimed. "That's Roger's birthday! Now I'll have to shop on my way home! Really, Todd, you could have picked a better day!"

Todd was still smiling. "It can't be helped, Mrs. Runkel. If you want to file a complaint, wait until after June eleventh. I'll be in Europe then."

Vida stared at Todd over the rims of her glasses. "I thought it was your in-laws who were going to Europe," she said.

"They are, later in the summer." Todd looked very pleased with himself. "But Wendy and I decided we needed a getaway as soon as school was out. We're heading for Greece and Italy for a month." He glanced at his watch. "Hey—it's almost nine. I've got a meeting. See you."

Ed was still conferring with Francine Wells. Carla had resumed filing her nails. Ginny was checking the coffeemaker which seemed to have stalled on us. Vida was sitting with her chin on her fists, staring at the door that had closed behind Todd Wilson.

"Greece and Italy for a *month*?" Vida rubbed furiously at her eyes. "Now that's ridiculous! Todd only gets two weeks' vacation. What's he doing, taking a leave?"

Francine's perfectly coiffed head raised from the dummy she had been studying with Ed. "I could have told you about their trip," she said, obviously pleased to know something Vida didn't. "Wendy was in the shop yesterday buying me out. She must be taking a steamer trunk."

Vida's gaze darted from Francine to me and back again. "Did she spend more than a thousand dollars?"

Francine feigned shock. "Vida—you know I can't tell you how much a customer spends!" She winked in an exaggerated manner. "Let's say you're lowballing me by about a third."

Disgusted, Vida swung around in her chair. "Oh, good heavens! And I thought I knew the biggest fools in town!" She gave me another quick look. I was beginning to feel less guilty, not only about the money I'd blown, but about not spending it with Francine.

"She must have gotten some nice things," I said in a weak voice.

Francine nodded. "She did. But Wendy's hard to dress. Her posture isn't great and she's awkward. We worked at it, I'll tell you. But by the time she left, we were both happy. If nervous," she added with a little laugh. "Me, I mean. I don't usually have that much cash in the register, and the way things are going these days . . ." She made a graceful gesture with one hand, the diamonds in her wristwatch glinting in our sickly fluorescent lights.

Vida pounced. "Wendy paid *cash*?"

Francine's fine eyebrows arched. "Why, yes. She usually does." Leaning on Vida's desk, her voice dropped to a confidential level. "It must be Todd's father who has the money. Isn't he a big-shot Everett businessman?"

Vida gave a snort. "He owns a muffler shop. How many mufflers do you have to install to get rich?"

Francine moved toward the door. "Somebody in that family is well-off. Lloyd's done all right, but the appliance store must be hurting in these hard times. Jean's dad worked at the mill, didn't he?"

Vida nodded. "Dust Bucket Cooper, they called him. I never knew why. After the original mill closed, he helped build the ski lodge. Then he drove a truck for one of the other logging companies, I forget which. Died in 'sixty-three. Heart."

Having received the capsule biography of Dust Bucket Cooper, Francine left. Vida was still fuming.

"I don't understand it," she seethed. "Where do the Wilsons get so much money? Cash! If Lloyd and Jean were rich, they'd give more to the church. So what are Todd and Wendy up to?"

Carla had finally finished her nails. "Prostitution," she said calmly. "Wendy is selling herself to students."

Ed, halfway to the door, stopped to stare. "Carla—that's a terrible thing to say! You're joking, right?"

"No," Carla answered blithely, "not really. I mean, I don't think she's selling *herself*. Grades, maybe. I've heard some of those kids talk about her when I've been up at the high school taking pictures and doing stories."

I had perched on Ed's desk. "What do they say?" I asked.

Carla was looking vague, a familiar expression. "Oh—it's not *what* they say; it's *how* they say it. Knowing looks and stuff."

Disappointed in Carla's lack of specifics, Ed went on his way. Ginny, carrying the mail, almost collided with him in the door. Carla sought Ginny's support.

"Wendy Wilson," Carla said, holding up both hands to halt Ginny, and at the same time, admire her newly filed nails. "What did Rick Erlandson say about her the other night?"

Ginny looked thoughtful. "Wendy ... Let me think. ... Oh, it was what his sister said to him. About something her husband told her ... That Wendy's students would do anything for her." Ginny's high forehead puckered. "Something like that, and that Steve—Rick's brother-in-law—couldn't understand it because he said Wendy wasn't that great of a teacher." She gazed at Carla. "Is that what you mean?"

Carla nodded vigorously. "Right. We're trying to figure out what Wendy has going on with the students."

I was at sea, trying to figure out the source of Ginny's gossip. Vida noticed and took pity on me. "Rick, who works at the bank, went out with Ginny the other night, remember? Rick's sister is Donna Erlandson Fremstad Wickstrom. She's married to Steve, who teaches science and math at the high school." She folded her arms and waited for me to become enlightened.

"Oh! Sure, and Steve teaches with Wendy. The Wickstroms were with the Wilsons and the other two couples at Café de Flore."

Smiling benevolently, Vida nodded. The class dumbbell had finally come through with the right answer. It was Ginny, however, who drew Vida's next comment:

"So Steve Wickstrom thinks Wendy has some sort of hold over her students. That's interesting." Vida juggled her thermos of hot water. "Emma, why don't you assign me to a year-end story at the high school? We can use it in the special edition."

I glanced at Carla who was already slated for the assignment. Carla, however, didn't mind. "Go ahead. I'll do the photos, though, if you want."

Now that my staff had gotten down to business, I took the mail from Ginny and went into my office. I hadn't finished the first irate letter when Milo strolled through the door. Somehow, he had gotten past Vida. I assumed she was on the phone.

"Don't ask," he said in a glum voice. "There's nothing new in the homicide investigation."

"Then why are you here? Did you find out who's been sending Marilynn Lewis ugly mail? Or who's been writing me anonymous letters? Maybe you've recovered Bucker Swede from those teenaged gangsters in Sultan."

Milo sat down in one of the two chairs on the other side of my desk. He looked as if he'd like to put his feet up, but there wasn't room. Taking a big handkerchief out of his pocket, he blew his nose.

"What I don't get," he said, ignoring my comments, "is that you can't scratch your ass in this town without six people knowing it. But blow some guy away in broad

daylight—and nobody sees a thing. It's damned aggravating."

Idly, I started flipping through the rest of the mail. "If
you came here just to bitch, I'll give you something to do.
Check out a convicted murderer named Wesley Charles.
He's down at Shelton, waiting to be transported to Monroe."

Milo jerked forward in the chair. His long face lost some
of its color. "Wesley Charles? What about him?"

Puzzled by Milo's reaction, I put the mail aside. "I told
you, he's a convicted murderer. Kelvin Greene testified at
his trial. Damn it, Milo, do you ever do your homework?
Why don't you hire Vida and me and deputize us? We
could use the extra money."

But Milo wasn't listening. He had placed one hand on
the edge of my desk, and his hazel eyes were riveted on my
face. "We just got an APB, Emma. A Wesley Charles escaped this morning as he was being brought to the Monroe
Reformatory. Now go over what you just said, and do it
slow. You talk too damned fast."

Milo wasn't entirely clear about how Wesley Charles had
managed his escape. There had been a traffic tie-up involv-
ing an accident with an eighteen-wheeler full of produce, a
U.S. Forest Service truck, and a school bus from Snohomish County. The first concern was for the children, none
of whom had suffered serious injuries. But during the dis-
ruption, Wesley Charles had fled, presumably chains and
all.

"So you're saying this Charles guy whacked Marilynn
Lewis's boyfriend?" Milo asked, taking notes.

"That's right," said Vida, who had joined us. "That is, he
was convicted of shooting Jerome Cole. Charles maintained
his innocence. According to Winola Prince, Marilynn's
former roommate, Jerome and Marilynn had been romanti-
cally involved for some time. Jerome was a drug addict, I
might add, and didn't treat Marilynn at all well. Kelvin
Greene testified at the trial."

Milo was exhibiting both amusement and admiration.
The latter trait seemed strained, but at least it was there.

"You two were busy in Seattle yesterday," Milo remarked. "What was Wesley Charles's motive?"

If Milo thought he had stumped us, he was wrong. Vida answered promptly: "Jealousy, it would appear. He was infatuated with Marilynn, or so Kelvin Greene testified. Kelvin, if you want to know, and of course you should, was seeing Winola Prince."

Milo, who had been sitting with one leg propped on the other knee, planted both feet on the floor. "I've got to talk with Marilynn Lewis again. Damn." He glanced at Vida, then at me. "I wonder if this Charles will try to see Marilynn?"

"More fool he," Vida replied. "But don't discount it."

Getting to his feet, Milo wandered over to gaze at my map of Skykomish, Snohomish, and Kittitas counties. It also included the northeast corner of King.

"It's over forty miles from here to Monroe," Milo noted. "If Wesley Charles has any smarts, he'll head back for Seattle and lose himself."

"This is weird," I said. "Wesley Charles insists he didn't kill Jerome Cole. We know he didn't kill Kelvin Greene, because Charles was down at the Shelton correctional facility at the time of the murder. Milo, what do you make of all this?" I hated to ask, but I had to know.

Milo turned around, his shoulders sagging. "You don't want to hear it," he said. "Oh, hell, nobody hates to disagree with a jury, but once in awhile a bad verdict comes down. Maybe this was one of those times. So we've got a common denominator in both homicide cases. Marilynn Lewis. Who else?"

"Cyndi Campbell," Vida snapped. "Really, Milo, you don't believe her trumped-up story about giving directions? If you don't question that young woman more closely, you're a bigger fool than I thought."

Milo showed no enthusiasm for grilling Cyndi Campbell. "Face it, Vida, Cyndi probably got a big bang out of drinking beer with a black dude. I figure her for somebody who likes to give people a shock now and then, especially her folks. He asked how to get someplace, she said let's talk it over. No big deal."

Vida leaned back in the chair, and made a strangled

sound. Her green velvet toque fell off. "Milo! Try to convince me you're not an idiot! Hurry! You're almost out of time!"

"Vida . . ." Milo threw up his hands. "Okay, okay, I'll talk to Cyndi. Look, you two, I'm not a total incompetent. We may not have interviewed Winola Prince, but we got some background on Kelvin Greene, other than his rap sheet."

Vida lifted her head. "And?"

"He was a borderline kind of guy," Milo said, leaning against the wall next to the map. "If he'd kept away from the drugs, he might have been all right. He used, he dealt. But he finished high school, got married, had various jobs. His wife left him about five years ago. Then he moved in with some woman and had a kid. The woman took off a couple of years ago. Grandma Greene has been raising the little boy, who's about three and a half. Kelvin held his last job for almost a year before he got laid off in April. He was working in the stockroom at Fred Meyer up on Broadway. Winola Prince moved in with him just before Marilynn Lewis left town. Now how's that for background?" Milo looked pleased with himself.

I had been watching Vida as well as Milo. I waited for a reaction. It came more slowly than I expected, and on a lower key.

"Well now." Vida retrieved her hat and plopped it back on her head. "So what conclusions do you draw?"

Under Vida's close scrutiny, Milo didn't turn a hair. "It's too soon to draw any conclusions. Especially with this new information about Wesley Charles. We're going to have to check that out with King County. In fact, I'd better get going." He started for the door.

"Milo." Vida didn't move in the chair.

The sheriff paused, leaning against the doorjamb. "What?" A note of impatience rose in his voice.

Vida let out a big sigh. I knew what she was going to say, and had to hide a smirk. "It may not mean a thing," Vida began, now turning around to look up at Milo, "but Shane Campbell worked at that same Fred Meyer store when he lived in Seattle. It seems to me that you have a connection not only between Kelvin Greene and Marilynn

Lewis, but between Kelvin and Shane—and thus, all of the Campbells, right down to Wendy and Todd Wilson. While you're at it, Milo," she continued, her voice rising, "you might also want to check on where the Wilsons get their money. We're hearing some pretty strange rumors. I don't want to tell you how to do your job, you understand, but I also don't want to see you make a public fool of yourself." Vida turned back to face my desk, picked up a State Wildlife news release about endangered pigeons, and began to peruse the copy.

Over Vida's head, Milo gazed at me with a bemused expression. "Gee, Vida, thanks. I appreciate it."

"Mm-hmm," Vida replied, still reading the release.

Milo left. I waited until I was sure he'd exited the front office before I spoke. "If I'd said all that, he would have killed me," I noted.

"Age has its privileges," said Vida, sliding the news release back onto my desk. "The truth is, Milo needs more help. He's shorthanded, his budget is too small, and I suspect his technology isn't as up-to-date as it should be. Instead of getting annoyed with us for interfering, he ought to be grateful. Deep down, I rather suspect he is." Moving with her own peculiar brand of splayfooted dignity, Vida returned to the news office.

I returned to opening the mail. There were a half-dozen letters decrying the recent violence in Alpine, all blaming it on big-city influences, and four of the six specifically mentioning the matter of race. None, fortunately, brought up Marilynn Lewis by name, though the implication was there in two of the missives.

Then came my anonymous correspondent. I groaned as I unfolded the plain white piece of paper. "Dear Publicher," it began again. "You are ignoring my complaints. These people have a languege all there own. They don't even talk like the rest of us. Once they worm there way into this town, they will take over. Look at Seattle to see if what I say isn't true. It all starts there, and it will creep out over the rest of the state like a playge. Yours, A Loyal—getting more upset—Reader."

Annoyed, I called Milo. He was busy, Jack Mullins informed me in his cheerful voice. "We had a homicide last week, remember?" he chided and chuckled.

"Right, right," I acknowledged. "Can you get finger-prints off of paper? I'm getting fed up with this anonymous letter writer."

"They're usually pretty smudged," Jack replied. "We tried to take a set from the hate mail that black nurse got. No dice. Did you know that crow had been shot with a .22?"

I didn't. "You mean somebody shot the bird purposely and then sent it to Marilynn Lewis?"

"Maybe." Jack's voice conveyed a shrug. "Lots of people shoot crows. They're pests. Whoever mailed the thing might have found it someplace."

Noting the indifference in the deputy's voice, I decided to surrender, at least temporarily. If Milo and Company had struck out on discovering who had sent hate mail to Marilynn Lewis, I couldn't expect any better results. I thanked Jack Mullins and hung up. It was, I realized, more important that the sheriff's office devote its efforts to the homicide investigation.

My staff—or part of it—was devoting itself to arranging interviews at the high school. Vida and Carla would join forces Friday morning.

Meanwhile, Ed had some exciting news. "Starbuck's has made an inquiry about that vacant space by the railroad sta-tion," he announced. "You know, where Stuart's Stereo was located before they moved to the mall."

At the corner of Front Street and Alpine Way, the site was perfect for a quick caffeine stop. Commuters heading out of town could breeze by on their way to Highway 2; those who stayed in town during the day wouldn't have far to go no matter where they worked.

Carla was elated. "Oh, too cool! Now I can get a double skinny extra tall or a one-twenty-five-degree extra foamy without having to explain it to those yokels at the Venison Inn! I can't wait! Alpine may hit the big time yet!"

Her reaction to the possible advent of Starbuck's and all its glorious coffees reminded me of Marlow Whipp's new es-presso machine. I conveyed the message to Ed. His freshly found enthusiasm didn't carry over to Marlow, however.

"Well now, Emma, I'd be the last person to turn up my nose at a potential advertiser," he said, resurrecting his more familiar mournful face, "but Marlow's always been a wash-out. I tried to get him to advertise after he took over from his folks. Three, four times I asked him, but he always said *no*. Heck, I was in there as recently as last winter—I needed some breath mints—and Marlow was downright surly. He couldn't wait to get me out of there, mints and all. I'll admit, he was busy then—must have had ten, fifteen kids in there. It was crowded, I'll say that for him."

I decided not to press Ed further. Still, if Marlow wanted to make a go of his espresso machine, he ought to have the opportunity to get the jump on Starbuck's. The Spruce Street Grocery was sufficiently removed from the railroad station to nab potential customers on the east side of town. I'd bring the subject up again when we heard something more definite about Starbuck's intentions.

Around three o'clock, I was debating with myself over whether to write an anticensorship or a pro–L.I.D. editorial. Deciding that Alpine needed sidewalks above Cascade Street more than it needed obscene music, I started with the safety factor. I was fumbling around with funding when Marilynn Lewis called. Her voice was muffled, and she sounded agitated.

"Ms. . . . Emma," she said into the phone, "is it possible to talk to you after work? We can meet somewhere. Maybe one of those little cafés at the mall?"

I suggested my house, which was infinitely more comfortable than the mall's two hole-in-the-wall fast-food eateries, one of which featured ersatz Chinese and the other, semi-Tex-Mex. Marilynn paused briefly before saying she'd be over around six.

It was only after I hung up that I realized she'd have to walk from the clinic. I called her back and suggested that I pick her up sometime after five. Shyly, she asked if I could make it five-thirty. I said I could. It was no problem to kill time at the office for thirty minutes.

I had no reason to think that something besides time might get killed in that half hour.

Chapter Ten

It HAD STARTED raining early in the afternoon, but the air was warm. After three years of summer drought, I didn't complain. I never do when it rains. A typical native Pacific Northwesterner, I feel invigorated by damp weather. It's the sun that depresses me. When the days of cloudless skies spin out and the heat beats down like a hammer and the grass goes brown and the evergreens droop and the earth turns to dust, my own roots crave water, too.

So I didn't curse the gray skies or the need to use my windshield wipers. Marilynn got into the Jag as if she were being chased by demons. She actually sighed as she settled into the bucket seat next to me.

"What a day," she murmured. "Dr. Flake had thirty-four patients. Doc Dewey saw twenty-six."

"Egad," I said, doing some quick mathematical calisthenics, "that's sixty people. Well over one percent of Alpine's entire population."

"Babies and arthritis," Marilynn replied. "Those are the major complaints around here. You can't do much about either one."

Braking at the Third and Cedar intersection, I glanced at Marilynn. "And you? What's your complaint? You sounded a bit frazzled when you called."

Marilynn's perfect profile was on display as she leaned back against the leather upholstery. "Wait until we get to your place. Have you got any white wine, or am I being pushy?"

I laughed. "White wine, bourbon, Scotch, beer, vodka, and maybe some gin shoved to the back of my so-called liquor cabinet. Oh, and rum, I think. I keep the Scotch for the sheriff and the beer for my son."

Marilynn turned to gaze at me inquiringly. "Where did you say your son was? Alaska?"

I nodded as we crossed Tyee Street. "He's at the university in Fairbanks. His father and I never married, but we keep in touch." The newly acquired assets of my closet leapt before my eyes.

Marilynn displayed polite interest. "It's good for parents to get along, whether they're married or not. My folks didn't, and it was much better after my dad died."

"Did you have brothers or sister?" I inquired as we passed a couple of young fishermen who had apparently walked up from the river.

Marilynn nodded. "Two younger brothers. They moved back to California with my mother when she remarried. One works for Kaiser. The other's in college."

I turned onto Fir Street. We were less than a block from my house when we heard the sirens. I pulled over next to a vacant lot with a tipsy FOR SALE sign that had been there since before I'd moved to Alpine. In the rearview mirror, I could see the ambulance right behind us. The driver slowed as he passed my driveway, then turned into the cul-de-sac where Fifth Street dead-ended.

"What's up there?" Marilynn asked, as a couple of people came out on their front porches.

"Nothing," I replied. "It's all forest. The woods begin in back of my house." I was about to release the brake when I heard another siren. Sure enough, a sheriff's car had pulled onto Fir. I stared into the window as it passed: Dwight Gould was behind the wheel, with Bill Blatt at his side. Milo must have gone off duty at five.

Marilynn and I exchanged curious looks. This time I waited to make sure that the fire department wasn't also racing up Fourth Street or coming along Fir. As far as I could tell, it wasn't. I waited for a van filled with Little Leaguers to pass, then pulled back out and crept up to my driveway. Once in the carport, I picked up the pace.

"Marilynn," I said, jumping from the Jag, "I'm going to let you in, and then I'm afraid I'd better check out the action around the corner. I'm sorry to be such a bum hostess, but I'll point you to the white wine. I shouldn't be long."

Over the top of the car, Marilynn gazed at me through

the rain. "Hey—I'll come, too. I'm a nurse, remember." She pulled her tan all-weather jacket aside to reveal her white uniform. "It looks to me as if there's been an accident, right?"

Fueled with professional zeal, we marched through the wet grass, past the older single-story home that stood next to my log house, beyond the skeleton of construction that had been abandoned by its private builder, and around the corner lot that was overgrown with blackberry bushes, huge ferns, and Oregon grape. We turned at the entrance to the cul-de-sac.

The rain wasn't coming down very hard at present, but earlier in the afternoon, it had been heavy enough to fill the potholes in the dirt road that led about fifty yards into the forest. Five vehicles jammed the dead end: the sheriff's car, the ambulance, a Forest Service truck, a white compact I didn't recognize, and a beater that might have been abandoned in the cul-de-sac a long time ago. We had almost reached the little knot of people when I heard another vehicle pulling up behind us. I turned to see Milo Dodge come to a stop in his Cherokee Chief. He was still in uniform.

"Emma! What are you doing here?" He acknowledged Marilynn with a brief nod.

"I live here, remember?" I waited for him to catch up. "We working girls are merely doing our duty. What's going on?"

Milo had loped out ahead. "We got another shooting," he called over his shoulder. "Stay back, I hear the guy's dead."

I obeyed; so did Marilynn. We were within twenty feet of the group which I realized included not only the two deputies and the ambulance attendants, but Libby Boyd, three boys about eleven years old, and a man in a bright plaid shirt who looked vaguely familiar. After only a few words from Milo, Libby, the boys, and the man were dispersed in our direction. I glommed on to Libby.

"Who is it?" I asked.

Libby put her hands to her head and twisted her upper torso, as if expelling demons. "Jesus, I don't know. It's another black man." She stared straight at Marilynn Lewis. "What's going on around here?"

Stiffening, Marilynn grabbed my arm, as if for support. "How would I know?" she retorted. I didn't like the hint of hysteria in her voice.

Libby hung her head. "Sorry. I found the poor bastard. That is, those kids found him, but they didn't realize he was dead." She gestured jerkily at the young boys who were standing with the man I barely recognized.

"Who's he?" I inquired in a low voice.

Libby brushed raindrops off her forehead. "Him? His name's Vancich. He was driving along Fir Street, and I waved him down to call for help. He stuck around because he knows one of the kids."

The man's identity clicked in. Verb Vancich was married to Monica, St. Mildred's CCD teacher. Monica was a faithful attendee of Sunday mass, but Verb was what was known among Catholics as a C&Eer. He came to church on an irregular basis, showing up usually for Christmas and Easter, and very little in between.

Wrestling with my handbag, I found a notebook and a pen. "The sheriff said he was shot. Is that true?" I asked.

Libby closed her eyes and gulped. "It sure is. Shot in the head. Just like that other one, over at the grocery store."

I felt the pressure of Marilynn's fingers on my arm. A quick glance told me she was as distressed as Libby Boyd. "You'd better come home with me, too," I murmured at Libby. "You could use a drink."

Libby nodded, a distracted gesture of assent. I patted Marilynn's hand, pried her loose, and doggedly marched over to Milo.

"Okay," I said, trying to sound as coldhearted as journalists are portrayed in fiction where they don't ever really look at dead people and feel like throwing up, "let's have the facts, Dodge."

Milo had just returned from viewing the corpse. "He was shot in the head at close range. I'm guessing he's been dead for no more than an hour, maybe less. I wouldn't say that much, if I didn't know you can't print this until next week." He paused, waiting for Bill Blatt.

Vida's nephew was flushed with excitement or possibly repulsed by the sight of a dead man. Bill was young enough that it was hard to tell.

"All those ferns are pretty well trampled, Sheriff," said Bill. "Do you think that shows the signs of a struggle?"

"No," Milo answered bluntly. "It just shows the poor devil thrashed around for a while before he died. Have you combed the area?"

Bill nodded. "Nothing, so far. Well," he amended, "footprints. The kids', I'd guess, and Libby's. It's pretty hard to tell, with all the rain."

"Right." Milo sounded disgusted. "And all I wanted to do was go home and have a beer and watch the NBA playoffs." He voiced the latter complaint in a low voice as Bill Blatt trudged back to the victim.

I tugged at Milo's sleeve. "Tell me this much and I'll go away, taking two disturbed young women with me," I promised. "Is the dead man wearing leg shackles?"

Milo gritted his teeth. "Yes. But they've been sawed through. So have the chains attached to his waist. By all means, call Vida. Call me a horse's ass. It's probably Wesley Charles. See that old car?" His long arm lashed out at the beater. "He stole that, maybe in Monroe, possibly Sultan. Now take your black and white broads, and get the hell out of here!"

In spite of the proximity of a dead man, in spite of Milo's latent racism and chauvinism, in spite of my own revulsion in the face of violence, I laughed. Milo Dodge was impossibly small-town. But somehow, I sensed that under his clumsy veneer of various prejudices, he wasn't small-minded.

"Milo," I said, not entirely sure that I, too, wasn't a trifle hysterical, "I could kiss you."

Milo loomed over me, his hazel eyes boring into mine. "Then why don't you, you dink?"

I felt myself being swept off the dirt road, pulled against Milo's big, lanky frame, and kissed in a style I hadn't remembered since a drunken fraternity party in 1969. I shuddered; I shook; I reeled even as he parked me back on the ground.

"Milo!" I squeaked, staggering just a little, and putting a hand to my mouth, which felt as if it had been smacked by a wet fish.

But Milo had already turned away and was giving orders

I THINK I KNOW WHO IT IS

to Bill Blatt and Dwight Gould. The ambulance men were awaiting further directions. Libby Boyd and Marilynn Lewis were standing ten yards away, as wary of each other as they were of the impulsive action between Milo and me.

Angrily, I stalked toward them. "Get your truck, Libby," I ordered. "Marilynn and I will walk."

Libby stared at me, her fair, wholesome face stunned. "You should have done that two minutes ago," she declared.

I gave her a fierce look. "Speak for yourself. Maybe Milo should have done that two years ago." Taking Marilynn by the arm, I stomped out of the cul-de-sac.

My guests sipped white wine, while I drank my standard bourbon. Yet neither of the two young women who sat at opposite ends of the sofa relaxed much. Libby seemed nervous; Marilynn appeared distressed. I had not mentioned Wesley Charles's name out loud, and wouldn't until after Libby was gone. Marilynn couldn't have seen the body from where she was standing in the cul-de-sac. Indeed, I hadn't seen it myself. It was possible, however, that she had heard me ask if the victim was wearing shackles. She might have heard of Wesley Charles's escape on the radio. Or, I thought with a pang, she might know about it on a more personal level.

Conversation was stilted and mundane. Not that murder is mundane, but our comments certainly were. Libby had pulled into the cul-de-sac because of a report that someone had set a snare, presumably for deer, in the woods between the cul-de-sac and the Tolberg farm. The Snoqualmie National Forest took a rectangular jog behind my property to the south and as far west as the Burl Creek Road. Libby Boyd had been checking to see if the trap was on federal land. She hadn't found it, but on her way back to the truck, she had come across the three boys who had discovered Wesley Charles's body.

"They had just found him," Libby explained. "They didn't know what to make of it. I'm used to the city, so I thought at first it was a drunk, passed out. Then I saw the blood."

I kept waiting for her to mention Wesley Charles's

shackles or his prison uniform. But she didn't. Perhaps Libby hadn't seen the shackles; maybe she didn't recognize convict clothes when she saw them. For all I knew, the state Department of Corrections transported prisoners in tuxedos. Real life didn't always work like the movies or TV.

Until now, Marilynn's remarks had been limited to exclamations and murmurs. Suddenly, she shuddered and spoke in an uncertain, frightened voice: "Shot in the head—it sounds like a gangland execution. But that can't be, can it?"

The thought had never crossed my mind. I stared at Marilynn. "Do you mean gangland as in the mob, or as in a gang?"

Marilynn's gaze was still frightened, but now it was also wary. "The mob. I've read about how they kill people. I like true crime stories. They're much better than fiction, where everything is too neat and tidy."

Chastened, I gave a murmur of assent. What did Marilynn know about gangs? I felt like an oaf for my insinuation.

Libby Boyd was helping herself to more wine, pouring from the bottle I'd placed on the coffee table. "Oh, great! Now you tell me—there are gangsters in Alpine! What next, a back street I haven't seen yet with hookers and drugs and porno stuff like they have in Hamburg?"

The concept made me smile. I envisioned Milo and his deputies, stalking along River Road, passing not warehouses, but whorehouses; seeing not a loading dock full of lumber, but a bay window with scantily clad females; stopping not at the game warden's office, but at a shuttered storefront where high rollers played low-down and dirty.

"We're too tame for any of that," I finally said, closing the door on my fantasy. "If these two men had any connection with crime, then someone from Seattle must have followed them to Alpine." I sounded sanguine, but somehow, the words didn't ring true.

Marilynn and Libby didn't appear to notice. I offered Marilynn more wine, but she declined, instead asking to use the bathroom. As soon as she was out of the room, I expected Libby to make some comment about the fact that both victims were black—and to ask if I thought Marilynn had any connection with them.

But Libby didn't. She looked at her watch and announced that she had better get going. "I'm still officially on duty. I mean, it's after six, and I was through then, but I ought to check in before I go home. I'd better run, I'm meeting someone at seven-thirty."

I saw Libby to the door. "Did you give the sheriff your statement?" I asked.

Libby looked blank. "No. Should I? I mean, I told him what happened, but it was all pretty informal." She made a rueful face.

"Check with him tomorrow," I said. "Milo Dodge likes to go by the book."

Libby leered at me. "Really? What book was he reading before he came up to the cul-de-sac? It must have been hot stuff."

In the wake of a second homicide in less than a week, I had been able to put Milo's kiss out of my mind. My response to Libby's impertinent question was a toss of my head. "An etiquette book," I replied. "That was Milo's macho way of apologizing for being a dumb shit."

To my surprise, Libby Boyd looked satisfied with the explanation. Maybe she knew a man like Milo. Most of us did.

It seemed to me that Marilynn looked relieved to return from the bathroom and find Libby gone. I explained about Libby having to report in at the U.S. Forest Service office and that she had a date. Marilynn's eyes narrowed.

"A date? She hasn't been here any longer than I have. I can't even find an apartment, let alone a *date*."

"That makes two of us," I retorted, "and don't give me any dirty looks. What you saw with the sheriff wasn't the sign of a hot romance. We've never shared more than a pizza until now."

Marilynn was not only more relaxed, but she seemed a trifle giddy. Sitting back down on the sofa, she laughed in her musical manner. "Well, you could have fooled me! If I hadn't been so upset, I would have applauded. It was cute."

"Cute! I'm too old to be cute." I grabbed my glass and

realized that, except for a few shrunken ice cubes, it was empty. "I should feed us," I announced, getting up to fetch myself a refill. "I've got boneless chicken breasts, rice, asparagus. It'll take less than half an hour. Don't argue—we haven't had our talk yet."

"Then let me help," Marilynn insisted. "I know a great recipe for asparagus with shirred egg and buttered bread crumbs. Have you got a hardboiled egg in the fridge?"

I did, having had an urge earlier in the week for egg salad, which I'd never gotten around to fulfilling. The urge had now passed. Side by side, Marilynn and I set to work in the kitchen. It felt good to have another female to man the stove. Vida didn't count—her efforts were always diligent, but erratic, and sometimes downright disastrous.

"You never said what was bothering you," I began, unwrapping the package of chicken breasts.

Marilynn uttered a noise that was part laugh, part groan. "It was your friend, the sheriff. He came to see me again. At least he was nice enough to use the clinic's rear door."

"What this time?" I inquired, not looking at Marilynn for fear she'd see that I already knew.

She sighed, resting her hands on the sink counter. She had been cutting the coarse ends off the asparagus and she held my sharpest kitchen knife. It occurred to me that I should be afraid. Marilynn, after all, was supposedly a suspect in a murder case. Two murder cases, for all I knew. But I felt no sense of alarm.

"I don't know what to say . . . not now." She bowed her head. "The sheriff asked if I knew a man who escaped from prison this morning. Well, not prison, exactly—he was on his way to Monroe. I did know him, but not very well." She sighed again. "And unless life is even weirder than it seems to be, I'd bet my last dollar he was the one who got shot over here in the cul-de-sac." She turned to give me a resigned look, her classic features somehow askew.

I wondered if I dared to level with Marilynn. She had sought my help; I had given her hospitality. She wasn't quite young enough to be my daughter, but she could be a kid sister. Our personalities seemed to mesh. She was a big-city girl trying to make it in a small town. So was I. We had a great deal in common; we could be friends.

I took a chance, knowing that in the process, I was starting down the road toward friendship—but also risking losing Marilynn at the first intersection.

I talked as we cooked, I with my chicken breasts and rice, she with her asparagus and chopped egg. I explained about going to Seattle with Vida, about meeting Winola Prince, about reading microfiche at *The Times*, about Milo and his APB. And finally, about Kelvin Greene and Shane Campbell both working at Fred Meyer's Broadway store on Capitol Hill.

Marilynn had listened without comment, her eyes occasionally darting in my direction and giving away her distress. I reached my rationale, explaining my need to know, the public's right to be informed, the whole fulsome excuse for being a meddlesome snoop.

Marilynn interrupted me before I got to the part about a journalist's search for truth. "Emma—you're on the wrong track." She took my hand and made me sit down in one of my mismatched kitchen chairs. I caught a glimpse of Marilynn Lewis, R.N., dealing with a recalcitrant patient. "Yes, I used to go out with Jerome Cole. Yes, he was often a jerk. Yes, I was shattered when he was killed. No, I wasn't there when it happened. I knew Kelvin, of course, because of Winola. But I certainly didn't know he was coming to Alpine, and I couldn't tell you why he did. I practically fainted when I heard he was the one who was killed at the little grocery store."

"Actually," I began, feeling chagrined, "he wasn't killed there, he . . ."

But Marilynn was shaking her head. "Wherever. It doesn't matter. It doesn't even surprise me. Maybe I always knew Kelvin—like Jerome—would come to a bad end. Drugs do that to people, one way or the other." Her dark eyes turned moist. "It's terrible, Emma. The person you know becomes somebody else—a stranger, even a monster. When Jerome wasn't being a creep, he could be the most wonderful, charming, fascinating guy around. He was a musician—he knew all kinds of music, not just jazz, but classical, pop, the blues, even country and western. He played the saxophone like you wouldn't believe, and he was just fine on the clarinet and trumpet, too. He had talent, that man—but he had a drug habit and he dealt. For over two years, I tried to talk him into rehab. I got nowhere. Oh, he made promises, he had plans, he sounded good. But he never carried through. When you're doing drugs, today is yesterday, tomorrow never comes. It's a world you and I don't understand, thank God. I knew I was the one who had to make the changes—but I didn't do it soon enough. He got killed before I could make the break."

Marilynn paused, her head in her hands. I had found my second, untouched drink, and took a deep sip. "Do you know why?"

Marilynn's attitude turned evasive. "Why? Who knows? A drug deal gone wrong, maybe. A misunderstanding. A fight. Jerome could turn violent. It's hard to say."

I dared to ask another ugly question: "Was he violent around you?"

The evasion intensified. "He could lose control," she said slowly, her chin quavering just a bit. "Jerome didn't always know what he was doing."

I let the answer go and decided to shift gears for the moment. "Cyndi Campbell had a beer with Kelvin that afternoon at the Icicle Creek Tavern," I said. "Do you know why?"

Falling back in her chair, Marilynn gaped at me. "*Cyndi Campbell?* Why, no! That's ridiculous! Cyndi didn't know Kelvin."

Marilynn seemed genuinely flummoxed. "But Kelvin and Shane worked together at Fred Meyer," I pointed out.

"I guess they did." Her eyes grew shadowy. "I knew Shane in Seattle. That's why I moved in with his family." She didn't look at me, but stared at the oilcloth table covering with its cheerful pattern of red poppies.

In my mind's eye, I could see myself weeding in the garden: a shoot of morning glory sprouted from the ground, then sent out new runners, creeping into the flower bed, entwining my rose bushes and day lilies and maidenhair ferns. So it seemed with Kelvin Greene—his life, which had at first seemed isolated, now reached out to touch so many others. And like the morning glory, it threatened to choke those with whom it became entangled.

"How did you know Shane?" I asked quietly.

Marilynn was still nervous, but her speech wasn't self-conscious. "He was the assistant manager at Fred Meyer. I had a complaint. I'd bought a clock radio that didn't work. He made the adjustment for me. We got to talking about appliances, and he said his dad owned a store in Alpine. I said my stepdad had one in Oakland. The next time I went into Fred Meyer, I ran into him, and he asked me about the new clock radio. It was fine, I told him. He was just going on break and asked me out to coffee. So I went." She gave me an ingenuous smile.

I was puzzled. "So you . . . sort of dated Shane?"

"Not really. We had lunch a couple of times, and I'd run into him grocery shopping at QFC. I was going with Jerome, and Shane had a girlfriend. We were just friends. Really," she added, her dark eyes begging me to believe her. "When I decided to break up with Jerome, I started looking for jobs out of town. The opening in Alpine came up, and by coincidence, it was about the same time Shane was moving back home. It just worked out that I was able to stay with the Campbells."

Coincidences happen, of course. They seem to happen more often in a small town than in the Big City. "And Kelvin? Did he and Shane know each other very well?"

The red poppies in the tablecloth again seemed to consume Marilynn's attention. "I doubt it. Kelvin usually worked nights in the stockroom. It was okay with Winola— she often took the night shift at the hospital." Her gaze wandered to the stove. "Your rice—it's boiling over."

So it was. I leaped up to turn the heat down. "And Wesley Charles? What about him?"

Marilynn gave an impatient shake of her head. "Wesley lived across the hall from the apartment I shared with Winola. He was sort of strange—the kind who didn't have many friends, but kept trying to insert himself into other people's lives. I was nice to him, which may have been a mistake." Marilynn made a wry face. "Isn't it terrible how being kind can backfire?"

I'd adjusted the burner and mopped up the rice water. "It is. You swear the next time some weirdo comes along, you'll cut him—or her—off. But you don't, which I suppose is a good thing."

Marilynn nodded, obviously relieved to be on philosophical, rather than factual ground, however briefly. "That was
the trouble with Wesley—he kept trying to butt in. It bothered him when he'd hear Jerome ranting and carrying on.
One night, Jerome went wild." Pausing, Marilynn shifted in
the chair. "Winola came home . . . she'd gotten off at
eleven. She was afraid of Jerome when he was . . . like that.
She made me leave. We went to . . . a friend's. Nobody was
home at first, but a few minutes later we got in." Marilynn
licked her lips and frowned at the bright poppies. "After
about an hour, I called the apartment to see if Jerome had
calmed down. Somebody I didn't know answered. It was
the police. Jerome had been killed. They arrested Wesley
Charles."

I had returned to my place at the table. Marilynn sat with
her forehead resting on her fist and her eyes closed. I
thought she was going to cry, but she didn't. "I didn't go
to the trial. I couldn't stand it. I went through every emotion in the book in the three months between Jerome's
death and Wesley's trial. I was angry—at Wesley, for killing Jerome, at Jerome for getting into a mess where he got
himself murdered, at myself, for getting involved with
Jerome in the first place. Then I began to grieve—oh, how
I grieved!" She paused in mock dismay, then uttered a
small, self-deprecating laugh. "I turned Jerome into a saint,
I wiped out all his faults. Reality set in around Valentine's
Day. Shane invited me to a party."

I raised my eyebrow. "Shane? What about his
girlfriend?"

Marilynn gave a quick shake of her head. "Oh, it wasn't
a real *date*. Some of the people at Fred Meyer were giving
the party, and Shane's girlfriend was out of town. We had
a nice time, I guess. It was my first social outing since
Jerome died."

"Was Kelvin there?" I asked, keeping an eye on the
clock. Our dinner should be almost ready.

"Yes, he and Winola came. There were about thirty of
us, I think. It was at somebody's apartment on Capitol
Hill."

"How," I inquired, aware that the question was painful,
"was Jerome killed?"

Marilynn made an agitated motion with her hands, then stood up. "I really should melt the butter for the bread crumbs and egg." She moved to the stove. I guessed she was more at ease talking while she worked. "I gather what happened was that after Winola and I left the apartment, Jerome was still smashing up things. Wesley went across the hall, and Jerome let him in. There was an argument, I think, and then they started fighting. Jerome was killed by a blow to the head. Wesley hit him with an ivory carving from Cameroon. Jerome died almost instantly. Or so I was told." Again, she looked as if she might weep.

"Why," I asked, "do you think Wesley Charles insisted he was innocent?"

"I don't know." Marilynn straightened her shoulders, then sprinkled bread crumbs into the melted butter in the frying pan. "His fingerprints were on the figurine. He admitted he'd been in the apartment. But he said Jerome was already dead when he got there. He thought maybe he'd picked up the carving in the excitement of finding the body."

I was removing the chicken breasts from under the broiler. "The evidence sounds a little flimsy. Who called the police?"

Deftly, Marilynn transferred the asparagus from the steamer into the skillet. "Another neighbor had already called—maybe before Winola and I left. They lived below us and had heard Jerome and me fighting. But the police didn't get there right away. They came along just after Wesley killed Jerome." Making a brave attempt to keep her face impassive, Marilynn dished up the asparagus concoction in a serving bowl. "If only they'd arrived five minutes earlier . . . Jerome might still be alive."

"So," I noted, "would Wesley Charles."

Marilynn's dark eyes met mine. Her long-lashed lids drooped. "Yes. Yes," she repeated, almost in a whisper, "he would." Slowly, she opened her eyes and again stared at me. "Isn't it strange? I've never thought much about Wesley Charles. He was sort of like a . . . cipher. And now he's dead."

"We can't be sure—yet," I reminded Marilynn.

Grimly, she sat down at the table. "I'm sure. It makes sense."

Surprised, I spilled rice on the oilskin cloth. "Why do you say that?"

Marilynn's face had grown very earnest. "Why would someone kill Wesley Charles? He always seemed so harmless. But what if he told the truth and he didn't kill Jerome? Then there would be a reason to get rid of Wesley."

Annoyed with myself for not having come to the same conclusion, I immediately started to punch holes in it. "First of all, we're not absolutely sure that it was Wesley Charles in the cul-de-sac. Second, if it was, some loose cannon might have heard about the APB and shot Wesley in the hopes of getting a reward. Third, it would mean that Jerome's real killer is right here in Alpine. That hardly seems likely to me."

Marilynn didn't say anything. She didn't have to. Her shrewd expression told me everything I needed to know. And, I realized, with a sinking sensation, more than I wanted to hear.

The Fifth Street cul-de-sac had become the biggest attraction in Alpine, at least for the rest of the evening. Hearing a steady stream of cars and pedestrians pass by on the usually quiet street in front of my house, I realized that I had a job to do. I called Carla, relayed my skimpy information, and asked her to take a picture. She's a better photographer than I am, and I'd left my camera at the office.

Carla, of course, had heard about the shooting from Libby Boyd. Expressing horror, shock, and excitement in a series of squeaks and squeals, my reporter said she'd be over in ten minutes. It was still light, and although the body had been removed, Carla would be able to get a shot of the murder site and the milling curiosity seekers. People love to see their picture in the paper, even when they're being ghoulish voyeurs.

Marilynn and I had spent the rest of our dinner talking about the three murders that had touched her life, and now mine. The conversation was mostly speculative. She insisted she knew nothing more than she had already told me—or Milo Dodge. Around eight-thirty, I offered to drive

her home. It was still raining, but the Campbells live only
six blocks away. I half expected Marilynn to say she'd
walk. She didn't. In fact, she asked if I would go in with
her.

"There'll be questions," she explained with apprehension. "I don't blame the Campbells for asking, but it's awkward."

Marilynn was right. Jean and Lloyd met us at the door;
Cyndi came downstairs as soon as we got inside. Shane, we
were told, was out for the evening. I presumed that Wendy
and Todd Wilson were at their home in the Icicle Creek development.

"You're just the person we want to see," Lloyd Campbell
said to me in a jovial manner that seemed forced. "Everybody's saying that the murder happened right by your
house."

After being ushered into the comfortable living room, I
explained how Marilynn and I had arrived at the cul-de-sac
shortly after the victim had been discovered. I didn't use
Wesley Charles's name, but mentioned that the sheriff
thought the dead man might be a convict who had escaped
that morning from a prison bus outside of Monroe.

"It wouldn't be the first time we've had prisoners hiding
out around here," Lloyd said with a dour expression. "Let's
hope the state settles on a site in Snohomish County for
that new work-release facility. I sure wouldn't want to see
it built here."

Earlier in the month, I'd run an article about the proposed sixty-bed facility that was supposed to be constructed
at Paine Field outside of Everett. Protests had been lodged,
however, and it was possible that the state would choose
another site. Skykomish County would be a logical alterna-
tive, but local residents wouldn't like it. Given the events of
the past week, they'd probably march on the capitol in Olympia.

Jean Campbell was perched on the edge of a green-and-
white-striped armchair. "Is it true," she asked in a hushed
voice, "that this man was black, too?" Jean avoided looking
at Marilynn.

Cyndi Campbell, who had been sitting cross-legged on
the floor in front of the dormant fireplace, jumped to her

feet. "Mother! What difference does it make if he was black, blue, or purple? The poor guy got shot, probably by some nervous old fart living up in the woods. Aren't there a couple of hermits around Carroll Creek?"

If local lore could be believed, there were several recluses who lived in old shacks not only near Carroll Creek, but Burl Creek, Icicle Creek, Deception Creek, Surprise Creek, and various isolated areas in between. Indeed, I had seen a couple of them in town over the years, elderly men with long hair and bushy beards, coming down the mountainside to stock up for the winter. Vida referred to one of them as Al Pine, the only name he'd ever given out to whoever had been bold enough to ask. But I didn't think any of the hermits lived so close to civilization.

Lloyd Campbell wasn't moved by his daughter's assertion. "It's damned queer, if you ask me," he said in a worried voice. "I turned the radio on at eight to get the news from Everett. They said this fellow was a murderer, so I suppose he got what was coming to him. But who would have shot him? Do you suppose one of the deputies did it, and he hasn't owned up to it yet? That stuff gets tricky these days. Look at that Rodney King deal in Los Angeles."

Cyndi was dancing around the hearth, darting her father caustic looks. "Forget Rodney King," she persisted. "This has got to be some kind of accident. Maybe that other one was, too. People panic. They see a strange . . ." Her eyes lighted on Marilynn's quizzical face. ". . . a stranger, I mean, and go nuts. This town is gun happy. They ought to ban handguns everywhere."

Lloyd grunted. "Not mine, they won't. I keep one of them under the counter at the store and another in my desk. If some guy comes in to hold us up, I'm prepared to defend myself. Hell's bells, I insist Shane keeps that SIG-Sauer in the truck. Todd carries a gun on the job, too. What if he's working on the PUD lines 'way up Tonga Ridge, and a bear comes after him?"

Unimpressed, Jean Campbell curled her lip. "That's crazy, Lloyd. I've always said so. You're all lucky you don't get yourselves shot. And don't think that after all these years I'm not still nervous about sleeping with that awful pistol under the mattress!"

Lloyd chuckled. "It doesn't keep you awake, Jeannie. You snore like the Burlington-Northern, climbing up through the Cascade Tunnel."

Jean was aghast. "Lloyd! I don't snore! I've *never* snored! But *you*," she raged on, pointing at her husband, "sound like a donkey engine!"

Lloyd's laughter had become full-blown now, and it broke the tension in the room. Jean's irritation was genuine, yet its cause was a refreshing change from murder and racial innuendo. I decided it was time to leave them laughing. Marilynn offered to see me to the door.

"Thanks for having me over," she said with her charming, slightly diffident smile. "I didn't like the murder much, but dinner was good."

I studied her as she stood next to a small cherrywood credenza in the entry hall. Still wearing her white uniform, she looked very young and all too vulnerable. "Are you sure you're okay?"

Marilynn nodded. "I'd like to think I've buried the past, but it's caught up with me. I suppose it always does. Unfinished business, I guess. I just wish I knew what it was all about."

I made a droll face. "Don't we all?" An idea popped into my head. I didn't much like it, but I couldn't keep it to myself. "Marilynn, do you think you need protection?"

Her dark eyes grew wide. "Me? What for?"

If Marilynn Lewis had leveled with me and knew only as much as she'd related thus far, she was in no danger. But if she had kept something back, even a small fact she didn't realize might be important, then her life could be at risk. I tried to say as much without frightening her.

But Marilynn assured me there was no reason to worry. "I wasn't even asked to testify at Wesley's trial. I gave a deposition about Jerome, but that was all. If Wesley Charles didn't kill Jerome, I haven't any more idea who did it than you do."

There was nothing else I could say. I moved uneasily on the threshold, wishing I could free my troubled mind. Marilynn read my thoughts and put out a hand. "Hey—stop fussing." She glanced into the living room where the Campbells were still arguing. "If anything happens, I can take care of myself. I've got a gun, too." She gave me a rueful little smile.

My mouth fell open. "You do?" I whispered back. "Why?"

"Why?" Marilynn's expression turned ironic. "A lot of the hospital staffers carry guns. I even took lessons and practiced at the range. How would you like to get off work at midnight and go through a deserted parking lot on Pill Hill?"

Pill Hill certainly isn't the safest spot in Seattle. Marilynn was right: A woman alone—or a man, for that matter—stood at risk anytime of the day or night. It had never occurred to me, however, that Marilynn would carry a handgun. It was beginning to sound as if everyone connected to the Campbell house was armed, if not necessarily dangerous.

"Let's hope you don't have to use it," I finally said. "I trust you don't carry it to the clinic here."

"No," Marilynn replied firmly. I half-expected her to turn defensive, but instead, an impish gleam danced in her eyes. "I don't have to. Dr. Flake has a Desert Eagle."

I knew all about Peyton Flake's Desert Eagle. He and my brother, Ben, had done a little male bonding with guns the previous December. I flinched at the memory. Shaking my head, I started to say goodbye, then noticed that Marilynn was eyeing a stack of mail on the credenza. Her mood suddenly changed as she picked up what looked like a dozen or more envelopes.

"This is mine," she said in a hollow voice.

"Bills?" I suggested, knowing better.

"I don't think so." Her face had taken on a haggard look.

"Don't read them," I urged, holding out my hand. "I'll give them to Milo in the morning."

But Marilynn was made of sterner stuff. "I'll do it myself. Good night, Emma."

I bit my lip, and walked out into the spring rain. This was only my second visit to the Campbell residence, but I was beginning to think that it was not a good luck house.

At least not for Marilynn Lewis.

Chapter Eleven

I WAS OVERCOME with guilt, good old-fashioned pre–Vatican II Catholic guilt. This was Ascension Thursday, a holy day of obligation, and I'd flat-out forgotten to attend Mass. Or communion service, if a visiting priest didn't show up, and we got stuck with one of our eucharistic ministers stumbling around on the altar. Maybe I hadn't really missed much, but I felt penitent. I called my brother in Tuba City and confessed my sin.

"Stick it in your ear, Sluggly," said Ben, using his childhood nickname for me. "It was an honest mistake. Did you really want to hear Ed Bronsky read the gloomiest readings in the New Testament?"

"Ed's not a euke," I retorted. "At least now I know why he was late for work—he went to church. Ed probably wondered where the hell I was. Damn. Besides," I added, "Ed's improved. He's actually exhibiting a positive attitude."

"Wow," Ben exclaimed. "Talk about a miracle! Maybe you should build a shrine in back of the newspaper office. Off the top of my head, I can't remember who's the patron saint of advertising revenue."

I hadn't talked to Ben in three weeks. As always, it was wonderful to hear his crackling voice and feel the warmth flow over the phone line. He regaled me with his latest adventures on the Navajo reservation, and I, in turn, told him about our recent murders. Ben shed his flippant attitude.

"This is not good," he said. "What's Milo up to?"

I tried to explain the sheriff's conduct of the investigation. I tried to rationalize his small-town racial prejudices. I tried to excuse his lack of progress on the grounds of the case's complexity and the county's lack of resources. I tried to keep the entire conversation on an analytical, objective plane.

"Milo kissed me."

Ben's laughter exploded in my ear. "Milo *what*? Why? When? Where? How?"

"Oh, shut up, Stench," I retorted, resorting to my own nickname for Ben. "It was all very silly. Milo's under some heavy pressure, and he'd been sort of rude to me earlier, and I think he was just trying to show me that I was a woman and he was a man."

Ben was still laughing. "What about birth certificates? You know, the box where they check *M* or *F*?"

"Stop it, you jerk." I was growing testy. "I'm sure Milo feels like an idiot. Which he should. I haven't had the nerve to call him, and I ought to, because I need to know the facts about this last murder. He hasn't called me, either. I'm sure he's embarrassed. Now let's talk about something else, like why St. Mildred's parishioners are a bunch of bigots."

At the other end, Ben paused. "No surprise there, Sluggly. Christianity embraces everybody. Christians don't always do the same. It's okay to love your brother—or sister—as long as they're the same color as you are. Want to hear some tales from the reservation? And I'm talking about both sides of the coin. Don't ever think that white people are the only ones who can work up a hatred for the other guys."

"I know that," I said, bristling at Ben's accusation of naïveté. "Racists come in all colors. I expect better of Catholics, that's all. I mean, lowercase the word and it means universal, right?"

"Right. Wrong." Ben sighed. "It's a great theory. It might even work someday. The key—and don't quote me, especially not around Tuba City—is love. Don't laugh, you cynic. I mean romantic love, as well as the spiritual kind. Intermarriage. A hundred years from now, I wouldn't be surprised if racism was passé. Look around you—but not in Alpine. Not yet."

"You paint an optimistic picture," I mused. "What are you puffing down there in Tuba City? Is it strong enough to let you take Adam on for a few weeks this summer?"

Ben chuckled. "Adam's okay, Emma. You deserve to pat yourself on the back."

My brother was right. Being a single parent is rough, but Adam and I survived. There had been big sacrifices for both of us. It was harder on me because I knew what I was giving up. Never having had a father, Adam didn't know what he'd missed. Or so I'd always rationalized.

The chat with Ben lifted my spirits. I cleaned up the kitchen, ran the dishwasher, put in a load of laundry, and postponed calling Milo until morning. Shortly before ten, Vida called me. She had spent the evening at her Cat Club, a dozen or so women in her age group who'd started out sewing for the needy, moved on to playing cards, and now used their monthly gathering to stuff their faces and wag their jaws. Or so Vida claimed.

"This is too much," Vida exclaimed after I'd filled in the details she hadn't yet heard. "Dot Parker said Charlene Vickers told her that Irene Baugh thinks a gang has moved into Alpine. She wants Fuzzy to issue a proclamation or some fool thing. Irene swears she's seen at least six African-American men loitering around the mall."

"Has she?"

"Of course not! Irene sees black men the way Averill Fairbanks sees UFOs. But I don't like the sense of panic she generates. Dot Parker believed every word of it. So did my idiot sister-in-law, Lila Blatt."

I mentioned the letters Marilynn had received, adding that I assumed they contained more hate messages and that I felt partly responsible. "It's Thursday—those lamebrains probably read yesterday's story in *The Advocate* about Kelvin Greene and dashed off some more ugly stuff to Marilynn."

"Don't be silly," Vida admonished. "The news was all over town days before the paper came out. But Marilynn's theory is intriguing. About Wesley Charles, I mean. It doesn't speak well for Alpine, does it?"

"We've had murderers here before," I pointed out.

"Yes, yes, I know that." Vida sounded exasperated. "It's the *kind* of murder. If I didn't know better, I'd think it's a racist. Neo-Nazis, or something. But I suppose it's not."

I was making a wry face into the phone. "Would you like that better than homicide with a motive?"

"No," Vida retorted. "I'd like it even less. But it might be easier to solve."

In the background, I could hear Vida's canary, Cupcake, chirping up a storm. "There sure are a lot of guns around here," I remarked. "You don't have one, do you, Vida?"

"As a matter of fact, I do," Vida replied blithely. "Ernest's old .45, from World War II. He enlisted on his eighteenth birthday in 1944. There's a shotgun and a .22 around here someplace, too. My husband used to hunt."

I sighed. "I must be the only unarmed resident of Alpine."

"Possibly." Vida seemed unperturbed by the idea. "I must run, Emma. I forgot to cover Cupcake before I left, and he's getting fractious. I'll see you in the morning. Oh— don't let Milo kiss you again, at least not in public. It's not good for either of your reputations, and Tommy wouldn't like it." She hung up.

Ginny Burmeister had a new hairdo. The thick auburn mane had been cut close to her head, with natural, artful curls clinging to her temples. Her fair skin was free of makeup, but there was a hint of brown eye shadow on her lids, mascara had been applied, and her lips were outlined in a subtle, but becoming shade of bronze. Overnight, Ginny had been transformed from a plain young woman into almost pretty.

I complimented her, and predictably, she blushed, which added to her new attractions. "Rick and I are going to Seattle tonight with Carla and Peyts. Carla talked me into getting a new do. I'm not sure about it—my head feels bare."

"It's not," I said with an admiring smile. "You look wonderful."

"That's what Rick said." Ginny blushed some more. "He's thinking of changing his hair back to its natural color."

"Well." I wasn't quite sure how to react. "Maybe he wants to move up in the banking business."

Ginny turned skeptical, then slapped a hand against her cheek. "Oh! I forgot to tell you! Rick says he heard Wash-

ington Mutual is going to open up a branch here in the fall.
You might want to check that out."

Naturally, I would. The First—and only—Bank of Alpine
had no competition within a thirty-mile radius. Another financial institution would hit the Bank of Alpine hard. Nor
did the timing seem right, with so many people in the timber industry out of work. I made a note to call Washington
Mutual's corporate headquarters in Seattle.

The mail had not yet arrived, so girding myself, I decided to amble down the street to the sheriff's office.
Maybe I imagined it, but I could have sworn that Milo's
deputies leered at me when I came through the door. Milo,
however, seemed preoccupied.

"It's a good thing you didn't try to call," he muttered
into his mug of coffee. "I'm not talking to anybody this
morning. Every crank in Skykomish County wants to know
why the morgue is filling up with black guys from Seattle."

"Wesley Charles was on his way to Monroe," I pointed
out.

"Yeah, right, you know what I mean." Milo set his mug
down on the desk and gave me a sheepish look. "Damn,
Emma, I don't know what got into me last night. I'm
stressed. Honoria's talking about going back to California.
She misses her family."

Jarred, I rested my elbow on the desk and held my head.
How had I become a sub off the bench for Honoria
Whitman? "Well . . ." I began, trying to be tactful and actually wanting to punch Milo in the chops, "I gather you
two aren't all that serious?"

Milo's long face seemed to droop onto his chest. "I don't
know. Sometimes I thought we had a future, but when I remember what it was like being married to Old Mulehide, I
don't think marriage is a good idea."

"Honoria isn't Old Mulehide," I noted, referring to the
unfortunate nickname Milo had given his ex-wife. "And
you aren't like her first husband who made her a cripple.
There are lots of happy second marriages. And they
wouldn't be second marriages if the first ones hadn't gone
sour."

Milo's hazel eyes were fastened on the ceiling. "After six
years of being single, I'm used to it. I'm married to the job,

I guess. It wouldn't be fair to Honoria, especially with her
. . . problems."

It seemed to me that problems or not, Honoria coped
very well from her wheelchair. She lived alone in a quaint
little house near Startup, she drove a specially rigged car,
and she was busily involved with her pottery. I said as
much to Milo.

He lifted his hands in a helpless gesture. "It's up to her.
I can't move to California."

I wondered if Honoria was giving Milo a shove by
threatening to return home. They had been going together
for almost a year. Knowing Milo, it was possible that he
and Honoria had never discussed a future together. But this
time, I kept my mouth shut.

"She hasn't left yet," I pointed out.

"Mmmm." Milo gave a slight nod, then gazed directly at
me. "You're not mad about last night?"

I was more amused than mad. I supposed that wasn't the
thing to say, either. "Forget it, Milo. Given the circumstances, we'll chalk it up as comic relief."

It was Milo's turn to look hurt. "Jeez, Emma, you make
it sound like we're a couple of clowns."

"We are. We all are. Now skip it, and let's talk about the
murder investigations."

We did, and as it turned out, I had more news for him
than he had for me. Perhaps Milo was doing penance for
kissing me, but he actually seemed interested in my background on Wesley Charles, in Shane Campbell's work relationship with Kelvin Greene, in the account of the arsenal
that was kept by everyone in the Campbell family as well
as Marilynn Lewis.

"Wesley Charles was shot with a .45 caliber," Milo said,
digging a roll of mints out of his pocket and following up
with a couple of sniffs on his inhaler. "Fairly close range,
no cartridge found, so it probably wasn't a revolver."

I was frowning. "Two killers?"

Milo shrugged. "Maybe."

"Nobody saw anything?"

"Nope. Who would? The houses on Fir Street don't look
into the cul-de-sac. Coach Ridley had his kids working out

on the other side of Fifth at the field, but they didn't see anything. Or hear it, either."

I felt my shoulders slump. "The damned starter gun again," I murmured.

"Probably. Your next-door neighbors are the closest, but they weren't home."

My neighbors to the east were from Alaska, and not overly friendly. They had a couple of kids, around ten and thirteen. The kids weren't friendly, either, at least not since I'd scolded them for using my front yard as part of their touch-football field.

I was fingering my chin and diving deep into speculation. "Why did Wesley come here, I wonder?"

Milo was shaking his inhaler. I gathered it was almost empty. "You'd think he'd head back to the city. But the truth is, he could only go east. There was a roadblock at Monroe and another one at Sultan. He must have gotten through before the second one could be set up."

It was my turn to borrow a map. Unlike the one in my office, Milo's was full of red, blue, and green pins. "There's a back road into Sultan out of Monroe. Have you traced the stolen car?"

Milo nodded. "It belongs to some kid from Maltby. He left it parked—with the keys in it—at Dan's Mainstreet Grill across from the high school in Monroe. The only problem is, he did that three days ago."

I gaped at Milo. "So where did the kid go?"

"Back to Maltby with some buddies. Dan's discourages high school kids from turning the restaurant into a hangout. The kid had to leave in a hurry. He was going to collect the car over the weekend."

"So why didn't Dan's have the car towed?"

Milo bestowed a half smile of approval. "Good point. Maybe that's because it got stolen by somebody else before they could get hold of a tow truck."

I tried to picture the scene. An escaped convict flees from a prison bus on a major highway, hobbles off right past the reformatory in full daylight, goes to a busy restaurant on one of Monroe's main drags, and drives off in an abandoned beater that just happens to have the keys in the ignition.

"This is making no sense," I said flatly.

"It sure isn't," Milo agreed. "That's why I'm guessing somebody else swiped that car first. The people at the restaurant don't remember seeing it after Tuesday afternoon."

"Who took it first?"

"Who knows? Kids, I suppose. But it means that car could have been anywhere—I figure someplace close to the site of the stalled prison bus."

I tapped the map. "Show me exactly where the tie-up took place."

Milo pointed to the long, downhill curve of Highway 522 just before the first Monroe exit. "It's steep, it bends, it's kind of narrow. People tend to go too fast in there, especially when it's raining. There've been so many accidents that the locals call it The Highway to Heaven. Ever notice all the skid marks between Monroe and the Paradise Lake Road?"

I hadn't, of course. I suppose I was usually too busy trying to keep from skidding. "There's a guardrail in here," I said, etching the accident site with my thumbnail. "Where could Wesley go? He's practically on top of the reformatory." The road into the Twin Rivers Correctional Center was less than a hundred yards from where the tie-up had occurred.

"According to the people from Shelton, the guards herded the prisoners off the bus and had them stand on the shoulder," Milo explained in his painstaking style. "The guards were supposed to be watching, but they got distracted by all the commotion from the school bus. Kids yelling and crying—you can imagine. The next thing they knew, Wesley Charles was gone."

I was slightly incredulous. "What about the other prisoners? Didn't they notice him clanking off down the road?"

"Hey—imagine the scene. You got cars, trucks, that school bus. You got people rear-ending each other and raising hell. In this day and age, it's more likely that some of the drivers are going to be armed and dangerous than it is that a bunch of shackled convicts will cause trouble." Milo glowered a bit. "Everybody's looking out for their own backside—or else they're worried about those kids. These prisoners weren't considered high risk. Not even Wesley

Charles. They said that he'd been a model con during his stay at Shelton."

I put my hands together in a prayerful attitude. Maybe I felt that only divine intervention could help solve this case. "Milo—the key to this whole thing has to be Jerome Cole. Why don't you get a transcript of the murder trial?"

I expected Milo to balk, at least a little, but he didn't. His agreement demonstrated how lost he felt. I wasn't exactly heartened by his attitude. When I left him a few minutes later, he was dialing his liaison in King County.

On my way back to the office, I saw Bill Blatt and Sam Heppner going into the bank. It wasn't yet ten o'clock, so they weren't on personal business. I paused at the corner by the toy shop and wondered if I should follow them. But I'd find out later from Milo what they were after, I told myself, and headed on to *The Advocate*.

The mail had arrived, and with it, a pile of outraged letters about the murders. Not all of them were blatantly racist; most were signed. They would have to be published, since that was my policy. I decided to start my editorial for the coming week. The music censorship issue could wait. I would blast people of prejudice, and let the chips—and another stack of letters—fall where they would.

"We see people as one dimensional," I wrote, "and what we see are always the most obvious, if superficial, things about that other person. Is she skinny? Is he a dentist? Does that girl wear glasses? Is this man bald? In a wheelchair? Have a stammer? Where do nicknames like Lefty and Tubby and Rusty come from? Our visual perceptions are swift, and always incomplete. We pigeonhole people, and it's not fair."

I paused, marveling at the quiet that reigned in the office. Vida and Carla had gone up to the high school to do their picture story and a bit of sleuthing. Ginny was in the front office, and Ed was out selling advertising. I kept writing, working up a full head of steam. I recalled what Ben had said over the phone. It wasn't fair to blame Alpiners for all the ills of the world.

"There was a time when prejudices were strictly tribal," I wrote in my moralistic frenzy. "Indeed, there are still places in the world where that remains true. In Saxon England, for example, members of one village didn't trust—or like—villagers from across the ford. As the years went by, they hated the invading Normans. Still later, they despised the Dutch and the French and the Spaniards. Then came people of a different color and religion. Meanwhile, those villagers had mingled, married, and produced new bloodlines. The Saxons melded with the Normans. The English nobility forged matrimonial alliances with the French, the Spanish, the Portuguese, and the Scots; a homosexual king led the Crusades against the so-called infidel; later, another monarch rebelled against the very church he'd sworn to defend and set off centuries of religious persecution. The Western world went to war to fight for freedom, to foil aggression, and to halt anti-Semitism. For two thousand years, the human race has struggled to be worthy of its name: the *human* race. Not the black or white or brown or yellow race, but a world peopled by *people*: unique, diverse, good, bad, talented, stupid, kind, grasping, and often, all of it in a single individual."

I paused, wondering how much I would have to cut before I jumped off my soapbox. Like most of my editorials, it probably wouldn't change anybody's mind. The people who agreed with me would nod in a self-righteous manner, and those who didn't would snort in disgust. Either way, I'd end up in the bottom of the birdcage.

The most encouraging attitude I'd heard so far had come from Regis Bartleby at Trinity Episcopal. Harvey Adcock, of Harvey's Hardware, had told Ed Bronsky that the rector planned on giving a sermon urging members of his congregation to invite minorities to visit Alpine. The concept was noble, but Bartleby had a reputation for speaking far over the heads of his parishioners. I hoped the message wouldn't be lost in a sea of intellectual theology. The rector's heart was in the right place, but his delivery was on another planet. At least I knew that he'd applaud my editorial efforts.

Going out to the news office to get more coffee, I glanced through the window by Vida's desk. Bill Blatt and Sam Heppner were coming out of the bank. On a whim, I zipped through the door and hailed them as they crossed the street.

"Coffee?" I offered, brandishing my mug. "*Real* coffee?" I knew from sad experience what pathetic brew passed for coffee at the sheriff's office.

Sam Heppner started to demur, but Bill Blatt was eager. The two deputies followed me inside *The Advocate* where I played the gracious hostess.

"This is a bribe," I declared, handing each man a steaming mug. "I can get a court order and force you to tell me what you found out at the bank, or I could go see Milo and throw a tantrum or," I added with a flinty look at Bill, "I could send Vida to do the job. But how about taking the easy way?"

Bill Blatt, who had shown alarm at the reference to his redoubtable aunt, started chattering like a magpie: "The sheriff told us to check out Wendy and Todd Wilson, but I'll be darned if I can see why. What have they got to do with these shootings?"

"Maybe they don't." I bestowed my most winning smile on the deputies. "But they're part of the family that's given shelter to your boss's favorite suspect. And never mind that your boss may be nuts. What'd you find out at the bank?"

Sam Heppner uttered a wry chuckle. He was in his midthirties, with slicked-back brown hair, pale blue eyes, and a nose that would have looked more at home on a buzzard. "Not much. The Wilsons don't have an account there."

I stared. "What? But the Bank of Alpine is the only game in town!"

Sam gave me his dour look. "That's right, ma'am. But so what? The Wilsons could bank in Sultan or Monroe. It's not a crime."

Vida blew in the door, her straw skimmer askew. "Crime? What crime?" Her gaze fixed on her nephew.

I started to explain, but Vida waved her hands. She whirled on Bill Blatt. "You went through the accounts at the bank? No Wilsons? That's ridiculous!" She shot me a smug look. "Especially under the circumstances."

"Which are?" I asked.

Vida's expression became owlish. "Odd." She turned back to Bill. "You actually looked at the bank records?"

Bill nodded, looking not unlike a new recruit being inspected by his first sergeant. "They had an account up until October of 1992. Then they closed it. At the time, they had about two thousand in savings, another four hundred in checking."

"Oooooh!" Vida whipped off her glasses and rubbed her eyes. "Interesting! Revealing!" She glanced again at me.

"Uh—where's Carla?" I asked, suddenly realizing that Vida had returned alone.

Vida gave a quick shake of her head. "She forgot to drop the roll of film off at Buddy Bayard's. She'll be here in a few minutes." Collaring her nephew—literally—she stood nose-to-nose with Bill Blatt. "Wilson," she said in a low, coaxing voice. "W-I. What about Marlow Whipp: W-H?"

Bill Blatt squirmed. "Aunt Vida—we weren't asked to check into Marlow Whipp's account."

"Nonsense!" snapped Vida. "You must have seen it." She gave Bill a little shake. "How much?"

I saw Bill Blatt's Adam's apple bob. "Uh . . . twelve grand and change."

With an air of triumph, Vida released her nephew. "Well! If that doesn't beat all! This is a monkey-and-a-parrot-time if I ever saw it!"

Bill Blatt and Sam Heppner were both looking mystified. I, however, was beginning to see the light. "So what did you learn at the high school, Vida?"

My House & Home editor all but simpered. "Very interesting, I assure you." She progressed to her desk, where she glanced at her mail and turned up her nose. "Wendy Wilson's colleagues find her popularity with students highly suspect. They think she's too easy on them. As for the students themselves, it all depends on who you talk to. Grace Grundle's granddaughter, who is a fine upstanding Presbyterian girl, doesn't think much of Wendy as a teacher. She says she plays favorites. But some of the others"—Vida leaned on her desk, and her gaze flickered from me to Bill to Sam and back again—"sing her praises to the sky. Their eyes are out of focus and they don't know Charles Dickens from Slim Pickens. What does that tell you?"

Bill Blatt looked as if it didn't tell him much. But Sam Heppner slapped his hands together. "Mrs. Wilson isn't just a teacher. She's got other irons in the fire."

Vida nodded sagely. "I can only guess. But it would be wise to keep Marlow Whipp's store under surveillance. If Milo Dodge wants to discuss it with me, please have him call."

Bill and Sam all but saluted. Gulping down their coffee, they hurried away. Vida was already typing up a storm. Calmly, I sat down in the chair next to her desk.

"Well?"

Vida didn't look up. She rattled off four more lines on her battered upright, slamming the carriage back so hard that the machine shook. At last, she stopped and eyed me squarely:

"It's got to be drugs," she said. "Pot, at least. Marlow Whipp is the middleman."

Her deductions made sense. Running drugs through the little grocery store would account for the Wilsons' affluence and Marlow's ability to stay in business. I had objections, however.

"If there's a widespread drug problem in this town, why haven't we heard about it?" I objected.

Vida didn't dismiss my quibble out of hand. "There have been stories about certain young people with problems," she pointed out. "The Nielsen boy. One of the Gustavsons. Jessie Lott's granddaughter, though at the time, we assumed she went away to have a baby. Oh, if I thought about it, I could name a dozen in the past year or two. But parents often don't know what to look for. Into denial, as they say. And the youngsters can be clever, I'm told." Sadly she shook her head. "It's a terrible thing to raise children these days. Much harder. I look at my grandchildren, and my heart goes out to my daughters and their husbands. Why, to think of Roger exposed to drugs!" Her face grew horrified. "What would become of him?"

A vision of Roger, dealing crack out of a moving van came to mind. Roger, in a loud suit and a broad-brimmed hat with a big feather, cuddling two curvaceous cuties and clenching a cigar between his teeth. Roger, at the head of a long, polished table, giving orders for reprisals against the other dons and their families. Roger, hanging by his thumbs in a Turkish prison. I liked the last picture best.

"Don't worry, Vida," I said in my most sanguine voice.

"I'm sure Roger—and your other grandchildren—will turn out just fine." The Turkish prison evolved into a scaffold with a large noose.

Looking temporarily reassured, Vida returned to the matter at hand: "We don't know how long this has been going on, of course. Except for buying the house in Icicle Creek, Todd and Wendy's wealth seems to have accumulated quite recently. Until last autumn, their savings were modest. School started in September. So, perhaps, did Wendy's drug sales. Thus, the Wilsons moved their growing hoard out of town to avoid suspicion."

"I gather you didn't talk to Wendy herself this morning?"

"No. She was in class." Vida had turned pensive.

I got out of the chair. "Let's hope Milo follows through with the surveillance. It's too bad he doesn't have more personnel at his disposal."

Vida agreed. "If we're right about this drug thing," she said, causing me to stop in midstep, "how does it tie in with Kelvin Greene and Wesley Charles?"

I swiveled around to face Vida. "That's obvious, isn't it? The part about Kelvin, I mean. He used drugs, he dealt them. Maybe he was Wendy's connection."

"Or Todd's." Vida's face froze. "Wendy may be the baglady or whatever it's called. Emma, call Milo right now. If he can't afford to have someone watch that store, we'll volunteer."

"Vida!" I was aghast. "Are you crazy? I'm not going to disguise myself as a shrub and lurk across the street at the high school field. Neither are you. This is police work, not journalism."

Vida, however, remained firm. "It is, too. We're after a story. Good heavens, Emma, didn't you ever use a cover to get a story when you worked on *The Oregonian?*"

I had, of course, on several occasions. Once, I'd masqueraded as a student at Reed College to check out rumors of sexual harassment by the faculty. Another time, I'd been a phony whiplash victim, trying to get the goods on a shady chiropractor. My most memorable guise was a shoplifter at Lloyd Center. The article was intended to show the public how severely criminals are treated, and thus, to prevent crime. I managed to walk off with over seven hundred dollars worth of merchandise from nine stores before I finally got caught. My arms and my feet ached so much that I was tempted to keep the stuff I'd stolen.

But this was different. This was Alpine, not Portland, and I had to maintain my dignity. So did Vida. I called Milo immediately.

"Yeah, yeah, I already heard Vida's idea from her nephew," Milo said in an impatient voice. "Forget it. Surveillance! That's for law enforcement bodies with staff to spare. If we want to check out Marlow Whipp, we'll get a search warrant."

"So do it," I suggested.

"On what grounds? That Wendy Wilson's a shitty teacher and chews gum she buys from Marlow Whipp? Listen, Emma, old Mr. and Mrs. Whipp ran that store for fifty years. They saved every dime. Vida should know that. Maybe they invested their money. Marlow lives in the family house, and the old folks are in the Lutheran retirement home. Marlow's wife gives piano lessons, their daughter lives in Wenatchee, and their son's a meter reader for the PUD. Now how respectable can you get?"

Somewhere in the back of my mind, I knew that the Whipp grandson was a meter reader. Until now, however, I'd never made the connection between Frankie Whipp and Todd Wilson. Maybe there wasn't any, except for their employer. Maybe it was just another of Alpine's coincidences.

Vida mulled over Milo's response. "He's right, in his way," she allowed, then heaved a huge sigh. "All the same, there's something very peculiar going on between Marlow and the Wilsons. Maybe I should pay a call on Marlow's mother at the hospital. She's still recovering from knee surgery, you know."

Vaguely, I recalled that Peyton Flake had done a knee replacement on Mrs. Whipp the previous week. "Give it a try," I said, not sounding very hopeful. A glance at the clock told me it was going on noon. Carla still hadn't returned from Buddy Bayard's Picture-Perfect Photography Studio. "Where is Carla now? Did she go on a story?"

Vida was typing again. "Just a minute. I'm adding a couple of items to 'Scene Around Town.' Mrs. Whipp and her knee. The Wilsons' vacation trip."

I arched my eyebrows. "Scene" was Vida's weekly gossip column, filled with snippets of local happenings. Often, they could be expanded into feature stories. Even though we buried the column on an inside page, I'd been told it was the best-read item in the paper, right up there with the obituaries. People loved to see their names in print. Readers supplied at least half of the material, usually with gleeful reports over the phone. But during a slow news week, Vida had to scratch to fill the column: "Carrie Starr seen browsing in the cereal section at Safeway . . ." "Henry Bardeen's car parked two spaces down from his usual spot at the ski lodge . . ." "Polly Patricelli sporting a new bandanna and crossing Third Street with a sprightly step . . ." Such were the meaty bits that made Alpiners sit up and take notice—of themselves, caught unawares, and suddenly thrust into the limelight.

Vida was finished. She had no idea where Carla had gone. "It's lunchtime," she said calmly. "Maybe she's meeting her heartthrob."

"Dr. Flake?" I rolled my eyes. "If so, this romance is really heating up. They're going to dinner in Seattle tonight."

"Yes, yes, I know. With Ginny and Rick Erlandson. They'll have a nice time, but it won't be romantic. Not with all four of them." Vida's expression turned puckish. "Speaking of which, I forgot an item for 'Scene.' " She poised her fingers over the keyboard. " 'Sheriff Dodge seen kissing Publisher Lord at murder site. Do we hear wedding bells chime?' Now there's some news!" She made as if to start typing.

"Stop!" I yelled, just as Carla came through the door. Vida smirked. Carla stared.

"What's happening now?" she asked, sounding resigned.

I moved in front of Vida's desk. "Nothing. Where were you? I thought you'd been stolen by Gypsies."

Carla leaned sideways, the better to see Vida. "I was on a stakeout. It was Vida's idea."

"Now, now," said Vida, also leaning around me. "I merely mentioned the idea. Well? Did you see anything?"

With an impatient step, Carla walked over to her desk. "Hardly. I stayed there, parked by the stupid football field, for an hour. Nine kids—nobody I recognized—went into

the store. All but three came out with soft drinks. Two of
the others were carrying little bags. One of them didn't
seem to have anything, which meant he probably bought
cigarettes."

"Hmmmm." Vida mused a bit, rocking back and forth in
her chair. "Little bags. Drugs." Her head snapped up.
"That's it? No adults? No car traffic?"

Sorting through her mail, Carla shook her head. "No
cars. One adult, a white male in his seventies, bought a *P-I*.
Oh, Shane Campbell pulled up in his Alpine Appliance van.
He took a big box into the store and came out about five
minutes later."

Vida was on the alert. She gave me a quick glance.
"Shane? Could you see what was in the box?"

Carla shot Vida a rebellious look. "Do I have X-ray vision? It was a box—like this." Carla framed a two-foot-
square piece of space with her hands. "It had writing on it.
Script letters, starting with an *M*. I couldn't read the rest of
it from across the street."

I gazed at Vida. I couldn't resist. "*M* for morphine?"

Vida pursed her lips. "*M* for moron. Emma, you're not
taking this seriously." She glared at Carla. "Neither are you,
young lady."

Carla had moved on to her phone messages. She started
punching numbers into her phone. "Vida, you're crazy.
Hello, is this the Baptist Church? May I please speak to
Reverend Poole?" She put her hand over the mouthpiece.
"The censorship thing. The Baptists have joined the Meth-
odists and the Pentecostals and both our Mormons."

I laughed, a bit lamely. Vida, however, was looking grim.
In retrospect, she was right and I was wrong. But at the
time, neither of us knew why.

Chapter Twelve

MAYOR FUZZY BAUGH's voice had dripped Southern syrup when he'd called to ask me to confer with him over my L.I.D. editorial. A native of Louisiana, Fuzzy had lived in Alpine for going on forty years. By rights, he should have lost his accent, but he resurrected it when he wanted to get his way. This was one of those occasions. The mayor didn't feel the time was right to suggest a bond issue for civic improvements. There were too many people out of work in Alpine. We needed jobs, not sidewalks. It was up to me to prove that building sidewalks could create jobs. Knowing how hard-headed Fuzzy could be under that soft, gallant exterior, I figured I was whipped before I walked into his office.

Before I reached city hall three blocks away on Front Street, I spotted Shane Campbell. His van was parked by the Clemans Building, and he was wheeling a dolly along the sidewalk.

At a trot, I called to him. He stopped, a hand on the dolly. Passing the Upper Crust Bakery, Daley's Cobbler Shop, Alpine Ski Hut, and Stella's Styling Salon, I struggled to come up with a conversational gambit. By the time I caught up with Shane, I'd concocted a reasonable excuse.

"Shane!" My smile was a mile wide and probably twice as phony. "Do you carry thirty-cup coffeemakers?"

Shane Campbell considered the question carefully. "I'm not sure if we have any in stock, but we could order one."

My relief was exaggerated. "Great! Ours has been acting up. I don't know if it'd be cheaper to fix it or get a new one. What do you think?"

Shane gave a slight lift to his shoulders under his official

Alpine Appliance jacket. "I can get our repairman to take a look. I'm no expert myself."

"Great," I repeated, wildly searching for a path to Marlow Whipp's grocery store. "The coffeemaker is pretty old. Marius Vandeventer probably bought it ten years ago."

Shane ran a hand through his fair hair. "Gosh, that could be a parts problem. We'd have to send to Seattle, and they might not even have it. Even if they do, it could take a couple of weeks."

I gaped at Shane as if he'd just told me the world was going to end in ten minutes. "Oh! Well—we can't go without the coffeemaker that long. . . . Of course, it still works. But Ginny and Carla have trouble getting it going in the morning. . . ." My voice trailed off as I frantically sought an opening to inquire about Shane's visit to Marlow.

"If you order a new one," Shane said in his quiet, bland voice, "we can UPS it up here in two days. Overnight, if you want to pay the extra delivery charge."

"Ah!" I exclaimed, as if deliverance were at hand. The world wasn't going to end after all.

"It's not cheap," he went on. "We just got a milk steamer for Marlow Whipp's new espresso machine, and he wouldn't put out the extra twenty bucks to hurry it along. It took a week to get here because it had to come out of a warehouse in California."

"Oh." The disappointment in my voice had nothing to do with Marlow's tightfisted attitude. "A milk steamer? What kind?"

Shane screwed up his face in the effort of recall. "Melitta. He wanted me to set it up, but as I said, I'm no technician."

Feeling silly, I gave Shane a half-baked smile. "Okay, thanks. I'll see how it goes Monday. If it's still balky, I'll call you or your dad."

Shane made appropriate noises of agreement. I stalked past the Clemans Building. The red brick facade of the county courthouse and city hall loomed across Second Street. Fuzzy Baugh awaited, in all his civic splendor. Shane Campbell had delivered a milk steamer to Marlow Whipp. Vida and I were grasping at straws. For once, it seemed that Carla Steinmetz wasn't as dizzy as her coworkers.

Unless, I suddenly thought, as I walked through the echoing granite-and-marble lobby of city hall, there was something else in that box. An innocent milk steamer from a reputable company like Melitta would make a perfect cover for running drugs.

Again, I didn't know what was really perking in Alpine.

Carla wanted to leave early to prepare for her big date in Seattle. Ginny hinted that if Carla left to get ready, she should do the same. Ed, claiming exhaustion and a leaky bathroom faucet at home, took off at four. Vida had to hurry home and fix dinner for "just us girls." By four-fifteen, I was alone in the office, writing up Fuzzy Baugh's interview about why this would not be a good year to call for a special election on a L.I.D. bond issue. I had lost an editorial battle, but gained a lead story for the coming week.

Even in retrospect, Fuzzy's drawling comments bored me. I had no quarrel with his rationale, nor did I resent his refutation of my arguments. Rather, it was his penchant for using phrases such as "In the public interest . . ."; "To take a longer view . . ."; and "Matters that weigh heavily upon the mayor's mind . . ." He had had no comment on his wife's alleged sighting of gang members at the Alpine Mall. Thus, I had no invasion story. I was glad.

I wrapped up the L.I.D. piece in under ten minutes. It was not quite four-thirty. Who would drop by or call at such a late hour on a Friday in May? The rain had stopped during the night, the clouds had blown away by early afternoon, and the office felt stuffy. On an inspiration, I called Stella's Styling Salon. I didn't have much hope of getting an appointment, but Stella herself answered. She was willing to stay late if I could come over right away.

Stella Magruder is a bubbly woman with gleaming gold locks and a wicked walk. She is close to sixty, looks fifty, and carries her extra twenty pounds with pride. "No man," she once told me, "wants to worry about finding his woman in the dark. My Richie tells me he'd rather have ample than a sample." With four grown children of her own, Stella has had plenty of experience being a mother. She also has been rumored to have counseled other people's offspring over the years when their parents and professionals failed them.

"A gamine cut?" she asked, gazing at our reflections in the big mirror. "Show me, in a picture."

It didn't take long to find the right look in a hair styling magazine. Stella studied the photograph. It would work, she said, but I'd lose most of my permanent.

"I don't care," I replied. "If I like it, I'll keep it short. I promise."

Stella made a face. "You always go at least three weeks too long. You're too busy, Emma. You don't take time for yourself."

"Single moms get used to that," I answered lightly.

Stella made a disapproving noise in her throat as she began shampooing my hair. "Your son's away at school. He doesn't demand that much of your time, sweetie. You got in the habit of shortchanging yourself when he was younger, but now Adam's all grown up. Pamper yourself a little."

"I am," I countered, staring up at the ceiling with my head in the washbowl. "That's why I'm here."

Stella rinsed the shampoo out of my hair, and dried her hands. "Hold on—I've got a foil job to check. See you back at my station." Hips swaying, she went into the adjoining room. As I wandered back to Stella's domain, I saw Cyndi Campbell looking like a space cadet, with her head full of silvery tissues. Stella was examining a strand of Cyndi's hair. She pronounced her client ready, then propelled her over to the chair next to mine.

"I'll get Laurie to take these out," Stella announced, gesturing to her lion-maned associate who was heading for the laundry area with a load of dirty towels.

Cyndi greeted me with a languid wave. "I'm playing hooky from the PUD," she said, then offered a quirky smile. "It's okay if your brother-in-law is your boss."

I smiled back. "How are you all going to get along without Todd while he's gone for a month?"

Cyndi's smile disappeared. Laurie started removing the foils. "It won't be easy. I think it's selfish of Todd to take off for so long. If you ask me, it's Wendy's brainstorm. She gets some big ideas. It's time she got her head together and had a baby or something."

"Maybe this is their last fling," I remarked as Stella began to snip at my overgrown coiffure.

Cyndi sniffed. "Maybe. My folks don't think much of it. They'd like some grandchildren. It looks as if Shane will have them before Wendy does."

Stella stopped snipping. "Shane? Hey, Cyndi, what's up with your brother? Is he getting married?"

Cyndi's smug gaze locked with its mirror image. "I wouldn't be surprised."

Laurie, who was artfully made up and definitely pretty, had a bovine expression. Still, her face evinced interest. "Your brother's cute, Cyndi. Who's the lucky girl?"

Cyndi remained cagey. "Oh—somebody. It's not official. I can't blow it for him."

Stella was again concentrating on my hair. "A hometown girl? Is that why he came back to Alpine?"

In reply, Cyndi hummed. Laurie giggled. Stella took two inches off the top of my head. I began to wonder if the new me was going to scare the old me out of my wits.

"Let's say she's a mystery woman," Cyndi finally replied. "No, she's not from Alpine."

"Then we don't care." In the mirror, Stella gave Cyndi an arch look. "She must be somebody Shane met in Seattle."

Cyndi hummed some more. Stella had clipped away everything but an inch or so of straight hair. Laurie was down to the last few foils. My nose itched. Stella trimmed the nape of my neck. Her face suddenly hardened. She turned to Cyndi.

"The nurse?" Stella's voice had a faint rasp.

Cyndi swiveled her head, causing Laurie to drop the last foil. "Did I say that?"

"No." Stella's expression was somber. "I sure hope you didn't, sweetie. Your parents would have a fit and fall in it."

Cyndi resumed admiring her newly highlighted hair. "So? They like to talk about being broad-minded. Equality, and all that. What difference does it make?"

Stella was running a comb through my shorn, damp

locks, or what was left of them. She didn't notice my horrified reaction. "I'll tell you what difference—it's one thing to treat other people equal. It's another to intermarry. You end up with half-breeds, that's what. And those poor kids go through life not knowing what race they belong to. It's hard, believe me. My brother married a Korean girl. He met her in Seoul after the war, and they've got two kids. They live down in the Willamette Valley in Oregon, and I can tell you it's been rough. Of course, they're grown up now, and one's a computer programmer in Portland and the other's an orthodontist, but they put up with plenty of guff along the way."

Cyndi said nothing; I felt obligated to comment: "It sounds as if they turned out fine."

Stella gave an eloquent shrug. "Oh, sure, now that they're grown and have families of their own. But as kids—I'm telling you, it was one thing after the other. They got called Slant Eyes and Sloop and everything else." Quizzically, she stared at her own image. "Or was it Slop? Slope? I forget."

"It was the Fifties," I noted dryly.

"It was *rough*." She moved to Cyndi's chair as Laurie stepped aside. "That looks terrific, sweetie. You've got nice hair, but it needs just that extra touch of color to make it shine."

Cyndi nodded. Relaxing in the chair, she allowed Laurie to style the gleaming gold tresses. The effect was charming. "I like it," Cyndi announced, untying the smock she wore over her clothes. "Now let me out of here. I need a cigarette."

Cyndi and Laurie proceeded to the front desk. Stella watched them out of the corner of her eye. "Marriage is tough enough without going into it under a handicap," Stella muttered. "I hope Shane knows what he's doing."

In the mirror, I saw my closely cropped hair and wondered if Stella knew what she was doing. With a flick of the wrist, she created a sweep of bangs, then flipped a tendril of hair in front of each ear. A bit of brushing heightened the whole effect, and a swish of spray held it in place. Suddenly, I smiled. I looked younger, even prettier. Well, younger, at least. Stella stood back to admire her handi-work.

"Can you manage that?" she asked.

"Maybe." I didn't sound very certain.

"Try it for a week," Stella urged. "If you can't, we'll do a really soft body perm." She turned to the front of the shop, where Cyndi Campbell was about to make her exit. "Thanks, sweetie. Knock 'em dead. But don't forget what I told you about Shane and his bride-to-be."

Cyndi inclined her newly highlighted head and gave us an enigmatic smile.

I had forgotten that Cyndi was also invited to Vida's dinner party. It didn't surprise me that she turned out to be a no-show. I was, however, surprised to find her sister standing in for her.

"Cyndi has a hot date with a guy from Everett," Wendy Campbell Wilson explained to Vida. "It was a last-minute thing, and Mom was afraid Cyndi had screwed up your planning. Besides, Todd is working late tonight, getting caught up before we go on vacation."

Vida's reaction was reasonably gracious—for Vida. "Your mother should have come. Now why didn't I ask her in the first place?"

But Jean and Lloyd Campbell were already going out to dinner, in Sultan. The original guest list had dwindled from six to three, with one substitute. It was not Vida's style to linger over hors d'oeuvres and cocktails. Wendy and Marilynn arrived two minutes after I did. We were immediately hustled into Vida's dining alcove, with its Duncan Phyfe table and chairs, matching breakfront, and small buffet. Vida had made a crab casserole that tasted like glue. I suspected she hadn't used real crab, but the artificial kind that looks like surgical tubing. The green salad was fine, since it's hard to ruin lettuce, tomato, onion, and radishes. The poppy-seed rolls had come from the Upper Crust Bakery, and were delicious. I speculated about dessert, and hoped it was also store-bought, rather than homemade.

Halfway through the glutinous casserole, Marilynn complimented me on my hairdo. Vida had mentioned it when I came in the door, asking if I were trying out for a part as

Prince Valiant. "It's more Peter Pan," I informed her haughtily. Vida said she liked it. She thought. It would take some time getting used to.

"It makes you look like a pixie," Wendy declared. "It's really cute."

I thanked her, and mentioned seeing her sister getting a foil job. Wendy said that was for the special date. Marilynn wished she'd seen the results, but by the time she got home from work, Cyndi had already left.

"Cyndi was hinting that there are wedding bells in the offing," I said, an eye on Vida. I hadn't yet had an opportunity to break the news to her.

Wendy threw back her head and laughed. As ever, there was something ungainly about her manner. "That's a joke! Cyndi hasn't even gone out with this guy before. She's jumping the gun."

I explained that I meant Shane, not Cyndi. My eyes darted to Marilynn. She looked mildly interested, but composed.

Wendy brushed crumbs off her blue cotton camisole. "Really? I didn't think my brother was serious. That serious, anyway. Well!"

Vida, who had been arrested in the act of passing more of her odious casserole, gave me a reproachful look, then turned her gaze on Wendy. "I didn't know Shane was going with anyone. Who is it, Wendy?"

Wendy's deep blue eyes rested on Marilynn. "Is it a secret? What do you think, Marilynn?"

Still maintaining her composure, Marilynn gave a shake of her head. "It's not up to me to say. I'm not family."

Wendy made a helpless gesture. "You see? No formal announcement is forthcoming. We'll have to wait for Shane."

Vida looked as if she'd just as soon wait for Judgment Day. "That's not fair. I can't abide it when people bring up topics and then let them dangle. It's a tease. More than that, it's a challenge when you're dealing with newspaper people. We can't stand secrets. Can we, Emma?"

"Uh . . . No, we can't." I shifted uncomfortably in my chair. "Basically, we're snoops. But we snoop in the interest of truth."

Wendy seemed unperturbed. She also didn't seem to mind eating Vida's casserole. "Then let's talk about our murders. If you're looking for truth, there's where you should start. Who did it? I'll bet you two know more than the rest of us."

Our hostess wasn't diverted from her original purpose. Wendy had thrown down the gauntlet, and Vida was ready to joust. "Very well. Let's put our cards on the table. As far as we can tell, the only people in Alpine who knew Kelvin Greene were you, Marilynn—" Vida nodded to the guest on her right. "—your brother, Shane—" She nodded again, this time at Wendy on her left. "—and probably your sister, Cyndi. With all due respect, that means the three people who knew Kelvin live under the same roof. Shane and Cyndi were both at home about the time Kelvin was shot. Cyndi met us in the living room when we arrived for dinner, probably within fifteen minutes of the shooting, which very likely took place in the cemetery a block away from the house. Shane appeared shortly thereafter. You, Marilynn, arrived later, claiming to have been with Dolph Terrill at his apartment house by the clinic. Dolph is addled. He couldn't be precise about time if his life depended on it. Thus, none of you has a real alibi for the murder."

Marilynn and Wendy had both listened to Vida with a growing sense of alarm. The difference between them was that Marilynn looked hurt; Wendy seemed angry.

"Are you saying my brother or my sister could have killed that jerk?" Wendy demanded.

Vida wore her most owlish expression. "Somebody did. And murdered Wesley Charles as well." Vida offered me more casserole. I took it only to keep the peace, such as it was.

Still appearing offended, Marilynn spoke to Vida but looked at me. "I certainly didn't shoot Kelvin—or Wesley. As far as Wesley is concerned, Emma knows I was with her—or still at the clinic when it happened."

"That's true," I admitted, thrusting aside a nagging doubt. Something bothered me, but I couldn't think what it was.

"I can't speak for my brother or my sister," Wendy huffed. "I wasn't there. Todd was late getting home from the PUD, and I was grading papers to kill time. If you want alibis for Shane and Cyndi—which is ridiculous—ask my folks. They were there."

Vida inclined her head. "So we think. But we don't know that, do we?"

Wendy had crumpled her linen napkin, which she now hurled onto the table. "Oh, for God's sake! Now you suspect my parents? Vida, you're out of your mind!"

"I didn't say I suspected Lloyd and Jean," Vida replied calmly. "I'm saying that if your siblings are relying on your parents for an alibi, we don't know if they can provide one." Ignoring Wendy's irate expression, Vida turned back to Marilynn. "Do you know why Kelvin Greene was laid off by Fred Meyer?"

Marilynn frowned. "I thought he quit. Winola said he never stayed anywhere very long." She stared at her plate. Considering what was on it, I marveled it didn't stare back. "Now that I think about it, there was some trouble. Winola said it was unfair. She ... ah ... thought it might have been racially motivated."

"Do you remember the trouble?" Vida had lowered her voice. She sounded coaxing.

Marilynn shook her head. "No. I was all wound up in my own troubles. I suppose I was ready to make the break with my old life and didn't want to take on any new garbage. I guess I ignored Winola's complaints."

"Jeez." Wendy Wilson plunked her elbow on the table and almost upset her water goblet. "What's Kelvin's job got to do with his murder? I'm sorry I brought this up. Let's talk about something nice, like who got knocked up lately around here." She leaned toward Marilynn. "Hey, you'd know that. You work at the clinic."

Marilynn looked aghast. "I can't breach patient-doctor confidentiality," she retorted. "Why can't we talk about something other than scandal?"

Vida stared at Marilynn. "Why should we?"

I felt it was my duty to intervene. "People do, in other places. You know, art and books and music and politics."

Vida lifted her chin. "You aren't in other places, Emma. You're in Alpine."

So I was. With Vida around, I couldn't forget. Even when I wanted to.

I can't say that dinner was a success. On the other hand, I suppose it wasn't a failure. There were no deaths. Dessert had been a delectable plum crisp from the Upper Crust. The conversation had dwindled to a predictable discussion of marriage, divorce, remarriage, and the intertwining relationships that resulted thereof. I'd felt that Marilynn would be excluded, but she was an eager student. She had been in Alpine just long enough to know some of the parties involved, or at least a few of their relatives.

Wendy and Marilynn left around ten. I offered to stay and help Vida clean up. She demurred, but not vehemently, so I began clearing the table.

"Why," I inquired when we both reached the kitchen, "did you ask that question about Kelvin and Fred Meyer?"

"A hunch," she replied, rinsing off plates under the faucet. "Shane and Kelvin both left Fred Meyer about the same time. Now is that a coincidence or what?"

The thought had not occurred to me. "Winola would know," I suggested.

Vida nodded. "You have her number, don't you? It's Kelvin's phone, as I recall."

It was eight minutes after ten. "She might be up," I ventured.

Vida's response was to stare at the white Trimline phone that hung on the opposite wall. I shoved a handful of silverware into the dishwasher and went in search of my handbag, which was in the living room. Winola's number was on a notepad in a side pocket. Two minutes later I was waiting for Winola to answer my call.

On the fourth ring, her drowsy voice came over the line. I wasn't completely prepared. Vida and I hadn't parted from Winola on amicable terms. The bilge I'd concocted about asking how Kelvin's funeral had gone was dismissed in favor of honesty:

"Winola, this is Emma Lord in Alpine. As you may have heard, another man you knew has been killed up here. Wesley Charles?"

There was a little shriek at the other end. It seemed

Winola didn't know. Maybe she didn't watch the news on TV. Perhaps she didn't read the papers. The story was only twenty-four hours old, and word might not have filtered down through the big-city grapevine.

"You mean that dude who killed Jerome?" Winola's voice sounded hollow.

"That's right." I explained about the escape and the shooting. I told her how Marilynn Lewis and I had been at the scene. If Winola had doubts about my acquaintanceship with Marilynn, this anecdote surely should put them to rest. "I'm worried about Marilynn," I said, and it was true. "This case needs to be solved quickly, if only to stop the hate mail she's getting." I didn't mention the more ominous reason. "I only have a couple of questions."

Winola now sounded fully awake, if sullen. "Like what?"

I took a deep breath. "Do you think Wesley Charles killed Jerome Cole?"

Vida was watching me closely. Winola took her time to answer. "They say he did," she finally replied. "If I had to decide, I say he didn't, 'cause he got no balls. But maybe it was an accident."

I signaled to Vida, showing her that Winola was being ambivalent. "Why did Kelvin get laid off last April?"

Winola uttered a half snort, half sigh. "*That.* He was set up. They say he stole from the stockroom. They lie. Kelvin did some bad things, but he never stole stuff. What's to steal? Toys? Lawn furniture? Slug bait?"

"The store carries some big-ticket items," I pointed out. "Jewelry. Electronics. Cameras, I think." I tried to visualize the last Fred Meyer I'd been in, a store near Richmond Beach in Seattle's North End. "Nintendo games. CDs and tapes and calculators and radios. Small appliances."

Winola wasn't impressed by the inventory. "Kelvin didn't work with that stuff. He stocked the clothes and the toys and the garden section. Christmas trees, too, and decorations during the holidays. I tell you, he was set up by some white guy that didn't like him 'cause he was black." She sounded emphatic.

"Who was the guy?" I asked, an idea buzzing in my brain.

"Some kid in the stockroom. I don't know his name." She'd turned sullen again.

My shoulders sagged. My idea wasn't panning out. I had one last inspiration: "Winola—where did you and Marilynn go the night Jerome got killed?"

"A friend's place," she answered. "A friend of Marilynn's."

I pressed on. "Who was it?"

"A white dude. That Shane she kind of liked. I don't know why. I never thought he had it goin' on."

Maybe he didn't, in Winola's estimation. But Shane Campbell definitely had something going on, somehow. As I hung up, I felt the first of the pieces begin to fall into place.

Chapter Thirteen

LETTERS FROM BIGOTS hadn't struck me as appropriate dinner conversation. Neither Vida nor I had brought up the subject during the evening. It wasn't until Milo called Saturday morning that I learned Marilynn had turned the latest mailings over to his office.

"The usual bilge," he said in his laconic voice. "Mostly unsigned, though I can figure out who some of them are."

I pounced. "Who?"

"You don't want to know, Emma. In fact, you could probably guess. They're typical, mainly written out of fear. These people have nothing against Marilynn Lewis as a person. It's what she represents. You know—stereotypes. I'm not very good at putting it into words, but you get the idea."

I did. Marilynn Lewis was a symbol, mostly of negativity. Why did people always think of the bad, rather than the good? Why think in stereotypical terms at all? Marilynn Lewis wasn't a gang member, on welfare, or working the streets. Neither was she a famous singer, dancer, or athlete. She was Marilynn Lewis, R.N., educated, middle class, and, like too many women of every race, religion, and creed, inclined to fall in love with the wrong man. It could happen to anybody, and didn't I know it. The human heart didn't care what color of skin hid its wayward beat.

"You don't think those letters have anything to do with the murders?" I asked, coincidentally sorting through the mail that I'd just collected from my streetside box.

"No," Milo replied firmly. "To be sure, I'm sending them over to an expert in Snohomish County. It'd be nice if we could afford our own nut wizard. This county doesn't even have a shrink."

It was true. There were no practicing psychologists or psychiatrists in Skykomish County. The closest thing we had was a part-time counselor at the high school. Rumor had it that she also read palms and tea leaves.

"I don't think the correct term is *nut wizard*," I chided Milo. Before he could retort, I went on in a more serious vein: "What about my letters? Any ideas?"

"I let Dwight Gould go through all of them," Milo said. "He's kind of shrewd when it comes to figuring out people. In his way," Milo added hastily, lest I get the wrong idea. "He doesn't think your letter writer has written any of the stuff to Marilynn. Your guy—or gal—is sort of incoherent. Not that I'd hold up some of the ones to Marilynn as models of composition. But it's different—yours don't seem to be fueled by the same kind of hate and fear. Dwight can't explain it, so neither can I. Call it intuition."

"More personal?" I ventured.

"Personal? I don't know about that. I'm not sure what you mean."

Neither was I. Furthermore, I was distracted. The WNPA had mailed me my confirmation, as well as the official program for the weekend at Lake Chelan. On Friday, June 18, from ten-fifteen to noon, the scheduled presentation was "Where are we headed?—What will community newspapers be like in the future, and what will they expect from the WNPA?" The featured speaker was Tom Cavanaugh.

"Say, Milo," I said in an overly bright voice, "why don't you drop by for a beer? I should tell you about my most recent chat with Winola Prince." It would be a more stimulating way to pass the time than cleaning the oven, which had been my original Saturday plan.

Milo evinced interest, but said he was driving down to Startup to see Honoria. They might go to Wallace Falls for a picnic. Or maybe drive into Seattle for dinner and a movie. Or up to LaConner to see some of the local crafts. Or just have a long talk. Milo's voice dropped a notch with each option.

My initial reaction was that Milo's priority should be his murder investigation. Or, I asked myself, did I mean that *I* should be his priority? That was nonsense. Milo and

Honoria had reached a turning point. It was vital that he spend his time with her and try to resolve the crisis.

"Good luck," I said, amazed that I sounded sulky.

"Hey—Emma. Haven't you noticed something about me the past couple of days?"

"Huh?" Was Milo being cute? "Extra ears? You grew a beard? A new nose?"

"That's it! My allergies went away. You noticed!" Milo was elated.

"Oh! Oh, right, you're cured. Good. I wonder what set you off?"

"Pollen, I suppose. Plenty of it around here this time of year. Hey, I've got to get changed. See you."

Milo. He was *impossible*, as Vida would say. I looked again at the WNPA program. Tom. He, too, was impossible. What was he getting out of his marriage to Sandra, other than hassles, heartaches, medical bills, bail postings, complaints from irate merchants, and bad publicity? Sandra's money? Early on, yes. But Tom had established himself as one of the West's leading newspaper entrepreneurs. With Sandra's money. Tom was grateful; he had a strange sense of loyalty. Honor, he'd call it. I called it fear. Tom was afraid to face a different future. Most of us are like that. Milo was. I was. Milo was afraid a second marriage would turn out as badly as his first. I was afraid of marriage, period. That must be the reason I clung to Tom. As long as I could file him away in the back drawer of my emotional life, I had an excuse to stay out of other entanglements. Most of all, I could keep my independence. I'd fought hard for it. Why surrender it now when Adam was grown and I was on my own as a newspaper editor-publisher? Being lonely wasn't a good enough reason. As Vida said, "There are worse things than not being married."

And Vida said into my ear five minutes after I finished talking to Milo, "There aren't any funerals this week. Would you like to join me at the cemetery?"

"What for?" It seemed to me that Vida wasn't making sense.

"See here," she said earnestly. "The two murdered men were shot with different caliber bullets. That could mean two killers—or two guns. Wouldn't a man like Kelvin

Greene be armed? Yet no gun was found on him or in his car. Now where would his gun be? With his killer? Wouldn't that be too dangerous? I suggest we go dig around up at the cemetery. If we don't do it now, there will be oodles of folks coming around for Memorial Day. And if anybody sees us, we'll just say we're remembering our beloved dead a bit early. I'll bring some foxgloves and poppies. Oh—and a shovel. You bring one, too."

As far as I was concerned, Vida still wasn't making sense. "Vida—even if you're right, that gun could be six feet deep. Wouldn't it be smarter to ask Milo to have the regular grave diggers search for the weapon?"

"Of course it would," Vida agreed. "But Milo won't do it. He'll think it's a waste of time—and money. I'm sure the county would have to pay the grave diggers. It's the Peabody brothers, and they do it part-time, when they're out of work in the woods. They charge the world."

If I thought Vida was on a wild-goose chase, Milo certainly would, too. But the lure of cleaning my oven wasn't that strong. Shortly before noon, I picked up Vida and her bouquet. She'd stuck one of the poppies in the band of her straw hat. Along with the flowers and the shovel, she'd brought a metal detector.

"It's Roger's," she explained. "He hunts treasure with it. Isn't that darling? You should have seen my brother, Ennis, pitch a fit when Roger found the steel plate in his head! Honestly! You'd think it was some sort of state secret!"

Fortunately, it was only a three-minute ride from Vida's house to the cemetery entrance. Thus, I didn't have to listen to more adorable tales about Roger the Terrible. Vida, however, was wrong about the cemetery being deserted on this particular Saturday. There were several cars parked along the winding roadway, and I guessed that they were mourners who had come early to pay their Memorial Day respects.

"Out-of-towners," Vida grumbled. "Ex-Alpiners. They flee to the city and come back once a year with a piddling plant. I'll bet they don't even bother to call on the living."

I didn't argue. I hadn't visited my parents' grave site at Holyrood in North Seattle for almost two years. I felt remiss. They had been dead for two decades, taken too soon in a car accident returning from my brother's ordination. Ben, who hadn't lived in the vicinity since, had a better track record than I did—he offered a memorial Mass every time he came to town. I'd been absent from all but three of them.

Fortunately, there were no other cars parked near Axel Swensen's grave. That, I assumed, was because Axel had outlived any mourners. While the funeral flowers had been removed, the marker hadn't yet been set in the ground, nor had new sod been laid. Apparently the Peabody brothers had other fish to fry. They certainly didn't have many trees to cut during the present logging hiatus.

Vida was working with the metal detector. At first, I'd thought it was a mere toy, but now that I took a good look, I saw it was fairly sophisticated. Roger, naturally, must have the best, the little spoiled wretch.

"We don't want to get confused by the casket," Vida remarked, moving slowly around the bare earth that delineated Axel's grave. "We should have brought sandwiches. My father-in-law, Rufus Runkel, loved to have family picnics in cemeteries. He always found them so quiet. And the flat markers were very convenient for spreading out a lunch. We'd go from here to Skykomish to Gold Bar to Sultan to . . . Well!" The detector let off a couple of beeps.

"Are you sure it's not the casket?" I asked, shielding my eyes from the midday sun.

Vida shook her head. "Too far to the left." She stomped on the ground in her sensible shoes. "Axel's right under me. Let's get the shovels."

It was too late to protest. Still, I didn't much like what we were about to do, for various reasons. First, it was ghoulish. Second, it was probably illegal. Third, I was certain we would come up empty-handed.

Vida, however, had no such qualms. She dug vigorously, dirt flying in all directions. I relieved her at intervals, during which she put her foxgloves and poppies in a vase and then stuck the bouquet at the head of the grave.

"Nice," she remarked. "How are you doing?"

We had dug straight down, about three feet. "Okay, but I don't see anything."

Vida tried the metal detector again. This time it beeped

more loudly. She took over with the shovel. The sun was growing warmer, and so was I. Another foot, then she let me have a turn. Luckily, the ground was fairly soft, no doubt from the numerous springs that trickled through the mountainside. At the five-foot level, Vida relieved me. She dug more efficiently than I did, probably because of her vast gardening experience. Now standing in the narrow hole, Vida seemed oblivious to the dirt she was getting on her gray slacks and print blouse.

"Hand me that detector," she commanded.

I obeyed. The detector made loud, insistent noises. Vida kept digging. A minute later, she was rewarded with the sound of metal on metal. Looking up out of the hole with a triumphant grin, she handed me her shovel.

"I don't suppose we should worry about prints," she called in a muffled voice as she bent down to retrieve whatever she had hit.

"Probably not," I replied as a car drove by slowly. The driver stared, but passed on. I wished we hadn't brought the Jag. It was too easily identifiable in Alpine.

In the hole, Vida was chuckling. "I told you so—one gun." She held up a pistol, waving it like a trophy. "Yoo-hoo, take this, Emma."

Gingerly, I complied. The weapon wasn't particularly heavy. I peered at the lettering. "It's a Beretta, Model 87," I informed Vida.

"Yes, yes, I could see that." Her voice was still muffled as she remained bending over in the hole. "Here, I found another souvenir. Give me that metal detector."

Along with the gun, I was now holding a watch. It was a Timex with a round face and a black band. The band had worn through. I retrieved the rest of the imitation leather. To its credit, the watch was still going: The hands showed that it was twenty-seven minutes after twelve.

From the hole, I could hear the metal detector sending off low little beeps. "It must be the casket," said Vida. "Or the fillings in Axel's teeth."

I winced, but Vida seemed unperturbed. Her efforts were now concentrated on getting out of the hole. This was not an easy task. Vida clambered up the side while I held onto her arms. She was no featherweight, and I practically threw out my back trying to hoist her. In the end, she created a couple of footholds and heaved herself on top of the grave site.

"Oooooh! That was a job!" Vida leaned on her shovel, shaking off dirt like a pup and rubbing her eyes. "Let's fill in the hole and get out of here."

This time, we could work together. The job went swiftly, if a bit slapdash. Somehow, we ended up with too much dirt. Vida spread it around, then tamped it down with her feet. If anyone had driven by, they would have thought she was dancing on Axel Swensen's grave.

Hot, tired, and dirty, we headed back to her house, which was closer to the cemetery than mine. Vida immediately put the teakettle on.

"I've got some casserole left from last night," she called to me from the kitchen while I washed up in the bathroom. "Would you like a bit of lunch?"

I declined. "I had a huge breakfast," I lied, coming out to sit at the dinette table. Behind me, Cupcake was singing his head off. "Let's have a look at the gun and the watch."

Vida had placed both items on a towel. "I doubt that at this point Milo can tell if this gun has been fired recently," she mused. "But he should be able to match the gun with the bullet they got out of Kelvin Greene."

I was no ballistics expert. "Maybe," I allowed. "What you're saying is that this is Kelvin's gun, and somehow the killer got hold of it, shot him, and dumped it in the open grave, right?"

Vida stared at the gun. "I guess so. That would indicate a struggle. Yet Milo made no mention of it. But how else would the killer have gotten hold of Kelvin's weapon? We must assume a person of strength." Over the rims of her glasses, she raised her eyebrows. "A man."

"We don't know for sure that this was Kelvin's gun," I objected. "The killer may have had two guns—if the same person actually shot both Kelvin and Wesley. If you meet someone in a cemetery and end up shooting him, it's probably premeditated, right?"

Slowly, Vida nodded. "A cemetery isn't the usual place for a rendezvous."

I was stymied; so was Vida. "The watch," I said, pointing to the round face. "Somebody lost it. That backs up the theory of a struggle."

Vida had picked up the watch and was patching it together, broken strap and all. She held the timepiece in the palm of her hand. "I fastened it in the hole that was most worn. Small, wouldn't you say?"

"Try it on," I suggested.

Vida did. Holding the broken band next to the crystal, we could see that it would be too tight. She handed the watch to me. It was too loose. I was beginning to feel like Goldilocks. "A woman," I conjectured. "Or a small-boned man."

"Which makes no sense." Vida sounded irritated. "Could a woman—or a rather slight man—overcome an armed Kelvin Greene? That's what we're saying."

"Maybe the watch belongs to one of the Peabody brothers. Or one of the mourners at the funeral."

Vida gave a shake of her gray curls. "Have you ever seen the Peabody brothers? They're great hulking things. At the interment, nobody got close enough to the grave to lose a watch except the pallbearers, and they were all big rawboned Scandinavians."

For several moments, we sat gazing at our find. "We'll have to turn these things over to the sheriff," I said.

"You told me Milo was gone." Vida stood up as the teakettle boiled. "I'll call my nephew, Billy. He's on duty this weekend."

Vida served our tea in bone-china cups. It refreshed, but didn't inspire. The best I could come up with was the suggestion that there were indeed two killers. Perhaps both of them had met Kelvin Greene in the cemetery.

"Then who?" Vida asked. "We're having enough trouble figuring out the identity of one."

"The key is Wesley Charles, not Kelvin Greene." I spoke with a conviction I didn't really understand. "Both men were linked with the Jerome Cole killing. Bear in mind that Jerome wasn't shot. He was bludgeoned, and it could have been an accident. Wesley Charles could have claimed self-defense, and maybe been acquitted. But he didn't. He insisted he was innocent. Was his attorney an idiot, or was Wesley a man of principle?"

Vida sat hunched forward, one hand resting on the other. "A public defender, wasn't it? You'd think he—it was a man, as I recall from the newspaper articles—would have plea-bargained. Do you remember the name?"

"Zerbil," I answered, off the top of my head. "It reminded me of gerbil."

Vida made a face. "As in having the brains of. Let me get my Seattle phone book."

There was only one Zerbil listed in the directory, on Phinney Ridge. The first name was Stanley. Vida dialed, but got an answering machine. She didn't leave a message.

"Drat," she said, replacing the phone. "He may be gone for the weekend."

Another silence fell between us. I was getting hungry, but didn't dare admit it for fear of being force-fed the leftover casserole. Vida sipped her tea, staring with unseeing eyes at Cupcake's cage.

"What you're trying to articulate, Emma," she finally said in a careful voice, "is that Wesley Charles did not kill Jerome Cole. Someone else did, and Kelvin Greene knew it. Perhaps Kelvin was paid to testify against Wesley. Bribed, if you will. Kelvin then . . . oh!" She looked startled.

"What?" I leaned forward, setting my cup and saucer aside.

Vida had grown excited. "Kelvin was blackmailing the real murderer. His demands became too great. That's why he was killed." She folded her hands and sat up straight, looking very pleased with herself.

Vida's theory fit in with the vague ideas I'd been forming on my own. "And Wesley Charles?"

"Wesley knew the truth. He may have been bribed to take the rap or whatever they used to call it in crime fiction. A twenty-year sentence? He might not serve ten."

Vida's hypothesis didn't convince me. "It'd take big money to make up for Wesley Charles's loss of freedom, then to pay off Kelvin Greene as well."

"True." Vida frowned, concentrating on our puzzle. "Who has oodles of money? The Wilsons?"

I disparaged the idea. "What have they got to do with Jerome Cole? Shane and Cyndi may have known the whole cast of characters from Seattle, but not Todd and Wendy. I can't see any connection there."

"The drugs." Vida refused to give up her pet theory. However, she saw the skepticism on my face and made an impatient gesture. "All right, let's skip that for now. Let's go back to Wesley Charles. At least he knew he wasn't the killer. Maybe he knew who the real murderer was and maybe he didn't. But as long as he was still alive, he was a danger to whoever killed Jerome Cole."

I was still bothered by Vida's deductions. "Wait—we've already said Jerome's death could have been an accident, or the result of a fight. Why would the real killer be so upset about getting caught?"

Vida grimaced. Then her eyes scanned the ceiling, which, like the rest of her house, was free of dust and grime. "Because it wasn't an accident," she declared. "Or if it was, the killer is a coward."

"A coward?" I was taken aback. "Does a coward then go out and shoot two more people?"

Vida considered. "No, you're right. Whoever killed Jerome Cole did it in cold blood. And then did the same to Kelvin Greene and Wesley Charles. It's Wesley's murder that bothers me most. The man was in chains. How did he get off the bus and make his escape?"

"I gather the prisoners were taken off the bus, to check for injuries," I said, trying to recall precisely what Milo had told me. "There were only a few—ten, at most. There are two armed guards and the driver who travel on those buses. Wesley slipped away in the confusion over the school children and the other vehicles."

Still thoughtful, Vida wagged her head from side to side. "Slipped away to where? I know that highway like I know the back of my hand. He would have had to walk along the shoulder, straight into town or on to the Stevens Pass junction."

"He could have gone over the guardrail," I argued. "Through the trees, and out across the street."

Vida gave me a caustic look. "In full daylight, in a well-populated area, within view of the Twin Rivers guard tower? Really, Emma, I expect better from you."

"Well, he went *somewhere*," I retorted, on the defensive.

"Yes, he did," Vida allowed, again very serious. "But did he go there alone? Was there an accomplice, say, in a car? Was this whole thing preplanned to get at Wesley Charles?" Behind her glasses, Vida blinked twice in rapid succession.

I caught my breath. "My God!" I whispered. "It would have to be an elaborate—and very daring—plan!"

"Everything about these murders is daring," Vida declared. Showing an uncharacteristic sign of anxiety, she ran her tongue lightly over her lips. "I believe we're facing an extremely ruthless killer, Emma."

Impressed by Vida's alarm, I grew subdued. "Maybe we should leave this up to Milo."

Vida was gnawing on her thumb. "No. We can't do that."

"Vida . . ."

"It's not that Milo is stupid. He's not. At least he isn't any more stupid than most men," Vida amended. "Milo has got an idea in his head. Regardless of what he says, he sees this as a racial situation. That is, somehow it's confined to one race. Marilynn's alibi for Wesley's murder notwithstanding, if Milo were forced to make an arrest, he'd haul her in. He's got no imagination. Most of all, he doesn't have the means."

As much as I didn't like to think it, Vida might be right. There was also the nagging doubt I'd experienced at dinner the previous night: I was Marilynn's alibi for Wesley Charles's murder. But when I told Marilynn I'd pick her up at five o'clock Thursday evening, she had asked me to wait until five-thirty. I'd assumed she had unfinished business at the clinic. But what if she had had other, more deadly, unfinished business, such as Wesley Charles? I suppressed a little shiver, and didn't mention my misgivings to Vida.

Later, I realized my mistake.

Chapter Fourteen

CARLA AND LIBBY stopped by shortly after I returned from Vida's house. Carla was agog, full of her evening with Peyton Flake in Seattle. They had gone to Palisades, the glitzy restaurant at Smith Cove overlooking Elliott Bay and downtown. They had eaten wonderful food, drunk marvelous drinks, and capped the evening with a jazz session in Pioneer Square. Ginny and Rick had had fun, too.

Libby Boyd listened to her roommate's giddy recital with an indulgent attitude. "They must have had a good time," she finally said when allowed to get a word in edgewise. "It was almost three A.M. before she got home."

"We practically closed down Jazz Alley," Carla exclaimed, getting her second wind. "Peyts knows all about jazz. He chose the wines, too. He even wore a tie!"

"Did Rick wear his orange hair?" I inquired.

"Oh, sure, but it doesn't matter in Seattle. It's okay to be weird there." Removing her sunglasses, Carla turned sober. "I wish I were back in the city. Alpine is so *dull*."

Despite the growing body count, I had to agree with Carla. I, too, missed the city. Before moving from Portland to Alpine, I had consoled myself with the fact that Seattle was less than two hours away. I could drive in anytime for the opera, the theatre, and sporting events. But I rarely did. I stayed in my rut, spending my weekends working around the house and getting caught up with the rest of my life.

"You want some excitement?" I asked on a sudden whim.

Carla looked dubious; Libby was wary. "Like what?" asked Carla.

We were out in the backyard where I'd been wiping down the lawn furniture I'd hauled out of the carport.

Swiftly, I brushed off a couple of the chairs. "Here, sit down, let me make a proposition to one or both of you."

My brainstorm would serve two purposes: One, it might prove or disprove Vida's theory about the Wilsons and Marlow Whipp. Two, it would perk up Carla's life, and maybe Libby's, too. Though why Carla should need a diversion when romance had finally come to her, I couldn't guess. It was, however, in character for my flighty staff reporter. Her attention span was notoriously short.

"Wait a minute," said Carla, after I had related my plan. "You want one or both of us to go to Marlow's store and hint that we want to buy drugs? Why us?"

"You're young, you're not locals," I explained. "Frankly, it would be better if Libby did this. Marlow knows who you are, Carla. He might be suspicious. Have you ever been in Marlow's store, Libby?"

Libby shook her head. "I've driven by it, though. It looks like a dump."

I studied Libby in her casual clothes. She was wearing cutoffs, a striped tank top, and sandals. With her wholesome face, her curly fair hair, and no makeup, she could pass for considerably younger than what I guessed to be her twenty-five years. Marlow might not notice the tiny lines around her eyes.

Libby shrugged. "I'll do it. When?"

I glanced at my watch. It was after three o'clock. "Now is as good a time as later. There shouldn't be any students hanging around because it's a Saturday. In fact, I don't know why Marlow bothers to stay open on weekends."

Carla was pouting. "Hey, I thought this was supposed to be exciting for me! What do I get to do, drive the getaway car?"

Momentarily stumped, I sat with my mouth open. "No," I finally responded, talking fast. "You can go in a few minutes later and ask about the espresso machine. Make sure he really has a steamer. Tell him Ed would like to talk to him about an ad."

"That sounds like work." Carla was whining. "Why can't I search the premises or something while Libby distracts Marlow?"

It wasn't a bad idea. "If you do, don't go in together," I cautioned.

Now full of enthusiasm, Carla sprung to her feet. "Let's go, Libby. We'll be like spies. Undercover stuff. Maybe you should use a foreign accent."

I shuddered, picturing Carla in false whiskers and Libby dressed like Mata Hari. "Report back to me," I called after them. "I'll give you a beer."

I was watching them drive away in Carla's secondhand Honda when I heard the phone ring. Hurrying into the house, I caught the call just before it switched over to the answering machine.

"Mom—the sun's out!" Adam's voice crackled over the line, making me smile. My son was beginning to sound like Ben. "I need shorts and tees and a whole bunch of stuff!"

My smile faded. "Did the bears eat your old wardrobe?" I asked in my sarcastic mother's tone.

"No, but Rich Tallfirs sat on my boom box. The lid for the CD player broke off. Can you send me a new one?"

"A new lid? Why not just get it fixed?"

"No, a new boom box. This one sounds funny sometimes."

"They all sound funny to me. Maybe it's what you're playing on it."

"Don't be so uncool, Mom. I've had this thing for almost two years." Adam's tone was aggrieved.

"I've had the TV for six, the stereo for five, and my small, modestly priced radio for twelve. Forget it, Adam, I'm broke. Just like your boom box. And don't tell me there aren't any stores in Fairbanks. You don't need much, you're leaving in less than two weeks."

"But that's just it!" Adam cried, not so much on a crackle as a wail. "I'm headed for Tuba City, and it's going to be a hundred and ten degrees in the shade! Do you want me to die of heatstroke? I need to pick up some stuff in San Francisco."

"Now hold on," I persisted, thinking how many times my son and I had carried on similar arguments—and how few of them I had won. "You're stopping in San Francisco on the way to Arizona?" Adam mumbled his assent. I wondered if he'd talked to Tom again. I wouldn't ask. "Could it be that you want lots of money to spend at the tremendously cool shops in San Francisco as opposed to Fred Meyer in Fairbanks? Could it be that you have visions of parading around the Navajo reservation as Mr. Hip Dude?"

Adam made some sort of noise that was possibly obscene. "Don't be dumb, Mom. Sure, I'd rather look for stuff in San Fran. Who wouldn't? But I don't want to ask . . . *him* to pay for it. Do you?"

Adam had hit me where it hurt. He knew of my fierce desire for independence. And I knew that despite the amicable meetings, despite Tom's generosity with plane fares, despite Adam's natural yearning for a father, my son—*our* son—still wouldn't call the man who had given him life anything but *sir*—and *him*.

"I'll send a money order for two hundred dollars," I stated firmly. "Not a penny more. Got it?"

"Not yet," Adam replied glibly. "When do I pick it up at the post office?"

"What's wrong with the regular mail? Did Rich Tallfirs sit on your postal box, too?"

"He's there now with my boom box, listening to the only FM station between here and Anchorage." Having gotten some of his way, Adam was now inclined to become jocular. I asked him if he had scrapped his plan to stop off in Alpine on the way south. He wasn't sure. It was a real mess dealing with the airlines. As of right now, he was booked on a flight from Fairbanks via Seattle to San Francisco. If he had a layover, the price would go way up. Maybe it'd be better if he waited until August to come to Alpine. That, he reminded me, had been his original plan.

Naturally, I was disappointed. Was Adam choosing Tom over me? Or San Francisco over Alpine? I recalled Carla's comment about small-town dullness and decided that maybe after the better part of a year in Fairbanks, Adam needed a good stiff dose of a big, bustling metropolis. He certainly wouldn't get that in Tuba City. Our conversation continued on less controversial lines than money, clothes, boom boxes, and Tom Cavanaugh. By the time we hung up, I was feeling proud of my son, pleased with our ability to communicate, cheered by the bond he was forging with both Tom and Ben. I was also feeling poor, but at least I was used to that.

I was making inroads on my oven when Carla and Libby returned. They came up the walk like a pair of conspirators, whispering and giggling. I let them in and offered cold beer before the interrogation began. Carla accepted, but Libby asked for bottled water, if I had any.

I did, and brought out three glasses. I joined Carla in having a beer, which tasted surprisingly good after my exertions with the lawn furniture and the oven.

"Well?" I asked, settling into my favorite armchair. "Did Marlow Whipp offer you a line of coke?"

Carla giggled some more, that ear-rattling sound that always made me grit my teeth. "Vida is losing it! How in the world could she think some dud like old Marlow could be peddling crack? Tell her, Libby."

Libby sat forward on the sofa, shaking her head. "I was terribly coy. I went in and strolled around and didn't say anything for a long time. Finally Marlow asked if I needed any help. I said, 'Yeah. What did he have in mind?' I sort of wiggled my eyebrows." Libby demonstrated, while Carla giggled anew. "Marlow looked embarrassed. I think he thought I meant something sexual."

"*Gack! Gack!*" Opening her mouth wide, Carla made thrusting movements with her index finger. I was beginning to think my bright idea was pretty dim.

Acknowledging Carla's clowning with a smile, Libby resumed her account: "I decided I'd get more specific. I noted that Marlow carried beer and wine and cigarettes. That was great, I told him, but tame. Didn't he have something a little stronger?"

"How did he look when you said that?" I inquired, ignoring Carla who now had her finger in her mouth, pulling down her jaw, and making an idiot noise. I trusted that she was imitating Marlow Whipp. At least I hoped so. It was unsettling to think that she was merely being herself.

Libby considered my question briefly, but carefully. "Puzzled, really. Then he said he did, but it wasn't ready. I got sort of excited, figuring I was on the right track. But he pointed to that espresso machine and told me he still didn't know how to operate it. Or the steamer that had just arrived yesterday." Libby looked aggravated; Carla rolled her eyes.

I was disappointed. "Was that it?" I asked.

Libby gave a quick shake of her head. "I made one last try. I acted indignant, said I'd heard that he sold more than what was out front. I got out my wallet, showing him a fifty. He couldn't tell it was the only money I had."

Carla was squirming around on the sofa next to Libby. "Now we get to the good part," she murmured in an aside.

"Marlow looked interested," Libby continued. "At least I *thought* he did. He just stood there though, so I told him I wanted good stuff, nothing that was cut with cheap crap. Marlow seemed worried or maybe confused. He said it was all cut the same, in mint condition. What was I talking about? I said, 'You tell me, and we'll see if we can do business.' Marlow said to give him a name. That threw me. Did he mean a contact or a password or a drug? I've heard drugs called all kinds of things, but I don't pay much attention. It's all poison as far as I'm concerned. I took a wild guess and said, 'Grass.' Marlow said he didn't know that one. I believed him." Libby tucked her feet under her bottom and sighed. "I blanked. I couldn't think of anything but crack and pot. I had a feeling that if I asked for coke, he'd have offered me diet or regular."

The room fell silent, except for Carla's twitching around on the sofa. The Burlington-Northern freight whistled as it passed slowly through town. The train rarely stopped in Alpine these days.

"He's either very cagey or else he's not dealing drugs after all," I finally concluded. "I wonder why he perked up when he saw the money? What did he mean about a name?"

Libby had no idea. It struck her as an odd question, too. I turned to Carla. "Did you get a chance to do anything?"

"Well, sure!" Carla bounced a couple of times for emphasis. "While Libby was inside, I went around back. There's a storage room attached, but you can only get at it through the store. No windows, either. But he has a Dumpster between the store and the alley. I went through it as well as I could. I didn't have much time, and I had to keep watching for Libby to leave."

"And?" Silly me, I was being hopeful.

Carla's enthusiasm finally dwindled. "I didn't find much. Old cartons, pop cans, rotten produce, newspapers. What you'd expect, I guess."

I suppose I was expecting small plastic bags, hypodermic syringes, and roach clips. I said as much. Carla shook her head, the long black hair sailing around her shoulders.

"Not a sign of that stuff. I told you everything I saw—mostly cartons and newspapers. I don't think he sells many copies of *The Times* and *P-I*. Maybe everybody around here would rather read *The Advocate*."

If Carla thought to cheer me, she was wrong. Instead, I was discouraged that so few people read a daily newspaper. It wasn't a good omen for weeklies.

But something she had said did pique my interest. "Cartons? From what? Marlow can't have tons of stuff shipped to the store because he doesn't have much turnover."

Shoving the long hair off her face, Carla turned pensive. "Gee—I don't know. . . . I didn't pay much attention. He'd mashed them down, to fit into the Dumpster. I don't mean there were zillions, or anything—just quite a few. You know, a couple dozen or so."

That still seemed like too many for Marlow Whipp's atrophied business. The Dumpster would be emptied every Tuesday. In five days, Marlow Whipp had received two dozen cartons of what? I couldn't think of a single item in his store that would move that fast, except dairy products, pop, beer, and cigarettes. As far as I knew, only the cigarettes would be shipped in a cardboard box.

I praised Carla and Libby for their covert operation. They finished their drinks, then decided it was time to leave.

"No hot dates tonight?" I inquired at the door.

Carla grew sorrowful. "Peyts is on emergency call the rest of the weekend."

I turned to Libby. "You've got the weekend off. Don't tell me you and Carla are going to sit around and watch videos."

Libby grinned. "I've got four whole days off, in fact. No videos for me, at least not tonight." She pointed to her watch. "Come on, Carla, it's after five. You're the one who wants to stop at the Grocery Basket on the way home."

"I have to eat," Carla pouted, following Libby out to the car. " 'Bye, Emma. See you Monday."

I went back into the house, determined to finish cleaning the blasted oven. I got only as far as the dining area when I heard the frantic rapping at the front door. It was Carla. She'd forgotten her sunglasses.

"Thank God!" she exclaimed as fervently as if she'd lost the family jewels. "I thought I might have dropped them in the Dumpster!" Whirling around, she headed for the door.

"Carla!" I called after her. She stopped on the threshold. I beckoned her to come a step closer. "Who's the guy? Libby's guy, I mean." Over Carla's shoulder, I could see Libby sitting in the passenger seat of the Honda. There was no way she could hear us.

"You don't have to whisper," Carla chided. "It's not a secret. I thought you knew." Carla put her sunglasses on, took them off, wiped the lenses with the tail of her cotton shirt, and replaced them on her nose. "She's going with Shane Campbell. They've been dating for months."

"And you thought I was crazy!" Vida huffed as we climbed up Sixth Street from her house to Marlow Whipp's store. It was after six, and Marlow had closed at five. "Cartons! Carla! The girl can't even count properly! She probably saw two! Dog food, I'll bet!"

"You're tall and I'm not. Carla's shorter than both of us. I would have brought Milo along if he hadn't gone off with Honoria." We cut down the alley, a dirt track lined with garbage cans, tricycles, garden implements, and an occasional cat. Blackberry vines grew helter-skelter over sagging fences. Morning glory wound around clothesline poles and trellises. There were nettles, too, and great clumps of weeds that threatened to choke out the ferns. We were a mere block away from Vida's neat bungalow and only two from the Campbells' handsome home, yet the neighborhood changed drastically between Tyee and Spruce Streets. It was probably because the houses were not only old but small, and too close to the high school. Parking had long been a problem in the area. If Alpine had a slum, this was it. Fortunately, the blight covered no more than three blocks.

"And Shane!" Vida's voice rang out on the quiet May evening. "Are he and Libby getting married? Is that what Wendy and Cyndi have been hinting? How did they meet? Oh, I know—in Seattle. But *how*? Did she get herself transferred up here to be near him? It *must* be serious."

It was pointless to try to hush Vida. Her voice sounded like a trumpet, and over the fences, I saw at least a couple of heads turn in our direction. But we had almost reached the rear of Marlow's store, and Vida grew silent.

The lid of the Dumpster was heavy, but we managed. I marveled that Carla had opened it on her own.

"We should have brought Roger," Vida mumbled, holding onto her straw gardening hat as she leaned into the Dumpster. "We could have lifted him in here."

And left him there was the evil thought that flashed through my mind. Dismissing such cruel notions, I concentrated on the task at hand. "Well? How many cartons? Two? Or two dozen?"

Vida harrumphed. "Carla's right, for once. There are quite a few. You're right, too. Cigarettes. Wrigley's gum. More cigarettes."

I could see into the Dumpster, but I couldn't reach as far as Vida. She was bending way over, and I tried not to think about the target her rear end was providing for any of her local detractors. "What's that?" I asked, motioning at a flat piece of cardboard on her left. " 'Death Something-or-Other.' It doesn't sound like groceries to me."

" 'Death Row/Interscope,' " Vida replied promptly. "Goodness, how gruesome! It can't be canned goods. Whatever happened to the Jolly Green Giant? Here, a box marked 'Tommy Boy.' 'Jive.' Hmmmm . . ." Vida continued to rummage. " 'Atlantic,' " she called from deeper yet in the Dumpster. " 'Warner Brothers.' It seems these are recording companies. Since when," she demanded, straightening up and resettling her hat on her head, "does Marlow Whipp sell records?"

I felt as mystified as Vida looked. "I didn't see any records—or tapes or CDs—when I was in the store the other day. Surely he'd have a big display. Especially with that many." I pointed to the Dumpster that contained the empty cartons. "Can you tell if the boxes held tapes or what?"

Vida shot me a scathing look. "Oh, good heavens! What's wrong with a regular record? Long-play or forty-five or seventy-eight? What's all this nonsense about teeny-weeny discs and tapes that come unwound like so many snakes all over the place? Roger is starting to listen to music, and his room looks like a ticker-tape parade!" Catching herself in a rare criticism of her grandson, Vida looked chagrined. "It's not his fault, of course. I'm sure the companies make those tapes so that they can't be reused, and the poor children have to buy more. Roger is the victim of a Madison Avenue marketing ploy."

Roger as victim of anything short of a Scud missile struck me as unlikely. This, however, was not the time to argue the point. Indeed, it never was with Vida. "Kids don't buy records anymore," I pointed out. "Tapes and CDs— that's it. But Marlow would have them prominently displayed. Maybe even some promotional material."

Foregoing my assistance, Vida closed the Dumpster. "He might be just starting," she suggested. "Like the espresso machine. Marlow's such a dunce he probably hasn't figured out how to sell music, either."

A couple of eight year olds came roaring down the alley on small dirt bikes. They paid no attention to us, but we couldn't count on that kind of indifference from adults. I suggested we leave. Vida concurred. She asked if I'd had dinner. Fearing yet another reprise of the casserole, I lied and said I had.

"That's too bad," she lamented as we trudged back down the alley. "I thought we might drive down to the Venison Inn and have supper together. We could mull."

Taken aback, I allowed that I hadn't eaten much. "I could have something light and keep you company," I offered, sounding uncommonly meek.

Vida paused to examine her soiled gardening clothes. "I should change," she muttered.

I was still wearing the old clothes I'd had on while doing my Saturday chores. "It's Alpine. It's us. Nobody will care."

But Vida cared. She would not "go downtown" looking like a slavey, as she put it. "We'll change, and I'll meet you there in twenty minutes," she said, checking her small jeweled watch. "Seven, straight up."

I agreed. My car was parked on Tyee Street in front of her house. It needed washing, and I felt guilty. The Jag was my only material pride and joy. I'd neglected it for the sake of my oven, which was low on my list of personal priorities. It served me right that during my absence someone had etched FUCK YOU on the hood.

"Really," said Vida, "how can these youngsters be so crude? Though words are words, and if they'd written 'Partake in marital relations' you would be amused, not offended."

"I'm not offended," I said with a grin. "I've raised a son. There's nothing I haven't heard."

"Thank heavens my girls were grown before all this filth became so ordinary. Of course, the shock value is debased by common usage. I'm wearing slacks," Vida added as she headed through her garden gate.

"Okay," I called back. I paused in the act of wiping off the obscenity with a Kleenex. "Vida!" I shouted. She stopped at the steps to her porch. "That's it! Obscenity! Explicit lyrics! Censorship!"

At a trot, Vida came down the path. "Emma, are you out of your mind?" She glanced up and down the quiet street. "What will the neighbors think?"

Making feverish hand gestures, I waved her into silence. "The recordings. Tapes, CDs, whatever. The do-gooders who've banned rock and rap music. The kids can't buy that stuff in Alpine. Except," I added, on a note of triumph, "from Marlow Whipp."

Chapter Fifteen

IF VIDA WAS surprised when I ordered the steak sandwich with a side of fries and a green salad, she gave no sign. Rather, she was too intrigued with my theory about Marlow Whipp's grocery store. After giving our order, her first question was what Marlow's illicit trade had to do with Wendy and Todd Wilson.

"As before," I told her. "They provided the stuff, in this case, not drugs, but recordings. Marlow is indeed the middleman, peddling to the high school, maybe junior high and even grade school kids. Alpine Middle School is only a block away from your house. That's two blocks from Marlow."

Vida absorbed the information. "The grade school is across town, though. But," she added accusingly, as if I should be personally responsible, "your parochial school is much closer, on Fourth and Cascade." Obviously, Vida felt that Catholic morals were far more likely to be corrupted than those of the public school—Protestant—children.

I didn't argue the point. There were Catholics who would be every bit as hidebound as their Protestant brethren. There also would be those inclined to greater liberalism. "It takes all kinds," I murmured. And we had them at St. Mildred's, for better or for worse.

"Where," Vida asked, after drinking half her ice water at a gulp, "do the Wilsons get these recordings?"

I shrugged. "They've got a contact someplace. Seattle, maybe. Of course, they have to pay up front. I don't know what the profit margin would be, but I have a feeling they aren't as rich as we think they are. I mean, they've got extra cash, but X-rated records don't bring in what drugs would."

Vida nodded. "Marlow makes something, too. We've been thinking in the thousands. Hundreds would be more likely. Still, it would explain why the Wilsons moved their bank account. They didn't want anyone around here to notice how much money was coming in and going out."

"Coming in, anyway. I bet they deal in cash at the distributor level." I gave Vida a sheepish look. "I don't even know if any of this is illegal. The legislature has tried to make it a criminal act to sell offensive music to minors, but the state supreme court is expected to rule otherwise. Fuzzy Baugh and the council haven't passed any laws. It's mainly a boycott at this point, and the churches have enough clout to make it work."

Vida, who had ordered pot roast, waited until our waitress had delivered the salads before speaking again. "It's a letdown," she complained. "If it had been drugs—and, of course, I'm glad it's not—that would have been dreadful—then we might have had a connection with Kelvin Greene. But there isn't any. Unless . . ." She brightened a bit. "Jerome Cole was a musician, wasn't he?"

I made a gesture of dismissal. "Jazz. I doubt he had any contacts with the recording business. At least not with distribution."

Vida deflated. "We've made no progress. I'm ashamed of us."

Silently, I agreed. How long had Wendy and Todd Wilson been in the black-market record business? Probably not long, I mused. Perhaps since the start of school; maybe only after the ban had been observed in the past few months. Any previous signs of affluence were no doubt due to the fact that they had no kids. I could understand that. I took a notepad from my handbag and wrote, "Go to bank Mon. A.M. M.O. $200." Yes, I, too, could take a long trip if I weren't shelling out big chunks of my income for Adam every month.

My steak sandwich arrived along with Vida's pot roast. We were both unnaturally quiet. The Venison Inn, however, was busy as usual with Saturday night diners. The dentist, Dr. Bob Starr, and his wife were in the opposite booth, no doubt girding for their daughter's wedding, which was coming up over the Memorial Day weekend. On our way in, we had seen Stella and Richie Magruder. Stella had stopped me, advising that I hadn't quite gotten the knack of the new haircut yet. I told her I'd been cleaning my oven. Vida, of course, had known just about everybody present, including one of her nephews, Ross Blatt, and his wife, Lynnette.

"The carrots aren't done," Vida remarked, eating them anyway.

"I don't have carrots." Neither of us sounded very interested in our food.

"Is there any point in telling Milo about Marlow's sideline?" Vida wondered aloud. "All it would do is raise a hue and cry with the antismut people."

I forked up some rare steak and soggy toast. "We've got to let him know, just to keep him filled in. Vida, how do the Presbyterians feel about this issue?"

Vida pursed her lips. "It's come up."

"And?"

Stirring gravy into her mashed potatoes, Vida threw me an icy look. "We're divided. You'd be surprised how divided Presbyterians can get. It didn't used to be that way."

I suppressed a smile. "Really? Like how?"

"Well," Vida began, knife and fork poised, "there are traditionalists and there are ... ah ... modernists. As a rule, I adhere to tradition. It's always so much more sensible. But on this music to-do, I felt bound to support free speech. Being a journalist, and all." Vida gave me an appealing look. "At the last Women's Institute meeting—the first Tuesday of May—we had quite an argument. I didn't tell you about it because ..." She actually blushed. "I didn't want it to get into the paper. It made us sound foolish."

"Vida!" I didn't know whether to laugh or scold.

"If it were your Wild Eyes or whatever you Catholics call it, you'd do the same," Vida asserted.

"I don't belong to the YLIs," I said, not even sure if the Young Ladies Institute existed in the post–Vatican II Church. If it did, it was probably called something like Single-Again Christians. SACs. It figured.

"The discussion got quite heated," Vida continued. "Jean Campbell called for a vote on whether or not to join the boycott. We tied, eleven to eleven. Grace Grundle—she chairs—was asked to cast the deciding ballot. Grace abstained. We're going to reconsider when we meet the first Tuesday in June."

My distress over Vida's own form of censorship was diverted by her mention of Jean Campbell's role. "Was Jean for or against the boycott?"

"Oh, all for it. She can be a terrible bluenose." Vida smirked. "It's funny, isn't it? Her own daughter smuggling ribald recordings into town! Oh, dear—I mustn't gloat!"

I swallowed my last french fry and put down my fork. "Not her daughter," I said abruptly. "Her son."

Vida stared. "What?"

"Shane." I waited to see if Vida had joined my wavelength. She hadn't, but it wasn't her fault. Vida hadn't shopped as much in the city as I had. "Fred Meyer sells recordings, tapes, the lot, in all their stores. That's the connection. I'll bet Shane Campbell was getting those shipments through his former contacts in Seattle."

Vida's eyes made a circuit of the restaurant, floor to ceiling. "Well now. And Wendy was the marketing device, spurring on the students. My, my." She savored the deduction, then frowned. "It still doesn't help us find our killer."

"No." But my voice didn't carry conviction. It seemed to me that our discovery should lead us closer to the murderer. I just couldn't see how. Then.

Sunday's priest was from Wenatchee. He was tall, thin, and dry. It had started to rain again while Vida and I had eaten dinner, with the clouds gathering in over the mountains shortly after six o'clock. However, the church seemed stuffy that morning, and the congregation grew restless.

"At least," Francine Wells asserted in the vestibule after Mass, "we haven't had to put up with any Jesuits. They're so damned patronizing. They think they're such hot stuff, and they look down their noses at everybody else."

Never having met a Jesuit I didn't like, I kept quiet. Betsy O'Toole, who, with her husband, Jake, owned the Grocery Basket, sidled up to Francine.

"Relax, Frannie. My cousin's daughter works at the Chancery office in Seattle. She saw the tentative new assignment list. We're getting Father Dennis Kelly. Incredible as it seems, he's young, he's smart, he's a great guy. I hear he's good-looking, too."

Instead of cheering, Francine groaned. "Father What-A-Waste! I know we're short of priests, but we're also short of men! Why can't the ugly ones have the vocations?"

Roseanna Bayard patted Francine's chic shoulder. "They do, Francine. When was the last time you saw a handsome priest under fifty?" Roseanna glanced at me and looked sheepish. "Except your brother, Emma. He's cute. But he wasn't here very long."

"Ben was on vacation," I responded. "Where is this marvel of a Father Kelly coming from? I can't believe we're getting a real pastor."

Again, it was Betsy who was in the know. "He's been teaching at a seminary in California. I guess they had to close it down, and he was surplussed. He's originally from Tacoma, so he asked to be assigned to a Pacific Northwest parish. We got lucky. If we didn't have the school, we'd probably be stuck with visitors and lay people."

As usual, the post-liturgy crowd was growing. In Father Fitz's time, we'd always had coffee and doughnuts after Mass in the school hall. But without a pastor to guide us, we were relegated to social gatherings in the vestibule. Ed and Shirley Bronsky were standing next to me. Shirley wore a red-and-white checkered sundress that revealed a lot of flesh. But Shirley *had* a lot of flesh, and it would have been pretty hard to hide. Ed wore a Budweiser T-shirt with tan shorts. He was not a pretty sight. But he also wore an air of enthusiasm.

"Betsy! Francine! Roseanna! You're just the people I want to see! We've got to set up appointments for the school special." He shot me a quick look, probably to make sure I was paying attention. Next to him, Shirley beamed with pride. "Groceries for graduation parties, clothes for Mom and the grad, photographs of the happy occasion. You're all going to make a mint off of this, but you've got to advertise!"

The three female merchants looked as astonished as I felt. Obviously, they weren't acquainted with the new Ed Bronsky.

"Ed," Francine said in a soft voice, taking him by the short sleeve of his T-shirt. "It's *Sunday*."

"Hey," Ed replied, still full of enthusiasm, "no rest for the wicked. I'm just getting my second wind in this wild and crazy world of advertising! It's sell, sell, sell! Ask Emma. She'll tell you how I'm single-handedly picking up the beat for Alpine's economy."

Smiling weakly, I acknowledged Ed's assertion. "He's been a real go-getter lately. New accounts, bigger, better-looking ads—he even chased Lloyd Campbell up a dead end the other day. Ed just won't quit."

Betsy O'Toole was laughing in her deep, rich style. "Oh, good grief! The Grocery Basket may have to go to color inserts—like Safeway! What will Jake think?"

Briefly, Ed lost some of his bloom. But he remained game. "Inserts, special editions, color—we can handle it, Betsy."

Betsy looked as if she were seriously considering the idea. The advent of Safeway the previous year had definitely provided real competition for the O'Tooles. "We've been thinking about staying open twenty-four hours," she said thoughtfully. "I'd hate to do it—so would Jake—but it seems to be the trend. Good grief, Lloyd Campbell's working Saturdays now. I saw his van last weekend parked up by First Hill, and it wasn't even nine o'clock in the morning."

"There you go," Ed exclaimed with enthusiasm. "Don't let up. Offer the customer convenience, service—and a quality product." He plunged deeper into his sales pitch. As Monica Vancich and Jake O'Toole and Buddy Bayard and the organist, Annie Jeanne Dupre, joined the circle, I edged away. Ed had achieved his goal, impressing both his wife and his employer. I would leave him to it, and stop worrying about *The Advocate*'s revenue. At least for a while. Ed might want to work on Sunday, but I didn't. There were letters to write and the Sunday paper to read. I had decided to spend the day being semi-lazy.

Just finishing the first section, I was interrupted by Todd Wilson. I was so surprised to see him on my doorstep that I assumed he'd come to tell me about a power failure. I was wrong.

The premature creases in Todd's forehead deepened as he took the armchair I offered him. I'd taken over the sofa, with the Sunday paper spread out on the cushions. My offer of coffee was declined; Todd seemed anxious to get down to business.

"What's going on with *The Advocate*?" he asked, his close-set brown eyes filled with worry. "I understand you had a couple of your people at the high school Friday asking some strange questions about Wendy."

His reference to my staff made it sound as if I had hordes of employees. Perhaps Todd felt that way, fearing Vida and Carla's invasion of Alpine High might trigger a veritable media blitz.

I played innocent. "It's a year-end story. We're doing a special issue the second week of June."

Impatiently, Todd slapped the upholstered arm of the chair. "Right, sure, you've done stuff like that before. But this is different. Wendy heard that both Vida and that girl you've got working for you were zeroing in on my wife. We were out last night with some of the other teachers and Principal Freeman. They told us about it. Wendy's pretty upset. What's going on?"

Wendy had a right to be upset. Vida wasn't always the soul of tact, and Carla could be downright heedless. Now that we had discovered the secret at Marlow Whipp's grocery store, I felt embarrassed at our over-zealous snooping. On the other hand, it *was* a story. If Milo carried through, he might find grounds for criminal prosecution. My understanding was that a judge would have to rule on whether or not the lyrics were obscene. I guessed it also would depend on how the recordings were obtained and what Marlow was charging for them. But the truth was, I didn't want charges brought. It was the self-styled censors who were wrong, not the Wilsons and Marlow Whipp.

I decided to be honest. Without mentioning our earlier suspicions of drug dealing, I told Todd what we believed was going on across from the high school. His dismay couldn't be concealed. He immediately went on the defensive.

"What's the difference if those kids buy the music in Sultan or Alpine? There's a market, and we fill it. Should

Marlow have advertised? Hell, no, he'd have been boy-
cotted by all those stiff-necked church people and the rest
of the Nazis around here. Are we corrupting young minds?
What do you think?" Todd had grown very red, his freckles
seeming to spread all over his face.

I wasn't about to get into a philosophical debate with
Todd Wilson. In fact, I didn't know whether or not teenag-
ers could be influenced by rap or rock or any other music.
If everybody who'd ever heard "The Battle Hymn of the
Republic" was inspired to march out the door in search of
Truth, I might believe that Art could shape Life. But there
was a big difference between being moved and being made
to move. One song doesn't create an attitude.

"Look, Todd," I said quietly, "I've been planning to do
an editorial on this issue for some time, but I haven't gotten
around to it. The problem needs more than a column on
page two, with me extolling the virtues of the First Amend-
ment. We could do several pieces, maybe a series. We need
input from parents and teachers. I know Wendy has some
real concerns about illiteracy. Is this her way of striking
back at complacency? Is she trying to tell people that ignorance and repression are wrong? We could give her a fo-
rum. I don't intend to crucify her."

Todd's expression was skeptical. "Teaching jobs are hard
to come by these days. How long do you think she'd last
at the high school if this got out in the paper?"

"Why," I responded, "would she think it wouldn't get
out? If not in *The Advocate*, then via the grapevine? Good
grief, Todd, I can't believe it's been a secret this long!"

Todd shifted uncomfortably in the chair. He drummed his
fingers on the arms, tapped one foot, then ran a jittery hand
through his wavy brown hair. "It's been about four months,
I guess. Oh, there're students who don't approve, but peer-
group pressure gets to them. But it wasn't Wendy's idea.
All she did was make sure the kids knew where to get the
recordings. I don't suppose she had to tell more than one.
Word got out—the kids thought it was real cool that a
teacher would side with them when it came to banned music."

Cool teacher, cool subjects, cool classes. The students
might learn something. Maybe that was the way Wendy's

mind had run. I wanted to credit her with good motives, not greed.

"If it wasn't Wendy's idea, whose was it?" I thought I already knew.

Todd frowned. "Her brother's. It started when Shane was still working at Fred Meyer in Seattle. They got a shipment that was flawed. There was a hassle with the recording company, then they replaced it, but never collected the first batch. It was tapes. There was nothing wrong with them, only the plastic boxes they were stored in. Shane brought them home at Christmas and gave away some of the really good ones as presents. We kidded him and said he ought to sell the rest on the street corner and pick up an extra buck. He told his dad to sell them at Alpine Appliance. But Lloyd had tried that once, back in the '70s, and said he'd been robbed blind. Too much shoplifting with kids. He didn't want kids in his store anyway because they screw around with the TVs and VCRs and stuff."

"So you came up with Marlow Whipp?" I remarked.

"Sure. It was a natural. Right by the high school, with kids hanging around all the time. But we didn't really start until a month or two later, when the busybodies began raising a ruckus over the explicit lyrics and what was being sold at Platters on the Sky. Shane made contact with the distributors in Seattle. They couldn't get their stuff in up here and were afraid maybe the whole Stevens Pass corridor would chicken out, from Monroe to Leavenworth. It was all on the up-and-up."

"So it's a four-way split," I mused. "Is there really big money involved?"

Todd looked offended. "Big money? What's big money? The most Wendy and I've cleared in a week is around seven hundred dollars. The same for Shane. Marlow makes his profit just as he would on any other item he sells in the store. It's nice extra income, but we're not getting rich. And," he added on an unhappy note, "it won't last. But then we never thought it would."

Still, the Wilsons had enjoyed a good ride. So had Marlow Whipp. And Shane. "What's your brother-in-law doing with his share? Shane seems to keep a low profile."

For the first time, the hint of a smile played on Todd

Wilson's wide mouth. "Shane's like his dad. A typical Scot. He salts it away. Cheap, cheap."

I gave a faint nod of agreement. Scots were tight, Gypsies stole, Germans were stubborn, Italians had mob connections, Scandinavians were rawboned, Japanese excelled at self-discipline, African-Americans got mixed up with street gangs. It wasn't a matter of being politically correct, because in a democracy, no one is right or wrong, and taboo word games only muzzle the English language. It was the stereotyping that bothered me—the old, stale, tired labels that we were too lazy to discard. When would those clichés end? In the past two weeks, I'd heard them all, even from my own mouth.

Todd had lost his smile; he was looking very earnest. "You see the problem, Ms. Lord. Wendy and I are doing fine right now. But this music thing will blow away when Platters on the Sky gets enough guts to stand up to the fascists. If Wendy is canned at the high school, what do we do? Move away to a new school district? I can't quit the PUD. I've got ten years in there."

I ventured a guess. "You've got Principal Freeman on your side, don't you? Coach Ridley, Donna Wickstrom—several members of the faculty. Who are you afraid of on the school board? Isn't Lloyd Campbell a member?"

"He's only one out of five," Todd replied, still looking downcast. "Pastor Phelps from the Methodist Church is on it, too, and he's dead set against music he thinks will corrupt kids. Then there's Richie Magruder, Doc Dewey, and Grace Grundle. Mrs. Grundle is a retired teacher. What could be worse?"

Doc wouldn't be narrow-minded. Richie Magruder would be the tool of his wife, Stella. And Vida had Grace Grundle in her pocket. I liked Wendy's chances. I said so, but Todd wasn't cheered.

"Everything's happening at once," he lamented. "If it's not Wendy, it's Cyndi. Have you heard what people are saying about her?"

As a journalist, it seemed I was always the last to know. "What?" I asked in a hollow voice.

"That she knew this Kelvin guy. Sure," Todd went on, waving his hands, "maybe she'd met him in Seattle. Shane gave parties, he went to parties. Cyndi liked visiting him and having a good time. Big deal. Shane knew plenty of people. That's the city. But it wasn't some kind of romance. Kelvin had a girl. She was Marilynn's roommate. Hell, Cyndi wouldn't date some black dude! She's got pride in being white."

"Really." Todd's remark bounced off of me, like so much bird doo. My mind was elsewhere, sorting through the intricacies of the Campbell ménage: Marilynn Lewis, Jerome Cole, Kelvin Greene, and Wesley Charles ... "Todd, has your family been questioned about the murders?"

Todd practically reeled in the armchair. "Hell, no! I mean, Cyndi was asked about talking to Kelvin Greene at the Icicle Creek Tavern. But that was it. Why should we? Oh, Milo Dodge gave Marilynn Lewis a bad time, but that doesn't count. She's not family."

Family. What was family? Todd probably felt closer to Marlow Whipp than he did to Marilynn Lewis. He was in business with Marlow; Marlow was a native of Alpine; Marlow was white.

"The fact remains," I said, sounding stern, "Shane and Cyndi knew Kelvin Greene. Nobody else in Alpine did, except Marilynn Lewis. Come on, Todd—for all I know, Kelvin was in on the music deal. He worked for Fred Meyer, too."

Todd's surprise seemed genuine. "He did? I never met the guy. I thought he was just some dude Cyndi ran into at a party. You know, a friend of Marilynn's. I figured Kelvin got hold of Cyndi because he didn't know how to get in touch with Marilynn."

My guest was getting up from his chair, obviously about to leave. I jumped off the sofa. "What do you mean? 'Got hold of'? You mean Kelvin contacted Cyndi?"

The telltale flush began to creep over Todd's face again. "Right, yeah. He came to the PUD office that afternoon. That's when he and Cyndi went out for a beer."

While Todd backpedaled toward the front door, I pursued him. My index finger waggled in the direction of his chest. "You knew that? You knew your sister-in-law had gone off with Kelvin Greene?"

"No!" Todd burst out at me. "No, I didn't know it! I was

out hacking down trees at the fish hatchery. She told me later. After dinner, in fact, when you and Vida had gone home. Cyndi wondered . . . you know, if the guy who got killed might be Kelvin. She thought it was funny that Vida said it wasn't anybody we'd know. This is Alpine—everybody knows everybody."

Todd's rationale made sense. Still, it raised some questions. After a few more reassurances that I wasn't about to launch an exposé of his wife, he left. Todd Wilson wasn't happy, he didn't believe me completely, he was as worried as when he'd arrived—but I'd done all I could. I returned to the sofa and got caught up on the sports news.

The Mariners were losing; the Sonics were winning. I expected that before May was over, the tide might be running the other way in both cases. I hadn't been to a baseball or basketball game in four years. It was too late in the NBA season to catch the Sonics, but maybe I could go into Seattle and see the Mariners. I had a schedule in my handbag. Texas was coming in the third weekend of June. But I would be at Lake Chelan. With Tom Cavanaugh. I corrected myself: Tom and I would be at Lake Chelan. We wouldn't necessarily be together. I'd wait for Toronto in August. Why not? I'd waited for Tom for over twenty years.

The sound of sirens tore me from the comic section. Sure enough, the ambulance was speeding past my house. A sheriff's car came next, but from my window, I couldn't tell who was in it. I rushed outside to the street. To my astonishment, the emergency vehicles were once again pulling into the cul-de-sac.

Bill Blatt and Jack Mullins were standing beside the squad car when I arrived on foot. A young couple I vaguely recognized were making excited gestures and talking at the same time. She was, I thought, Dot and Durwood Parker's granddaughter; he was the Rafferty who tended bar at the Icicle Creek Tavern.

Jack Mullins spotted me and waved. "Hey, it's the press! Calm down, guys, we're not doing anything until Sheriff Dodge gets here. I've got a squeamish stomach." Jack was all smiles, though his eyes were wary. "Hi, Ms. Lord. Where'd you come from?"

"My house," I replied, gazing around and seeing nothing out of the ordinary. If Milo had put up any crime-scene tape after Wesley Charles was killed, it was now gone. "What's happening?"

The Parker granddaughter—who was not a Parker as it turned out, but an Eriks, since her mother had been the Parker—began to babble incoherently. She was joined by young Mr. Rafferty, whose first name I later learned was Tim, and who was working his way through spasmodic quarters at Western Washington University in Bellingham, and who made as little sense as Tiffany Eriks. Bill Blatt took pity on me. Or perhaps he feared repercussions from his aunt Vida.

"Tiffany and Tim went for a hike," Bill explained, his earnest young face showing the strain of the past few days. "They started out up on Second Hill and took the trail that winds back into town." Bill paused, swallowing hard. "Just before they reached the cul-de-sac, they found a body. It looks like we've got another murder on our hands."

Chapter Sixteen

IT SEEMED TO me that things were getting out of control in Alpine. On a per capita basis, it appeared that we must have the highest homicide rate in the state for the month of May. Maybe that statistic would keep the dreaded Californians out. Except that in this season of clear-cut bans, we could use some new blood, even from L.A. and other such sun-drenched, overcrowded environs.

". . . just lying there!" Tiffany Eriks cried, leaning on Tim Rafferty and threatening to stifle him. "A logger, I'll bet!"

"Right, right," Tim agreed. "Maybe he's been there for a long time. An accident in the woods. We didn't want to get too close. You know, dead bodies smell bad."

"No!" Tiffany shrieked. "Not an accident! An environmentalist! Somebody who probably thought this guy was cutting down an owl's nest! Those people go crazy! They don't care about human life, just a bunch of birds! Oh, my God, it could have been Uncle Deekey!"

Not having the faintest idea who Uncle Deekey might be, I felt a surge of relief when Milo's Cherokee Chief pulled into the cul-de-sac. He emerged looking both weary and grim. Nor did he seemed pleased to see me, though I couldn't tell whether it was because of the situation or the memory of our last, quasi-passionate encounter under similar circumstances.

"Is he black?" was Milo's first question.

He wasn't, Tim and Tiffany chorused. At least they didn't think so. He looked like a logger, Tiffany asserted. Why? Milo asked. Because he was wearing a plaid shirt and work pants, Tim responded. Big, too. And wearing a hat, which made it impossible to see his face. Not that they wanted to, Tiffany put in hastily, because maybe the birds had eaten it. She wouldn't put it past a bunch of spotted owls.

"Show us," Milo said, sounding dismal. He turned to me. "Why don't you wait here, Emma?" Milo knew my delicate stomach.

But faced with a major story, I couldn't be such a coward. "I'm coming," I replied, setting my jaw. "I don't have to get up close."

We plunged into the forest, which was overgrown with ferns, berry vines, and nettles. There were a few deer runs, which made the going easier, but no real pathway existed. Tim Rafferty explained that the trail from Second Hill actually continued on to the ski lodge. He and Tiffany had tired, however, and decided to cut back to town and grab a snack.

We had gone about fifty yards into the woods when Tim and Tiffany exhibited confusion. They weren't exactly sure which way they had come. Tiffany remembered a pair of big cedars; Tim recalled a stand of devil's club they'd avoided.

It took us almost half an hour to find the spot. Meanwhile, I waved away mosquitoes, deer flies, and no-see-ums by the dozens. Bill Blatt fell in a gopher hole. Jack Mullins tripped over a root. Milo muttered that it was a hell of a way to spend a Sunday afternoon. He'd planned on replacing some shingles that had blown off his roof during the winter windstorms.

"How's Honoria?" I inquired as we trudged up a steep hill, which was choked with ferns and huckleberry bushes.

"Fine," Milo responded tersely.

"Are you engaged?" I couldn't resist the barb.

"I'm on probation." He kept walking. "Don't keep so close to my butt. It makes me nervous."

A sudden shriek halted us. It was Tiffany, standing under a hemlock tree and pointing jerkily at the ground. "It's him! He's dead! Omigod!"

"He was dead before," Milo grumbled. "What does she expect now?"

Jack Mullins was the first of our party to reach Tiffany and Tim. I held back, while Milo and Bill continued on to the site of the body. To my amazement, Jack Mullins burst into laughter. Tiffany started shrieking again. Tim took her in his arms and clasped her close to his chest.

"Hey, sheriff!" Jack exclaimed between fits of mirth, "this guy's not dead! He's a dummy!"

Milo, who had been about to sneeze, held a finger under his nose. "Huh?"

Jack Mullins bent down and lifted the alleged body. It swung lightly from his arms. Tiffany pressed her face against Tim. Bracing myself, I stared. Now Bill Blatt was laughing, too.

"Jack's right, Sheriff! It's Bucker Swede!"

It was indeed. The plaid-shirted, brown-pantsed dummy seemed to cuddle up to Jack Mullins. The high school mascot had been found. I began to giggle, but Tiffany Eriks was infuriated.

"A dummy? From the high school? Oh, shit! I remember that thing—but he never had a hat!"

Tiffany was right. Bucker Swede was wearing a hat taped to his melonlike head. He looked like Smokey the Bear. To add to the absurdity, a tourniquet had been applied to one of his bulging upper arms. The comical effect only made the rest of us laugh the louder. Until, of course, we realized that there was nothing funny about it.

It was natural that Milo Dodge wouldn't believe me. He didn't operate on guesswork; he didn't believe in half-assed theories. Beside, it was Sunday. He had to finish nailing down those shingles.

"Tomorrow, I'll ask a few questions," he promised. "Let's thank our lucky stars it wasn't another stiff. I'd be up for recall if we had any more murders around her. I need evidence, not ideas out of left field."

I knew that Vida wouldn't be so obtuse. But Vida wasn't home. I had forgotten that she planned to drive up to Bellingham for the day to visit her daughter, Meg, and her family. Indeed, she had warned me that she might stay over, and be a bit late arriving at work Monday morning.

Stymied by my lack of an accomplice, I called Carla. Libby Boyd informed me that her roommate was sunning herself by the pool.

"She envies my tan," Libby laughed. "Little does she know I got it from a salon in Seattle. The original one, I mean. Carla's dark by nature. Why doesn't she skip the bad rays and be herself? Now that I can be outdoors, I wouldn't dream of roasting my body on purpose."

"If you're not doing anything, why don't you drop by?" I asked. "Sundays in Alpine can be dull."

But Libby had to catch up on her laundry, her checking account, her paperwork. She rang off, and I sat with my chin on my chest, wondering what to do next. Shortly before five, I drove over to the high school.

It was a whim, and probably a silly one. But I had to see it through. The Buckers' trophy case was inside the main doors that faced First Hill Road, an offshoot of Highway 187. The highway itself curved eastward around the bottom of First Hill and continued to the ranger station and the Icicle Creek campground. First Hill Road climbed up the mountainside, past the Tolberg farm and the Dithers sisters' horse ranch. About a mile out of town, it turned into a dirt logging road, then ended somewhere on the face of Mount Sawyer.

Eight stone steps led up to the broad walk. A wider, longer staircase ended under a portico. There were three sets of double doors, and I knew they'd be locked. On a late Sunday afternoon, the high school was deserted, except for a few kids horsing around on the field. They were a block away, however, in back of the school building.

Across the street, several of Alpine's larger, older homes on First Hill could be seen through the trees. They were shielded, however, by the tall evergreens. And I was shielded from the nearby residents' prying eyes.

Secrecy wasn't my primary concern. At least not *my* secrecy. Still, to prove my theory correct, it was important to know that any activity in front of the high school usually would not be noticed. The First Hill residents demanded their privacy. They had ensured it by keeping the original stands of fir, hemlock, and cedar as a bulwark against the rest of Alpine.

The shrubbery that flanked the front of the school building consisted of rhododendrons, mountain laurel, and Japanese yews. I searched carefully on each side of the main staircase. Gum wrappers, pop cans, paper cups, lunch bags, cellophane. While the grounds were clean, the shrubbery cried for a litter crew. I wished I'd brought a bag so that I could collect the junk and throw it away.

But junk was all I did find. Discouraged, I stood at the head of the steps that led to the street. At each side of the walk was a circular bed where someone with more imagination than taste had planted pampas grass. The stuff looked out of place in Alpine, and I was amazed that it would grow at such an altitude. But grow it did, each clump almost as tall as I was.

Delving into the thick green foliage, I found something. It was a U.S. Forest Service first-aid kit, wide open and almost empty. More burrowing unearthed some compresses and antiseptic. I had found what I was looking for, though in the beginning I wasn't sure what it would be. Buoyed by my discovery and armed with the kit, I went to the hospital.

As I'd hoped, Peyton Flake was there, having just finished setting an arm broken in a fall off Mount Baldy.

"Rock climbers," Flake groused. "City types, trying to pretend they're outdoor fanatics. Shit." He glared at me through his wire-rim glasses. "Why don't they take lessons? One foray up a rockery in their backyard and they think they're frigging experts."

Dr. Flake was holding forth in the all-purpose office that served whoever was on call at the hospital. As usual, he wore jeans and a beat-up shirt under his white coat. His long brown hair was pulled back in a ponytail and his six-foot-four frame looked as if it could use a good meal.

"Okay, Ms. Emma Lord, what's up? Am I on trial for seducing your star reporter?" His blue eyes twinkled, though his jaw was set. Peyton Flake was no man to mess with, and he knew I knew it.

I laughed, though without humor. "Carla can take care of herself. At least as far as you're concerned." I hesitated, waiting for his reaction. There wasn't any. That came as no surprise. "Who do you think has been sending your nurse ugly messages?"

Flake snorted. "Everybody. It's this town. They don't know their asses from a hole in the ground. Ignorant bigots, most of them. Hey, I came from Ellensburg. I know small towns. Oh, they have a college over there, they like to think they're broad-minded. But I didn't know jack-shit until I got to Seattle and the UDUB. I thought a crib was something you put a baby in." He chortled at his own naïveté.

I laughed, too, though I wasn't feeling very merry. "Dr. Flake, I've got a favor to ask." I asked it. Flake looked puzzled at first, then turned serious.

"You aren't kidding around, are you?"

"No," I replied, equally somber. "I'm scared."

"It won't be easy," Flake said, fingering the stethoscope that hung from his neck. "Christ, I'm on call until tomorrow morning."

I stood up. "You'll think of something. You have to."

Peyton Flake gave me an odd half smile. "Yeah. I guess I will. I took an oath to save lives."

"Then save one," I urged him. "For your own sake, if nobody else's."

I left him with a worried look on his face. It wasn't half as troubled as my mind.

It was almost dark when I pulled the Jaguar up at The Pines Village Apartments. I had no plan. I was taking a terrible chance. All that was going for me was sheer opportunism. But fear was the motivator.

The apartment house was five staggered stories, with the pool on the roof. Carla had told me it could be covered in winter. The balconies sported a variety of greenery, from evergreens in planters to window boxes with bright geraniums. Chimney pots indicated the existence of fireplaces, and gave the building a European air.

C. Steinmetz and L. Boyd lived on the third floor. It was Libby who answered when I punched in number 307. She cheerfully directed me to wait for the door to buzz, then come inside and take the elevator.

The carpet, a serviceable but handsome mauve, still smelled new. The elevator was tiny and quiet. No children, I guessed; no pets. On my way in, I had noticed a sign indicating that there were some vacancies. No one bedrooms, I mused—or nothing for the likes of Marilynn Lewis? Maybe the owners were violating the Federal Fair Housing Act.

Libby offered me something to drink. I accepted, though blackberry-flavored water isn't my idea of a shot in the spine. And that was what I needed. I'd come to ask Libby some difficult questions.

"Carla took off on a run," Libby said, after we'd sat down in the living room. A fresh breeze blew in through the sliding glass doors that led to the small balcony. The fireplace had glass doors, too, and looked as if it had never been used. The decor was eclectic, a mélange of Carla Steinmetz and Libby Boyd. A navy blue sectional sofa, a glass-topped coffee table on brass legs, a big lamp with a floral ceramic base—these objects belonged to Libby, I guessed. The refinished Victorian rocker, the mohair armchair that held a Raggedy Ann doll, the old-fashioned three-way floor lamp all smacked of Carla.

"Where'd she go?" I inquired, trying to keep my voice calm.

Libby shook her head. "She didn't say. Often, she doesn't. She got a phone call after she came down from the pool and raced off. I think it's better to keep tabs. I mean, you never know what might happen. It's a good thing to let somebody know where you are, just in case."

I agreed. "That's the way I was raised. Maybe Carla wasn't."

"*I* wasn't," Libby said, sitting cross-legged on the navy sofa. "My parents believed in being free. What they really meant was they didn't want to be bothered. That's why I'm the opposite, I guess."

Fumbling around for an opening, I found one in Libby's remark about her parents. "You don't have family close by, do you, Libby?"

Libby fingered a carved crane on the end table next to the sofa. "No. My mother's dead. I don't know where my father is. I had a brother, but he ran away when he was fifteen. I was twelve. I wished he'd taken me with him." She sounded wistful.

"I gathered you didn't have anybody around here," I said, aware that I was treading on painful ground. "That's why I'm barging in. You've been fussing over Carla. Now I'm fussing over you."

Libby didn't look keen about the idea. "That's nice, but don't. I'm not used to it."

I gave a short nod of assent. "Then I'll have my say and take off. It's about Shane—how well do you know him, Libby?"

Relief flooded Libby's tanned face. "Well enough. We've been seeing each other for a year. Shane's great. Oh, he'll never set the world on fire, but he's basically a good guy. If that's what's bothering you, forget it."

"It's Shane's feelings I'm worried about," I said, and it wasn't exactly a lie. It just wasn't the whole truth. "I'm wondering if he knows his own mind. And heart."

Now Libby looked perturbed. "What are you getting at?"

"I think," I said boldly, "that he's infatuated with Marilynn Lewis."

Libby threw back her head and laughed. "That's crazy! Shane hardly knows Marilynn!" Giving into her amusement, she laughed herself into silence. "Really, Ms. Lord, the only reason Marilynn is living at the Campbells is because Shane's so good-hearted. Soft, like mush. It was all so casual—she was in the Fred Meyer store one day, and they got to talking, and she mentioned moving to Alpine, and—well, one thing led to another. Shane put his foot in it. He does things like that."

I wanted to believe Libby, but I wasn't convinced. I had seen the smitten look on Shane's face when Marilynn entered the dining room at the Campbell house. I had watched the flush grow on his cheeks when I mentioned Marilynn's name. Most of all, I detected latent animosity between Libby and Marilynn. As far as I could tell, Libby was no racist. Any hostility she felt for Marilynn grew out of a more primal fear—one woman's jealousy of another over a man.

"Okay." I sighed. "Let me ask one more question and then I'll be out of here. Do you remember the night Jerome Cole was killed and Marilynn and her roommate came over to Shane's apartment in Seattle?"

Libby tilted her head, eyes on the ceiling. "I remember that it happened. But no, I wasn't at Shane's that night. He told me about it later."

"How did he tell you?" I kept my voice even.

Perplexed, Libby gazed at me. "How? I don't know what you mean. I guess he said the two nurses had run away from their apartment, and then he heard that Marilynn's boyfriend got killed." She shrugged. "It was too bad, but from what I could tell, the guy was headed for some kind of big trouble. I think a neighbor took him out."

I was perched on the edge of the navy blue armchair that matched the sofa. "Are you sure?"

Libby shifted on the cushions. "That's what happened. The guy was sent to prison."

I gave a sad shake of my head. "I don't think so. That guy was Wesley Charles, the man you and those kids found near my house. He didn't kill Jerome Cole." I took a deep breath. "I hate to say it, but I believe Jerome Cole was bludgeoned to death by Shane Campbell."

Libby Boyd's face was horror-stricken. Afraid, too, I thought, and I didn't blame her. "That's awful!" she finally gasped. "Shane wouldn't—couldn't—do such a thing! And why would he?"

"Because he was nuts about Marilynn," I replied doggedly. "He was trying to protect her. Jerome Cole was a violent drug addict. He made a habit of beating up on Marilynn."

Libby still looked afraid, but her expression also conveyed defiance. "No. No, I don't believe Shane felt that way about Marilynn. Oh, he *liked* her. But there was nothing romantic there." Her eyes grew desperate. "God, Ms. Lord, don't you think *I'd* know it?"

I did, and Libby's obtuseness baffled me. It takes either a very stupid or a totally self-absorbed woman not to sense when her man is straying. Unqualified trust is as rare as it is naïve. Libby didn't seem to fit into any of those categories. I began to wonder if I might be wrong about Shane Campbell.

The phone rang. Libby answered it in an abrupt voice, then switched to her more natural tone: Her half of the conversation was mostly monosyllables. When she hung up, she gave me a smug smile.

"That was Shane. He wants to catch the late showing of *Jurassic Park* at the Whistling Marmot Theatre. I'd better change if he's coming here for a drink first." She glanced at her watch. "It's after seven. The last show starts at nine-forty."

It seemed to me that Libby and Shane would have more than enough time for a drink. Or for whatever else they planned as a short feature before the movie. Which, I realized, was none of my business. Obviously, Libby was politely telling me I'd worn out my welcome.

Maybe I'd spent too much time around Vida. Perhaps I'd appointed myself Libby's guardian angel. Possibly I was acting like a pigheaded fool. But I had to make one last stab at keeping Libby away from Shane, at least until Milo Dodge had had time to do some serious police work.

"Libby—what would it take for you to break this date?"

Libby's expression was scornful. "Why should I? Ms. Lord, how many times do I have to tell you . . ."

Waving my hands, I interrupted. "Stop calling me Ms. Lord! And stop and think for a minute, *period*. I'm certain Shane went to meet Kelvin Greene at the cemetery. He left his van parked up on First Hill Road by the Tolberg farm. I was at the Campbells' that night for dinner. Shane was late getting home, and I don't think he brought the van with him. He must have walked down First Hill Road to the cemetery so his van wouldn't be seen, and after he shot Kelvin Greene, Shane ran home, right through his mother's flower garden. It's only half a block." I steeled myself for the next question: "Libby—did you meet Shane at the cemetery and help him get rid of the gun?"

Libby looked stunned as well as angry. "Of course not! That's a terrible thing to say! You're way out of line!"

I was. Libby's vehemence jarred me. "Okay, okay," I soothed. "But you've got to be realistic. There's a murderer loose in Alpine. Maybe I'm wrong. Maybe Shane didn't kill Jerome Cole. But somebody did, and somebody—maybe the same person—killed Kelvin Greene and Wesley Charles within the last week." Briefly, I considered tipping my hand and revealing why I was certain that the recent murders had been committed by someone in the Campbell ménage. I bit my tongue. Libby's rigid face told me that nothing I could say would convince her. Indeed, for a fleeting moment, she actually looked as if she'd like to slug me. I couldn't blame her. Not only had I condemned her for collusion, I'd accused the man she loved of murder. Worse yet, I'd baldly stated that he was infatuated with another woman. Libby Boyd had every right to throw me out of the apartment.

Apparently Libby saw the uncertainty on my face and put out a hand. "Hey—Ms. Lord, forget it. You're taking your job too seriously. Remember, I'm a city girl. I'm used to looking out for myself. Given the way I was brought up, in a sense I've always been on my own. I've been going with Shane for a year. He's never done a single thing to upset me, let alone scare me. If anything, he's too laid-back. Now go home and stop worrying."

I didn't have any choice. I smiled at Libby as I left, but inside, I felt grim. By the time I got to the lobby, Shane was coming up the walkway. On a whim, I jumped back into the elevator and pushed the button for the fourth floor.

I waited about five minutes, then walked down the fire stairs to three. Libby and Carla lived in the second unit from the end of the hall. Feeling silly, I knocked on the neighboring door. There was no answer. I tried the door; it was unlocked.

The apartment was vacant. Judging from the pristine condition of the carpet and the walls, it had never been occupied. It was a two-bedroom unit, identical to Carla and Libby's. Carefully, I opened the sliding glass doors to the balcony and stepped out. I could hear Shane and Libby, if barely.

"It's up to you," Shane was saying.

Libby's response was muffled. I suspected she might be in the bedroom, changing.

"I'd rather have more privacy," Shane said, his voice now a notch louder.

"Well?" Libby sounded much closer. "For once, you decide."

There was a pause. "Let's go," Shane said. A moment later, I heard the faint click of the door.

I waited only as long as I dared. Peeking into the hallway, I found it empty. Shane and Libby had gone down to the lobby. I hurried along the corridor and caught the elevator as it came back up. To my chagrin, it stopped at two on the way down. A middle-aged couple I'd seen around town got in, smiling and nodding.

Fortunately, the trip wasn't long enough to encourage conversation. They moved at a stroll; I raced out of the building ahead of them. Libby and Shane were just pulling away from the curb in a turquoise Pontiac compact. I hoped they didn't see me head for the Jag two spaces down the street.

Following someone in a small town like Alpine isn't easy, especially in a semi-exotic foreign automobile. Surely Libby had noticed the Jaguar still parked outside of The Pines Village. On the other hand, I might bank on the mutual absorption of young lovers. As I followed the Pontiac down Alpine Way, I kept a block's distance between us. There wasn't much traffic at seven-thirty on a Sunday evening.

Lulled into thinking Shane and Libby would go all the way down Alpine to Front, I was caught by surprise when they turned right onto Fir Street. This wasn't a logical route to the Whistling Marmot. Indeed, this would lead us straight past the mobile-home park, a block of condos, and into my own neighborhood. It was still broad daylight. What would Libby and Shane think if they saw me in the rearview mirror and I didn't pull into my driveway?

But just before I reached the intersection at Fourth and Fir, I saw the Pontiac's right turn signal go on. The car slowed as it turned into the Fifth Street cul-de-sac.

My heart leapt. Shane and Libby weren't going to the movies. It was too early, for one thing, a good two hours before the next showing of the feature film. From the balcony, I'd overheard them talking about *privacy*. Were they going to hide out in the cul-de-sac and make love? Given the recent discovery of a corpse there, it seemed like an odd choice.

One thing was certain—having turned off Fir Street, there was nowhere else they *could* go. I pulled up in front of the unfinished construction near the corner and got out of the Jag. Feeling like a grade C detective in a grade B movie, I skulked through the tall ferns and flowering berry bushes that separated the construction site from the cul-de-sac.

Shane and Libby had gotten out of the Pontiac. They

were walking hand-in-hand toward the woods. What was their intention? I could hardly traipse after them and embarrass all three of us by interrupting a tryst. But I was still fearful of what could happen next. Heedless of my black slacks and gray blouse, I ran back through the brambles, racing for my car.

I shot up Fir Street, turned onto First Hill Road, and sped all the way down to the Icicle Creek development where Milo lived in one of the older, more modest houses built in the tract. Fortunately, his home was also among the closest to Highway 187. I made the drive in under three minutes.

Milo wasn't up on his roof but he was down on his couch. There was no time to argue, I blurted. He must get in the Jag and come with me. Was he armed?

Milo Dodge rarely moves in haste. His first reaction was to scratch himself under his T-shirt and yawn. I guessed he'd been taking a nap in front of the TV.

"What're you talking about, Emma?" he demanded in a cross voice. "I'm off duty."

I yelled; I nagged; I pushed; I shoved. In the end, we got into Milo's Cherokee Chief. I drove. He put on a flannel shirt that was lying on the floor, loaded his Colt King Cobra .357 Magnum, sneezed twice, and muttered incoherently.

". . . bunch of bullshit . . . Shane Campbell . . . good kid, little slow . . . black troublemakers . . . Marlow Whipp? I must be nuts . . ."

We'd reached the cul-de-sac. Shane's Pontiac looked innocent with the setting sun gleaming off the metallic turquoise finish. As I'd feared, Shane and Libby were nowhere to be seen. Milo and I jumped down from the Cherokee Chief, heading up the makeshift trail that was actually a deer run.

"Milo," I whispered, after we'd gone about fifty yards into the forest, "should we not *tromp*?"

"I don't give a damn if I bellow," Milo retorted. But in fact he began to watch his step, pausing to peer between the evergreens.

We had gone well beyond the site where Wesley Charles's body had been found. However, there was still a trail of sorts, no doubt the same one that Tim Rafferty and

Tiffany Eriks had followed from the Icicle Creek campground. As we climbed up higher on the mountainside, the underbrush gave way to tall cedars, fir, and hemlock. There was pine, too, and clumps of huckleberry and stands of fern. It was beautiful, yet menacing. The quiet overwhelmed us. We were also losing the light as the sun began to slide down behind the mountains.

We reached the Forest Service trail, which ran in an east-west direction. Milo and I had no idea which way to go. Shane and Libby had almost a ten-minute head start. I was now certain that lovemaking wasn't their object. If that had been the case, they would have stopped much farther down the hillside. Soft ferns and gentle earth would have been more conducive to romantic purposes. Apprehension made my heart pump faster.

I was standing at Milo's elbow while he stifled a sneeze. "Should we split up?" I whispered.

He gave me a disdainful look. "You're the one who wanted me to bring a sidearm. What're you going to use? Your thumb?"

Milo, of course, was right. The west-bound trail led to the ski lodge, more than a mile away. To the east lay the Tolberg farm and the Dithers Sisters' horse ranch. The Tolberg property was nearest, perhaps only a couple of hundred yards away. I guessed that Shane and Libby would have taken the long route, in the direction of the lodge. Their chances of meeting anyone this time of night would be almost nil.

Milo didn't argue. We picked up the pace on the trail—the sheriff with his long, loping strides; I, virtually running to keep up. Within three minutes, we saw movement ahead of us: two figures were standing by a wooden footbridge that crosses Alpine Creek. The trail dips down to the bridge where the stream tumbles among moss-covered rocks, then takes a deep, dizzy plunge, and eventually joins Burl Creek just west of the mall. Flanked by tall ferns and dogtooth violets, it was a perfect sylvan setting.

But now it was filled with menace. As we approached on tiptoe, we could see Libby's back turned to us. She was at the edge of the trail, a step from the bridge. Beyond her, we could make out Shane's head and the left side of his body.

I was Right!

They appeared to be in earnest, even heated, conversation.

"He's going to push her off the bridge," I breathed. "She'll go right over the falls!"

Milo quickened his step. I followed. Shane looked up and saw us. He shouted something I couldn't hear. Libby craned her neck, then screamed. Shane lunged at her; they struggled, teetering at the edge of the bridge. We were within twenty feet of the pair, and now Milo was yelling at them to desist.

Libby was strong: She had managed to break free from Shane, but to my horror, instead of fleeing the bridge, she pressed forward. Now it was Shane who appeared to be on the defensive. Milo had pulled his King Cobra Magnum.

"Stop!" he shouted once more. "Stop or I'll shoot!"

It was not an empty threat. As Shane again grabbed Libby, Milo fired into the air. Then he dropped to one knee, the gun fixed on the battling couple.

A second shot shattered the mountain's natural peace. I jumped, then stared at Milo. He hadn't budged, but was gaping at Shane and Libby. Shane had fallen onto the bridge, clutching his side. His head dangled over the edge. Libby whirled around, and I saw the gun in her hand. I uttered a little shriek; Milo swore.

"Don't do it!" he warned. "Drop it! Now!"

Libby threw Milo one last defiant look. She didn't drop the gun. Instead, she turned again and jumped. I could have sworn I heard her scream all the way to Burl Creek.

Chapter Seventeen

IT WAS MIDNIGHT and Milo was sneezing his head off. He sat behind his desk with a bottle of Benadryl in one hand and an inhaler in the other. The fluorescent lights flickered above us. Carla and I were seated in the two visitors' chairs while Peyton Flake lounged against a filing cabinet.

"Shane'll be up and around tomorrow," Flake assured us for the third time. "Take your guilt trip somewhere else, guys. You did your best."

But neither Milo nor I was feeling very proud of ourselves. The sheriff had been unable to prevent Shane from getting shot and Libby Boyd from committing suicide. And I, the dreadful dunce, had picked out the wrong murderer.

Or, at least, the wrong person who had killed Kelvin Greene and Wesley Charles. I could only console myself that I'd been partly right: Shane Campbell had indeed bludgeoned Jerome Cole with Marilynn Lewis's ivory figurine. His motive had been gallant; perhaps he'd acted in self-defense. But what had followed was completely without honor and utterly indefensible.

Carla was still shattered by her roommate's treachery. "She seemed so nice!" Carla wailed. "She was always fussing over me and she never argued about expenses and she even vacuumed!"

Peyton Flake moved away from the filing cabinet to rub Carla's shoulders. "Hey, babe, get over it. The big thing is that you're safe. Now you know why I called and asked you to come down to the hospital and help me file charts."

Leaning back in the modular plastic chair, Carla gave Flake a big-eyed, adoring gaze. "I just thought you wanted to be near me!" She giggled, though on a less jarring note

223

than usual. Turning away from Flake, she looked at me. "But I still don't get why you thought I was in danger."

Sadly, I shook my head. "I thought both you and Libby were in danger. And I didn't want you around when I confronted Libby about Shane. I knew she wouldn't discuss their relationship in front of a third person, even her roommate. I was panicky. There'd been too many murders, and it seemed to me that anybody connected to the Campbells could be next."

Milo wore his musing expression. "And Shane *was* next. Or was that because you put a scare into Libby?" His hazel eyes were watery as he waited for my reply.

I gave a halfhearted nod. "When Libby found out I knew Shane had killed Jerome Cole, she panicked, too. She figured it was just a matter of time before somebody filled in the rest of the gaps and pinned the other two murders on her. Shane had to go—preferably as a suicide. He said she was trying to force him to jump off the bridge. She didn't want to shoot him, just threaten him. The gun went off by accident, while they were struggling."

"Gosh." Carla's voice was faint. "How pathetic. Libby wanted to marry Shane so much. He was her first real chance at security. Oh, she didn't talk about it often, but sometimes she'd let things slip. Like, having her own house and a family and belonging to somebody. I could cry, really, I could."

I didn't blame Carla. I felt sort of weepy, too. Libby Boyd was a tragic figure, an unloved child who had been utterly ruthless in her search for safe harbor. Instead, she had wrecked several lives, including her own.

But while I felt terrible pangs for Libby, I still had a need to exonerate myself. "So much pointed to Shane," I persisted. "Not just with Jerome Cole's death, but the other two, as well. The night that Jerome died, Marilynn and Winola went to Shane's apartment. He wasn't there. I suspect he'd gone to Marilynn's and they'd crossed paths, but missed each other. He found Jerome, still ranting and raving. Shane, feeling obliged to defend Marilynn, got into a fight with Jerome and hit him with that carving. Shane doesn't have much backbone—Libby told me that, and I believe her. He fled, and let Wesley Charles take the blame.

Wesley came along later and picked up the murder weapon. Somewhere in there, Kelvin Greene showed up, probably to see Winola Prince. Kelvin recognized Shane from working together at Fred Meyer. He saw Shane leave, and put two and two together. That's when he decided to make things interesting and blackmail Shane. When Shane feels better tomorrow, I imagine he'll tell us he confided everything to Libby. She knew that Shane was falling for Marilynn—she didn't want to lose him. Libby probably told him to go ahead and let Wesley Charles take the rap and to pay Kelvin off. But Kelvin kept coming back for more. Shane got the idea to sell those banned recordings. He must have used the money he made to pay off Kelvin. But he wanted to be done with blackmail so he quit his job and came back to Alpine. He could live more cheaply at home, and he needed all the money he could get. But it wasn't that easy to shed Kelvin. He came up here to meet Shane and make even bigger demands."

Milo was trying to look enthused about my deductions. He was also trying to keep awake. "So Libby decided to call a halt," he murmured.

"Right," I answered, also feeling weary. "To Libby, security was financial as well as social and emotional. She couldn't stand seeing Shane drained of everything. I don't know exactly what Kelvin did when he got to Alpine that Friday, but he probably asked a few questions and found out that Shane worked for his father at Alpine Appliance. Maybe he figured it wouldn't be smart to head straight there. Lloyd Campbell might make trouble. But he knew Cyndi and tracked her down at the PUD. She probably told Kelvin to telephone Shane and arrange a meeting."

Peyton Flake was still standing behind Carla's chair, his manner protective. "Did Cyndi know what was going on?"

I shook my head. "I doubt it. She probably thought it had something to do with Marilynn. Cyndi was just the intermediary. She had no idea. . . ."

Milo's phone rang, startling all of us. Even from across the desk, I could hear Vida's voice shrilling in the receiver. Milo listened wordlessly, then said, "Oh, hell, why not. It's on the way home."

We gazed at him in curiosity. "Vida got your note,

Emma," Milo said, heaving himself to his feet. "She's put the teakettle on. Let's go."

Vida doesn't believe in answering machines. She also doesn't believe in being kept in the dark. Consequently, I had insisted that after leaving the hospital, we should swing by Vida's house and put a note on her door in case she came home from Bellingham before morning.

Carla and Peyton Flake declined Vida's invitation, however. "I'll take Carla home," Flake told us in the sheriff's reception area. He gave her shoulders a squeeze. "Seems to me she can use a new roommate, at least temporarily." They started out the door. "But I don't vacuum, babe. I won't even dust."

"Oh, Peyts," said Carla. And she giggled.

By one A.M., Vida was almost filled in. Refreshing our teacups, she nodded sagely. "Yes, yes, the psychology was there all along. I can't believe I missed it. Especially the part about the wristwatch. I ran into Libby at the mall the day after the murder and never noticed her bare arm. My eyes must be going."

"I missed that, too," I admitted. "What really misled me was Ed and the Alpine Appliance van. He had mentioned following it up First Hill Road that Friday, thinking it was Lloyd Campbell and that he could apologize for screwing up the co-op ad. When he got there, Ed said Lloyd was gone. But it wasn't Lloyd—it was Shane, delivering the Tolbergs' stove. I forgot all about that until this morning— yesterday morning—after Mass when Ed was doing his eager-beaver bit with the Catholic merchants. I remembered that the Tolbergs' new gas range was what made Shane late getting home that Friday. The Tolberg farm is right across from the high school. It's secluded up there, with the Dithers Sisters' horse ranch across the road. Maybe he met Libby to rendezvous over the meeting with Kelvin. Whatever, he left the van, not wanting it seen parked by the cemetery where he was going to meet Kelvin. It was still there the next morning. Betsy O'Toole saw it on her way to the Grocery Basket. She thought the Campbells had taken to working on Saturdays, but I knew better. By chance, Lloyd and I had talked about a six-day week earlier. Naturally, when Betsy mentioned seeing the van, I suspected the worst of Shane."

"Bucker Swede," Milo said doggedly. "That was a forest ranger's hat. Why did you think it had been put in Shane's van?"

I suspect my expression was as foolish as I felt. "I'd never seen Libby wear an official hat with her uniform. I figured she'd lost it in Shane's van while they surrendered to a fit of passion. The Alpine Appliance van had been parked by the high school, too—it just wasn't in the same place as Libby's truck. The pranksters could have put Bucker there just as easily. As I said, once I got on the right track, I kept going. I never noticed the detour sign that pointed to Libby Boyd. I think that must be what they call linear thinking."

Vida passed Milo a tiny English bone-china pitcher of cream, which he sloshed into his cup. Tea was not Milo's beverage of choice. "Now, Emma," Vida said sternly, "don't punish yourself. It's very late, and I've had a long drive, almost from the Canadian border. Did Shane meet Kelvin at the cemetery or not?"

Feeling rebuked, I nodded quickly. "Yes, I'm sure he did. I suspect Kelvin pulled his gun. Shane was—is—a bit of a coward. He wouldn't have fought Kelvin for it. Only a strong emotion like self-defense could goad Shane into violence. He struggled with Kelvin to protect himself. And tonight, with Libby, because she wanted him to die."

"Such irony." Vida looked disapproving. "First, Libby risks everything to keep Shane, then she tries to kill him. The primary instinct is always survival. My, my."

Milo drooped in Vida's maplewood kitchen chair. "No guts, no glory," he murmured.

I didn't agree. "Oh, Libby had guts. Having been alerted by Shane, Libby showed up, pulled her own gun—which Milo thinks is the same one that killed Wesley Charles—disarmed Kelvin, and shot him with his own weapon, then dumped it in the grave, losing her broken watch in the process. Shane may have run off by then. Remember, he was torn between his fading feelings for Libby and the awakening love for Marilynn. Having killed Jerome Cole, Shane was already in a terrible state of conscience. Given his lack of spine, flight would have suited his personality. Shane might never have been sure that Libby killed Kelvin."

Milo nodded in a vague way. "And Libby had parked her truck in front of the high school, across from the Tolberg farm. She didn't count on the kids who were hanging out around the practice field swiping the Bucker mascot, using her first-aid kit, and putting a tourniquet on the thing. Oh, and her forest ranger's hat."

"Ridiculous," Vida sniffed. "To think they blamed it on Sultan! Is there no end to rivalry on Stevens Pass?"

Milo shot Vida a nettled glance. "Keep to the murders. I'm already confused." He applied his inhaler, and expelled a deep breath. "So when did Libby find the damned Bucker?"

I made a self-deprecating gesture. "That was part of my problem. I thought it was Shane who had parked his van by the high school, until I remembered that Ed had seen it farther up on First Hill Road. It couldn't be in two places at once. Libby wouldn't have been observed by the people who live on First Hill—those houses are too secluded. She left her truck in front of the school, then walked across the street to the cemetery. While she was gone, the kids decided to play a prank. Let's face it, some Alpiners look at the Forest Service as a tool of the federal government. They don't like their stand on the spotted owl. The kids were getting back at the enemy. They put the dummy in the back of the truck, which was full of brush and tools and all sorts of stuff. I suspect Libby didn't even notice—until she hid Wesley Charles in there."

Vida pursed her lips. "It was very stupid of us not to think about that Forest Service truck being involved in the accident at Monroe." She gave Milo a reproachful look. "Working for the government, Libby must have had no trouble finding out when Wesley Charles would be transported from Shelton. Somehow she caused that tie-up, then liberated Wesley Charles while everyone's attention was focused on the school bus. Where did she take him?"

I shrugged. "Who knows? Probably a back road where she happened upon the stolen car. She had tools in the truck, including a saw. She cut through Wesley's shackles and let him drive up to Alpine on his own. Maybe she fed him some story about knowing that he was wrongly imprisoned and that she knew who really killed Jerome Cole. Wesley Charles sounds like a credulous soul, and he certainly didn't want to serve time for something he didn't do. I'll bet she had a map, directing him to the cul-de-sac. She met him there later in the day and shot him, then waited until he was discovered by those kids. It wasn't any coincidence that she was in the vicinity when they found the body. No doubt she was lurking in the woods, just biding her time."

"And getting rid of Bucker Swede." Vida sighed. "She went way too far. She didn't need to kill either of those poor men. Such a waste."

Milo was yawning widely. "I don't get the part about that watch. Where does that come in?"

My voice was growing tired; I was getting tired of hearing it. "After the murder I noticed that Libby had a tan line on her arm. Then Vida and I found the broken wristwatch in the grave. I also realized that the next time I saw Libby, she was wearing a watch. A new one, or a spare, I suppose. But I didn't put the whole picture together until later."

Vida gave a shake of her head that set the graying curls dancing. "Libby planned things so carefully. She would have been very good at organizing Presbyterian bazaars. It's such a shame she was homicidal."

Milo grunted. "She was hell-bent on saving Shane's reputation—along with his money and her future. People like that are out of kilter. They don't think the way we do."

Vida concurred. "Terrible. Just terrible. Shane would never have gone to prison. He still won't."

Milo didn't look so sure. "He withheld evidence. He impeded justice. I don't think Shane will get off scot-free."

I slapped my hand on Vida's kitchen table. "There you go! More ethnic clichés! Stop it, Dodge! Hasn't this whole sorry mess taught you anything?"

Clumsily, Milo got to his feet. "Yeah, it sure has. I've got to break up with Honoria. At least until she changes perfumes. I'm allergic to that stuff she wears. My sinuses cleared up when we didn't see each other. Come on, Emma, I'll take you home to my place."

Half out of my chair, I froze. "*Your* place? What are you talking about?"

Milo gave me an innocent look. "Huh? Your car. You left the Jag at my place. Don't you want to collect it to-night?"

"Oh!" I flushed. "Sure, let's go."

Behind us, Vida snickered.

Monday was frantic at *The Advocate*. I took the tricky murder investigation story upon myself. It was noon before I finished the main article and the sidebars. By then, Libby Boyd's corpse had been retrieved from Alpine Creek and sent to the morgue. Doc Dewey ruled the death accidental. No one claimed the body until Carla came forward and said she'd see to the burial. I told her I'd help. Vida chimed in, and so did Ed and Ginny. Somehow it didn't seem right that Libby, who had been abandoned in life, should be alone in death.

It was almost two P.M. before I got to the mail. To my disgust, there was yet another letter from my anonymous nemesis. "Dear Publicher," it read. "I hear more rumores about the invazion. They are going to bewich us and make us slaves. From dawn to dark, we'll carry those ugly paper cups and drink, drink, drink. BEWARE!!! The end is near, and its name is LATTE."

I laughed. Uncontrollably. This was no wild-eyed bigot, fearing interracial marriage, demonic drugs, and gangland warfare. This was a man with an espresso machine he couldn't master and a dread of competition from Starbuck's.

This, I realized, was Marlow Whipp.

The WNPA program didn't start until eleven A.M. on Thursday, June 17. But since Wednesday was my off day, I decided to make the two-hour trip that afternoon. The past month had been hectic, not only with too many murders, but the burgeoning battle between the pro– and anti–explicit lyrics factions. There was rage at the school board, anxiety over the unveiling of the federal plan for the forests, argu-ments about the L.I.D. proposal, rumors that the Seattle Po-lice Department had brought Shane Campbell in for questioning, disappointment that Fred Meyer had chucked its Alpine outlet for a new store between Fremont and Ballard in the Big City, a great debate over Ginny Burmeister's brainstorm for a summer solstice celebration, and rampant buzzing about whether or not Mayor Fuzzy Baugh had taken to wearing a girdle.

Thus, I was well pleased to escape from Alpine for a few days. Adam had flown directly from Fairbanks to San Francisco. I would not see him until August. From Tuba City, he had called to announce his safe arrival and to inform me that he and Tom Cavanaugh had spent two days going to see a Giants game at the Stick, visiting the wine country in the Napa Valley, and taking a tour of Alcatraz. Considering that I'd had my fill of criminals recently, the last item seemed like an odd choice. But at least it would make for the opening gambit in a conversation with Tom when, and if, I saw him at Lake Chelan.

So that Wednesday, after waving the paper off to the printer in Monroe, I spent an hour making sure I wasn't leaving any loose ends. The school special had come out the previous week, and we were now setting our sights on the Fourth of July edition. Vida and Carla had plenty on their plates, while Ed continued to bustle about town in search of advertising revenue. I had a right to feel good about my professional life. My personal world, however, was a mess.

But Marilynn Lewis was putting her house in order. She showed up in my office just as I was about to leave for Chelan.

"I'm on a break," she said, then laughed. "I don't get breaks, except for lunch. Dr. Flake's in surgery and Doc Dewey is delivering a baby." She settled into one of my visitors' chairs. "I haven't had time to thank you properly for everything you did. I've been so busy getting moved in with Carla and worrying about Shane and trying to keep out of the hassle over those dumb recordings. . . . It's funny how easily you get caught up in small-town life."

"Funny," I echoed. "Right, it's hilarious." I grinned at Marilynn. "Hey, I didn't do much, except put my foot in it."

But Marilynn disagreed. "You wrote that editorial about

bigotry. That was a brave thing to do in this town. I appreciate it, and I imagine there are some broad-minded people around here who were glad to see it, too."

My modesty was unfeigned. "What I wrote won't change a thing. Only time will do that." I gave Marilynn a quirky little smile. "And newcomers, like you. Maybe it won't be long before the locals look at you and see a nurse instead of an African-American. Then, if you stick around long enough, they'll get to know you for who you are, not what you are. For now, I'm glad that you and Carla are going to be roommates. Try not to let her drive you crazy."

Marilynn gave a short, sharp snake of her head. "After Winola, Carla will be a snap." She shot me a rueful look. "I shouldn't criticize Winola. She's a decent person, but frankly, as long as I was seeing Jerome, I had a hard time finding a roommate who'd put up with all the turmoil I went through. Winola didn't mind—she came from a rough background."

I inclined my head. "Plus, she was seeing a drug dealer. Winola couldn't afford to gripe."

Marilynn expelled a long sigh. "True. Poor Winola. She deserves better."

"So do you," I asserted. "What are you going to do about Shane once his lawyer gets through plea-bargaining him down to community service, which will probably include playing gin rummy with Crazy Eights Neffel for the next six months?"

Marilynn's beautiful face turned thoughtful. "I don't know. I think Shane has a crush, really. I mean, for him I was different. Exotic, maybe?" She laughed. "He's nice, but he's not what I'm looking for. The best thing I could do for Shane Campbell is introduce him to one of the Chinese or Samoan nurses I worked with in Seattle. He's spent too much time with those tall, blonde Swedish and Norwegian girls."

Aghast, I stared at Marilynn. "Oh! Not you, too!"

Marilynn's black eyes grew wide. "Me what?" Suddenly she burst into laughter. "Oh, no! I'm a racist!"

I was also laughing. "Yes, you are. We all are, I guess. As I said, it's because we see with our eyes, not our minds."

Still making merry noises, Marilynn nodded, then shook her head. "Well . . . no. It's because we see what we want to see."

I had grown serious. "We see what's there. What do you see when you look at me?"

Marilynn sobered, too. She tilted her head to one side and studied me carefully. "I see a white woman who runs a weekly newspaper. I see a mother. I see a person who lives alone and thinks she likes it. I see . . ." Again, a smile played at her lips. "I see someone who deserves better. Don't we all?"

Campbell's Lodge at Lake Chelan was in a lovely setting, with every possible facility to make a conference run smoothly. Situated right on the lake, there were also swimming pools, an excellent restaurant, and private patios. The owners, I discovered, were not related to Lloyd and Jean Campbell, unless you were willing to dig back into the clan for several centuries. I certainly wasn't. They were entitled to wear the same tartan, but other than that, I was trying to put ethnic clichés aside.

I was also trying to figure out when Tom Cavanaugh would arrive. According to one of the WNPA hosts, he was scheduled to check in that evening. He was also expected to attend a private dinner that had been arranged exclusively for the officials and guest speakers. As far as I was concerned, Tom was off-limits until Thursday when he made his appearance at the midmorning session.

I ate in the restaurant with four of my fellow weekly publishers. We were a buoyant group, filled with the trials and tribulations of the newspaper profession. Anecdotes unraveled; rounds of drinks turned us maudlin; night fell over Lake Chelan.

I tottered out of the restaurant shortly after ten o'clock, feeling more unsteady from my brown mock-crocodile platform shoes than the four bourbons I'd consumed. Despite the air conditioning, I had perspired in my new taupe short-sleeved sweater; the elegant striped slit skirt was badly wrinkled. I was tired. I was disappointed. I was over forty and all alone.

And there, in the lobby with its soft lighting and bountiful potted plants, stood Tom Cavanaugh. He was shaking hands with one of the WNPA luminaries. His light blue chambray shirt was casual, as were his dark gray linen slacks. The profile was noble, the blue eyes keen, the brown hair going gray lent him an air of distinction. He had never been lean, but I'd settle for trim. Indeed, I'd settle for anything, as long as it was Tom. Damn.

I thought I had a good chance of getting to the elevator unnoticed. But, of course, I tripped over the blasted platform shoes and fell into the umbrella plant. Tom and the luminary turned to see what had caused the commotion. So did one of the resort workers, a fresh-scrubbed youth who couldn't have been more than eighteen.

"Ma'am!" he exclaimed, worry and liability written all over his face. "Are you okay?"

"Yes, yes," I replied through gritted teeth. "I'm not used to wearing shoes. I live in Alpine."

The youth helped me to my feet. "We have a doctor on call," he said, sounding solicitous. "Would you . . . ?"

"I would not," I stated firmly, making sure that the ankle I'd injured six months ago wouldn't give way under pressure. Or maybe I was waiting to see if *I* wouldn't give way under pressure. "It's fine. I'm going to my room."

The young man had obviously been well schooled in resort insurance procedures. "Maybe you'd like to come into the office and sit . . ."

I was growing testy. "I would like," I declared firmly, "to go to bed."

Backing off, the youth still wore an uncertain expression. "Uh . . . if you think . . ."

I don't know where the WNPA luminary went; I never saw him leave the lobby. But behind the resort employee stood Tom Cavanaugh, giving me his wide, off-center grin.

"It's all right," he said, touching the young man's sleeve. "The lady is tougher than she looks. I'll see to her."

Like a zombie, I limped off into the elevator with Tom. We were alone inside the small car. "Hello there," he said. "What's new?"

My brain was operating on low. "We're getting a new pastor," I blurted.

"Really." Tom sounded vaguely curious. "What's he like?"

The car stopped at three, which Tom had punched and which happened to be my floor. "I don't know. He's Irish, from California. Father Dennis Kelly."

Tom laughed, one of my all-time favorite sounds. "Dennis Kelly? From the seminary? I know him. He's pulled vacation duty at our parish in San Francisco. Nice guy—but he's not Irish."

We were out in the quiet corridor. "I mean, Irish extraction," I said, wondering what was going to happen next.

Tom shook his head, a touch of mischief added to his grin. "Not that, either. Dennis Kelly's ancestors may have *known* an Irishman. But Den's black."

My jaw dropped. And then I laughed. And laughed and laughed. I think Tom wondered if I was hysterical. He put a hand on my shoulder, and his blue eyes showed concern. I started shaking my head.

"No ... I'm not losing it. But all those crazy Catholics in Alpine think ..." I laughed some more.

Tom's grip deepened. I swore I could feel it all the way to the pit of my stomach. "Tell me about it later. Where did you say you were going?"

I looked up. It was quite a distance. Tom is tall, and he always makes me feel like a midget. Or at least like a fragile, delicate woman. "Where? Oh!" I put a hand to my cheek. "To my room. It's just down the hall. And ... to bed." Abruptly, I lowered my eyes.

Tom's hand moved to my waist. He steered me along the carpeted hallway. "That's right. I'm your guide. At the rate you're going, you'll never make it on your own."

"I will," I protested. Suddenly, I stopped, almost causing us to crash into each other. I gazed up at him, obstinacy written all over my face. "I *have*. For over twenty years."

Tom bit his lower lip, cocked his head, and leaned down to rest his chin in my gamine haircut. "So you have. But not tonight."

We stood very still, almost but not quite pressing against each other. "No," I breathed, "not tonight."

Coming to bookstores everywhere in
March 1995 . . .

THE ALPINE ESCAPE

by Mary Daheim

Published in paperback by Ballantine Books.
Read on for the exciting opening pages of
THE ALPINE ESCAPE . . .

Chapter One

I HAD BEEN warned. Sooner or later, it was bound to happen. My beautiful secondhand Jaguar would develop mechanical problems. Apparently, it finally had. It wouldn't start. To me, that's a mechanical problem.

I'd parked the Jag at the end of a long row of cars in the lot reserved for the Three Crabs Restaurant & Lounge on Dungeness Spit. On an overcast July day, the Strait of Juan de Fuca looked gray and dull, as if it were bored with its endless passage between the Olympic Peninsula and Vancouver Island.

I, however, was not bored, but agitated. And confused.

My car wasn't my only problem. With great reluctance, I'd abandoned by duties as editor and publisher of *The Alpine Advocate* in an attempt to reassess my life. Maybe it's naive to think that forty-two years of eluding reality can be rectified in three days, but I had to start somewhere. The Olympic Peninsula seemed like a good place for soul-searching.

Now my priority was a tow truck. I marched back inside the restaurant, found the pay phone, and scanned the local directory. The towing service in Sequim would be out in an hour. Where did I want to go?

That was a good question. I had no idea who could handle Jaguar XJ6 repairs on the Olympic Peninsula. Just off Highway 101, I wasn't exactly stranded in the middle of nowhere. The town of Sequim was a bustling place, chockful of dissatisfied and retired Californians who had found an authentic Sunbelt in the Pacific Northwest. A few miles to the west lay Port Angeles, with a population of 18,000. Surely one or two of these people owned a Jaguar. Surely someone could do the repairs.

"Gee," said the friendly voice at the other end of the line, "I don't know who fixes those things around here. There used to be a bunch of hippies at Happy Valley who worked on foreign cars. Good mechanics, too."

"It might be something simple," I said, sensing the onslaught of a panic attack. "The Jag's green. My name is Emma Lord. How about taking me to a Chevron or a BP station here in Sequim?" I had plastic for the two oil companies. My budget for the three-day trip was two hundred and fifty dollars. If the repair was over fifty bucks—and when was it ever under?—I'd have to charge it.

"We'd better haul you into Port Angeles," said the man at the other end. "You'll have better luck there with that Jag. See you around two. More or less."

Back outside, I prowled the sands, feeling a cool breeze on my face and hearing the tide slap against the shore. Dungeness Spit snakes five miles out into the strait, with one of the last two manually operated lighthouses in the continental United States. Recently, I'd heard it was scheduled for conversion to a computerized operation. So much for romance. But I, too, was trying to convert. Outmoded romantic notions were impeding my personal progress as well.

Some seventeen miles across the strait, I could make out the cluster of buildings that was Victoria, British Columbia. I hadn't been to Victoria in twenty years. Indeed, I hadn't been on the Olympic Peninsula since then, either. My plan to drive around the loop was hitting a snag. Trying to avoid added pressure on myself, I'd resolved not to make reservations. I dealt with deadlines every day on the job in Alpine. But the ferry from Edmonds to Kingston had been full; traffic heading across the Hood Canal Floating Bridge had been heavy. Maybe I should go back to the restaurant and call ahead to book a motel room. If nothing else, it would help kill time while I waited for the tow truck.

With my short brown hair tousled by the wind—and sand in my open-toed shoes—I trudged the long, narrow spit, my eyes straying to the rugged bulk of the Olympic Mountains that seemed to rise almost directly above the highway. I was accustomed to mountains. In Alpine, I live among them, eight miles west of the Cascade summit, in a town built into the rocky face of Tonga Ridge. Fleetingly, I thought of my little log house. Already I missed it. But, as my House and Home editor, Vida Runkel, had advised, I needed to get away. Alone. I went back into the restaurant which was still busy. Judging from the license plates in the parking lot, most of the lunch crowd were tourists like me.

The motels were also doing a brisk business. They were all booked, except for the ones that were out of my price range. The bed and breakfast establishments were full, too. Discouraged, I went into the bar and ordered a Pepsi, then felt my mouth twist with irony. Here I was, Emma Lord, forty-two years old, mother of a twenty-one-year-old son, never married, university graduate, newspaper owner, fairly bright, reasonably attractive, and sitting alone at a bar on a Tuesday afternoon drinking soda pop. No wonder I needed time to reflect. I felt like a real loser.

The woman tending bar was younger than I, but not by much. She was pretty, her makeup carefully if generously applied to hide a sallow complexion. At the moment, I was her only customer.

"Where you from?" she asked after giving me my Pepsi. I told her. She looked vague. "Idaho?"

"No." I explained where Alpine was located. It didn't surprise me that she hadn't heard of my hometown. With only four thousand residents living in relative isolation off Stevens Pass, Alpine isn't exactly a Washington State hub.

"Traveling alone?" she asked, trying to sound casual. I nodded.

She looked vaguely shocked. "That takes guts these days. Too many creeps out there." Using her white ceramic coffee mug, she gestured in the general direction of the entrance. "You're not camping, I hope?"

It was my turn to look shocked. "Oh, no!" I've always felt that if I had a sudden urge to sleep outdoors, I'd join the army and get paid for it. On the off chance that the bartender might have a brother or a friend in the hostelry business, I told her of my dilemma.

The best she could do was suggest places I'd already called. Frowning into her coffee mug, she shook her head.

241

"You don't know anybody around here?" Apparently, it seemed inconceivable that a stranger should have no local connections. As a small-town dweller, I understood her thinking. Everyone knows everyone else, and half of them are somehow related. It was no different in Clallam County than it was in Skykomish County.

The bartender's question jolted my memory. "As a matter of fact, I do. Sort of," I added lamely. Before buying *The Advocate* and moving to Alpine, I had toiled for seventeen years on *The Oregonian* in Portland. My best friend on the paper was Mavis Marley Fulkerston, now retired and living in Tigard, Oregon. But Mavis's daughter, Jackie, had gotten married on St. Valentine's Day and moved to Port Angeles. I hadn't attended the wedding, but I'd received an invitation. I racked my brain trying to remember her husband's name. With a dawning sense of doom, I decided that I could hardly barge in on someone whose last name I didn't know. On the other hand, I'd sent Jackie and her groom a toaster oven.

The tow truck arrived just as I was finishing my drink. Overtipping the sympathetic bartender, I hurried outside. After checking the battery and finding it wasn't the cause of my trouble, we hit the road to Port Angeles. My gloomy mood persisted all the way past Morse Creek and into town. Things weren't looking up half an hour later when the mechanic at the Chevron station announced that he couldn't find the trouble. Could I wait for Jake? He knew a little something about foreign cars.

I didn't have any choice, but since Jake and his knowledge were off somewhere in the mysterious West End, I resumed cudgeling my brain for Jackie Fulkerston's married name. I went halfway through the alphabet in my mind, and stopped at *M*. With my eyes locked on the Jag which was up on the hoist, I snapped my fingers. One of the mechanics darted me a curious look.

"Melcher," I said firmly. "Do you know a young couple named Melcher? They moved here late last winter."

The mechanic, who was young and needed a shave, closed one eye and wrinkled his thin nose. "Melcher. 'Ninety-two Wrangler. 'Eighty-nine Honda Accord. Yeah, they come in here. She had a lube job on the Honda last week."

Figuring that the newlywed Melchers wouldn't have made it into the current Port Angeles phone book, I trotted over to the corner booth and dialed Directory Assistance. Jackie's husband was named Paul. Their phone was answered on the second ring.

"Emma!" shrieked Jackie Fulkerston Melcher. "How *funny*!" To my dismay, she began to sob.

"Jackie, what's wrong?" I asked, alarmed.

Two gulps later, she replied: "I'm pregnant! Isn't it wonderful?" She sobbed some more.

"Well ... it sure is." I frowned into the stainless steel pay phone panel. "I ... uh ... just thought I'd call and say hi since I'm passing through."

Jackie sniffed loudly before speaking again. "You've got to stop in and have a drink or something. Where are you?"

I told her, then added that my car was temporarily out of commission. I was beginning to feel embarrassed.

Jackie, however, was a font of sympathy. "Oh, how awful when you're on a trip! I *hate* it when that happens! Remember the time Mom had to drive down to Coos Bay and her wheels fell off?"

I did, but my version wasn't quite the same. Mavis had hit a deep rut while trying to turn around off the highway and had jarred her axle. I'd forgotten that Jackie was inclined to dramatic exaggeration.

"Cars are such a *pain*," Jackie was saying, and I could envision her wide mouth turning down at the corners and her gray eyes rolling heavenward. "Listen, I'll be down to get you in five minutes. We're right up here on Lincoln Hill. Oh, I'm so *glad* you called! It's like the answer to a prayer!"

I was properly surprised. "It is?" Not having seen Jackie since her mother's retirement party two years ago, I couldn't imagine why she'd been invoking divine intervention to hear my voice.

"Yes! It's incredible, the next best thing to having Mom show up. Paul and I need an inquiring mind."

I was beginning to think Jackie could use any kind of mind that operated on a more even keel than her own. "Oh? How come?" My tone was neutral.

Jackie lowered her voice, and instead of a tearful vibrato,

243

she giggled. "It's so *weird*, Emma. You won't believe this!" She tittered, she gasped, she let out an odd howling sound. "We found a body! In our basement! Isn't that *great*?" Jackie burst into fresh sobs.

There was a bit of comfort in finding someone whose mental state was more unstable than my own. Or so I mused, as I leaned against a lamp post at the corner of Ninth and Lincoln, waiting for Jackie Melcher to pick me up.

I wasn't alarmed. The alleged body could be anything, including a dog, a squirrel, or a gopher. Jackie's sense of high drama was probably exacerbated by pregnancy. She'd always been a volatile girl, full of energy one minute, given to morose moodiness the next. She would often exasperate her mother but never her father who doted on his daughter.

Fortunately for the Fulkerstons, their two sons were rock-solid specimens. One was an oceanographer in California; the other produced films for the City of Portland. Jackie, as I recalled, had majored in French at my alma matter, the University of Oregon.

But, I reminded myself, while Jackie was young and pregnant, I had no such excuses for capricious behavior. After twenty-two years of waiting for the father of my son to get up the nerve to leave his wife, I'd come to the realization that while Tom Cavanaugh might care for me as much as I cared for him, he put duty above love. Of course he'd call it *honor*, as men often do, but it boiled down to the same thing. Sandra Cavanaugh was the mother of his other two children, and when it came to mental instability, I couldn't hold a candle to her. But then neither could Napoleon. Sandra suffered from a variety of emotional problems, all no doubt caused by the fact that she was born rich. Or so I'd always told myself.

Tom and I had met when I interned on *The Seattle Times*. Sandra's mental disorders were only beginning to surface, but living with her had become sufficiently difficult that Tom had sought comfort in my arms. He'd also apparently sought something in Sandra's because we both got pregnant about the same time. Not without regret, Tom had chosen to stay with his wife. I chose to leave Seattle and have my baby in Mississippi where my brother, Ben, was serving as a priest in the home missions. I also chose—fiercely and proudly—to raise Adam alone. If Tom wouldn't give me his name, he wasn't going to give me any help, by God. For almost twenty years, I shut him out of my life. And out of Adam's, which wasn't entirely fair to either of them.

In the past two years, I'd relented. Tom had shown up in Alpine, and I'd succumbed to his entreaties to let him meet Adam. Father and son had gotten along very well.

Father and Mother had, too, so much so that when I'd attended a weekly newspaper conference at Lake Chelan in June, Tom and I had ended up in bed.

For three days and three nights, we pretended it was forever. We knew better, though. Tom no longer needed Sandra's fortune as a base for his newspaper ventures, but Sandra needed Tom. He wouldn't forsake her, and I would have loved him less if he had. Tom neither loved nor lived lightly, which I suppose is why I could never quite let go. We are too much alike.

But there was no future in it. If I wanted to marry, maybe even have another child, I had to put the past aside. "Keep your options open," Vida Runkel had counseled. "You've put up a barrier to everyone but Tommy."

Only Vida could get away with calling Tom *Tommy*. And only Vida could speak so frankly to me. Even my brother, in his kind but indecisive manner, wouldn't take such a resolute stand. Ben not only sees both sides of every issue, he considers all the angles and contours. I am prone to do the same. Ben vacillates; I'm objective. Either way, the result is that it's very hard for both of us to make crucial decisions.

Thus Vida was right. I needed a shove in order to get going. Over the years, there had been a few other men in my life, but never one I really loved. I wouldn't let myself love them, asserted Vida. I had built a dream house on sand, and the tide was coming in fast.

Watching traffic pass by, half of which bore out-of-county license plates, I thought of Sheriff Milo Dodge. Like me, Milo was afraid of letting go. Divorced for the past six years, Milo refused to commit himself to his current lady-love, Honoria Whitman. Honoria was getting impatient. I didn't blame her. But I didn't blame Milo, either. Like me, he was afraid. Sometimes I wondered if Milo and I were afraid of each other. We spent quite a bit of time together but had only kissed once, which was sort of an accident. Or so I had thought in the heat of the moment.

A white Honda Accord pulled up at the curb. Behind the wheel, Jackie Melcher waved frantically, her heart-shaped face wreathed in smiles. I jumped in and we shot across the intersection before I could fasten my seat belt.

"Emma, you look great! You got your hair cut!"

I laughed, patting the gamine style I'd acquired not long before going off to Chelan. "It's nice and cool for summer," I said noncommittally.

Jackie was heading through the main part of town, past the handsome old red brick courthouse I remembered from my last visit. A large new modern building stood next door. Apparently it now housed the county offices.

"The old courthouse is a museum," Jackie said, following my gaze as she stopped at a traffic light.

"How do you like Port Angeles?" I inquired, having decided to hold off asking Jackie about her alleged body in the basement. It was the sort of question best discussed over strong coffee or a weak drink.

Jackie wrinkled her button nose. "It's okay. The setting's great. But I miss Portland."

"Me, too," I replied. After four years in Alpine, I still missed the vitality and the variety of the city. My plans to spend as many weekends as possible in my native Seattle had never quite worked out. I was lucky to get into the city once every couple of months.

But Jackie was right about her surroundings. Port Angeles was nestled at the base of Mount Angeles which seemed to glower over the town like a sullen guardian angel. The outskirts were dense with evergreens, signaling the start of the vast Olympic National Park. While new businesses seemed to abound on the long stretch of highway that led into the heart of Port Angeles, the mountains to the south and the strait on the north were a reminder that residents lived close to Nature.

We turned on First Street, which is also Highway 101. The houses were sturdy and old, though none reached quite as far back as the Victorian era. Like Alpine, Port Angeles was built into the foothills of the mountains. Unlike Alpine, the ascent was more gradual, starting at sea level.

Jackie pulled into a paved driveway that led to a detached garage that couldn't have held more than one modern car. I stared. The house that was set back among the Douglas firs was huge. The style suggested a Spanish mission reinterpreted by a late Victorian mentality. A giant monkey tree stood in the middle of the front lawn, with a smaller, less imposing oak near the corner of the house. A concrete retaining wall separated the newlyweds' house from a two-story ramshackle edifice that looked deserted. Jackie followed my gaze and emitted a little snort of disgust.

"That was the old livery stable that served the whole neighborhood. It's a *wreck*. I don't know why it doesn't fall down in a strong wind." She led me back onto the sidewalk so that I could get a better view of the house from the front.

Several of the camelia bushes appeared to be at death's door. The magnolias didn't look much better, and even the peonies seemed lifeless. Three stories of faded amber paint, a wraparound porch with peeling Moorish arches, a big lawn choked by weeds, a scarred river rock foundation, and a roof with missing shingles all combined to validate Jackie's description.

"You must have gotten a real deal on this place," I said.

Jackie laughed immoderately. "We sure did. It was free." She started back toward the driveway. "Paul inherited it from his uncle," she explained, leading the way to the back door. "Uncle Arthur lived here until about fifteen years ago when he got Alzheimer's and had to go into a nursing home. Uncle Arthur died last year. Aunt Wilma bought a condo in Sequim, but she died before he did. We decided to move here and fix the place up. That's how we found the body."

The interior of the house appeared to be in much better shape than the exterior. We were in the kitchen, which had been renovated and enlarged. I guessed that Jackie and her groom had enclosed the back porch. Gleaming black appliances were set off by red and white accents. A white tiled island stood in the middle, with a rack of stainless steel cookware suspended overhead. The basic design was orderly, but the counters were cluttered with pizza boxes, old newspapers, grocery bags, and empty bottled water containers. Jackie headed straight for the refrigerator and pulled out a jug of white wine.

"I can't drink but you can," she said, waving the bottle at me. "I'll have some mineral water."

I didn't question her abstinence, though I recalled downing reasonable quantities of Canadian whiskey with Ben while I awaited the birth of Adam. Neither Ben nor I ever got seriously drunk, and my son seemed sober enough when he finally arrived. But this was over twenty years later, and perhaps medical knowledge had made progress. Then again, doctors were still practicing. They probably never would get it perfect.

Carrying a delicate long-stemmed glass, I followed Jackie into what she called the den, but what I suspected had once been a library. This space was also littered, with magazines, videocassettes, tapes, CDs, and more newspapers. It appeared that Jackie didn't spend her spare time cleaning house.

The room was freshly painted in a soft shade of green. A tiled fireplace was flanked by glass-fronted bookcases that contained mostly paperbacks. Along the middle molding were the brass heads of monks, at least a dozen of them, their expressions ranging from puckish to surly. The furnishings were sparse, befitting a monk's cell. The absence of more than a small sofa, a huge cushiony footstool, and a TV set didn't bespeak a disdain for worldly goods, but rather a credit limit on a charge card.

Jackie collapsed into the footstool that seemed to devour her small frame. The flannel shirt she wore over her jeans concealed any signs of pregnancy. Running a hand through the natural waves of her taffy-colored hair, she sighed.

"It's going to take forever. I hope we get the roof replaced before winter sets in. The baby's due at the end of December." Jackie had turned pensive. The topsy-turvy emotions she'd displayed earlier over the phone seemed in abeyance. "We've already spent a fortune on making the house livable. Paul can do some of the work himself, but not the major stuff."

I tried to remember what Mavis had told me about Paul

Melcher. She and Roy liked their son-in-law, I knew that much. It seemed to me that Paul was some sort of engineer. I fished a little, hoping not to show my ignorance.

"Paul was lucky to get a job here," I remarked, thinking that the bare green walls cried out for a framed print or two.

Jackie nodded enthusiastically. "It was a near thing. We thought we'd have to move here and wait it out for a while, but then that opening came along at Rayonier. In fact, he actually started work right after New Year's, before we got married. That's why we couldn't go on a honeymoon. He didn't have any vacation yet."

ITT Rayonier was the big pulp plant down on the water. I'd seen its billows of smoke from the tow truck. Like Alpine, Port Angeles was still dependent on the timber industry, though it had been able to diversify over the years. Fishing and tourism also contributed to the town's economic base.

"He gets off at four," she said, glancing at her watch. I did the same. It was just three fifty-five. I postponed asking the inevitable and switched to baby-related inquiries instead. Jackie beamed and glowed, discussing plans for the nursery upstairs and promising to take me on a tour of the house when I finished my wine.

The phone rang as she was listing potential names for both girls and boys. Jackie heaved herself out of the cushioned footstool and left the den. A moment later, she shouted for me. It was the Chevron station. Jake had finally returned from the West End. He didn't have the foggiest notion what was wrong with my car. Could I have it towed over to Dusty's Foreign Auto Repair?

I could, of course. I'd have to. I wondered if my towing insurance covered two trips in one day. I sought the Yellow Pages and called a local tow company. Then I turned glum.

"They can't possibly fix it before evening," I moaned out loud.

"Big deal." Jackie shrugged and led us back into the kitchen. "Have some more wine. We've got tons of room. Five bedrooms, take your pick. Except ours." She showed me her dimples.

I started to make the usual demurs about not wanting to

249

impose, but Jackie ran right over me. "Hey, why not? We haven't told you about our body yet. I'll send for pizza." The light behind her eyes went out. "I usually do lately. I get sick every time I look at the stove."

She was pouring my second glass of wine when Paul Melcher came home. A stocky young man in his early thirties, he sported a neatly-trimmed blond mustache and a faintly receding hairline. His handshake was firm and sincere.

"I've heard Mama Mavis talk about you," he said with a diffident grin. "You two used to get into a lot of trouble at *The Oregonian*, right?"

If trouble was sneaking out for a beer and a burger while working after hours, then I guess we qualified. But I merely laughed and tossed my head as if Mavis and I were indeed a couple of scamps.

Jackie poured wine for Paul, another mineral water for herself, and we adjourned to the den. Paul seemed mesmerized by the sad story of my Jaguar. He speculated upon its problems.

"Those Jags—they're a wonderful piece of automobile," he said with a serious expression on his face, "but they don't call the head of their engineering department Dr. Demento for nothing."

"Really?" I winced. But I had been warned. In fact, it was Mavis who had told me that if I couldn't afford the price of a new Jag—and I couldn't, not even with my unexpected inheritance which had also allowed me to buy *The Advocate*—then I probably couldn't afford the repairs. It appeared that I'd been lucky. So far.

My eyes glazed over as Paul presented a litany of possible cause. The starter. The stick shift. The electrical system. I wondered what kind of pizza Jackie would order. Pastrami sounded good to me.

". . . With parts. Now over in Victoria they'd probably be able to get . . ." Paul seemed unusually talkative for an engineer, rambling on while carefully piling the magazines and stacking the videocassettes. He finally shut up. Jackie was weeping. "Sweets, what's wrong now?" He reached over from his place next to me on the small sofa and patted her knee.

Jackie wiped her eyes and sighed. "All this talk of fancy cars. How many people live in an old beat-up Volkswagon van? It made me think of the homeless. Why do they have to live under bridges? Do you think anybody is living under a bridge in Port Angeles? We have so many of them, with all these gullies."

Gently, Paul soothed her. There weren't that many homeless people in town. It was July, and while the summer weather had been cool and uncertain, nobody would take cold even if they had to sleep under a bridge. Shelters were provided. The churches were helping out. The United Way was doing its best. Jackie shouldn't worry. The baby would get upset. Paul's arguments were logical, orderly.

Wanly, Jackie smiled at her husband. "You're right, Lamb-love. Let's talk about something cheerful. Like the body."

Paul rubbed her knee. "That's my Sweets." He gave me another big grin. "Emma would like to hear about that. It's pretty interesting."

"I'll bet it is," I said, bracing myself. "When did you find this . . . ah . . . body?"

Paul's grin faded only a mite. "Yesterday." He stood up. "We're keeping it in the basement. Want to see it? Afterward, we can order pizza."

MARY DAHEIM

Published by Ballantine Books.
Available in your local bookstore.
